PENG

The SHATTERED LANDS

Brenna Nation resides in a crowded old row home in Baltimore, MD. After graduating from the University of Maryland with an English degree, Brenna began her career as a marketer for media companies. Her first book, *The Shattered Lands*, was born from early morning wake-ups. When she's not writing, she can be found petting her dogs, getting tattoos, searching for the spiciest food in the room or crying to Taylor Swift songs while she drives around aimlessly. You can follow her writing journey on TikTok at @brennawritesnow.

The SHATTERED LANDS

BRENNA NATION

PENGUIN BOOKS

For you, my reader.
You deserve to have your stories told.

PENGUIN BOOKS

UK | USA | Canada | Ireland | Australia
India | New Zealand | South Africa

Penguin Books is part of the Penguin Random House group of companies
whose addresses can be found at global.penguinrandomhouse.com

www.penguin.co.uk   www.puffin.co.uk   www.ladybird.co.uk

First published 2023

001

Text copyright © Brenna Nation, 2023
Cover illustration copyright © Kii W, 2023

The moral right of the author has been asserted

Typeset in 10.5/15.5pt Sabon LT Std
Printed and bound in Great Britain by Clays Ltd, Elcograf S.p.A.

The authorized representative in the EEA is Penguin Random House Ireland,
Morrison Chambers, 32 Nassau Street, Dublin D02 YH68

A CIP catalogue record for this book is available from the British Library

ISBN: 978-0-241-64526-0

All correspondence to:

Penguin Books
Penguin Random House Children's
One Embassy Gardens, 8 Viaduct Gardens, London SW11 7BW

CHAPTER ONE

The Saints no longer heard their pleas for mercy.

That much she knew. The thought pushed her forward as she gripped the hilt of her dagger more tightly. The Home could not afford another night of her returning empty-handed. As she positioned herself against a large tree, she looked up to the sky. It was a deep shade of grey – as it had been for months now, but it seemed darker . . . sinister even.

It would make her hunt that much more difficult.

Sapphire tugged the sleeve of her ill-fitting tunic back on to her shoulder and tightened her cloak. To her right, a gaunt squirrel rustled the leaves, attempting to burrow into the damp soil, hunting for scraps just like she was. Dagger in hand, she focused her eyes and mouthed a fool's prayer to the Saints, hoping they would allow her this one favour.

The dagger pierced the creature's abdomen and it let out a desperate cry. She wasn't sure she would ever get used to taking a life, but morality had no place in barren lands. Gathering her kill, she headed out of the woodlands.

When she stepped into the Home, she could tell something was different. No one met her at the door. And the musty smell she was used to had been replaced by something sticky, something sweet enough to almost make her stomach turn.

It did not fit the weathered and draughty walls of this place.

As she slipped off her cloak, no one rushed to help her. There was no hum of voices.

Something wasn't right.

She pressed her thumb into her palm, tracing the thin, jagged scar that ran across it. As she moved deeper into the hall, she noticed a tiny flickering light in the centre of the makeshift dining room.

Cautiously sticking her head through the doorway, she sighed in relief as she took in the smiling faces.

'Happy birthday!'

On a table in the middle of the room was a small cake that must have taken months of rations to make.

'I – this was not necessary,' Sapphire sputtered. The images worming their way into her mind were uninvited and unrelenting. These now-smiling faces staring up at her, twisted in pain. Their bodies hunched, curling inwards on themselves as spasms of hunger overtook them. Those rations were worth more than some silly cake. Worth more than her. She wanted to cry – and scream – that she was the only one that saw the truth. Martia should have known better.

'It is your eighteenth birthday. It was necessary.' Martia's tone was sharp, and Sapphire bit her tongue in an effort to swallow the poisonous feeling welling up in her. 'Take this as an expression of our gratitude for –' . . . a pregnant pause filled the air as Martia's eyes scanned her, finally landing on the fallen creature tucked into her bag – 'bringing dinner.'

Sapphire offered Martia a tight-lipped smile, knowing she should be grateful – but the words she wanted to say, about how foolish and short-sighted this all seemed, weighed like ashes in her mouth. Still, when her eyes found Lyna's, she felt the smallest tug of peace. The eleven-year-old's face was lit up with excitement. A spark of joy she hadn't seen there in years.

That might be worth some wasted rations.

When Sapphire was given her piece of cake, she quickly passed it to Lyna and Susanna when Martia wasn't looking. The draughty room warmed slightly as the twins hugged her tightly before running off with their extra serving.

Sapphire was eighteen now, the age at which Martia had thrown many before her out into the world. Their beds were given to children who could not defend themselves from the cruelty of Witrotean. Sapphire had always known that the land was overrun with orphans. The Home was one of the few places those children could find refuge.

But, out of desperation, Martia had made a rare bargain with her. A bed in return for meat. A bed in return for victuals. A bed in return for whatever forageable scraps existed out in those Godforsaken plains. Sapphire was to provide in a way Martia no longer could thanks to age, and war. The Home needed her, and both women knew it. But there was no telling for how long. Nobody was guaranteed a bed or a home in Witrotean any more. She pushed away from the table, rushing to the washroom, seeking relief from the pressure building in her chest.

There, she stared at her reflection. Haggard and tired. Her brown skin dulled by the constant cloud cover of the Witrotean sky. Deep-set bruises had settled beneath her mahogany eyes. Her long, thick hair was tangled from the hours spent in the woodlands' unforgiving wind. Her face was gaunt, a sign of the famine and the nights she could not find rest. Too withered and worn to be so young.

In the hours that followed, she prepared her kill from the day. The small animal hardly offered enough meat to be worth her time, but it was better than nothing. Then she cleaned the kitchen, willing to do anything to distract herself from the thoughts that consumed her.

Martia found her standing near the window later that night and offered her an extra blanket.

'I have been given more than enough today,' Sapphire reasoned, but Martia shook her head.

'You will accept the kindness I extend to you, child.' Martia shoved the blanket forcefully into her hands. 'Now, get to bed. The candles must be blown out before midnight. You know that.'

Sapphire accepted the blanket and obeyed.

She had not earned such kindness, she knew that. The meal she had provided that night was hardly enough. She could see in Martia's face that it was only a step short of failure but still, it was more than anyone else had offered.

As she approached her bed, she saw that something was out of place. A small stack of objects she didn't recognize was sitting on her thin mattress. As she picked it up, she noticed that it was a mix of charcoals and one jar of red paint – a gift from the girls who slept around her. Tears spilled over, hot and heavy with guilt.

When she could no longer tolerate the weight of the guilt she shouldered, she walked over to where Lyna and Susanna slept. It was winter and the timeworn walls of the Home were little protection from the chill. She placed the large blanket over their sleeping forms and Lyna hummed with satisfaction.

'I hope you had the best birthday, Saph.'

Sapphire bent forward, placing her lips to each of their foreheads in turn and listening to their murmured thank-yous before getting into her own bed.

She sighed, rolling over in the small uncomfortable cot. Anger and grief swelled inside her; the weight of the others' hunger resting on her shoulders was crushing her. She had been carrying that burden since war arrived at their doorstep two years ago. The memory was still vivid in her mind, the Mothers locking them in hidden rooms as Beasts tore down doors and took lives.

Martia was the only Mother to survive.

She had come to Sapphire the day after the Fall, grasping her chin in a wrinkled hand.

'You are a few years short of adulthood – I've tossed far more useful girls from this place at your age. But,' she added, her exhaustion obvious in a way it never had been before, 'I will make you an offer. I train you how to wield a blade, you gather food for all of us, and you may remain.'

And so they began.

Sweat and tears filled the following weeks. She worked with the dagger, razor-thin slices coating her fingers like lace gloves, but she refused to give in. Sapphire knew she wasn't ready when Martia sent her into the forest, but the desperation in the Home was nearly suffocating. The burden of stopping the slow death march of starvation from claiming them all now sat firmly on her shoulders.

She dug her nail into her scar as she recalled the memory, potent resentment coursing through her, as familiar as the worn scrap of fabric she pulled tighter around herself as the damp chill of the room began to settle into her bones.

It was then she heard the ringing of the bells, signalling the midnight hour. A warning to all those who lingered in the dark to return home and lock their doors.

The Beasts were hunting.

At the twelfth toll, she allowed herself to accept the other thing it signified as well.

Her birthday.

A deep breath in. A deep breath out. She closed her eyes tightly and willed her mind to slow.

Then the world fell away.

Mercy, not another vision . . .

The scene in front of her was familiar. Too familiar. A mostly felled willow, half tilting optimistically towards the sky, half splintered and shattered, rooted next to the girl she could never reach. It was dark, the world shrouded in frightening shadows, but as always, the girl's cardinal red hair caught her eye, a guiding light in the storm.

Sapphire stared for only a moment longer before beginning the trek forward.

Her chest swelled as the pathway gave way to tall grass, each blade trailing against her skin. It only took the smallest brush at her back to let her know she wasn't alone. Something nearby was watching her. Watching and waiting. Her heart rate spiked, as a spark of fear ignited her body. She was always the observer in these visions. Never noticed, never seen.

She took another step and finally saw the flowing hem of the girl's black dress. She paused as she always did, waiting for the thunder to roll. She felt her shoulders relax slightly at the familiar sound. She knew what came next. She waited for the lightning that tore through the sky to strike the girl and end her life.

Sapphire would be left alone. And then she'd wake in a cold sweat, and spend the rest of the night staring out of the small window of the bedroom.

It always happened that way.

But today the girl spoke. Her voice was like a siren's song. 'Help me.'

Sapphire froze, fright rooting her to the spot.

'Help me, Sapphire.'

The second time, the voice was harsher, no longer a plea but a demand, and Sapphire's fear swelled. Still, she felt the pull between them. She allowed the tension to force her forward.

The sky above her began to swirl, the storm coming to life. She hesitated, eyes wild as they took in the scene.

The girl spoke once more. 'The storm is you. It will obey.'

Sapphire attempted to block out the voice. The mysterious words only caused her panic to grow.

Three paces. That was all she needed to reach the girl.

The shadows parted slightly, and Sapphire was close enough to see her outline. Her stomach clenched at the thought of being this close as the lightning struck. Close enough to hear what it sounded like when the electricity split her bones.

From the shadows, she saw a pale hand emerge, the crack of thunder filling the air, and in an act of desperation and terror, she lunged for the girl.

The second their hands touched, lightning struck – and the world went black.

When Sapphire awoke, the musky scent of a campfire flooded her senses. Despite her poor excuse for a bed, whatever she was lying on now somehow managed to be even more uncomfortable.

She groaned and rubbed her eyes, taking in her surroundings.

No draughty windows that let in too much winter air, no row of beds that she and the others had long outgrown, no Martia yelling that they were already behind on their morning chores. This was not the Home.

The world around her was vivid, with large raised plateaus and basins formed from brilliant stone varying in shades of deep red, tans, and oranges in every direction. This was nothing like Witrotean. She pushed off from the ground, and on to her feet.

Mercy, nothing about this was familiar. Sapphire breathed the smallest sigh of relief when she felt the familiar weight of her dagger at her hip. She picked a direction at random and began to walk.

The old makeshift nightgown that draped over her thin frame was ripped and ruined. Martia would be livid. Her shoes were missing as well – mercy, she might as well never return.

There was no clear direction. No obvious pathway. But she continued to move forward – turning right . . . and then left . . . but nothing looked familiar.

After about a mile, her feet begged for relief. The terrain tore her skin and a trail of bloody footsteps now stretched behind her.

In her despair, she almost missed the movement to her left – *almost*. She hurried to slip behind a tall tree, peeking around the trunk to get a better look.

A dark-skinned girl, who looked around Sapphire's age, was sitting on a quilt with her legs stretched out, reading. Her lips were slightly parted, brows knitted in focus as she hurried to turn the page, engrossed in the story.

Sapphire watched for a few more moments as she smiled at the book with such innocence that Sapphire felt guilty.

She looked away, unable to handle the thought that she could not prevent what was about to happen; convinced this was just another vision – just another person she could not save. Sapphire stepped backwards in an attempt to gather herself but stumbled over a large rock, almost falling over.

The girl closed her book quickly at the noise, jumping to her feet and frantically searching until her eyes found Sapphire. Although her face showed fear and intrigue, her features were elegant and Sapphire admired how lovely she was. But when she met the girl's eyes, she was taken aback by the sight of irises that burned red like the embers of a dying flame.

With her book clutched tightly to her chest, the girl took a careful step towards Sapphire.

Panic.

Sapphire knew her visions well. They came at all times of the day and night. She had adjusted, memorized them. But this . . . this was not like what she knew. Never once had a victim approached her. Sapphire stepped back, feeling for her dagger. She blinked a few times, attempting to adjust to the hot sun on the back of her neck, the warm breeze that felt so foreign to her.

'Who are you?' The girl's voice was steady and calm.

Sapphire did not want to answer.

'What are you doing here?'

The girl's lips twitched, and she gave a heavy sigh when Sapphire refused to answer her.

'I'm Evera.' She closed the distance between them by a few inches. 'Now, can you please tell me your name? What you're doing out here . . . dressed like that? Anything?'

Sapphire took a deep breath before speaking.

'That all depends.'

'On?' Evera pressed, intrigue instantly overcoming her caution.

'On where exactly I am right now.'

Evera's expression shifted, but she held her ground.

'You are in the fields of Aleburn.'

'Aleburn?'

'Yes. The southwest territory.'

'Of what?'

'The kingdom of Eriobis, surely.'

'Er-e-oh-bis? I've never heard of it.'

Evera gave a deep, shaky breath before taking a few steps forward. Her face was pinched in a frown, but her mouth fell slack as she met Sapphire's eyes.

'What?' Sapphire positioned herself to fight, her fingers dancing on the hilt of the dagger.

'Your . . . your eyes. They're . . .' Evera paused. 'Where exactly are you from?'

'Witrotean.'

'I've never heard of such a place.'

Evera shook her head, and now it was Sapphire's turn to feel overwhelmed. A sharp pain split her palm, and she looked at the scar that ran across it, red and risen.

She needed this vision to end.

She reached out for the girl's hand, hoping that contact would bring the nightmare to a close just like it had before. But in the blink of an eye, a flame erupted from Evera's palm.

Sapphire retracted her hand quickly, stumbling over the rock behind her. She hit the ground hard, a yelp escaping her lips, though her eyes never left the dancing flame.

Evera's gaze remained on her for a few more moments before she extinguished it.

'Sorry. I thought you were going to –'

'Attack you?' Sapphire got up, brushing the dirt off her nightgown. 'Well, if I was thinking about it – I definitely won't now.'

A small smile played on Evera's lips. 'What element do you belong to?'

'Element?'

'Yeah, I'm Fireborn, obviously. What are you?'

'I have no idea what you're talking about.'

Evera frowned. 'Are you OK? Maybe you hit your head and you're confused.'

'Where I'm from, people can't casually ignite a flame in their palm.'

Evera's eyes lit up. 'Are you a mortal?'

A mortal. Sapphire had only heard that word used in discussion of the Beasts and their prey. Her fear reignited as she realized she could very well be in the presence of a monster. Yes, she was a mortal, and mortals ended up dead when they found themselves in the presence of a monster.

'I –'

'But if you are a mortal, breaking the barrier would be impossible. How did you end up here?'

'That's what I've been trying to figure out.'

'This doesn't make any sense.'

Sapphire almost chuckled. Finally, something they could agree on; but the fear she still felt caused the laughter to die on her tongue.

An uncomfortable silence followed until Evera finally spoke. 'I think you should come with me.'

'I'm fine on m–'

'You're barefoot and in a nightgown,' Evera quipped back, taking in the girl's appearance once more, her eyes softening in sympathy. 'My mother will be able to help.'

Martia's voice rang out in Sapphire's mind: *Never trust a stranger, my girl. The woodlands are full of creatures born of deceit.*

'All I need is a change of clothes, then I'm on my way.'

Evera nodded. 'Yes, of course. Follow me.'

The walk seemed to last for miles. Sapphire began to pant under the hot sun, Evera tossing her worried glances as they journeyed towards her home. Finally, rows of small stone houses came into view: a village bustling with life. But Evera opted for the path that led around it. To their right was a large canyon, water glistening at its bottom. Further on stood an incredibly tall mountain with a fire burning at the peak.

Finally, her guide turned towards a small stone cottage that looked identical to the couple of hundred or so that they had already passed. Pausing at the gate, Evera gave Sapphire a half-hearted smile.

'Just wait for a moment. I need to let my mother know you're here.'

Sapphire watched as Evera disappeared behind the grey door. Sapphire did what she could to stay calm, tracing the scar on her palm. Several minutes passed before Evera reappeared with an older version of herself in tow. The woman's eyes mirrored her daughter's, red and apprehensive, but lacked the softness Evera's held.

For a fleeting moment, Sapphire wondered if she ran, how far her raw and blistered feet would take her.

'Hello. My name is Lelani. My daughter tells me you're in a bit of a bind.'

Sapphire met Lelani's gaze, and the woman tried her best to hide her flinch. Sapphire did not miss Lelani giving Evera the smallest push, putting her body behind her own.

'As I explained to your daughter, all I need is a change of clothes, and then I can be on my way.'

Lelani looked her up and down twice before she spoke.

'You are exhausted.'

Sapphire began to interrupt, but the woman raised a hand to silence her.

'You are exhausted, and your feet are in a state. Why don't you come inside and rest while we try and sort things out, hmm?'

Sapphire wanted to say no. She wanted to refuse the woman and her kindness, but as she peered around the village, she wasn't sure where she would go. She needed shoes, and water, as the thick burning in her throat reminded her. So she nodded and the woman allowed her to pass through the gate. Once inside the cottage, Evera led her to a small table, pulling out a seat before heading up the stairs. Lelani joined Sapphire, her face suspicious.

'What is your name?' the older woman asked.

Sapphire chewed on her lip, wondering if it would be unwise to reveal more about herself to these women. But exhaustion weighed on her. She had to trust them, even if she knew she shouldn't.

'Sapphire.'

'So, Sapphire, can you tell me how you came upon my daughter?'

'I was just trying to get home,' Sapphire snapped, her tone more defensive than she had intended.

'And where is home?' Lelani continued, her face unreadable. She was clearly unfazed.

'Witrotean.'

'I've never heard of Witrotean.'

The woman's tone spoke volumes. Sapphire knew what she was thinking: *liar*.

Still, the answer chipped away at her resolve. Witrotean was a war-torn hellscape, but for her, it was her only home, the place where she'd grown up and, more importantly, a place where she knew how to survive.

'How do you not –?' Sapphire choked on the words, the muscles along her throat clenching in tiny spasms from thirst, but Lelani did not move to comfort her.

'Is there anything you can tell us? Anything that could help us help you?' Lelani asked.

Sapphire considered the question, but when she met the woman's cautious expression, she knew honesty had no place at this table.

'No.'

Lelani pressed her lips into a thin line as her eyes narrowed.

Before her mother could continue the interrogation, Evera reappeared with a pile of clothing in hand. Sapphire pushed back from the table, needing to escape Lelani's heavy stare.

'Bathroom?'

'Second door to the left,' Evera answered with a small, sincere smile as she handed the pile to Sapphire as she passed. Once she clicked the door closed behind her, Sapphire felt herself coming undone and moved to grip the cold basin in front of her for support. A single sob shook her shoulders before she heard the whispers outside the door.

'We have to take her to the kingdom, Evera. We have no idea who she is or what her intentions are.'

'Can't we take her tomorrow? She's practically dead on her feet right now.'

'No. You've heard the whispers about the Shattered Lands too, Evera. You saw her eyes. I fear she's –'

Their voices turned even quieter, and Sapphire moved to the looking glass. Everyone seemed to want to talk about her eyes. When she saw her own reflection, she realized why. They were usually a muddy, chestnut brown, but now they glowed a vibrant violet. She stumbled away from the glass, trying to gather herself together.

This was not possible.

Eyes did not just . . . change, especially to a colour so unnatural and unsettling. Taking a few deep breaths, she summoned up the courage to look at herself once more. The violet was still there. She blinked, willing it to fade, but nothing changed – and as she stared, unable to turn away, a sick feeling began to settle into her bones.

She remained there for some time before a gentle knock broke her out of the trance.

'Sapphire? Are you OK?' Evera's voice was worried.

'Just a few minutes, sorry.'

Rushing, she forced herself into the odd garment Evera had given her. It seemed to be made of some type of heavy leather. She was too tall for the top half, causing the entire outfit to fit awkwardly. But still, it was better than what she had been wearing. When she finally stepped back into the main room, Evera went to gather her nightgown, but Sapphire snatched it away.

'I need to keep this.'

Evera nodded, stepping back towards her mother quickly. Sapphire knew better than to lose the gown she had slept in for almost two years. Martia would never provide another.

'Sapphire, I can't, in good conscience, allow you to just stumble through Aleburn on your own. Why don't you let us escort you to Astral – the queen's city? I honestly believe the royal family can help you find your way home. They can certainly help more than anyone around here can.'

Just the mention of others put her on edge. 'No. That won't be necessary.'

Lelani grimaced. 'I'm afraid it's more of a demand than an offer. I have some things to take care of, but in a few hours, we'll begin the trek.'

Lelani did not allow Sapphire to argue, heading straight up the stairs.

'It's better we take you to the kingdom than guards find you,' Evera said once they were alone.

'Why would the guards even bother? I've done nothing wrong.'

'Not technically, I guess.' Evera looked uncomfortable. 'But your presence is a slightly bigger deal than you might realize.'

Sapphire felt her temper flare.

'Was that your plan, then, all along? Bring me here just to hand me over to armed guards?'

'Of course not. I wouldn't – I was worried for you – you looked so out of place, I just wanted to help.'

'And what changed?'

Evera deflated slightly. 'My mother is a bit more cautious than me.'

'I hadn't noticed,' Sapphire scoffed.

To her surprise, Evera smirked.

'She means well . . . she's just protective of what is left of her family. You have to understand that.'

The words burned Sapphire from the inside out.

'Not all of us have the luxury of a family, much less a mother as fierce as yours.'

'Oh, I'm sorry.' And Evera's voice truly sounded so. 'It was unfair of me to expect you to . . .'

Sapphire felt her anger slip a little.

'It's fine.' She looked back to the washroom, remembering how it had felt to see her own eyes. She recalled Lelani's hushed tone. She recalled how, despite being afraid, Evera had offered her kindness, expecting nothing in return, and she sighed. 'My eyes . . . they're not usually this colour.'

The girl forced out the best smile she could.

'They're quite pretty. They suit you.'

'They make me look deranged.'

At that, Evera laughed loudly, and while Sapphire's hand still rested on the scabbard of her dagger, she felt herself relax slightly at the sound, allowing herself a moment of peace in the presence of such kindness.

CHAPTER TWO

As they made their way west, Sapphire learned what true exhaustion felt like. The weight of the leather made the walk excruciating, and she was covered in sweat. But despite the difficult terrain, Lelani and Evera barely broke their stride, slowing only to allow Sapphire to catch up with them.

She was too tired to be embarrassed. Evera kept her pace slow and intentional, remaining beside her.

'There's no need to be nervous, you know.' Evera said, shattering the silence that had existed for the past few miles.

'Who said I was nervous?' Sapphire snapped back, more venom in her tone than she actually felt.

Evera shrugged slightly, her eyes fixed on the path ahead. 'You're not as hard to read as you think you are.'

Sapphire studied the side of Evera's face, trying to piece together the girl's motives before Evera turned a gentle gaze on her.

'I work at the castle. In the library,' she continued. 'Everyone there is nice and I'm sure they'll just want to be helpful.'

Sapphire didn't reply. She just snapped her focus forward, not able to bear the weight of those kind eyes any further.

Sapphire was desperate for any ally – but Martia's avoidance of strangers was constantly in her mind. A few more awkward seconds passed before Evera turned her attention to her mother, accepting that the conversation was over.

They had been walking for what felt like hours when the view finally gave way to glistening water. Lush green trees and rolling hills followed. For a moment, Sapphire longed for the small charcoal set the twins had given her, and enough time to commit the landscape to paper.

'Astral – the city of water,' Lelani announced as they made their way down a stone path towards a canal. Ahead was a wooden dock, a small, weathered platform floating beside it.

The man that occupied it scrambled to his feet and smiled as they approached.

'Keep your eyes down, Sapphire.' Evera's voice was low and timid in a way she hadn't heard before.

Sapphire wasn't in the mood to argue, entirely taken by the scene unfolding before her. A world so rich with colour she once again convinced herself she was trapped inside a vision. Still, despite its beauty, her panic grew with every step. She had never felt comfortable in the water, and though she had tried to learn to swim she had never mastered the skill.

Evera held out a hand to assist her on to the rocking

platform. Once settled, she took a few deep steadying breaths and challenged herself to focus on the world around her. She dipped her fingers into the water and sighed. It was cool enough to feel like a balm across her hot skin, and clear enough that she could see straight through to the bottom, which helped settle her nerves.

But it was the man who directed the floating platform who truly enthralled her. With a simple wave of his hand, he sent them along the canal. At first, she didn't quite understand how the boat moved with such ease but then it dawned on her – this was another element. Astral was a city of water, and the people who lived there controlled it, as Evera controlled her fire.

The canal opened up into a much larger lake, and a huge castle came into view. She sucked in a breath as she took it in. The castle was perched upon a large hill, surrounded by water on all sides, pristine at every angle. As they moved closer, she noticed each white stone was even and square.

It was charming, but even the artistry of it all could not ward off the anxiety that built with every passing moment. She suddenly felt like a child as she bit back the urge to beg Evera to allow her a little more time before they handed her over.

The floating platform came to an abrupt halt in front of the castle, and as Sapphire's feet touched solid ground, she enjoyed her reconnection with dry land. The feeling, however, was short-lived as the guards noticed them and wasted no time in approaching. The shorter of the two spoke first.

'Can I assist you, ma'am?'

'May we speak privately?' When Lelani's eyes cut to Sapphire, the guard followed her gaze and nodded.

'This is all going to work out,' Evera said. 'The king and queen are powerful – powerful enough to get you back to Witrotean, I'm sure.' She gave Sapphire a small, forced smile.

Sapphire didn't respond, focused on tracking Lelani's and the guard's movements. They huddled together, the man's gaze darting to her every few seconds. Despite Evera's original advice, she refused to look away from him.

As Lelani rejoined them, Sapphire felt something shift. It was small, but as the older woman occupied herself with a frayed string on her cloak, Sapphire became intensely aware that the man's focus was now entirely on her as he crossed the stone walkway towards them.

The realization struck her a second too late, as two sets of hands wrapped tightly around her biceps. She attempted to break free of their grip, but they only held her even more firmly.

'You're hurting me!' Sapphire's voice was strained.

'Weapons?' the smaller guard asked, and Sapphire paled at the question. His eyes tracked down to the leather casing strapped around her waist. In a swift motion, he unbuckled her dagger, removing its scabbard as she fought against them.

The guards did not meet her alarmed gaze as they began to drag her along. The metal of Sapphire's boots made an unbearable noise as it scraped against the stone walkway.

As she realized escape was impossible, Sapphire's mind shifted to survival mode, studying her surroundings in an attempt to memorize the layout of the castle entrance. The bridge led straight to the water, and there was a window low enough to jump from and probably survive.

They were almost at the large double doors when she finally allowed herself to look back to the women who had delivered her. Lelani was pulling Evera back towards the platform, the girl's face stricken with panic as she watched Sapphire being taken away.

The last thing she saw before the doors slammed behind her was the blue sky slipping into grey.

They moved quickly through the castle, and Sapphire tried her best to track each turn they made. Large pieces of art adorned the walls, and the stone floors had given way to a shining marble. Everything was stark white, with greenery growing in terracotta pots that sat in the corners. Statues gleamed and vases shone in the late-afternoon sun that peeked through the large windows.

They took a left, moving into a dark stairwell, and the marble turned back to stone. With every step they took, the light faded until the world around her was entirely black. The warmth drained from the corridor, replaced by a bitter cold that caused her to shiver despite the heavy leather she wore.

There was a rancid smell accompanied by a stagnant heaviness that made her feel like she might choke. Finally, they entered a barren chamber with no natural light. There were no windows; flickering candles were the only source of illumination. Sapphire's eyes struggled to adjust to the dimness as stone walls and wrought-iron bars closed in around her.

No.

'You can't just throw me into jail.' Sapphire's voice was too loud, echoing off the stone. 'I want to go home. Please, I just want to return to Witrotean.'

One of the men grunted in response as he yanked her forward.

'Please, at least tell me how long I will be here.'

There was no answer as they escorted her to the third cell, and the larger guard pulled open the door before his partner shoved her inside. The lock turned with a deafening clunk, and she shut her eyes tightly, unable to bear watching them walk away. She followed the sound of their footsteps until they faded entirely.

Sapphire couldn't remember the last time she had been truly on her own. Always in the company of others at the Home – even in the woodlands – she was never truly by herself.

But she was here. Entirely alone.

Panic swallowed her whole as she stumbled backwards until she rested against the filth-covered wall of her cell.

Alone.

Alone in a world she didn't know. A world where she clearly didn't belong.

Sapphire clawed desperately at the tight collar of her borrowed tunic, ripping at the buttons in an attempt to find some relief. Still, panic built so rapidly she couldn't escape it. It twisted its way through her entire being as she leaned her forehead against the cold stone. Eventually, she turned to prayers, begging the Saints to hear her, but they didn't answer her pleas, and she slid down the wall as sobs racked her entire body until she felt empty.

There was nothing but darkness, a large puddle of standing water in the corner, and a small bench to her right.

She reached for her dagger instinctively before remembering it had been taken from her. Emptiness came with the realization. She wondered when her weapon had begun to feel as familiar as a limb. Was it her first kill? Or before? When she slept, clinging on to sharpened sticks just in case a Beast visited the Home?

She wasn't sure how long it had been when the man entered, holding a lantern.

'Hello,' he said, his voice gentler than expected. 'My name is Claye. And who might you be?'

She couldn't find any words as she stared at him, inching forward closer to get a better look. He was small with high cheekbones and a crooked nose. He allowed her time to take him in and offered her a small smile.

'My name is Sapphire and I just – I just want to go home.'

It was his turn to step forward and she fought the urge to flinch. She was taller than him, which forced him to look up at her. When he did, recognition passed over his face. The violet of her eyes was noticeable even in the dim light. Sapphire swallowed, her throat dry.

'Nice to meet you, Sapphire. But I do have a few questions first.' He waited for her to nod before continuing, 'Now, what business do you have in Eriobis today?'

'I wish I knew.'

The answer came out flat and angry, as desperation had left her too tired to remain polite, but Claye simply arched an eyebrow, entirely unfazed.

'This will be much easier if you're honest with me.'

A bitter laugh escaped her, and anger stirred inside her – actually a welcome relief from the panic.

'I am not lying. I wish I was lying. I wish I knew what I was doing here. I wish I knew anything. But I don't. Before today, I didn't even know Eriobis existed.'

'Where are you from, then?'

'Witrotean.'

He held her gaze for a moment before scribbling something in a notebook.

'I see. And do you belong to an element?' She stared at him, waiting for him to explain. 'Do you possess magic?'

'No. Where I am from, magic does not exist.'

Claye once again scribbled in his journal. Sapphire's irritation grew as he offered her no explanation in exchange for her honesty.

'Did someone send you to Eriobis, Sapphire?'

'I just told you that before today I did not know Eriobis existed.'

He licked his lips, his gaze lingering on her before returning his attention to the notepad. She sighed loudly, falling back against the bench.

'I am unsure of what to make of this situation,' Claye said.

'That makes two of us.'

She could've sworn that, for a fleeting moment, the man's lip tugged upward, amused.

When Sapphire traced the outline of the scar on her palm, Claye's eyes flicked to her hand, and he arched an eyebrow again before rushing to scribble more on the paper.

'Sapphire, have your eyes always been . . . the shade they are currently?'

'No. They're usually brown.'

He nodded before tucking his notebook into a satchel.

'Thank you for answering my questions. Regretfully, I do not have the authority to release you from this cell, but I will talk to the constable to see if we can move you somewhere more . . . comfortable.' He scrunched his nose like he was finally noticing how dirty the surroundings were. 'I am going to report my findings to the king and queen, and I will be back with an update as soon as I have one.'

'What?' Her voice broke. 'What findings?'

But he was already outside the cell and locking the door.

'Please! Don't leave me here.'

She sounded like a child, and he looked at her with more sympathy than she expected – but he still walked away. Hot tears flooded her eyes, and soon she started to sob again. She buckled over, fear and anger and exhaustion spilling out of her with every strangled breath.

She wanted Witrotean. She wanted to give Susanna her extra quilt. She wanted to find a tree that leaked sweet water and bring it home as a surprise. She wanted to thank Martia for her guidance. She wanted to provide for the Home again.

But wishes were fickle things, she knew that.

And long after her tears had stopped, she lay on the bench, staring into the darkness.

A gentle hand stirred her from her latest dream and she smiled.

A gentle hand.

Martia.

The vision was over. But as she peeled open her eyes, a soft cry escaped her throat. Claye's grey eyes were staring back at her. She scrambled away from him.

'Sorry if I scared you. But it's time to leave.'

She blinked a few times, the lingering ghost of Martia's touch making it hard to be present.

'Where am I going?'

'You've been summoned by the king and queen.'

CHAPTER THREE

The same two guards were waiting for her as she came out of the cell. They moved to strong-arm her, but Claye lifted a hand, insisting they let her walk freely. It was a small act of kindness, and she was grateful for it.

Claye moved with ease as they walked through the castle.

'What type of magic can you do?'

She knew she shouldn't ask that question. She had never been one for small talk, but despite her anger and fear, she was fascinated by the idea of magic. Claye gave her a warm smile, opening his palm and extending his hand to her.

She flinched as he twisted his fingers slightly, a cold breeze dancing over her skin.

'How –?'

'I'm from an Airborn household. My entire family are air manipulators. I wasn't always happy about it, but these days, it seems to fit me.'

She considered her response but quickly noticed that the two guards had moved closer to her, watching her carefully.

'The king and queen are very kind,' Claye said quietly, like he had read her mind.

'What magic do they have?'

'You'll be able to tell soon.'

He was right. As they moved through new corridors, the walkways were lined with shimmering water. Fountains bubbled in every corner. Flags in varying shades of blue hung from the wall.

'I told you,' Claye whispered, the corners of his eyes twitching.

At his words, she wiped away her look of bewilderment and fixed a scowl in its place, but he didn't seem to mind as he guided her to a small door. Inside was a washroom much larger than any she had ever seen. It was white with gleaming gold finishes, with not a towel out of place and not so much as a speck of dirt.

It was so perfect that it was almost infuriating.

'Please take a few moments to clean yourself up. A simple gown has been provided for you – if you should need assistance, simply knock twice on the door and it will be provided.'

The gown that had been left for her was made of the nicest fabric that she'd ever touched, soft against her aching muscles. She stared at herself in the mirror once more, never having a dress free of stains or wear before.

She opened the door to find Claye waiting.

'That is much better.' He began to usher her down the corridor.

Mercy, she was scared.

Dread settled upon her shoulders. And her fear intensified as she caught sight of two large gold-plated doors. Engravings of the Gods adorned them, and she couldn't pull her focus away because she knew, without a doubt, what – or who – resided on the other side. Would they order her to be returned to the dungeons where she would be left to rot? Or execute her as a show of power? Maybe they'd laugh, call her a silly child, and leave her to fend for herself in a world she didn't understand.

She wasn't sure which possibility scared her the most.

They paused in front of the doors for only a moment before Claye directed the guards to open them. He held out a hand, a signal for her to enter. She closed her eyes tightly, trying to push down the mounting panic in her chest, but the strong hand of one of the guards pressed against her back, forcing her to move forward. When she reopened her eyes, her vision filled with black spots as she struggled to keep herself upright.

In front of her was a large room full of light. It was brilliant white and reminded her of the days when you could feel spring giving way to summer, her favourite time in Witrotean, when food was more abundant and she could slip away to paint by the brook.

The memory brought her peace, but it dissipated quickly as she saw a man and woman seated in large chairs, looking directly at her.

'Move forward, Sapphire. We mustn't keep them waiting.'

She followed Claye's command, her eyes locked on the two thrones looming in front of her. He urged her forward, hustling her steps until she reached the king and queen and looked up to meet their gaze. Claye bowed his head, but

Sapphire did not follow suit, unable to tear her focus from the queen. Her brown skin was strewn with freckles and her eyes matched the colour of the green stones set into her crown.

She was ethereal.

'Hello, Sapphire.'

Her voice was melodic – sweet and commanding. As Sapphire watched the king and queen watch her, she stood a bit taller.

'Welcome to Eriobis,' the king said. His green eyes were as brilliant as the queen's. She wasn't sure what she had expected these two to be like, but not this. 'We hear you're in a predicament,' the king continued.

She couldn't find the courage to reply.

'Sapphire, how old are you?' the queen asked.

'I just turned eighteen before I arrived here.'

The pair exchanged a look that Sapphire couldn't understand.

'I'm sure your parents are so worried about you,' said the queen.

She shook her head, not wanting to explain that maybe no one at all was worried about her. She numbed at the thought.

The pair continued to stare at her, eyes flickering to each other every so often, and something shifted inside Sapphire, causing her to sweat. Her eyes darted around the room, which suddenly felt too small – she took a step backwards towards the door. If she ran fast enough, maybe she could escape. Run until her body gave out or they caught her and drove a sword through her chest.

She felt Claye's hand press against her back. He looked at her with a mix of warning and encouragement.

'Sapphire.' The queen's voice was quiet. 'I'm afraid we can't help you.'

No.

Sapphire ran her hands through her dark hair. She had known this could happen. She had known there was a possibility they would refuse her . . . but how was she supposed to return to Witrotean now? She bit her lip in an effort to quell the angry, heartbroken tears that threatened to spill over.

'Why not? I just want to go home.' Her voice cracked.

The queen stood, moving with ease as she made her way down the stairs. Her long dress flowed behind her, her eyes never leaving Sapphire's face.

Sapphire was unable to look away, nearly tripping backwards as the queen reached her. The woman placed a slender hand on Sapphire's right cheek.

Sapphire recoiled. Her blood ran cold at the queen's touch, her mind screaming at her to run. And despite the queen's kindness, her instincts urged her to put distance between them. She glanced over her shoulder, trying to calculate how far it was to the doors through which she had entered, but the queen's voice broke through the haze in her mind.

'We can't help you go home because . . .' The woman seemed to be struggling for words. 'Because you *are* home. Sapphire, I believe you are our daughter.'

Sapphire's vision blurred as she processed the words,

her heart pounding in her ears like a drum. She gripped the soft fabric that hung from her body in hopes of grounding herself.

Our daughter.

Oh, mercy, that couldn't be right.

She felt lightheaded as she rocked on her feet, unable to find her balance.

The queen's teary green eyes were the last thing Sapphire saw before she passed out.

CHAPTER FOUR

You will be Home. You will see grey, chipped walls. You will feel the light flooding through the open window on to your skin. You will hear Martia's sturdy footsteps as she moves down the hall to wake everyone. You will gather your dagger and your hunting cloak and you will head to the woodlands.

You won't be in Eriobis.

After repeating this mantra a few times, Sapphire forced her eyes open, then frowned as she took in the arched ceilings of the castle. To her right, the queen hovered with a worried look.

She immediately shut her eyes once more, willing it all to go away.

'Sweetling, did you hit your head?'

What a question to ask in a moment like this. And nobody had ever called her something affectionate like *sweetling*.

'I know this is overwhelming. But . . . you . . . you look so much like . . .' The queen choked back a sob, rubbing her arms as if trying to console herself. 'We lost our daughter eighteen years ago with no explanation. She simply disappeared from my arms only minutes after I first held her and you –'

'I fit the timeline,' Sapphire stated, slowly sitting up.

The queen eyed her closely, clearly unused to being interrupted. 'It's more than a timeline.'

She reached out an uncertain hand, intending to help Sapphire stand, but her eyes widened as Sapphire held up her own to accept. A loud sob escaped the queen's lips. Sapphire looked at the king in confusion, but he looked only at his wife. The air stiffened, a new tension enveloping the three as the queen continued to stare at her outstretched palm.

'Everyone, out.'

The king's voice was strained but commanding and everyone else in the room marched to the exit without even glancing back, except for Claye, who remained only a few steps away. At the sound of the door closing, the queen walked back to her husband. Her earlier grace had vanished as she collapsed against his chest, sobbing like a child.

'Araxia, what happened?'

The king held his wife closely, lightly rubbing her back, and Sapphire suddenly felt like she was intruding.

'Kip, it is her,' the queen sputtered. 'Her palm. Look at her palm. It's Aylara.'

His eyes found Sapphire, and they stayed there for a few heartbeats. The only sounds in the room were the queen's meek sobs and the king's heavy silence.

The tension returned to his posture, and he led his wife back to her seat before approaching Sapphire.

'Your palm again, please?'

'And if I say no?'

His eyes darkened at her words. Sapphire searched his face, trying to find clemency. Find clarity. Find herself.

'It wasn't a request,' he replied, reaching for her hand.

Her fingernails dug into her skin until she wondered if she had drawn blood.

'Please, Aylara.'

It was the queen who spoke now. Her voice was teetering on the edge of begging. Sapphire met the woman's tear-stained gaze for a moment but forced herself to look away.

'That's not my name,' she snapped.

'Please . . . Sapphire.'

Don't care, don't care, Sapphire chanted to herself. It wasn't her responsibility to care. But she couldn't help feel pity at the queen's desperate expression.

The king took his chance.

His left hand lunged forward, wrapping itself around her wrist. His right forced her fingers back one by one.

'Kip!' the queen cried.

'Aylara, we don't have time for games.'

As he bent back her last finger, the king paused, shooting Sapphire a look she couldn't quite read. Apologetic, weary, tired even. He ran his forefinger down the length of her jagged scar – leaving a burning sensation in its wake.

'You are hurting me!' she hissed through gritted teeth. Anger simmered deep inside her. Anger that now outweighed any fear that she'd felt.

He dropped her hand but his smugness was gone. His

face betrayed panic as he moved quickly, and silently, back to his throne.

'It's her.' There was no question in his tone. 'Call them. Let's get this settled.'

A quick flick of his wrist was all it took to send Claye out into the hall, shouting as he went. Sapphire did her best to track every movement, every word, trying to take stock, make sense, anything to understand the world around her.

She didn't hear Claye's soft-footed return.

'You fit.' He lowered his voice as he continued. 'You fit who they say you are more than you probably realize.'

Sapphire tried to ignore the meaning lurking behind his words and fixed her eyes on the two figures in front of them.

'They kept me in a cage for nearly two days.'

A small chuckle shook his body.

'Better than most are blessed with.'

He paused for another moment, craning his neck slightly to look up at her.

'And to be fair, the castle *guards* threw you in the cage. And myself, of course.'

Sapphire's eyes pinned Claye. 'I'll make sure I remember that.'

A grin spread across his narrow face. 'All I'm trying to say is, we put you in the cage. It was their decision to let you out. I'd make sure to remember that instead.'

He turned and walked away without another word, leaving her. It felt as if time dragged on for hours until the doors swung open again, and two women entered.

The younger one had fiery red hair and skin that was nearly translucent. She had a darkness about her, but even from a distance, Sapphire could tell she was unnervingly beautiful.

The older woman beside her looked more severe. She had the same red hair but her skin was nearly silver with scars running in every direction. When her eyes cut to Sapphire, she was startled to see they were pale blue.

'Your majesties.' The older woman bowed, her younger counterpart following suit. 'It's a long time since we've been issued an *imperative* court summons.'

The king took his place on the throne beside his wife. 'We need to get something straightened out,' his eyes jumped between the two women and Sapphire, 'quickly.'

The pair turned, their eyes settling on her at last. She squirmed under their gaze, unable to stop the shivers that ran across her skin as they took careful steps towards her.

This is –

It's too much –

She –

'We only want proof she is our daughter, Savina. Nothing more,' the queen called to the older woman from her throne.

'As you wish, my queen.' Sapphire did not miss the bitterness in the woman's tone. 'Though if I was you, your majesty, I'd want to know why this girl has eyes the colour of the flowers that cover the fields of Ciliria. Quite unusual.'

'That,' the queen's voice was sharper than it had been, 'is none of your concern. Just do as we have asked.'

Savina threw her hands up in mock defence. 'Nothing but a familial charm, my queen. There's no need to fret.'

Araxia held Savina's gaze with narrowed eyes.

'There is plenty to fret over, given our history. In fact, I want your daughter to do this.'

Savina smiled, turning to face the younger red-haired woman.

'Well, go on, Ashes. You've been requested.'

Ashes approached, her face unfriendly and guarded. The girl towered over Sapphire, making her feel small.

'Your hand.' Ashes' voice was unexpected – low and honeyed – and Sapphire could not focus. The girl arched a sharp brow. 'I need your hand to do the charm.'

Sapphire looked at her fist, unclenching it slightly while considering her next move. Finally, she extended her left hand, but Ashes shook her head.

'The scarred one.' Her voice was now laced with impatience and irritation. Sapphire remained motionless, staring up at Ashes.

'Please, Sapphire,' Queen Araxia spoke. 'If I am somehow wrong about this, you have my word . . . I will personally see to it that you return to Witrotean.'

Promises made in high-stake scenarios don't tend to be kept, but this was more than Sapphire had been offered since her arrival. So, begrudgingly, she offered her other hand, and Ashes accepted it, pausing slightly at the first sensation of touch until Savina cleared her throat and Ashes returned to the task at hand.

The girl's touch silenced the world around Sapphire.

Her mind and heart slowed for the first time all day.

Ashes pulled a small dagger from the bag hanging from her shoulder. Sapphire tugged at her hand, trying to free herself, but the girl's grip tightened, and she smiled.

'Why make this difficult? Obey, and it will all be over soon.'

'You don't command me,' Sapphire snapped.

'Your attitude surely suits your supposed status.' Ashes leaned in a bit closer, her voice dropping to a whisper. 'But you've been unable to take your eyes off me since I entered this room, so why don't you be a good girl and do as I ask?'

Sapphire froze at the challenge, and Ashes took advantage of her lapse to drag the blade across her hand. Blood trickled along the crease of her palm in a tiny red stream, and she watched as Ashes drew it out by magic, floating it in the air between them.

The girl began to chant deep, guttural words that rang through Sapphire's bones like chimes in the wind. Together they watched as the shallow trail of her blood drifted across the hall, moving towards the thrones.

The queen opened her own hand, silent tears rolling down her cheeks as the blood settled on to her palm, soaking into her skin.

'She is yours,' said Ashes.

The breaking of the spell felt like a twig snapping in Sapphire's mind; some unseen tether pulling free. Her eyes locked on the girl's hand in hers until the queen wrenched them apart, crushing her in a hug.

'My daughter. My sweet Aylara.'

'That's not my name,' Sapphire murmured into the soft fabric of the queen's dress, but the woman only tightened her hold. The king loomed a few steps away, watching them closely, his expression guarded.

Claye silently ushered the two red-headed women out of the room, but not before Ashes looked over her shoulder, catching Sapphire's gaze. The corner of her lip tugged upward ever so slightly before the doors closed behind her.

'I don't understand.' Sapphire's voice sounded sturdier than it had a moment earlier.

The queen cupped Sapphire's face with cold hands.

'There's time for that, my love.' A few silent tears dripped from her chin. 'We have time now. Eighteen years. Eighteen years I have waited for you. Where do we even begin? Claye, please send for someone to prepare Sapphire some lunch. Are you hungry?'

She nodded weakly, her mind racing as she was led out of the room.

A few steps from the large door, a ringing in her ears forced her to pause. Suddenly, the lights were too bright, and she shut her eyes tightly, feeling disoriented.

But just as quickly as it had come, the feeling disappeared, leaving nothing but the words:

Run. Run. Run.

That was the first time she ever heard the voice.

CHAPTER FIVE

There were no guards at her side as she was led back through the castle, only Queen Araxia. People who passed them bowed their heads in her presence.

King Kip had disappeared, citing a crucial matter that had to be handled, but Sapphire knew he was lying. His face had never lost the uncertain look he had worn from the second he laid eyes on her.

The queen, on the other hand, seemed anything but uncertain as she guided Sapphire to a large dining room. Ivy snaked up the walls, and the sun shone through large windows, casting golden rays throughout the room.

Servants awaited them, promptly pulling out the queen's chair and then Sapphire's to her right side. Sapphire felt awkward as she allowed the woman to perform tasks she could easily do on her own.

'Do you know what you would like to eat?'

Sapphire shook her head, embarrassed that she had no idea what to even ask for. It had been so long since she had the luxury of choice, as they ate whatever they could scrounge together at the Home. Araxia offered her a small smile.

'Please proceed.' She spoke loudly, and at her command, the door to the right swung open. Uniformed servants filed in carrying more food than Sapphire had ever seen together in one place.

She sat unmoving as she gaped at the spread, wondering if she could tuck small portions away in her dress to save for later, or maybe, if she returned to Witrotean, share with the other girls. Sitting with a feast in front of her planted the smallest seed of guilt in the pit of her stomach.

Araxia watched her from the corner of her eye.

'Is it not to your liking? I can send for anything you'd like.'

'I-I've never seen so much food.'

Araxia's face crumpled. 'One day, I hope you will tell me of the world you grew up in. I will never be able to offer you the time that was stolen from you, from us, but I will listen and try to understand if you give me the chance.'

'A chance?'

'Well, you are an adult, Sapphire. I must allow you to make your own choices no matter how badly I want you to remain at this castle.'

Sapphire paused, arm outstretched towards the food, unsure of how to respond to such kindness. So, instead of speaking she plucked an oddly shaped berry from a nearby bowl. The berry was a vibrant magenta with fantastic petals blooming from its top. She turned it over in her hands a few times before popping it into her mouth.

The flavour was sweeter than the most expensive berries in Witrotean and richer than the chocolate she had craved since stealing some from a merchant's cart when she was seven. The juice coated her tongue, rolling down her throat, and she reached for another quickly.

Her body sighed, grateful for an end to the hunger that had plagued her for most of her life.

When she reached for the dish of berries once more, she heard Araxia laugh.

'Roseberries have always been my favourite too.'

Sapphire didn't respond, focused on the food on her plate. But soon enough, she found herself uncomfortably full. Her body, unused to such a feast, warned her that it couldn't handle another bite, and she frowned.

Food was being offered, and she knew better than to waste it.

'It's perfectly fine if you can't eat any more, love,' said the queen. 'The staff will provide food for you whenever you need.'

Sapphire stared at her wide-eyed. The thought of food so . . . disposable was ludicrous. She imagined Susanna's tear-stained face as she begged for something to eat. Anything. Any scrap that could be spared.

She fought against tears as she leaned back in her chair, signalling that she was done, and watched as the table was cleared. The two women sat in silence for only a moment before Sapphire could no longer hold in her questions.

'I don't understand any of this.' Sapphire somehow sat up even straighter. 'I don't understand how I am your daughter. I don't understand how a baby simply disappears and ends up in another place. I – I need an explanation, answers.'

The queen stilled for only a moment before blinking a few times.

'You are bold, like all those who came before you.' She laughed, warmth filling her eyes.

Sapphire shook her head, refusing to be distracted.

'What others? Answers,' Sapphire pressed, 'please.'

Araxia took a deep breath, sinking back into her chair.

'I have rehearsed this conversation so many times over the years. I'm not sure why that practice is failing me now.' For the first time, Sapphire noticed that the woman looked nervous. 'Conceiving a child was not easy for me, Sapphire. And then you came – a gift from the Gods – and I felt so lucky to have a daughter. But something was not right; you were ill. Struggling to breathe, to cry – your wail hardly sounded. And I begged the Gods for any type of magic to save you. Magic that was forbidden. Magic that would cost me dearly. None of that mattered – I only cared for you. But the Gods are . . . well, they have their . . . reasons. They saved you, I suppose. I only wish I had known the price – the time with you we'd lose. I held you so tightly, but the room had gone quiet – the weight of your small frame was just . . . gone. And your father and I . . . we were alone.'

'But what . . . what did the Gods do?'

'They called upon a Shadow Witch. Their magic . . . the power that they wield . . . It eats away at the soul. But, in the moment, we were so desperate, Sapphire. So desperate that we broke a millennia-old rule – never trust a Shadow Witch. She . . . she cut open your small palm and the spell she uttered stole you away from us.'

47

Sapphire opened her hand, staring at the scar. She had always asked Martia about it, but got no answers – because it was caused by a witch. A shadow of her panic must have passed across her face because the queen reached out until her hand eclipsed Sapphire's own.

'Aylara, you must be tired.' Araxia paused, realizing her misstep. 'I apologize. I know that is not the name you are used to. You are Sapphire. I promise I'll get it right.'

Araxia held her gaze with hopeful eyes as if she was waiting for a response, but when it didn't come, she continued, 'I know this is overwhelming. So, I give you my word. As much space and time as you need will be offered. We will not rush into your presentation.'

Presentation?

Sapphire found that she was too tired to ask.

Araxia turned to whisper to one of the servants. 'I need Claye.'

It only took a few moments for his familiar face to appear in the doorway.

'You called for me, your majesty?'

'Ah, Claye. Yes – as you've been so . . . involved in this process, would you mind helping Sapphire get comfortable while we assign her a lady in-waiting? Simply show her to her room, help her learn her way around the castle. We will send handmaidens to assist with the day-to-day things.'

'Of course, your majesty. Anything you or her highness need, I am here.'

'Splendid.' The queen offered a small smile. 'Now, please

escort the princess to the guest room nearest to the water gardens. I want her to enjoy the view.'

'Of course, your majesty.' Claye gave another shallow bow before taking a small step back to give Sapphire more room to rise.

She stared between the two of them, uncertain, before Araxia gave her an encouraging nod. Pushing away from the table, Sapphire exited the dining room in silence together with Claye.

As he guided her down a corridor, she once again tried to memorize every turn they made.

'I will be here for whatever you need, princess. You don't have to worry about knowing the castle quite yet.'

'Please call me Sapphire.'

To her relief, they finally stopped in front of a large door – which looked like all the others they had passed their entire walk – and Sapphire wondered how Claye knew such a large castle so well.

'I apologize that your room isn't entirely prepared. We weren't expecting . . .' The man didn't finish his thought as he swung open the door.

The bedroom was four times the size of the room she shared with other girls at the Home. The far wall was lined with large windows that offered a view of the lake. Like most of the castle, the room was a stark white. Greenery grew from pots in every corner, climbing the walls and bringing much needed pops of colour. But it was the bed that caught her attention.

It was so large at least four people could fit. Comfortably.

'Is there anything you'd like at the moment, princess?'

Sapphire jumped, slightly startled by the female voice. She turned to find a woman no older than twenty standing by the door. Claye offered an encouraging smile.

'Whatever you need, Rayna will take care of you.' And then, he was gone.

Alone with the woman, Sapphire blinked a few times in the hope of acclimatizing herself.

'Rayna, right?'

'Yes, princess.' She bowed. 'Is there anything I can do for you?'

'I – well, would it be possible for me to take a bath?

'Of course. Whatever you need.'

Rayna disappeared through a side door, and Sapphire heard water running.

As the bath filled up, Rayna returned to the room, turning down the bed and starting a fire in the carved marble fireplace.

'I could do that, you know,' Sapphire protested. 'You don't have to waste your time with all this.'

'The queen requested that I aid your transition and make you comfortable, princess. I am simply following the orders I've been given.'

Sapphire returned her eyes to the windows, watching as a bird landed on the sill and pecked at the glass.

Rayna's hands began to work at the buttons she could reach, and Sapphire jumped from the chair, wrapping her arms around herself.

'What are you doing?'

'Preparing you for a bath, princess.'

'I–I am entirely capable of undressing myself. Please, I'd just like some time alone.'

Rayna stepped back, grimacing, and Sapphire kept an eye on her as she walked towards the washroom.

'I will be right outside the door. If you need me, please just –'

'I won't.' Rayna flinched and Sapphire felt guilty. Rayna bowed her head as Sapphire stepped into the washroom, avoiding the girl's gaze.

When she entered the bath, her hand stung and she quickly pulled it out of the water, staring at the fresh cut over her old scar. As she traced it lightly with her finger, she recalled the witch's touch – how it had lingered a second longer than necessary. How it had silenced every screaming thought in her head.

Sapphire half wished she'd held on a bit longer.

She remained in the bath with those thoughts for hours and the water never went cold. Magic, she guessed. She added that to her growing list of questions. Afterwards she collapsed into the large bed; it was soft and the pillows plentiful, so unlike the worn mattress at the Home.

The Home.

She wondered if they were looking for her in the woodlands; if they cried beside her bed; if Martia said a prayer to the Saints, begging for her return. Or if she had simply pressed the dagger into Kaila's hand, and Sapphire had become just another name on the growing list of those who never returned home.

The thought broke her, and she sobbed into the pillows until she fell into a restless sleep.

A soft knock stirred her the next morning, and when she opened the door, she found a small older woman standing there.

'I apologize for the interruption, princess. I have been asked to gather your measurements.'

The woman led her to her dressing quarters, assisting her as she stepped on to a box in front of a large, gilded mirror. The woman's hands worked quickly as she poked and prodded. A measuring tape was wrapped around Sapphire's waist, her bust, and her arms.

She couldn't stop fidgeting, but the woman never slowed, never sighed in frustration as she continued her task. Then the tailor wrapped the measuring tape around her waist once more, and studied the number.

'I-I come from a place of famine,' Sapphire rushed out, and the woman looked up, softening at the admission.

'I'll leave a few extra inches, princess. May you never know hunger like that again.'

Sapphire relaxed slightly but couldn't fully adjust to the feeling of hands on her skin as the tailor guided her through steps she did not understand, and it was only when the door shut, leaving her alone, that she allowed herself to truly breathe.

Heading back to the washroom, she noticed the leathers had been taken away and frowned.

She'd rather liked the leather. It made her feel like a warrior.

The dress that was brought to her a few hours later . . . did not.

Rayna and more new servants carried in the flowing garment. It was various shades of deep blue, much like the flags she had seen lining the castle walls. And she tried to focus on that as the maidens began to dress her.

Too many hands. Too many eyes.

As a maiden tugged the corset strings, she wondered if her ribs would crack under the pressure.

Rayna delivered one last crushing pull, squeezing the air from Sapphire's lungs before she scurried away. Sapphire took in her reflection and frowned. She looked ridiculous, like a child playing dressing-up. The blue of the dress made her new violet eyes even harsher, and her hair was coiled tightly atop her head. Sapphire unpinned it, then braided it in an effort to look more pulled together, but it did not help. And as she turned away from the looking glass, the word *run* rang out in her subconscious again.

Another knock at the door grabbed her attention. When she opened it, she found Claye waiting for her outside.

'Your highness, I'm here to escort you to breakfast.' Claye bowed quickly and Sapphire cringed.

'Please just call me Sapphire.'

Claye smiled but did not agree as he motioned for her to walk ahead. Sapphire held her ground, though, standing still in the large doorframe as she stared past Claye down the long corridor. Ever since she had arrived, she had been escorted around and told what she would do. But now Araxia had promised her space and promised to move forward at Sapphire's speed.

It was time to see if the queen was a woman of her word.

'I will not be attending breakfast.'

'I should've taken that bet,' he said under his breath.

She stepped back into her room, but Claye caught the closing door, giving her a small smile.

'I will inform the king and queen of your decision. Please let me know if I can assist you any further.'

Sapphire remained in the large armchair near the window, studying the world around her until the sound of movement came from the other side of her door. She waited a few moments before opening it, and was surprised to find a breakfast spread on a shiny silver tray.

Most surprising of all was the small bowl of roseberries in the centre.

She settled back into the chair with the food and began to slowly sample all the flavours until a piece of parchment on the floor caught her eye. It had clearly fallen from the tray as Sapphire had crossed the room.

In fine script, it read:

Take your time, sweetling. We will be here when you are ready.

She quickly tossed the note in the fireplace to her right and returned her eyes to a different parchment that sat in her lap – covered in her own sloppy handwriting. She had taken to writing down her thoughts and questions but she still needed some more time before she faced the king and queen again.

'Not yet,' she whispered, reaching for a pen.

It became a routine. Sapphire politely refused the invitation for meals, someone delivered food a few minutes later on another polished tray, and Sapphire counted to exactly two minutes before retrieving it.

Araxia's notes came daily. They never grew frantic, but they persisted.

Sapphire left her room a few times as well, sneaking down corridors and taking in the castle around her. She'd study the paintings, the pottery. Once, she even stepped outside and enjoyed the warm sun – but mostly, she remained in her room, partly as a form of rebellion and partly as self-preservation. She feared if she sat at the table with Kip and Araxia, she might unravel. Despite her efforts to organize her thoughts, she still felt entirely out of control of the situation.

It had been five days since she found herself in the deserts of Aleburn, and she had remained locked in her overlarge room for the majority of the time, riddled with anxiety.

Maybe that was why, when Claye visited on the fifth day to escort her to breakfast, Sapphire begrudgingly agreed. He reacted with brief surprise before rushing the maidens to prepare her. They quickly dressed her and fixed her hair with a blue gemstone clip.

'They will be so pleased you are joining them, princess,' Claye mused as he waited for them to finish.

Sapphire didn't respond as she stared at her reflection in the looking glass. She looked so unlike herself it was unsettling.

Claye was patient, offering a few much-needed moments of quiet before they began their walk to the dining room.

'If you are not ready, princess, I can inform them and deliver your breakfast.'

'No,' Sapphire pushed out, turning to face him. 'I can't stay in here forever, I suppose.'

'I suppose you can't.' He smiled slightly as she said it.

The walk to the dining room was shorter than Sapphire would've liked, and as they stood in front of the large double doors, she struggled to understand why she had made the choice to attend breakfast at all.

She couldn't stop hoping that this was the moment that would change everything. Change had, of course, been a consistent factor since the moment she found herself in Eriobis. But she could not shake the feeling that the second she crossed the threshold in front of her, she would be striking an unspoken agreement with the king and queen.

Acceptance of the situation.

Sapphire wasn't sure she was ready for that, but she was at the tipping point, walking on a tight wire with few options. Deep down, she didn't believe she could be the lost daughter they had mourned all these years. A princess. She had spent so many years being no one's daughter, that the adjustment was difficult.

And after a lifetime of weariness, she most certainly did not trust them; did not trust their kindness, their intentions, or their goodwill.

But if they were right . . . she needed answers. Answers to questions she had asked herself since she was a little girl. Questions that deserved answers.

So, with a deep breath, she decided to make an agreement with herself alone.

She would do as they asked, would sit with them at dinner and breakfast – but she would unravel it all – everything that had happened – and find out what was hiding beneath the unblemished surface of this kingdom.

And then, she'd return to Witrotean.

No matter what it cost her.

Chapter Six

At her arrival, the king and queen both sat up straighter in their seats.

'Sapphire.' Araxia smiled – a mix of surprise and relief – as the name rolled off her tongue. 'Good morning. How did you sleep?'

The pair sat at the far end of the table. The warm morning light cast them in an almost iridescent glow, and Sapphire once again had the overwhelming sense that she did not belong here.

'I slept well, thank you. The view was . . . everything you said it would be.'

'I knew you would love it. You are Waterborn, after all.' Araxia turned to her husband. 'Look, Kip, look how well the water territory colours fit her.'

The king gave her a tight-lipped smile and nodded.

'You look beautiful, Sapphire,' Kip said, staring at something on his plate.

Araxia clapped her hands as if she sensed the tension. 'Well, I am so glad you have decided to join us. Is everything to your liking? If not, I can request anything you like. I –'

'This is fine,' Sapphire responded as Claye pulled the seat out for her. She kept her hands in her lap, unsure if she could stomach food. 'When you say water territory, what does that mean?'

Araxia beamed at her while Kip shifted in his seat.

'A wonderful question. Eriobis is broken up into four territories: Aleburn, Ciliria, the Isle of Irobel, and Astral. In each territory, members of a single element reside. They each have a long, proud history, displayed through colours, crests, and more. You will learn all of this in your courses, though, so no need to memorize it all today.'

'I see.' Sapphire pushed a roseberry around her plate with her fork.

A few seconds passed before Kip cleared his throat.

'So, Sapphire, we'd love to know more about your life . . . before your return.'

'If you are comfortable sharing,' Araxia followed up quickly.

Sapphire stared at them with wide eyes for a moment, trying to figure out how to explain Witrotean.

'I – I grew up in an orphanage. Not really unusual, since most children in Witrotean do. As I got older, though, I learned how to hunt, wield a dagger, and take care of the younger girls.'

She met the queen's watery gaze.

'You have faced so much. You have my word that you will never know that type of life again. As the princess of Eriobis and the heir to the Canmore crown, you will know nothing but prosperity and good fortune. It is the Canmore blessing.'

'How long have the Canmores ruled?'

'For a thousand years, and many moons more, Gods willing.'

'Who ruled before the Canmores?'

'That is something you will learn all about in your courses,' Araxia replied abruptly. 'Tell me, Sapphire, was there anyone in Witrotean you were close to? That you would go back to, given the chance?'

Sapphire paused, her fork halfway to her mouth and stared at the queen for a moment.

'Is there even a possibility I might have that chance?'

Araxia went silent, dropping her eyes to her lap, and Sapphire almost laughed – they both knew the truth. Finally, the queen cleared her throat.

'How would you feel about beginning your training today?' Sapphire shot her a confused look before looking out of the window. 'Your elemental training . . . Training typically begins at a very young age, but I am confident you will adapt and excel quite quickly.'

'I-I am not ready for that. I can't simply just . . .' Her breathing caught slightly, and she counted to five before continuing. 'No. I do not want to do that today.'

Araxia placed her hand on top of Sapphire's to comfort her. She fought the urge to yank her hand away as her stomach clenched.

'I will be teaching you personally. And I'll continue to teach you for as long as it takes. There have been plenty of late bloomers in Eriobis. Every single one has grown to master their element. No need to be nervous.'

But Sapphire barely heard her, still staring at Araxia's hand on her own. The woman's touch was cold.

'I think you would do well to begin –'

Sapphire's attention snapped away from the contact and she shook her head.

'No. I'm not willing to start today.'

The queen stiffened at the response, her tension apparent in the lines around her mouth.

'I must ask you consider beginning training soon. We will, of course, wait for you to be ready – but I believe connecting with the water will bring you comfort. Perhaps instead you would like to use the library?'

Sapphire didn't feel like responding, so she simply nodded, and reached for a pastry to add to her plate and looked out of the large windows.

Instead of training, she studied. The queen's clear avoidance of the past had made her more curious than ever before. Sitting in the large, windowed room in the east wing, she was surrounded by an armful of books Araxia had allowed her to take from the library. Books about her history – about the kingdom she would supposedly inherit. She was ambivalent at the thought.

'There are better texts I could retrieve for you, princess,' said Claye. 'The ones you're reading are outdated and nearly ruined by time.'

'I enjoy the older feel of these books.' Sapphire sat down with the one she had pulled from a nearby shelf.

'The queen might –'

'The queen told me I was free to use the private library however I saw fit. I chose these.'

Claye sighed louder than he probably meant to before heading out of the door to give Sapphire some privacy. Turning her attention to the worn pages before her, she began to read.

The Canmore Dynasty, or *Blessed Queens*, read as if it was cut from the pages of Martia's favourite folktales. A thousand-year history of powerful women who never faltered when it came to honour and duty. The line was blessed by the Elders – the Gods who led Eriobis to victory during what they called the First War. Sapphire had yet to delve much into that war, as her attention was mostly taken by the original Canmore queen.

Queen Aylara. The woman Sapphire was named after. That sparked a feeling in her that she couldn't understand.

Aylara was chosen by the Elders to lead the country into the 'years of light' following the First War. The blessed queen, the beloved queen, the God-chosen ruler. Aylara's story read more like myth.

Queen Aylara, *the original*, was a beacon of hope and peace as she was a descendant of . . .

Sapphire turned the page and frowned when a new chapter about agriculture began. She returned to the previous chapter, ensuring she hadn't misread its ending, but the cut-off sentence remained.

Returning to the new chapter, she ran her finger down the gutter of the book, feeling the jagged edges of clearly torn pages. Someone had ripped them out. She flipped through the book once more, trying to recover the missing portion, but nothing came.

Turning to the next book, her frown deepened as she found more pages ripped from the seams of the book. Large sections were missing. Pages regarding the First War, Aylara, the Elders, and everything Sapphire desperately wanted to know about.

Opening the final book, she flipped through it looking for the missing history, but instead came across something that made her uneasy.

She was sure at one time it had been a lovely portrait of Aylara, but it was now distorted. Like someone had spilled liquid on the pages and not bothered to clean it up. But it was not the portrait that haunted her; instead, it was the words that had been written above the ruined image.

A throne that grows in unstable foundations is bound to rot.

'Claye?' she called out. A few moments passed before he entered the room.

'What can I do for you, princess?' Claye bounded towards her.

'What happened to this book? Do you know?'

Claye stared at the page a few seconds longer than he needed to before returning his attention to Sapphire.

'These books are very old and they have passed through many hands. I suppose it's time and use that have caused the decay.'

'But the image . . . it's entirely distorted. And what of the words here, written just above it?'

'What words, princess?' Claye leaned forward, squinting at the page.

Sapphire joined him before realizing to her horror that the writing was now gone.

'There was . . . someone had written words, right . . .' She trailed off, pointing towards the page.

Claye frowned, patting her on the shoulder.

Sapphire blinked a few times before reaching out a timid finger and running it over the portrait. For a moment, she could have sworn her skin burned at the touch. The sensation spooked her, and she quickly closed the book, then followed Claye out of the room, trying to ignore the sinking feeling that she was being watched.

Sapphire had been to the library for five days in a row but Evera still hadn't returned to her position there. Sapphire was beginning to feel unsettled. So, as she dressed for lunch, she decided today she would ask. The garment she wore was a lighter blue; her favourite dress so far, not as heavy or confining as the others that had been made for her. Rayna was ill today so three maidens she didn't know worked quickly, adding another jewelled pendant to her hair.

'I realized I've never asked your names,' Sapphire said.

'Their names are not important,' Claye interrupted as he entered the room. 'What is important is that we don't keep their majesties waiting. Do work quickly.'

Sapphire met the maidens' eyes, begging them to speak, but they never did.

Mercy, she wished they would, though.

Claye escorted her to lunch daily, prattling on about the castle. The art, the history of it all. But Sapphire barely listened, her thoughts nearly swallowing her whole.

Sapphire was playing along, but she needed to start putting a plan together if she wanted to return to the Home any time soon. Lyna . . . Susanna . . . Her thoughts always returned to their faces and the familiar mix of guilt and yearning overwhelmed her.

They arrived at the now-familiar double doors, Claye opening one for her, and she stepped in. Araxia gave a big smile when she saw her.

'I'm so glad you are joining us, Sapphire. Praise the Elders, my requests have been heard.'

Sapphire nodded as she took the seat she always did, and quickly spoke before the king and queen could say more.

'Is there a reason why Evera has not been working in the library?'

Kip and Araxia exchanged a guarded look. The seconds passed slowly before they returned their attention to Sapphire.

'We can control many things – but not how our staff spend their time off,' Kip explained.

Sapphire turned to Araxia, dismissing Kip's attempt to humour her.

'I will train. I will go into the water today, but only if

you give me your word that Evera will visit. Even if she does have time off, I am asking to see her as my friend.'

'There are no such bargains in my kingdom –' began Kip.

Araxia lifted her hand, silencing her husband.

'I will give you my word. If you allow me to train you today, I will make sure Evera is here later this afternoon.'

'You swear it?'

'I do.'

'Good,' Sapphire said over her shoulder as she stormed out of the hall and back to her room.

After slipping into her training uniform, a body suit made of a soft but sturdy material, Sapphire stared at the looking glass and tried to convince herself that she could do this.

Panic did her no favours, and she needed to get a grip before it swallowed her whole.

'I'm ready.'

Claye bowed, before guiding her out of the room.

The gardens around the castle were filled with bright shades of purple, blue, yellow and red. Large trees lifted their branches towards the sky, and sparkling water stretched for as far as her eyes could see.

To her right was a small pond filled with glimmering fish, and to her left, fruit-laden bushes lined the walkway. Roseberries grew on vines. The stones under her feet were smooth and shimmered in the warm sunlight.

But her wonder faded quickly as the training grounds came into view. Obstacles had been set out, and the queen awaited her in the middle of the lake. Claye escorted her to the shore.

He bowed slightly to Sapphire before bowing deeply to the queen, and then hurried away. To Sapphire's surprise, her stomach clenched as the man disappeared – longing to not be alone with Araxia.

'Sapphire, you are Waterborn, meaning you have a special connection with the water. And with a little practice, I truly believe that you will be one of the strongest water elementals in your age range, just like every Canmore before you.'

'Don't hold your breath.'

To her surprise, Araxia smirked. 'Funny you say that, because that's where we're going to begin.'

'What?'

'The first step of harnessing your power is holding your breath, though eventually you will be able to breathe underwater. This should be simple. The water is a part of you and should feel comfortable.'

Sapphire stared at her.

'Come on. You'll be OK. I'll be here.'

But Sapphire couldn't. She couldn't join Araxia in the water. For a reason that pained her to admit.

'I – I can't swim.'

Araxia softened.

'We'll stay where your feet can touch the bottom. But I think you'll be surprised by how at home you feel in the water.'

Araxia raised her hands and pushed them outwards.

Sapphire watched closely as the water followed the queen's movements, parting before her, allowing a clear passage for Sapphire to enter. She took a timid step forward and Araxia gave her an encouraging nod. She continued forward until she was standing a few feet away from Araxia.

'I am going to allow the water to return. But you are safe, Sapphire. Trust that you are in control.'

The water rushed back in, surrounding Sapphire up to waist level. She did her best not to acknowledge it, focused on calming the panic building up inside her.

Her body screamed out in protest. This was so foolish. She was not special. She did not have magic running through her veins. She was Sapphire: a hunter, an orphan. She was not a princess or a wielder of elements.

She took six paces backwards until she was standing on the shore.

'I can't.'

'You can, Sapphire. You may not trust me but you can trust yourself. Listen to your body. It understands even when you don't.'

Sapphire took a deep breath and stared down at the water before taking a tentative step forward, letting it cover her bare feet.

Two words fuelled her curiosity.

What if?

Martia had always said there was something about her that the others didn't have. That was why she had been chosen as the hunter, why Martia had trusted her to provide. That was also why Martia had been so stern – to shape her, to better her, to force her to grow.

Fear gets you nowhere, foolish girl. If you cannot summon courage, you are wasting my time.

Martia had told her that the first night she had returned from hunting empty-handed. She had run from the forest, terrified of the creatures that lurked around her. She had run like a scared child – and back then, maybe she was one. But she no longer wanted to be that young girl with tangled hair and tears running down her cheeks.

She might be a fool but she'd be a brave one.

Three more steps forward and the water met her chest. Her throat tightened slightly at the sensation and she planted herself on the spot, unwilling to move further.

'Good. Now, I want you to focus on the water. Understand it, trust it, make it part of you.'

'I don't think I'm ready for this.'

She blurted it out before she could stop herself and Martia's voice rang out in her head once more: *If you cannot summon courage, you are wasting my time.*

She flinched, awaiting the queen's disappointment. Instead, the woman offered her a soft, kind expression.

'I would be worried if you felt totally OK with all of this, having been away from it for so long.' The honesty shocked Sapphire. 'But you were born of this world. The power has always been inside you. You just didn't know it.'

The words sent a pang through her chest.

They kindled a warmth in her stomach.

For the first time since her arrival, she could tell that Araxia was meant to be a mother, so gentle and kind. So unlike Martia, the woman who had raised her, with her permanent frown.

'What if I fail?'

'You most likely will. But then we try again. And again. Until that failure is but a speck of a memory.'

The certainty of failure ignited a fire inside her. She was determined to buck against it. To be something more. Sapphire took one more purposeful step, the water nearly reaching her chin, and battled ever harder to push down her panic. Araxia smiled at her with more pride than anyone else ever had.

'So, what do I do?'

'Duck under the water. Hold your breath for as long as you can – and when your lungs begin to burn, trust that you are safe in the water. Rely on your magic to carry you through. Accept it.'

Fear wrapped around Sapphire. Squeezing her. Warning her. Taunting her.

But she took a deep breath and plunged down regardless.

The panic she had been fighting would not be silenced once she opened her eyes. The lake was clear for as far as she could see, and the silence that surrounded her put her even more on edge.

And her body sensed it. Her chest began to burn, urging her upwards. She fought against it, not wanting to fail so miserably on her first try, but a few seconds passed, and she could no longer handle the crushing pressure. She shot to the surface, coughing and gasping.

Anger flooded her senses as she backed away from the queen. She had not only failed but made a scene of it all. How could they believe she was their daughter when she could barely handle being underwater for a matter of seconds?

Mercy, she was not born for this.

The realization made the ache in her chest shift from panic to longing. At least in Witrotean, she had understood who she was. She had known her place. She had not been taunted by the idea of a family. She had no room for hope.

But here . . . here she . . .

She could not think about it. She could not consider it.

She was not their daughter.

She waited for Araxia to speak, to lash out, to throw her out of training, but the woman remained steady, saying nothing. She studied her with a look Sapphire could not read.

'Are you ready to try again?'

She wanted to say no, but she knew they had struck a deal. And despite her failures, she knew she had to continue to play the queen's game. She had to keep her word. She had to try and try until her attempts were deemed good enough.

So, back under she went.

Two hours later, she was exhausted. They had been training non-stop, and Sapphire was out of hope. Her chest ached and her lungs burned as she struggled to stay upright.

She had failed every single time; her arms flying about, a sputtering cough escaping her lips whenever she broke the surface. Araxia's ability to hide her disappointment was long gone.

Sapphire had tried to do what Araxia instructed. She had tried to connect, to feel at home. But every time, her anxiety overrode her senses, forcing her up with the need to fill her lungs with air.

Frowning, Araxia placed her hand on Sapphire's shoulder. 'One more time. And then you will be done for today. Evera should be here soon.'

With a heavy sigh, Sapphire ducked her head once more under the surface. She opened her eyes to see the familiar span of blue water. At first, it had been comforting; the silence it offered her had been peaceful.

And she repeated the mantra she had known for years.

You will not fail. You will not fall.

And she believed it . . .

Until doubt settled in.

You're running out of air.

Your lungs are going to explode.

You're not made for this.

Sapphire pushed upwards, desperate to break the surface. She knew it hadn't been long enough – her lungs were not even burning. But she needed this all to be over. Her pride was wounded, and her body was tired. But as she attempted to rise, she smacked into a hard surface – like the water had been turned to stone.

She looked up, but nothing had changed. Sapphire tried once more, slamming against the invisible barrier and bouncing back to the bottom.

She tried again with more force, pressing her hands against the surface only to feel it pressing back, and she clawed at it, trying to escape.

Her lungs had now turned to fire, begging for relief. She looked frantically around her, trying to find Araxia, but she could not see her.

She slammed her fist against the surface and a scream ripped from her throat as she did so.

Suddenly, two hands lifted her out of the water.

'Sapphire? Sapphire, you're safe. I have you.'

She pushed away from the woman, struggling to reach the shore. She needed to be out of the water.

'What is wrong with you? I could've died!'

'I was right there beside you. You just needed the push. You were choosing the easy option.'

'I couldn't breathe!' Sapphire cried.

'I was in complete control,' the queen said. 'It is not out of the ordinary that –'

'You are wrong! I am not like you. What else has this proven to you? I – I am not special.'

Araxia moved towards her, reaching out a hand, but Sapphire moved away.

'I'm going to my room. Please send Evera there.'

She stormed off, not bothering to look back at the queen, hoping she could recall the route that Rayna had brought her. But behind her she heard a voice call out.

'Sapphire? That time, you were down there for seven minutes. Don't tell me you're not meant for this.'

Chapter Seven

Sapphire was sitting in one of the armchairs when someone knocked on the door of her room.

'Come in.'

'Pardon the interruption, princess. Miss Viotto is here to see you.'

Evera poked her head around the door and Sapphire motioned for the girl to come in.

'Sapphire?'

'Close the door.'

Evera did so and made her way over to the second chair. Her expression was a mix of worry and curiosity.

'The last time I saw you, you were being dragged away by guards. I haven't been allowed to return to my job at the library. And now, you're living in the castle and sending a royal aide to request my presence.'

'I –' Sapphire's lip quivered. 'I'm sorry. I wasn't even sure if you wanted to see me. I felt like you were the only one I could trust.'

'As soon as you were . . . taken away, an aide appeared and asked that we sign a contract with so many stipulations . . . to not speak of you, of your appearance, your eyes, or things we had discussed. Guards surrounded us, and we feared if we didn't, we might be punished. And then they arrived once again, demanding my presence.'

Evera was angry. It was clear in her body language, her furrowed brow, and Sapphire understood why. The Viottos had never asked to be put in this position, and it was Sapphire's fault.

'I'm so sorry,' she rushed out. 'I'm sorry I got you into this mess. And I'm sorry I dragged you back in by inviting you here. I can send for someone to escort you home. I just –' She choked on another sob. 'I just needed someone and you –'

A warm touch on her skin brought her to a pause, and she found Evera's small hand resting on her forearm.

'It's fine, Sapphire. But I would appreciate knowing what is going on.'

Sapphire sucked in a breath in an attempt to steady herself. She needed this conversation to go well or she feared she might fall apart entirely.

'Tell me . . . have you heard of the Lost Princess?'

'Of course I have. I was a newborn when she went missing, but it is something that is talked about often.'

Another deep breath.

'Well, it appears I have returned.'

Evera's mouth fell open, and Sapphire dived into the events of the last few days. Evera didn't interrupt her until she arrived at the point in the story that still haunted her. The Shadow Witches who had arrived to perform the familial charm.

'They were terrifying – red hair, nearly silver skin. I was told they were Shadow Witches.'

'Shadow Witches,' Evera whispered, like she couldn't believe the words leaving her mouth.

'Why do you seem so shocked?'

'They are . . . citizens of Eriobis – but the history surrounding them is complicated. But they do practise other types of magic – forbidden magic.'

'The queen mentioned they practised magic we can't understand, but didn't explain what that entailed.'

'Shadow Witches push the limits of what is possible. Many moons ago, their magic was something to be marvelled at. But as time passed, they were consumed by a darkness. They passed that darkness down through generations and it carries a cost. It eats away at their souls and their physical bodies. I can't believe the queen and king would invite such an evil presence into the castle.'

Evera frowned. 'Shadow Witches are bad omens.'

Sapphire shrugged, but her mind was racing, her thoughts returning to the ripped-out pages of the book she had read and the harrowing story of her disappearance only moments after her first breath. She wanted to tell Evera what the queen had told her about the witches' involvement in her birth, and disappearance, but decided against it.

'If the Shadow Witches are so . . . Well, if they are citizens, then where do they reside?'

'They are known to move around but usually stick to the forest in Ciliria.'

'Ciliria?'

'It is the territory where those who control earth reside.' Evera shifted in her seat. 'It is the most uninhabited land, so it makes sense the coven would reside there.'

'And have you . . . ever seen a Shadow Witch?' She knew it was a fool's question – but she half hoped Evera had seen one. Maybe she too had met Ashes? The image of her unreal beauty burned in Sapphire's mind.

'No. And I pray it stays that way.'

The two sat in an awkward silence. Not enemies, but not friends. *Acquaintances*, she supposed was the word to describe them – she hadn't had many of those, and she wasn't sure how to proceed.

Evera leaned back against the chair and closed her eyes. 'What are they like? The king and queen?'

'They're nice. Emotional . . . always on edge. I can't bring myself to trust them.'

'I think that's understandable, just so you know.'

Sapphire gave her a grateful smile and looked out of the window.

'Perhaps I barely know you, but I feel as if you're the only person I can even begin to trust.'

'Is that your way of asking to be my friend?'

'Princess, your presence has been requested at dinner, so we should prepare,' Claye announced as he strode between the solid oak doors of her bedroom. 'Evera, I have arranged for a carriage to take you home.'

Sapphire ground her teeth. She had asked for space, and

Araxia had given her all of two hours. She narrowed her eyes as she spoke.

'I won't be attending.'

'Of course. I will inform the king and queen of your decision. Evera, I will escort you to the carriage, then.'

'She has to leave?'

Claye grimaced. 'I was instructed to ensure Miss Viotto returned home at sunset.'

'But I —'

'It's OK, Sapphire. I need to get home. It's my night to cook dinner.'

'I'll see you soon?'

'Of course, but next time, please send letters instead of guards.'

Sapphire laughed as they stood together, and Evera squeezed her hand.

'Until next time, then.'

CHAPTER EIGHT

Two weeks.

That's how long it had been since Sapphire stumbled into Eriobis. Did Martia still pray for her? Did their stomachs ache with hunger? Did Susanna and Lyna weep for her?

She threw herself into the one thing that would exhaust her.

Training.

She had been trying to master a simple task for a few days, but frustration was threatening to break her. When suddenly she had felt it – the magic in her veins coming to life felt like a rush of adrenaline straight to her brain. And she watched in awe as a tiny orb of water floated before her. Araxia's eyes had misted over with pride and even Sapphire herself had struggled to keep her composure.

It was the first time she had considered that maybe she might belong here.

But since then, her longing had consumed her. She became addicted to the smallest taste of power and she wanted more.

That was about the only thing she enjoyed, though.

She had begrudgingly agreed to etiquette training a few days ago, and it was exhausting. The identification of the proper utensils for dinner, the rigid posture, the conventional topics of conversation and those to avoid. She was tested, pushed, assigned lesson after lesson. She spent plenty of nights locked away in her room trying to memorize the steps to some ancient waltz and how to excuse herself from the table in a polite manner.

It was too much.

On top of that, the tension she felt around Araxia and Kip hadn't faded, but she tried to make an effort to spend some time with them. She asked them questions regarding the kingdom, the people she had yet to meet, the world she had yet to explore. They never refused her, telling her all about the town centre of Astral where merchants lined the streets daily, about the kingdom's orchards and gardens that helped feed the citizens throughout the year, about the Elders who offered prosperity and blessings. Despite it all, she listened, enchanted by a world she hardly knew. Kip remained standoffish but still present – still making an effort to connect with Sapphire. And Araxia? Well, she was kind. She was patient. She was accepting.

And for that exact reason, Sapphire didn't trust her.

She knew the queen's eagerness came from a place of longing . . . eighteen years without her child. But still, she never questioned her. She never looked at her sideways, like she was a stranger in their kingdom.

Outside that, they kept her impossibly busy. From sunrise to sunset, they moulded her to become a part of their world. A packed schedule left her no time to see Evera, to explore the grounds, to comb through the ancient books that lined her walls.

Shadow Witches. Dark Magic. Lost history. She needed to know more, but by the time she collapsed into bed at night, her eyelids were too heavy to read.

Today was no different, and as she walked into the chamber where her instructor awaited, she did her best to stifle a yawn. Exhaustion was ever-present.

'Good afternoon. I trust training went well?'

Fyra Pattaway had a stern look about her without even trying. The grey hair of the tutor Sapphire had been assigned was plaited tightly against her scalp, and a constant frown took up too much room on her face. Her voice was steady but not elegant. Her posture was rigid, and her clothes were always neatly pressed.

Sapphire nodded and the woman's frown deepened.

'Princess, as we've discussed, it is important to address questions verbally to show you are engaged.'

Sapphire fought the urge to roll her eyes, another habit she had been scolded for one too many times.

'Yes, Fyra. Training went well. I – well, I'm enjoying connecting with the water.'

'That is great to hear. But I hope you are prepared to focus on today's lesson.'

'I will do my best.'

Fyra narrowed her eyes.

'And I will focus.'

If there was anywhere that Sapphire struggled, it was in

this room. She had been lucky enough to learn to read and write – a privilege that was not awarded to most girls once the war came – but outside that, she had never attended school. She battled to keep focus, and to retain the information she was given daily.

Fyra patted the seat beside her, and Sapphire reluctantly sat. She liked to pace during their lesson, her body wound tight from her hours of training. Her disdain grew when the woman placed a large book in front of her.

'Turn to page three hundred and forty-five.'

Sapphire did and as she read the script on the page, her eyes lit up.

'Today, we will be learning more about the First War. Begin your reading, and then we will discuss.'

Sapphire turned her attention immediately to the text in front of her, trying not to appear too eager. She skimmed it for the most part, having already learned much of the history from the books she hoarded in her room.

As she read, she realized that it was the Shadow Witches who had plunged the country into battle. After years of peace, the witches' hunger for power grew too large, creating war that would tear apart the very land they walked on. The coven brought horrors to life, shadow creatures that threatened to swallow the world whole. And it was only the Elders who led humanity out of the darkness.

'The Elders were warriors born from powerful bloodlines,' Fyra explained. 'It was only after the war was won that the Elders travelled to the peaks of Wilhelma once more and used their combined power to pull the Gods from their thrones, taking their place, and sentencing the old Gods to a life of damnation for allowing the Shadow Witches to wreak such havoc.'

'And the Elders still exist today?'

'Of course they do. Foolish questions like that are not allowed in my classroom, princess.'

Sapphire lowered her head in false shame.

'Now, if you'd done your reading as I asked, you would know that following the war, the Elders constructed a barrier to banish Dark Magic and the coven who coveted it, from these lands –'

'But Shadow Witches still exist,' Sapphire interjected.

'Mind your manners, princess,' Fyra ran a hand over her hair. 'Yes, a new coven was formed through the passing of diadems and history. A contract was drawn to grant them amnesty in this country as long as they followed the code of magic outlined. Since then, peace has reigned in our homeland and –'

'But what of the original Shadow Witches? Of the creatures that roamed these lands?'

Fyra stiffened at the question, levelling her gaze at Sapphire.

'The witches of the first coven and the abominations they created are not the concern of this lesson. The Elders worked tirelessly to ensure that the barrier was strong and –'

'But what type of magic could they perform?'

'It is said that the Elders once helped form the cliff –'

'I know of the Elders' magic, Fyra. But the witches . . . Did they ever –'

Fyra slapped her hands on the table, her face red and splotchy.

'That's enough, princess. Rid your mind of such poison and recite the prayer of forgiveness in hopes the Elders take pity on your wandering thoughts. This lesson is over.'

Fyra marched out of the room, leaving Sapphire alone as she leaned back in her chair, looking around the room.

She would not pray for forgiveness. She would not apologize for curiosity. No matter what Fyra did. No matter what she said.

She could not stop Sapphire's growing obsession with the darkest souls of Eriobis' past.

And Sapphire would not stop until she had answers.

Chapter Nine

That night, Sapphire walked languidly among one of the gardens, pausing to look up at the sky.

'Do you often find yourself outside, alone and vulnerable, at night?'

Sapphire jumped, whirling around to find a familiar face.

'Do not speak to the princess, witch,' the taller of the two guards grunted, jerking the visitor by her arm, dragging her away.

'Wait.' The word left Sapphire's mouth before she could think it through. The guards halted and Ashes looked over her shoulder with a smirk. 'What are you doing here?'

'Does my presence offend you?' Ashes shrugged off the guards and turned to face Sapphire. 'That someone of such low status would sully the ground you walk upon?'

'Answer my question.'

'I am simply following orders and returning home.'

Sapphire stared at her, searching her face for a flicker of deceit, but could find none.

'Whose orders?'

'My king and queen's. They call, I answer.'

'Why would they call upon you?'

'To protect you, of course. Isn't that what we all were put in this world to do? Protect the beloved princess? What a blessing she has returned.'

'I don't –'

'As lovely as I find your violet eyes,' Ashes winked, 'those around you don't agree. My poor hands are cramping from crafting so many vials of potion.'

Ashes leaned against the stone wall as she took in Sapphire's confused expression, a lazy smile formed across her face.

Sapphire racked her brain – faintly recalling that Araxia had told her a potion would be coming. Sapphire had learned in her studies that members of each elemental faction had a specific eye colour. Earth was blue; fire, red; air, silver; and water a brilliant green. They had explained that something about Sapphire's disappearance must have affected her eyes – and that the potion would help her avoid prying questions about something so insignificant.

At the time, it had made sense. She certainly wasn't looking for a reason to field any more questions. But now, knowing that Ashes was the one who created it, she wasn't so sure any more.

'You made that potion?'

'Of course I did.'

The witch took a step closer. The guards tugged at her arms but it was as if she didn't notice. Sapphire felt entranced, leaning forward enough to catch a whiff of the girl's honey perfume. Her eyes fluttered as she drank it in, half wishing the guards would release their grip and allow the witch to do as she pleased. Do as Sapphire hoped she would.

Ashes' smirk grew like she knew every dark thought Sapphire had ever had.

'You would do well to ask questions, you know. About your court, your people, the very blood that runs through your veins.'

'That's enough, witch,' the taller of the two guards hissed, pushing Ashes along the path.

'Secrets are the bedrock that keep your kingdom steady, princess,' the Shadow Witch called over her shoulder. 'It's due for a reckoning.'

'What is that supposed to mean?' Sapphire couldn't mask the desperation in her reply.

'Stew in your curiosity. When you can no longer stand it, I'm sure you know where to find me.'

As quickly as they had appeared, the guards and Ashes were gone, leaving a sinister feel in the air.

She broke the surface once more.

'Where is your head, Sapphire?'

'We've been going non-stop.'

'This is for your benefit. It's how you must learn.'

'My benefit? I would be perfectly fine taking it slow. Instead, I am being rushed through this process so you can present me like a prize.'

Araxia's face fell.

'I do hope that's not what you really think.'

Sapphire chewed on her bottom lip. The woman's gaze was too heavy for her to endure, and picking fights would win her no favours.

'It's not. I'm sorry. I just – I didn't sleep well last night.'

The queen's shoulders relaxed, and she nodded. 'Let's take a rest, then.'

Sapphire watched as Araxia walked over to take a seat at the edge of the water. She patted the sand next to her, and Sapphire joined her.

'I'm sorry I've been pushing you so hard. Sometimes I forget how it feels to be your age. And I can't imagine . . . what you've dealt with.'

Sapphire shrugged, studying the smooth stones at her feet.

'You know, I trained in these same waters with my mother. I was always angry with her back then too. It was never enough. Never enough focus. Never enough drive. I spent most of my days wondering if she simply detested me.' A small, sad smile played on her lips. 'It turns out she just saw the potential I couldn't.'

'What was she like?'

It was not a question Sapphire had planned on asking. But while Araxia overwhelmed her most of the time, occasionally she found herself aching for more.

'Raya Canmore was a force of nature. She would've liked you, liked your fire. Your spirit. Your quick tongue. You're a lot like her actually.'

Sapphire smiled. She had seen Raya's portrait in the castle. She resembled Araxia but with furrowed brows and more anger in her eyes.

'She sounds incredible.'

Araxia's laugh vibrated against Sapphire's skin. 'She was a very polarizing woman, and queen. But she always did right by her people, all the way to the end.' Sadness dripped from Araxia's words as she stared up at the sky.

'A truth for a truth?'

It was a game Sapphire had played with Lyna and Susanna. A truth for a truth – a moment of honesty. She wasn't sure why the old memory had surfaced at this moment – but maybe it was a bit of childhood nostalgia, for moments like this when she was younger.

'Pardon?'

'It was a game I used to play in Witrotean. We don't have to –'

'Well, can you explain the rules?' Araxia replied eagerly.

Regret hit Sapphire quicker than she could stop it.

'It's simple, really,' Sapphire continued. 'Two parties volley questions and answers with only one rule.'

'Which is?' the queen pressed.

Sapphire turned to her, unblinking, and said in a serious tone, 'Both parties respect each other with honest answers.'

The amusement retreated from the queen's eyes for a moment before she finally nodded in agreement.

And so they began.

'Tell me your fondest memory of Witrotean.'

Oh.

Sapphire tucked her hands under herself and tried to consider the question.

Fondest memory of Witrotean?

Mercy, she wasn't sure there was one.

Still, she attempted to conjure up something.

'I was eleven. It was before the war, so times weren't as hard. Money had somehow found its way to the Home, and Loriana, one of the Mothers at the time, allowed us each a silver coin to buy whatever we pleased. I found a sketchbook at the market and bartered my way to a good price. I used the pages sparingly, until the day the war found its way into our home. We lost everything, my sketchbook included.' She wiped away a single tear. 'I enjoyed drawing very much. It helped me relax and get the thoughts out of my head. That was one of the last times I truly had something new of my own.'

Grief. Sorrow. Heartache.

Those were the words that came to mind as she watched Araxia falter to reply to her confession. The woman clenched her fist open and shut a few times as she tried to rein in her building emotions.

Finally, she spoke.

'Would you like some art supplies in your room?'

Sapphire ran her thumb along her scar in an effort to not give in to the urge to sob. 'It's my turn to ask a question, not yours.'

'Would you?'

A few quiet beats passed.

'I would love that.'

'Consider it done.'

Sapphire smiled, knowing it was now her turn.

'Tell me about the Canmore line. I read a bit with Fyra

91

in our lessons, but I'd like to hear it from you. What is our legacy, truly?'

Araxia's eyes brightened at the question.

'I've always wanted to pass on the legends to my daughter.' She settled against the sand, preparing herself. 'The Canmore line was and still is a miracle. Born from the Elders' blessings, they entrusted the original Canmore queen to lead Eriobis into a brighter age after the First War. Aylara was her name, and they blessed her with unmatched power. Each generation would bear an heir to the throne – the next queen in line. And it has persisted for a thousand years . . . and it will persist for the next thousand, and the next beyond that. The Elders' prophecy called for the reign of Canmore to continue till the end of moons.'

Araxia paused, staring out at the water.

'I am the youngest queen ever to take the crown. My mother and father passed unexpectedly when I was quite young. I'm not sure I was exactly ready, but I had Kip and a love for this country to guide me.'

Sapphire felt herself soften for the woman sitting beside her. The queen did not speak, but only continued to look out at the water.

'I bet she's proud of you,' Sapphire said. 'Queen Raya. I bet she loves what you have become.'

'Do you, now?' she asked, a small smile tugging at the corner of her mouth.

'I do,' Sapphire added softly. 'Do you think I'm fit to be the next queen?'

Araxia looked surprised. 'I thought it was my turn to

ask a question?' Amusement was warm and thick like a balm in her voice.

'Hardly,' Sapphire countered, a soft chuckle escaping her lips. 'Doesn't matter how small the question, a truth was offered. The rules are the rules for a reason.'

'I do,' Araxia replied with so much certainty it made Sapphire's chest ache, the smile finally reaching her eyes, warming them to a near clover green. 'What you feel . . . the doubt, the fear, the questions – it's all very natural. I'd be more worried if you didn't.'

'Why do you say that?'

'Because it would mean you're a fool. You're a Canmore queen, Sapphire. Or you will be, one day.' She looked back up at the sky. 'Canmores do not suffer fools gladly.'

The confidence in her voice, her conviction, and belief – those weren't things Sapphire was used to hearing.

'May I ask one more question?'

Araxia smiled, patting her arm.

'You may ask as many questions as you like. With or without the guise of a game.'

'Why did you name me after the original Canmore queen?'

'Aylara was always known as a reminder of hope and promise,' the queen started with a soft sigh.' A promise of a better, brighter future. She was a gift from the Elders . . . and to me, my daughter . . . you . . . were, are, my very own gift from the Elders. There was no other name that suited you.'

Sapphire paused, and a warmth she wanted to bottle up

93

and hold on to forever settled inside her. A few peaceful moments passed as the two women simply sat there together.

'Can we try again?' Sapphire finally asked, standing up. She extended her hand to the queen to help her off the ground. And the moment was right, good . . . but Sapphire didn't miss it: the queen's cringe when Araxia caught sight of the slender, raised scar across her palm.

CHAPTER TEN

Sapphire headed for the library the first free moment she got. Throwing open the doors, she stormed into the tranquil space. Searching the aisle, she finally caught sight of a familiar face.

'Princess? Hi.' Evera placed a book back on the shelf. 'I'm sorry. No one told me you would be visiting. Is there a text you'd like me to pull?'

'No, I just wanted to see you.' Sapphire leaned against the shelves. 'And it's not "princess". Call me Sapphire.'

'Ah, yes.' Evera returned her focus to the shelves.

'I'm sorry I didn't visit sooner,' Sapphire continued.

Evera offered a gentle smile. 'I'm just happy you're here.'

'How is your mother?'

Evera's smile grew. 'She's my mother. Busy, worried, incapable of resting for even a moment.'

'That sounds about right,' Sapphire replied with a soft chuckle.

Evera laughed softly and crossed her arms, studying Sapphire closely.

'Something is bothering you.'

Sapphire arched a confused brow while Evera levelled a stare at her.

'You haven't stopped fidgeting since you arrived.'

Sapphire closed her eyes, trying to decide if it was safe to be honest, to unload her burdens. As she opened her eyes again and looked at the girl, any doubt faded. Since the moment they had met, Evera had offered her nothing but honesty and kindness – and, mercy, Sapphire was desperate to talk to someone that wasn't hired to help her or related to her.

'If I say everything is bothering me, is that too dramatic?' Evera laughed and Sapphire relaxed. 'I have all these questions. Not only about my disappearance but just about . . . everything.'

'Including Shadow Witches?'

'That too.' Sapphire wasn't sure why but she felt embarrassed admitting it. 'I just – I feel like there is more to their story.'

'Shadow Witches are devils among men. Not a group you want to become entangled with.'

Sapphire mused, looking out of the window. 'I just want to understand them. Understand more about my disappearance. That's all.'

Evera looked at the floor for a moment before sighing.

'You know, as one of the royal librarians, it is my job to retrieve any texts you seek. Any information you may want.'

Sapphire couldn't fight her smile.

'So you think you could . . .'

'I'll see what I can do.' Sapphire heard someone clear their throat and Evera rolled her eyes. 'Now, I need to get back to work and judging by the look that man over there is wearing, I think you're late for something.'

Sapphire turned around to find Claye looking impatient, with his hands on his hips.

'You would be correct.' Sapphire pulled the girl into a quick hug. 'I'll check in soon.'

It was early when the knock on her door came, the kind of head-splitting knock that made her bury herself deeper under the covers.

'I do apologize – but we really must get moving. Please, princess. I will make today as easy as possible,' Rayna's voice pleaded with her.

'Go away.'

'That's not exactly an option.'

Sapphire stomped over to the door and threw it open. 'What?'

'Today is the big day, highness.'

Sapphire paled. Rayna was right.

Despite Araxia's spiel about her role being a choice, Sapphire had known from the beginning that it was not. For if she refused the crown, who would she be? Where would she go? This world was still new to her, her magic something she couldn't understand. She needed the guidance of the king and queen as much as they needed her presence.

So, she had agreed to the age-old tradition of the

presentation. Kip and Araxia had walked her through the ceremony. She could tell they were trying to gauge her level of comfort with it all, which was complicated, to say the least. Sometimes she craved to stay hidden in the shadows, free of duty, family, and expectation. But her curiosity gnawed at her, chipping away at the hesitation in her mind bit by stubborn bit.

She wanted to see Eriobis, with her own eyes – understand the land and its people. And she couldn't do that while hidden away.

Rayna gently pushed her towards the washroom, running a bath while Sapphire stared at herself in the mirror. Despite the put-together reflection that stared back at her, she wondered if the people would see right through her. If they would catch a glimpse of the girl she once was – feral and ill-mannered.

Her palms pressed against the cool marble of the basin as she tried to force herself to face the day.

You might not be a Canmore, but you need to act like one to survive. You will not fail. You will not fall.

Another solid rap against the outer door echoed around her suite. When she pulled it open, a team of six – and a kingdom – awaited her.

Together the six maids pulled and prodded, told her where to sit and then stand. Strings were pulled, buttons pinched, clasps clipped.

And the entire time she looked out of the windows, awaiting the sunrise. At the first lance of light shining through the glass, she heaved a sigh of relief. The sun was such a rare sight in Witrotean that she had come to appreciate each morning a bit more than most.

'Princess, I need you to sit and look directly forward.'

They painted her, retraced the lines of her face, and covered the bluish planes of her bruised body, until what was left was an immaculate little doll. Painted, polished, pure.

The perfect little prim and proper lie.

If she couldn't act the part, then, at least for today she looked it.

Her hair was braided and curled much like Araxia's, and a jewel-laden tiara balanced atop her head. The tiredness, the hunger, her failures, her shortcomings all carefully smoothed and polished away.

Then there was the dress.

It was the most brilliant shade of blue, hugging her body in heavy satin and velvet. Long sleeves. High neck. And encrusted with precious gems that cast small, fractured rainbows along the walls whenever she caught the light.

It made her feel powerful and delicate all in the same breath. As if somehow the Canmore women that came before her were woven into the laces, holding her steady. The gown's gems were like their eyes, watchful, guiding.

Rayna placed a tiny crystal bottle into Sapphire's hand.

Sapphire studied it. The bottle was unmarked, with no ingredients, no instructions, no indicators of its intended purpose. The potion made by Ashes.

Sapphire returned her gaze to the mirror – realizing, for the first time, just how out of place her eyes looked. A stark purple contrast to the pretty picture the servants had made.

She popped the top and tossed the contents back. It was bitter and thick, and she gagged as it slid down her throat.

But when she stared into the looking glass, Kip and Araxia's gentle colouring of soft moss and ryegrass already stared back.

'Green eyes, to match theirs,' Sapphire muttered.

She quickly averted her gaze, stepping unsteadily off the dressing platform. Claye knocked on the door, signalling that they were out of time. Rayna rushed to open it and he stepped inside.

'A vision you are, princess.'

Sapphire offered him a small smile.

'You look like her, you know.'

'Like Araxia?'

'No. Like Queen Aylara,' Claye responded. 'You look almost identical to the first Canmore queen.'

She wanted to ask Claye more, but the man was already ushering her out of the room. Araxia was waiting for her in the corridor, and at the sight of her daughter the queen began to cry. Even the king softened, his eyes misted.

'You – you are more lovely than I could have ever imagined.' The queen raised a hesitant hand towards her cheek, fighting to quell her tears. 'How are you feeling?'

Nervous, terrified, nauseous, anxious? A maelstrom of emotion caught together in the squall.

But out of all that, one fear weighed on her the most.

'I feel like an imposter,' she admitted, letting only a

quick silence grow between them before adding, 'does that upset you?'

A soft smile spread across the queen's face as she took Sapphire's hand in her own.

Sapphire lapped up the comfort of the touch. Today, she'd allow herself that much, at least.

'My sweet girl.' They shared a private smile. 'If it's of any comfort, if I doubted – even for a single moment – that you were ready, we wouldn't be here, standing together now.'

It was easy to be lulled by her words. But Sapphire's childish fear remained. The fear she had been trying to smother since the beginning. Approval. Rejection. Love. Acceptance. She stood at the precipice of them all.

'What if they don't like me?'

'How could they not?' the queen asked innocently enough. But all it did was send the dark, festering brew of feelings down to Sapphire's churning stomach.

'Would it help you to know that, when I was in your shoes, I felt very much the same as you do now?'

'You did?' Sapphire questioned, raising her eyes to meet Araxia's.

The queen offered a small nod in response.

'How did you manage it?' Sapphire whispered.

'My mother,' Araxia said, another small smile spreading across her lips. 'She told me something that I've carried with me every day since. I keep it close, chant it, breathe it, every time I feel doubt will consume me. *Their eyes may try to dismantle us, their thoughts cage us, but our own fear is the only thing capable of keeping us prisoner.*'

Sapphire bit her lip, letting the queen's words sink in as they neared the door to the terrace. She could feel Araxia's heavy gaze. 'Majesties, we should begin . . .' Claye's voice came out rushed, and Araxia shot him a look.

'Are you ready?' The king's green eyes were bright, clear, and expectant. Araxia took Sapphire's hand once again. 'I've dreamed of this day for eighteen years. I know you're nervous, but we'll be right there beside you. Today another Canmore rises. She will let us know when she is ready.'

Kip nodded his head in support of his wife. 'When you are ready, Sapphire.' His voice echoed out.

Outside, she could hear the crowds. The shouting. The cheers. The expectation. The air was thick with it. But Kip and Araxia were watching her so closely, one panicked and one stressed, that she knew she had already wasted more time than they could offer.

'I'm ready.'

At Sapphire's strangled voice the king's features softened even further, and he reached out to her, giving her shoulder an affirming squeeze before taking Araxia's hand and heading towards the terrace doors.

With every step, she felt her heart rate increase. The realization that she was about to emerge in front of thousands of people heightened the hollow feeling of anxiety that had bored its way into her chest.

She stood in the large French doors of the northern side of the castle. The same doors she had been seeing all week.

Sapphire's mouth was dry, her hands clammy. The world tilted, and the panic clung close.

Araxia tightly gripped the curve of her elbow, a silent question.

Sapphire met the queen's sincere gaze and tried to steady the hitch in her breath. Her knees wobbled but she remained standing.

Araxia gave her a proud smile.

Two guards pulled the doors open, Kip and Araxia stepping out a few seconds later. The sun was bright, blinding even, as it painted them golden. The crowd was deafening as the people of Eriobis celebrated their king and queen.

Claye stepped forward, in his robe with the cool silvers of the air lineage woven into it. As he began to wave his hand, a simple gust of magic was summoned, allowing Araxia's voice to carry out to the people below.

'It has been my greatest honour to serve the people of Eriobis,' she began. 'But, as you know, there was another honour I have always held dear to my heart – being a mother. Eighteen years ago, I was given that opportunity, and then, it was taken away in an instant. Since then, we have dedicated our efforts and time to finding our beloved daughter. It's been such a heavy burden to carry – the loss of a child – and I truly had started giving up hope. But the Elders are kind, generous, and have finally brought light back to our darkest times.'

The hum of whispers intensified. The air was electric. Araxia paused, allowing the crowd to process and speculate. She never wavered, though. She cleared her throat, and the silence returned.

'And that's why we have gathered you here today. It is a celebration beyond measure. Because we have regained the one title we thought we'd never hold again – parents. Today, I would like to introduce you all to someone very special. Our daughter, Sapphire Canmore.'

Stillness.

Unmoving and tense.

Sapphire Canmore.

She hadn't heard the names paired together before and couldn't tell if it sounded right. A hand pressed against her lower back and she turned to find Claye smiling at her, eyes narrowed.

'Go. They're waiting for you.'

Araxia and Kip turned her way, each with a hand outstretched. She thought of Witrotean, back to that small, dusty room, and Martia with her furrowed brow, Susanna and Lyna with their constant questions, her hand-me-down clothes. But there was no returning to what she had once known. There was no other path but forward.

So she took the first step forward – towards notoriety, scrutiny, and plenty of things she wasn't ready for.

Another step. Her panic rose. Another step. Her knees buckled. Another step, until her hands clasped theirs – her parents'.

They took the last step together. She was standing between them, head high, keeping her face impassive as she had been instructed to do. The crowd was mute: a demanding type of silence that made your ears ring. Araxia gave her hand another squeeze, but Sapphire did not falter.

She was trying not to bend to a silence that could kill. But then, the slow bristle of applause began to swell, the cheering and hailing growing with each breath. Sapphire smiled, curtsying to the faceless people below her, before kneeling at the feet of the Grand Prodigal just as she had been instructed.

The tiara was slipped from her hair, and a heavy crown settled in its place.

The crown of Canmore.

A circlet of heavy gold with a lattice of green gemstones, the weight of every Canmore before her bearing down from it.

The crowd's cheers intensified at the sight, and Sapphire thought she understood some of their enthusiasm. She was the princess they had mourned. A divine blessing returned to them. A good omen. But inside her, something stirred, and it made her feel undone.

She tried to ignore it as she stood up, and stepped forward to address the crowd.

'I wanted to take just a moment to express my gratitude for your prayers and wishes for my safe return. I have much to learn but I am excited and eager to immerse myself in our beautiful world.' Her hand shook as she raised it to the crowd, preparing to say the words she had practised with Fyra for weeks. 'Today, I take the Canmore oath to protect, to serve, and to prioritize you, my people. I am honoured to be the heir to the Canmore crown and am looking forward to our future together.'

At the words, a chill settled into her bones, a feeling that something had shifted, that a darkness lurked just out of sight. And her eyes moved across the crowd, trying to pinpoint the source of the dread, but there was nothing but the sea of smiling people before her.

But the feeling clung to her, even after the doors shut tight behind them and the roar of the crowd was silenced.

As if it had taken root inside her, spreading through her bloodstream. Then she heard the voice again.

An ill-boding voice that burned her from the inside out.

Time has a way of revealing all, child. But your patience will be rewarded.

Chapter Eleven

The large golden doors approached much more quickly than Sapphire would have liked.

Sapphire paused, wishing that Kip and Araxia were entering with her. But they were already seated. She pictured them, bookends at the impossibly long table, and it helped steady her.

Her nerves built as they waited for her signal that she was ready.

'Any advice?' Sapphire begged, with her eyes as well as her words.

Claye offered, 'I would be extra cautious regarding your conversations with the governing family of Ciliria, the Princeps. They come with forked tongues.'

'The Princeps. All right.'

'This day is all about rubbing elbows and gaining goodwill with people who have too much power for their own good. So, stick to your training. Smile a lot, be grateful, stroke their egos when possible, and try not to be so . . .'

'Me,' Sapphire said with a small laugh.

'Your word, princess, not mine,' Claye said, a small smile sneaking on to his face.

Sapphire nodded in gratitude, trying to stand taller.

She wondered if these powerful families were bold enough to question her legitimacy at dinner, or if they'd wait to whisper harsh words in dark corners where they thought she couldn't hear. She wasn't sure which was worse.

'I am nervous.' The words rushed out of her before she could stop them. 'I am nervous they . . . won't approve.'

Claye smiled.

'They should worry more about your approval. You are the next in line for the throne.'

'And yet I feel as if I'm the fool on a tightrope while everyone is gawking, waiting for a misstep.'

'Of course they are,' Claye continued. 'It's all a dance of politics and power struggles. But you've been trained by the best and prepared for the worst, princess. So, relax your shoulders, keep your chin high, and show them that you belong at that table even more than they do.'

A slight tapping signalled it was almost time, and she took a deep, shaky breath to steady herself.

On cue, the large golden doors swung open, and a guard banged his staff once again before clearing his throat.

'Presenting Her Highness Sapphire Canmore, Princess of Eriobis.'

An imposter in the presence of power, she gritted her teeth every time she heard her new title spoken.

Finally, she raised her eyes to meet the ones that looked back at her. Her training was like a knife to her back, pushing her forward.

'Hello, everyone. It's so wonderful to finally make your acquaintance.'

The group stared back at her with their own strained smiles, and Sapphire took her place in the appropriate corner of the room to greet and receive the families. Araxia and Kip joined her and signalled for the procession to begin.

The whole ordeal was carried out with a tense, rigid formality that grated on Sapphire's nerves. Each person would make their way to her, greet her. Some would offer gifts; most would offer her prayers. Words of goodwill would be exchanged, and then they could proceed.

The first to approach her were two dark-skinned women with bright green eyes – just like those of the king and queen. They bowed before her, taking her hand and praying over her for the Elders' guidance and gifts. They slipped beaded bracelets over her wrist.

'We are so proud to be a part of your future, princess. We hope you know we are always here for assistance, guidance, or support. Whatever you may need, you must simply ask.'

Sapphire felt herself offer the first untrained smile of the day. The two women brought her a sense of comfort that was hard to come by in Eriobis.

'Your support is appreciated. I would love you to show me Astral through your eyes. Perhaps we can schedule a tour together.'

The women bowed their heads, speaking hushed words of excitement. Kip offered her a small nod as the two women moved back to their seats.

Next came a man and a woman whose eyes were as red as Evera's and Lelani's. Their faces were cautious as they approached, eyeing her closely.

'Princess, an honour it is.' The woman spoke. 'I am Yila, and this is my husband, Abe. We are the governors of Aleburn.'

Sapphire reached out for Yila's hand, and the woman's eyes widened at her touch.

'Your beautiful territory is where I found myself when I first arrived. Aleburn will always have a place in my heart.'

The couple softened, Yila squeezing her hand gently.

'Whatever you need, princess. Any support we can offer – we are willing and ready.'

Sapphire gave them a close-lipped smile, the silence signalling it was time to move forward.

The next person stepped up alone. Her eyes were grey, almost milky in colour, hands frail, and skin seemingly stretched too thin. She wore a chain around her neck signifying her important status to those around her. A Prodigal – the highest level of enlightenment one could reach in the temple.

'Princess, I am one of the many Prodigals of this land. I have spent many years praying to the Elders for your return, and to see you here now is the honour of a lifetime. The power of the Elders in the flesh.'

Sapphire straightened a bit more, looking down at the small woman. There was something about the Prodigal that made Sapphire feel on edge. Her skin prickled under her dress and she shivered. The woman reached for her hand, and she begrudgingly accepted the grip.

At the contact, Sapphire clenched her teeth. The scar on her palm screamed in protest. The Prodigal's grip tightened, eyes locked on Sapphire's.

'Have you been saying your prayers?'

'Of course. Daily,' she lied.

'I insist you continue. It is of the utmost importance that you protect your mind from the evil that lurks in this world.'

Araxia stepped towards them, and gripped the woman's wrist gently but sternly.

'Thank you for your guidance. Do find your way to your seat as lunch will begin soon.'

The woman released Sapphire's hand immediately. The Prodigal's vision seemingly cleared as she blinked a few times.

'All blessings to you, princess.'

The procession continued to move forward but Sapphire struggled. The Prodigal's grip burned into her mind, as did the glassy look in the woman's eye, like she could see something nobody else could. Sapphire fumbled through stiff conversations and well-wishes. She forgot to express gratitude. She tugged at the corset that seemingly tightened with every passing second. Araxia and Kip eyed her closely as she did her best to not entirely embarrass herself.

But the rest of the room didn't seem to notice – offering her kindness. This relieved her, and the tension slowly eased from her jaw as she felt people's acceptance.

Kip and Araxia seemed pleased, meeting her gaze from time to time and giving her encouraging nods.

She prayed she might actually make it through lunch.

That was, until the next pair of eyes met hers.

An icy blue that was devoid of kindness – they bored into her, making her step instinctively closer to the queen.

The Princeps.

The woman approached her first. She was beautiful – but in a way that was almost unnerving. Her sharp cheekbones and angular jaw made her beauty seem harsh.

'Princess. What a miracle you're here in front of us.' The woman offered a thin hand, and Sapphire accepted it, startled by how cold her touch was. 'I am Sadara Princeps – the governor of Ciliria. This is my husband, Tyden.'

'We are honoured to meet the Lost Princess,' came Tyden's harsh voice. 'Who knew we'd ever have the privilege.'

His tone made Sapphire's spine stiffen as she turned to meet his gaze. He eyed her like a predator who hadn't decided if she was dinner or deadwood.

His long blond hair was pulled back into a low ponytail, and his prominent cheekbones made him appear gaunt and sick. The bags under his eyes were hollow, shaded a deep purple that made Sapphire wonder when he had last got proper rest.

A few seconds passed before his wife's hand wrapped around his thin arm, and the man's smile seemed to chill the air.

It was the type of smile that made you feel like he'd put

his hands around your neck right then and there if he could get away with it. Sapphire wondered how long he would wait to try.

'It's an honour to meet you as well. I've read about the wonderful things you've enacted in Ciliria. I can't wait to experience your beautiful lands for myself,' Sapphire replied, feeling tense under Tyden's piercing gaze.

Sadara smiled, before stepping aside to introduce another figure standing behind her. 'And this is our son, Kaian. I believe you two are the same age.'

Sapphire followed the woman's eyes, meeting the gaze of a boy who looked much like his mother. He was slightly taller than her with the same steel-blue eyes and icy-blond hair that was a bit longer on the top. His lips were pursed, thick brows furrowed, yet he still had a kindness to him that his mother could never muster. His moss-coloured suit complemented his pale skin.

It was only when Kaian stepped in front of his father, breaking his heavy gaze, that Sapphire felt she could breathe properly. She watched with wide eyes as the boy reached for her hand and placed his lips against the back of it.

'I echo my parents' sentiment. An honour to meet you, princess.' When she returned her eyes to him, he gave her a soft smile. 'I'm looking forward to getting to know you better.'

And then, Kaian Princeps tried to copy his parents – but he failed miserably as his taunting smirk looked more like a crooked grin. She stifled a giggle as he returned to his seat.

Her chest tightened as she spoke once again to the room. 'I am beyond grateful for the warm welcome and kind words. I know we'll be getting to know each other quite well over the next few months, but today, I truly want to express my gratitude for your acceptance. Without you, Eriobis would be nothing.'

The crowd shifted, the eyes of those around her softening, and she nodded, giving a smile before taking her seat. Araxia took her hand under the table, giving it a squeeze as pride overflowed from her. Sapphire allowed herself to bask in it, if only for a moment.

But as her eyes flickered to the Princeps family, Sadara and Tyden leaned in, heads bowed as they whispered to one another. Their eyes shifted around the room, finding Sapphire every few seconds, while Kaian stared at his hands in his lap.

The room hushed as Kip rose to his feet. 'I echo my daughter's gratitude for your presence today.' Sapphire's attention was taken by the new label she had just been given. *My daughter*. She caught his eye, and he gave her a knowing smile and she suddenly liked him more as he seemed to understand the alienness of the phrase for her. 'We are all grateful for your support and hard work that you offer Eriobis. Let us give thanks to the Elders as we have much to be thankful for.'

The room hummed and everyone bowed their heads.

'For the power in our veins. For the ground we tread on. For the air that fills our lungs. For the water that sustains us and the fires that fuel us. We praise them.'

Sapphire stared around the seats as the prayer continued, meeting another wandering gaze. Kaian smirked and they both looked away quickly. 'To the magic that binds us and the barrier that keeps us safe. May it endure for all of our days.'

Sapphire's eyes widened at the king's words as the prayer ended. Servants began to fill every inch of the table with dishes.

Before her was enough food to feed the Home for months. There were bowls of fresh fruit she knew had to have been picked from the trees and vines on the castle grounds, and fresh bread and pastries were stacked on tiered plates. There was meat – the kind of rich cuts Sapphire had dreamed of back in Witrotean. Nothing like the scraps she had pulled from the carcasses of the small woodland creatures she had hunted in the forest.

There was simmering soup, and sweets that made her mouth water from just looking at them. There was no space left on the table once the presentation was complete.

Overabundance to celebrate.

It was something she wasn't sure she would ever get used to.

Rayna began to plate her food for her. As she motioned to each platter, Sapphire gave her a simple yes or no, and the others waited as the king and queen's servants followed suit. Once their plates were filled, the questions began.

What was your childhood like?

Can you tell us more about Witrotean?

Were you aware of what had happened to you?

She played along, answering their questions as she had been trained to do. Otherwise she sat silently, studying the room and listening to their conversations. The governor of the Isle of Irobel was upset, seemingly offended by the lack of support and resources they were receiving for their transportation initiative. Then Aleburn was demanding more financial assistance for the rebuilding of villages affected by the erosion of the cliffs.

The guests slipped in their political plays any chance they got. But she also overheard things they might not have intended her to.

'The barrier is fracturing at a faster rate than they'd like us to believe,' whispered a man whose name she couldn't recall. 'If a simple girl can cross it, who is to say the monsters won't follow?'

'It's the Canmore way. Keep us all in the dark in an effort not to sully their perfect image.'

They cut their conversation short when they met her gaze, stiffening in their chairs.

It was all rather exhausting, but eventually, the room began to clear as attendees excused themselves, always offering the Canmores a bow as they left. Sapphire felt herself relax slightly. She wasn't entirely sure she had done well, but she had survived and that was good enough for her.

Soon enough, it was only the Princeps and the royal family left in the room.

'I'd love our children to get to know each other, my queen,' Sadara said, feigning a smile.

'Of course, Sadara. I'm sure Kaian could help Sapphire become more comfortable with Eriobis. He's such a bright boy.'

'Splendid. My attendants will send a letter soon. I feel they will become fast friends.' Sadara placed her hand gently on the queen's back. 'Do you have a few moments to talk about something more serious?'

Araxia nodded and the group of four parents tucked themselves closer to one another. Sapphire turned away from them, leaning against the wall. A sudden wave of exhaustion took her over.

'Long day?'

She jumped at the intrusion, turning to face Kaian. He smiled down at her.

'A good day, but a long one.'

'I can imagine. You did well, you know,' he said, no trace of sarcasm in his voice.

'I survived. I guess that's all I can really ask for.'

'No. You were really . . . rather impressive. Most of the other families were "happily surprised", if I heard them correctly.'

She bit back a smile.

'Most?'

'Well,' he said with a chuckle, pushing his hand through his hair roughly, 'my parents are impossible to impress. But I wouldn't worry too much about them.' He cut his eyes to the corner where the group remained huddled.

'They don't seem overly fond of me,' Sapphire agreed.

'They aren't overly fond of anyone. Except themselves, that is.'

Sapphire laughed loudly, and Tyden glanced in their direction. Kaian noticed, stiffening as he did.

'Ah, the joy of being the family disappointment,' he muttered, mostly to himself, before returning his gaze to her. 'Feel free to say I was horrible. Entirely vile. That you could barely stand to be around me. I have a reputation to uphold, you know.'

'You're the worst I've met in Eriobis, truly repugnant.'

He chuckled again, shaking his head. 'Your support is worth its weight in gold, highness.'

Their parents approached, breaking the conversation before she could respond.

'Kaian.' Sadara's tone was sharp. 'You darling girl, we are so happy you have rejoined us. The thought of the Canmore bloodline ending was . . . rather heartbreaking.'

Araxia took Sapphire's hand, stepping up beside her.

'Yes, well, luckily that is no longer a concern. The Canmore line continues, strong as ever.'

'Yes, I can see. What a miracle. Your arrival is truly an unbelievable gift from the Elders.'

The malice and ill intent in her tone set Sapphire's teeth on edge.

'The Elders' powers know no bounds,' Sapphire said.

Sadara nodded, clucking her tongue.

'Yes, well.' She looked Sapphire up and down once more. 'Time will reveal their intentions. Of that, I am sure.'

Araxia's hand tightened around Sapphire's, and she felt

it. Rage. It bloomed in her stomach and poisoned her blood. The surge, the pulse, a storm building inside of her.

Sapphire forced down the urge to reach out her hand to wipe the vicious smile from Sadara's face, and Araxia positioned herself between them with a firm step forward.

'It's been such a long day, and our family would like some time to gather after so much excitement. The guards will make sure your carriage is waiting out at the front.' Kip's face was impassive as he dismissed the group. Sadara's lips twitched as Tyden tugged at her arm, pulling her towards the exit.

'Your highnesses,' he mumbled, dipping in a slight bow as they made their way to the door.

Kaian looked back to meet Sapphire's eyes one last time, a goofy smile on his face.

'A pleasure,' he mouthed, and Sapphire shut her eyes tightly in an effort to not burst out laughing.

Once the doors closed, Sapphire's anxiety returned. Sadara doubted her enough to make it clear, and she wondered how far the woman would go to uncover whatever she was seeking. The feeling was a heavy weight on her chest.

Time will reveal the Elders' intentions. Sadara's words clanged like bells in her ears.

'How are you feeling?' Araxia patted her gently on the shoulder.

'Tired, excited, and in need of a long bath. But I do have a request.'

Kip and Araxia paused, looking at each other for a moment.

'I'd like to travel to Aleburn – to thank the Viotto family for helping me return to you. I think it is the least I can do after the part they played in my journey.'

The pride in Araxia's eyes was unmistakable and before Kip could even breathe a word of disapproval, she took Sapphire's hand and smiled.

'I think that is a noble idea. I will ensure a carriage is ready for you – but only after training.'

Sapphire mirrored her smile, offering a small bow of her head before excusing herself to her room.

That night, she could not slow her mind. All the day's events kept replaying, but one memory came to her most often. Kip's prayer. A prayer to the Elders to uphold the barrier and the magic. The barrier that kept the Shadow Witches away.

Mercy, how powerful must they be, to bring a king to pray for protection?

Sapphire pushed away from the bed, walking over to the windows, too many questions crowding her mind.

What was so detrimental about the witches' magic?

What if that magic returned?

Would she ever see Ashes again?

The last question grated on her nerves – and she hated how fear of the answer left her feeling hollow. She wanted – no, needed – to get answers, to unravel the mysteries that surrounded her.

She looked back out of the window.

She could swim to Ciliria, and find Ashes. Find her, ask her questions, and put this exhausting fascination to rest.

She had been studying the map of Eriobis. She knew that the large lake that extended from the training ground would eventually lead her to the shore of Ciliria's forest.

Pulling her cloak from the wall, she tiptoed down the corridor, sliding past the guards lounging at the main entrance, and exited through an unguarded servants' door that she'd noticed on a tour of the castle. Sapphire moved quickly, not slowing until she reached the lake's edge.

As she took a tentative step into the water, a chill breeze wrapped around her, reminding her of Ashes' cold touch on her hand. Her heart hammered in her chest at the memory, but she took another step deeper, pulled into the water at the memory. Then she thought she heard footsteps nearby.

Planting her feet a few inches deeper into the water, she forced her breathing to slow. No one who didn't live or work at the castle was allowed into the grounds. She was safe. She was the princess, and this was her realm.

And she was going to Ciliria to find Ashes before she went mad.

As her training uniform met the water, she forced herself to take another step. Then she thought she heard the distinct sound of someone clapping their hands slowly. Whirling round, she was greeted only by darkness and a gust of bitter wind. She shivered at the sensation, unable to shake the feeling that she was being watched. Looking back to the sky, she noticed that the moon had been concealed by thick cloud cover and in that moment, she had the sinking feeling that something wasn't right. And as badly as she wanted answers, as badly as she wanted to find the witch, something inside her screamed to run. Warned her that her questions could wait.

As she took a step towards the shore, the pressure on her chest grew, and she quickened her pace as she moved towards the doors of the castle, walking backwards to ensure nothing and no one was following her.

She spent the rest of the night in her room watching the moon, thinking of red hair and full lips until the sun rose.

Chapter Twelve

That morning, Araxia demanded small and specific motions from her: water shields, control, balance, and everything in between. Sapphire surprised them both by unintentionally causing waves to spread throughout the lake. Araxia beamed at her. But Sapphire knew she had plenty of work left to do.

Despite her aptitude, she hadn't adjusted to how exhausted training made her feel. And as soon as the nearly five-hour session in the water was over, she collapsed into her large bed.

They had moved her to her 'true' bedroom four days ago and she was beyond pleased with the progress in making it her own. Greenery filled every corner, a small pond bubbled by the window, allowing her to practise when she couldn't sleep, and the shelves were nearly bursting with gorgeous tomes about Eriobis history, their spines cracked with time and use. Their colours brought much-needed warmth to the space. In the far corner was the easel and sketchpad she had requested – fresh paints and charcoal sat ready for her use.

But best of all was her view.

She had thought the views of the lakes and the garden were the finest imaginable, but she was wrong. Because outside of her window was a large waterfall crashing over a cliff in the distance. She had a view of the sprawling gardens that she had come to love, the bright colours greeting her every morning. She had a partial view of the vineyards and groves as well. But she found that her gaze always wandered back to the large waterfall. She spent much of her time admiring it – and sometimes, for only a few moments, she even felt at home.

Still, she hadn't escaped the heaviness entirely. And sometimes, she found herself drowning in guilt and sadness at the thought of the Home crumbling while jewels were laid upon her neck. She wondered if they still searched for her. If they stumbled through the woodlands whispering her name.

Now, the thoughts of home made her exhaustion grow, and she crawled further into the overly plush bed, shaking the images of Beasts and hungry faces from her mind.

'Sapphire?'

A firm hand shook her awake, and she peeled open her eyes to find Claye standing over her.

'We're almost ready to travel to Aleburn. I'll call for the maidens to prepare you.'

The maidens worked quickly, forcing her into a dress, combing her hair, and making her presentable. An hour later, she was escorted out of the door heading towards the entrance of the castle.

'I am going to the governor's to collect a few things for

your father,' Claye said when they arrived. 'Sapphire, I am trusting you will be safe. Do not leave the Viottos' home. Do not discuss family business. And enjoy your time.'

She nodded, and Claye returned his attention to whatever he was reading, as a coachman opened the door, offering his hand. Sapphire took it, stepping out of the carriage with as much grace as she could. The neighbours' eyes were on her, and she smiled at them as she pressed the wrinkles out of her dress with her palms. As she walked, she noticed the hem dragging along the ground. The white lining turned a terrible shade of deep red.

She would be scolded for not lifting the dress. She knew that. It was probably ruined – the expensive fabric shredded by the terrain. But after weeks in the castle, everything so prim and pressed, it felt good to ruin something.

For a moment, she paused, recalling the first time she had approached this door, barefoot and afraid. It seemed like an entire lifetime ago.

As she extended her arm to knock, the door swung open to reveal Lelani standing in front of her, a surprised and confused expression on her face.

'Sapphire? I-I mean, princess?' Lelani looked over her shoulder at something Sapphire couldn't see.

'I apologize for the unannounced arrival, Mrs Viotto. I just – I just needed to come here. To say thank you for what you and your family have done for me.'

Something in the older woman's face softened, and she reached out with a gentle hand to pat Sapphire's arm. Sapphire clung to the woman's warmth, wishing she would linger a second longer. The touch was so natural and maternal it made her heart ache.

'You look very different from the last time I saw you.'

'I think this suits me much better than bare feet and a tattered nightgown, don't you?'

'I have to agree,' Lelani laughed.

Sapphire stepped inside and immediately relaxed. Something about the Viottos' was so comforting. The walls were filled with home-made art. The furniture was worn in and well-used. It smelled sweet, like they had been baking.

'Is Evera here?'

'Oh, Sapphire,' said Evera's voice, sounding slightly taken aback. 'I wasn't expecting to see you here.'

Sapphire whirled around to find Evera standing at the bottom of the stairs.

'I just came to thank your family for their kindness when I needed it most. I'm not sure what I would've done without you.'

Evera smiled as Lelani pulled Sapphire into a hug. Sapphire longed to remain there a bit longer but Lelani released her and Evera jerked her head, signalling Sapphire to follow her. Once in Evera's room, Sapphire studied every inch of the space. Pictures lined the wall, candles and books were stacked atop the bedside table and desk, clothes littered the floor. Sapphire smiled at the mess, enjoyed it even.

'Sorry,' Evera said, noticing her focus. 'I wasn't expecting guests.'

'It doesn't bother me.' Sapphire shrugged.

Evera sat down on the floor, offering Sapphire the bed, but Sapphire refused and joined her on the floor.

'My family attended the Introduction. You looked beautiful, I hear.'

Sapphire smiled at her.

'Thank you.'

'Yesterday was . . . something.' Evera shoved a pile of clothes under her bed. 'Now, tell me everything.'

Sapphire indulged her – telling her everything about training, rehearsals, etiquette, and roaming the castle grounds.

'It went well, I suppose,' she admitted, finally getting to yesterday's lunch. 'But there was one family – the governors of Ciliria – they weren't the most . . . welcoming.'

'The Princeps? Well, that's no surprise. I used to run into their son at training camps. He was always . . . odd. Standoffish.'

'Kaian was nice enough. But his parents . . . They put me entirely on edge. I felt like they could see right through me.'

'Well, I suppose that had to be expected, right?'

'Why would I expect that?'

Evera suddenly looked unsure of herself. 'Well, before your arrival, there was a big debate. With the king and queen having no children, many wondered who would take the crown. The Princeps believed they were the right choice, pushing for Kaian to be next in line.'

'How do you know that?'

'Gossip will do as gossip will do. The Princeps' eagerness was always a topic of conversation.' Evera shrugged. 'But now that you're here, I guess there's no question any more. So I'm sure the Princeps are angry.'

Sapphire chewed on her lip while she processed Evera's words. On the one hand, they explained the Princeps' behaviour, but on the other hand, she had never really thought about her next step. Never considered the expectations that came with her title.

Would Kaian Princeps do a better job? Kaian with his goofy grin and quick wit.

Araxia seemed to believe in her, at least.

The hour that followed was filled with whispered secrets and loud laughter and Sapphire, to her surprise, let herself relax – feeling like she belonged. But soon enough, Claye's knock resounded through the small house, alerting them that it was time for Sapphire to go.

After quick goodbyes, Sapphire headed for the carriage where Claye awaited her. But then she heard Evera's panicked voice.

'Sapphire! You almost forgot your book.'

She turned around, confused, just as Evera shoved a worn book into her hands without a word of explanation. Sapphire blinked a few times before nodding.

'Thank you. I'll see you soon.'

After an awkward hug, Sapphire turned to find Claye wearing a suspicious expression.

'You didn't bring a book with you.'

'Evera and I have a book exchange.'

He studied the object in her hands, and she tucked it behind her back.

'Are we ready to travel home?'

'We are ready.'

With assistance, she settled back in the carriage, and Claye took the other side, his eyes closing as soon as the carriage began to move. She watched him closely. His breathing was steady and slow. But only when she was sure he was asleep did she pull the book out from behind her.

She ran her finger down the cracked spine. There was nothing notable about it, no inscription or title. Nothing that indicated what might be inside.

Her eyes flicked to Claye once more, and she stifled a laugh. His mouth had fallen slack. He looked so worn down that she hoped the ride back to the castle would be longer than the one to Aleburn, allowing him to sleep more. And to offer her more time to explore the text Evera had given her.

With careful hands, she opened the book, the spine whining in protest, and thumbed the worn pages. In the front was a folded piece of paper. She watched Claye closely as she unfolded it, and then read:

Sapphire,

I found this as I helped my mother do our seasonal cleaning. This was my ancestor Linai's journal. She lived a hundred years after the First War. I know you have your questions regarding the Shadow Witches and the history of it all. I can't promise answers, but I believe these pages can help you understand the history of this land more, if only so you can be a better queen in the future.

Evera

She began to study the first page. The faded spidery penmanship was hard to read, but she focused. The carriage hit a bump, and Claye's breathing hitched, causing Sapphire to tuck the book behind her quickly once more. But Claye was lulled back to sleep quickly, and she returned to her reading.

The world continues to evolve each day, it seems. The Canmore crown seemingly carries us further into a new era with each rising of the sun. New fruits, new innovations, new temples. It is an honour to be a part of this world – but one must wonder how long it can last. New Gods seemingly watching our every move, scorned witches existing beyond a barrier made from magic no one can understand.

I cannot be the only one asking . . . how?
Why?
What comes next?
I cannot be the only one who is questioning the

Canmores, the crown, the new world.

And I cannot be the only one wondering what happened to the Shadow Witches.

Can I?

Sapphire was entranced by the words on the page – the musings of a woman who shared her curiosity nearly nine hundred years ago.

The carriage came to a sudden stop. Claye jumped awake with a panicked look, and Sapphire grinned at him.

'I'd appreciate it if you didn't mention I –'

Sapphire held up a hand, silencing him.

'Did you dream?'

He nodded as they exited the carriage.

'Then I demand you tell me of your dream.' She took the captain's hand as she stepped on to the platform, and it rocked slightly under her step. Claye joined her, sitting next to her with worried eyes. 'And your much-needed sleep is safe with me.'

He smiled as the platform began to move, and told her about his dream.

CHAPTER THIRTEEN

The hour was late, the staff long asleep, and a single candle cast just enough light for her to make out the letters.

When her eyelids grew heavy, Sapphire placed the journal under the mattress and lay on her back, slipping into a vivid dream.

Around her was a thick forest, the smallest bit of light allowing her to see a young girl. The child had long raven-coloured hair, braided back in pigtails. Her pale skin was jarring against the inky dress she wore. Her cheeks were flushed, her eyes wide, as she stumbled through the woods, breathing heavily in fear, searching for something Sapphire couldn't see.

Sapphire scanned the area, trying to spot what the girl was running from, but there was nothing except trees shrouded in shadows. The forest was familiar in a way she couldn't pinpoint.

Ahead of her, the girl leaped over a downed tree before sidestepping a large boulder. Her feet were bare despite the chill in the air, and Sapphire struggled to keep up with her.

Time seemed to move too quickly as the child stopped,

her delicate steps no longer echoing along the path, and she looked at Sapphire head-on.

'Help me.'

An ear-splitting scream followed, and Sapphire shot up from her bed – the forest falling away as she took in her room. Sweat coated her skin as she struggled to catch her breath.

She rushed out into the corridor to find where the scream had come from, the sound of it too real to be a dream. Stumbling from door to door, she threw them open only to find the rooms behind them empty. Her panic did not subside even after she returned to her chamber, as she half expected to find the child lingering outside the windows, but there was nothing besides the darkness.

She collapsed back on to her bed, her breathing ragged. She hadn't had a vision since she arrived in Eriobis, but the familiarity of it unnerved her. The connection to the forest and the small child was something she couldn't place.

And the scream.

Mercy, she could not shake it.

Needing to get out of her room, she pulled on her training uniform and headed to the water in the hope of silencing it.

Slipping down the hall, she could not escape the feeling that someone was watching her; a ghost nearby, waiting for her next move. The thought pushed her to move quicker, doing what she could to keep her footsteps silent.

Without breaking her stride, she passed the training grounds, headed to Lake Volta, which surrounded the left side of the castle and dived underwater.

Clarity.

That's what came as the water rushed over her. Clarity. Pride and happiness. She had found peace in what she once feared and it was an electric feeling. She could swim for miles without growing weary – she could bend the water to her will. What she felt most was power.

As she sank below the surface, the scream fell away, the sweat washed from her skin, and she finally understood what Araxia had meant when she said the water felt like home.

Here she was simply Sapphire.

No crown. No expectations. No questions.

She savoured the freedom of it all.

It is a part of you.

Here she truly could believe those words. Because she felt it – the smallest buzz against her skin mixed with the chill of the water. Magic surrounded her, coursing through her. It surrendered itself to her, and it vibrated against her core.

Accept me. Accept me. Accept me.

It was almost as if she could hear the magic begging for attention, for consent. And while it all still terrified her – the magic, the raw power, things that shouldn't be possible – the water was the one place that had started to make sense.

So, she allowed it, allowed the magic to carry her where it wanted her to go. It was only her there. It was only the feeling of water against her skin and the bite of a chilly night breeze when she broke the surface.

She blinked a few times as a shoreline came into view.

The trees were so tall they seemed to touch the sky. The shore was covered in smooth, slippery stones, and she struggled to stay upright as she clambered ashore.

This was not Astral. The forest before her was dark and loomed like it was waiting for its next victim to approach.

How far had she swum?

She whirled around to see that the lake stretched on for miles – the castle was nowhere in sight. As she walked closer to the treeline, the smooth stones gave way to a carpet of moss that squeaked under her boots. She squinted, trying to get a better look at the world around her, but could hardly see five feet in front of her.

Where was she?

As she racked her brain to recall her lessons about the territories, nothing came to mind. But then, the threatening sense of familiarity hit her hard.

The forest; she knew the forest, though she wasn't sure how – but familiar did not mean safe and her mind screamed for her to flee.

Leaves rustled to her left, and she stumbled backwards towards the water.

Terror raced up her spine. Further up the shore, amid the trees, the smallest ball of light shone dimly.

If she hadn't been looking for it, she might have missed it, but it was there.

'Leaving so soon, princess?'

From the shadows, a figure emerged. The woman was tall, with fiery red hair. The orb of light was balanced in her hand. Sapphire froze, immediately recognizing her.

The Shadow Witch.

Ashes' eyes were locked on Sapphire as she came down the shore, closing the distance between them. Sapphire struggled to look away, at the same time wanting to memorize every inch of her face.

'Now, what are you doing out here all alone?' The witch's voice was as calm and steady as it had been that day at the castle, and it grated on Sapphire's nerves.

'I got lost,' Sapphire said.

'Almost one hundred miles of black water lie between Astral and where you're standing, princess.'

'Like I said, I got lost.'

'Clearly.' The girl's lips twitched, and Sapphire chewed on the inside of her cheek, considering her next move.

'What are you doing out here?' Sapphire finally asked.

'I don't owe you my secrets.'

Sapphire felt off-kilter in this conversation, one step behind. 'You're a Shadow Witch.'

'A thrilling observation.'

'So, your magic . . .' Sapphire wasn't sure how to ask the question she so badly wanted answered.

Ashes tilted her head and fixed Sapphire with an unfaltering stare, stripping her bare, ripping back layers of flesh and psyche until she could have sworn she could feel her swimming in the marrow of her bones.

'I'll show you mine if you show me yours.'

A faint malicious laugh floated through the air, and Sapphire could have sworn the world around her darkened.

Sapphire tried not to flinch as Ashes stepped closer to

her, the orb in her hand shifting to something dark, radiating shadows.

Ashes looked amused.

'They should know better than to let you explore the forest at such a late hour. There are all sorts of vile monstrosities out here that would love to sink their teeth into something like you.'

'Speaking from experience?'

Ashes shook her head, laughing. 'Perhaps. But I'm a fair bit prettier than most, wouldn't you agree?'

Sapphire broke the witch's stare, attempting to gather herself together, before warm hands reached out in the dark, grabbing her by the chin and forcing her focus back.

'I could kill you, you know,' she whispered, her fingers tightening like a vice. 'My shadows could devour you whole. Can't you hear them begging me to let them?'

Sapphire tried to summon her courage, the courage that had earned her a dagger and a place at the Home. The courage she had desperately held to as she stared down the new world around her.

'But you won't.'

'Not tonight, little lamb,' Ashes agreed. 'But there's a time for everything.'

Sapphire blinked a few times, unable to follow what the witch could possibly mean. Ashes smirked like she could read Sapphire's mind.

'Do you always speak in riddles? Or does keeping me in the dark really excite you that much?' Sapphire finally asked.

'Are you interested in knowing what excites me, princess?' Ashes reached out, tracing her thumb across the back of Sapphire's hand. 'I'd be,' the smallest smudge of shadow lingered on Sapphire's skin before the wind carried it away, 'delighted to teach you.'

Sapphire recoiled, baring her teeth.

'Don't touch me.'

'Demanding, are we?' Ashes shrugged, pulling away, her hands pressed to her cheeks, feigning innocence. 'Time will tell how much you'll come to regret that.' A mocking laugh bubbled over her full lips as she spoke.

'Soon, princess,' she cooed. 'We'll see each other again soon.'

The shadows grew from her, blocking Sapphire's view, and when they cleared, she was gone, leaving only the bright moon above her. Long after she had disappeared, Sapphire could feel the witch's warm touch. The brush of her shadow had left a black speckle across Sapphire's skin.

The thought of Ashes consumed her, and she did not move from the rock until the sun peeked over the horizon, chasing off all the shadows. The water she stepped into washed away the witch's touch. But nothing could banish Ashes from her mind.

When Sapphire arrived back at the castle, her body exhausted from the long swim, the thoughts remained. She had floundered like an untrained toddler. Ashes had outpaced her at every stride. She brushed her thumb against the back of her hand, face warming at the memory of the girl's touch against her own skin.

Little lamb.

Princess.

The sound of the taunts rolling off the forked tongue was like needles against her skin.

She blinked hard a few times, attempting to banish the image of the witch from her mind, but she remained – smirking, and sinister, and beautiful.

The admission forced her off the bed, heading for the washroom closet to take out a journal. If she was going to be consumed, it might as well be by the history she so desperately wanted to know.

Evera had slipped her more journals over the last few days. Always careful to deliver them when she was in her room, careful that they would not be found. Sapphire had taken to reading them when she couldn't sleep, which was often.

There was a lot more anger in Eriobis' history than she had ever expected. Mikel, a member of Evera's family, recounted the anarchy. The clash of factions, the battle for territory, a world on fire, underwater, frozen, and destroyed. The coven at the heart of the pulsing undercurrent of a chaotic undoing.

Beasts of shadows are said to roam the land at night. The council advises people not to linger outside as darkness falls. No one has seen one, but it's as if you can feel the panic of the people growing, swelling to an unbearable level.

I fear what is to come.

She turned the page.

They found a witch bloodied and beaten. She died while being transported to healers. No older than fifteen, she begged for her life with her last breaths. A tide has turned, something has shifted. Darkness is here, and I'm not sure what will follow.

A new entry began.

The Shadow Witches returned the favour. An elemental was found strung up among the trees, eyes missing. In his blood was written: an eye for an eye.

Another.

Shadows plague the days now. They are inescapable, haunting, merciless as they rip through the streets. I knew of the witches' power . . . but never this. I never knew they could steal the light and consume the world.

They are almost . . . godlike. Able to do things I thought impossible. My fear grows with each day – but not for myself. For the future. We cannot go on like this.

Sapphire continued to read.

The council is advising vigilance. To lock doors and
practise protective magic. The Shadow Witches have
moved to the forest, dwelling among the trees. I hear
whispers of their evil as I walk the streets.

But what of us who know differently?

What of those who know the hearts of Shadow
Witches?

Mikel . . . She tore through pages until she found what
she was seeking.

His love for a Shadow Witch.

And the loss of that love as the tension in the world
swelled to an unbearable height.

I love her. I love her earnestly, and they demand
its end. They can control our money, our home,
even the land we stand on – but even Gods cannot
control our hearts.

But the uncertainty of what will happen next still
burns vicious and deep within me.

What will happen if I refuse to abide by the new
laws? If I say no? If I make a choice for myself for
all to see?

What then?

She is worth it. She is always worth it.

She is my heart. My soul. The entirety of my
being. Without her, there is nothing.

Destiny is all.

The words were too heavy – the taste of bile rising in her throat.

Mikel never wrote what happened. In fact, the journal ended abruptly, which unnerved Sapphire to her core.

She couldn't shake the swelling dread. War. Death. Loss. Heartbreak. Mourning. Mikel's words haunted her.

And then nothing.

How could all of that end in nothing?

CHAPTER FOURTEEN

'We're changing your schedule today,' Araxia told her abruptly. 'I think it's far past time we got out of this castle.'

Sapphire looked up from her plate, relief washing over her. Her body still ached from her long swim the previous night.

'I've committed to visiting Ciliria – the Princeps have extended an invitation for lunch.'

'Oh.' For a moment, Sapphire wondered how Araxia would take a refusal. What if Sapphire begged?

The idea of being on their territory, in their home, made her throat tighten.

As she was led to the washroom, she did not miss the small vial of potion on the counter. The bath was hot, the maidens' hands were rough, and the heavy fabric of the dress was uncomfortable against her skin. She wanted braids, but Araxia ordered curls. A monstrous necklace was clasped around her throat like a collar, a crown placed upon her head.

A reminder. A statement. A promise. To the Princeps or her, she couldn't be sure.

The potion was uncorked and placed in her palm. She

choked as she swallowed it, the bitterness biting the entire way down.

She turned to face the maidens and did not miss their pitying gazes.

She looked away from them and into the looking glass. The queen's brown skin, dark hair, and green eyes shone back. The sight warmed her, her heart betraying her mind at the thought of resembling her mother.

Mother.

The word still left her feeling conflicted.

Of course, at the Home, she had always had Mothers – but never one that looked at her the way Araxia did. With eyes that wished her all the good things in this life. One who would rather watch the world burn than have her suffer or labour. Who loved with abandon beyond choice or flaw. Unconditional. Universal. A bond of blood that no force, no magic could cleave.

When she was younger, the word *mother* had filled her dreams. A silent chant, a kid screaming in the dark, searching. Martia was the closest thing she had ever had. Even if the woman would've beaten her senseless for that insinuation.

But now, as she contemplated the word, she half hoped that one day, maybe, it wouldn't feel so heavy on her tongue.

The peaks of Wilhelma loomed to the north, the highest peak surrounded by grey sky. The jagged cliffs were capped in milky snow that reflected the sun, sending sharp bursts of light at the carriage. The mountain was a holy place, eternal.

The Elders had once hiked to the top in a quest for power to build the barrier. For six days, they fasted and prayed to the old Gods to look kindly on their cause.

Only the enlightened travelled to the peak these days. To the west was the Isle of Irobel, a large island floating in the sky, upheld by the very elemental magic that ran through its citizens' veins. She had read that Vasalis, the Elder of Earth, had once brought the Isle to its knees with an earthquake so powerful that it toppled temples and laid waste to the countryside.

The Gods had punished this abuse of power, weakening the earth bloodline. Many blamed Vasalis, refusing to pray to him. His temples were filled with offerings to other Elders, his altar ignored.

And finally, to the south, she saw the Volta Sea.

The dark water rushed to the shore, engulfing and pulling back anything in its path, devouring and all-consuming. The original child of water, Voltara, had made the eternal sacrifice for the sake of power that would be gifted to others. Barefoot, dressed in nothing but a nightgown, she had walked towards the furious waves.

A sacrifice to the old Gods.

Her body, made from water, returned to the very element she was born from. The Gods smiled down on her, granting the children of water more power, more abilities. And while Voltara was not an Elder, she was celebrated and honoured by all of Astral for her selflessness.

Always for the sake of power. Was there any line that wouldn't be crossed? Sapphire wasn't sure.

Soon enough, the view outside her small window gave way to tall trees and mossy ground.

Ciliria. In full view.

'It's beautiful,' Araxia stated, following her gaze.

'It is.' The air grew humid as they started on the path, the sun streaming through the branches of the trees above. 'It's a very different world from what I have known.'

'You must miss pieces of that world you once knew. If there is anything I can ever do –'

'Thank you but it is hard to miss a world that was so cruel.'

Araxia nodded. 'I hope you know that I am always here, if you ever need to talk.'

'I-I would hate to burden you. You're busy enough –'

'You aren't and never will be a burden to me, Sapphire,' Araxia interjected. 'We lost so much time, I'm not sure there will ever be enough left to make up for it. Whenever you need me all you must do is ask.'

Sapphire offered a rare, unguarded smile and returned her gaze to the window.

A thick fog had engulfed their carriage and she wondered what hidden monsters of Eriobis were lurking in the depths.

When they emerged from the forest, a wall of cold, indifferent stone came into view. Set into it was a large, grand door with sharp angles. Ivy slithered up the walls, masking it in a familiar vibrant green, only somehow this ivy looked mangled and like it might consume her whole.

A flag showing what must be the Princeps crest – a mix of trees and large bear-like creatures – flew high above the estate.

The carriage came to a halt before the stairs, and Sapphire reached for the door, but Araxia took her hand.

To correct her. For reassurance. To relieve the tension. Sapphire couldn't tell.

'It's the cost of the Canmore name, Sapphire. The true burden of the blood. Even opposition deserves our grace.'

A smirk broke across Sapphire's face. 'So, you admit it, then. You don't like the Princeps?'

'I said nothing of the sort, sweet girl,' the queen replied, patting her hand gently. 'Simply passing idioms.' But the upward tug of the woman's lips told Sapphire everything she needed to know.

The carriage door swung open, and Sapphire stepped out first, allowing the coachman to assist her. Araxia followed and, almost in unison, they took a deep breath, staring up at the house.

Sapphire felt Araxia's hand in her own, and let the moment just be.

Almost on cue, the Princeps stepped out to greet them. Sapphire was relieved to find that Tyden was absent but Kaian was there – a slight smirk on his face.

She had to wonder, as Sadara took them in, if the Princeps woman felt the same dread as she did. If so, she did not show it.

'Your majesty, princess. I am so glad you could make it.'

Sadara did not bow with Kaian, which Sapphire found surprising. She averted her gaze, but the queen looked straight ahead, unbothered by the disrespect.

Sapphire met Sadara's stare, and a smirk played on Sadara's lips.

An unfamiliar and jarring sensation struck Sapphire, an urge to move closer to the woman beside her. Her mother.

Sapphire squeezed Araxia's hand as they made their way up the stairs, and the queen gave her a grateful smile.

At least, it seemed, one thread united her two worlds.

Family.

She had learned early on that family came in many different forms: a room with too many beds, a dinner table that was overcrowded, and a list of chores that never seemed to end.

But maybe, she considered, family wasn't just . . . a checklist.

Together they followed Sadara into the main entry as Kaian veered off in a different direction. Sapphire handed her cloak to a cruel-looking man and shivered in the draught. The walls were lined with art, and the curtains were entirely drawn so no natural light bled through. She felt her breath catch as she recalled the darkness of the cage she had found herself in at her arrival. The crushing loneliness. A tug on her arm broke her rising panic, and she looked to Araxia, who gave her a gentle nod.

As they entered the dining room, Kaian immediately stood as any well-trained gentleman would. But as he pulled out his mother's chair, he smirked again, and Sapphire had to bite back a laugh.

'Lunch is running behind. Kaian, what a great time to show Sapphire the grounds.' Sadara turned to look at Araxia before Sapphire had a chance to sit too. 'I do have a few things I'd like to discuss with you, my queen.'

Araxia's jaw clenched as she gripped the chair's arm, but she delivered a tight-lipped smile in response. The queen's eyes searched Sapphire's face, allowing her the luxury of making her own choices. Sadara arched an impatient but amused eyebrow like she was enjoying the uncertain exchange.

'I think that's a great idea, Sadara,' Sapphire said, deciding to play along. The woman flinched at the use of her first name. 'Ready?'

Kaian met her gaze, nodding before standing to offer his arm. She took it and at once they made their way through the large glass doors in the back of the room. Neither spoke until they were ten paces away from the house, both welcoming the fresh air with deep breaths.

'Well, welcome to Ciliria.' He spread his arms out wide as if to offer her the world, and she chuckled at the sight. He looked like a child showing off his finest toy, and she couldn't help but notice that today he looked more like a boy than a man. His hair was more ruffled, and his formal robes had been replaced by a simpler tunic and trousers.

He grinned. 'When my mother is scheming, she can play nice.'

'Duly noted.' She looked out into the gardens – the forest rolling on forever. 'The forest seems . . . peaceful.'

'It rains a lot, and it's hard to get proper sunlight when I'm trying to paint. But I suppose I enjoy it.'

'You paint?' Something within her flickered.

'I do. But once again, if anyone asks, I bullied you nearly to tears and have never touched an easel in my life.'

'Right,' Sapphire replied with a laugh. 'Your reputation.'

'My family's reputation,' he corrected her with a cluck of his tongue. 'Not something I'm terribly interested in upholding, but life is much easier if I do.'

Sapphire relaxed on a bench, her body happy to have a break from supporting the heavy fabrics of her dress. They were quiet for a moment before Sapphire found the courage to ask the question that had been on her mind for some time.

'Kaian, were you hoping to take the throne before I arrived?'

He turned to face her quickly, his body rigid. He did not answer at first, as if he feared a careless answer would undo him. Finally, he joined her on the bench, running a hand through his hair and tousling it.

'The throne,' he said, heaving a sigh. 'Would you believe me if I said I never wanted it, no matter how much it was wanted for me? From the very first screaming breath I took in this world, I was meant to rule as Ciliria's governor, to keep these people, these lands safe. I look out at the clearings, the central temple in which I have prayed since I was a boy, and my blood sings. I never wanted to be king.'

'But . . .?' Sapphire pushed.

'But my parents saw an opportunity.' He blushed at the admission. 'So, while I wasn't hoping to take the throne, I was willing to.'

Sapphire chewed her bottom lip. 'Are you angry I came back?'

His hearty laugh filled the air around them. 'Angry? Princess, I am relieved.' He looked up to the sky thoughtfully. 'How to put this?' he started. 'Better your neck breaks beneath the burden than mine.'

'Well, that's comforting.'

He shrugged, patting her arm. 'The Canmores have a way with the world, Sapphire. You are no different. Trust me on that. The role suits you.'

She wondered how someone raised by Sadara and Tyden could be so charming. His crooked smile and now-rumpled tunic made him look entirely harmless. Nothing like the warnings Claye had offered her.

Much too soon, a voice called out that lunch was ready. Kaian bowed his head quickly before escorting her back.

Araxia did most of the talking during the meal, giving the most simple and well-rehearsed answers she could offer to Sadara's probing questions about Sapphire's return. Sapphire studied her hands as they chatted, picking at the beds of her nails, which were already chewed ragged. The conversation was stilted and moved slowly.

'Sapphire, how is training going? I am sure it is difficult to begin at a much older age than most.'

'Training is going smoothly. I am being trained by the best –' she smiled at Araxia – 'so while there are hurdles many did not face, my progress is swift, and I am well on my way to achieving the Canmore power we all know.'

'I think it's admirable, highness,' Kaian finally spoke. 'To come from a land of no magic, a childhood with no exposure, and to simply trust what is within you. It's impressive. You're impressive.'

Kaian's cheeks flushed slightly as he returned his eyes to the golden buttons on the cuffs of his sleeve.

'Impressive, indeed. You know, I was thinking that Kaian and Sapphire could duel.' Sadara cut her eyes to her son and he stiffened. 'Seeing that she missed so much with her absence, I'm sure it would be wonderful for her to flex her powers in a proper setting.'

Araxia's body went rigid. 'Sapphire is still growing and understanding her true potential. I'm not sure duelling would be beneficial.'

'But all children go through duelling practice, Araxia. You and I certainly did.'

At the use of the queen's first name all the air seemed to leave the room.

'Yes, but my daughter's path is quite unique, wouldn't you say?' the queen countered.

Right then, Sapphire realized Sadara had got what she wanted. She smirked, looking victorious while Kaian stared at the floor.

'Oh, we know.'

The way the woman stared down her nose at her. The way she refused to call Araxia by her proper title. The way the woman didn't believe she could hold her own in a duel.

'I accept.'

A fork clattered against one of the plates, but silence followed. Sapphire saw red as she met Kaian's panicked gaze. If they wanted a fight, she'd give them one.

'Sapphire, I'm not sure that's best. Maybe in a few months?' Araxia whispered.

'No, Mother. I can handle this. I want to do this.'

Mother. The word Araxia had so badly wanted to hear. An undeniable glow washed over Sapphire. She felt slightly guilty for using the word for her own gain.

'OK, then.' Araxia smiled. 'If my daughter believes she's ready, I trust her intuition.'

The Princeps looked surprised, and a cumbersome silence settled in.

'Sadara, I am so grateful that you are so concerned with my development. To know that the governing families are behind me as I make this transition offers me a sense of peace.' Sapphire's tone was dulcet, her smile gentle, and Kaian bit his lip like he was fighting back a laugh. But Sadara stared at her deadpan, unblinking.

'Of course, Sapphire. It is our duty to seek what is best for Eriobis.'

'Sadara.' The queen's voice was sharp. 'I will advise you only once to treat my daughter's and my own title with respect. I am your queen and she is your princess. And while we may have grown up together, you will refer to me properly. I'm sure you understand.'

'Yes, your majesty. I do apologize for the indiscretion,' Sadara muttered, not looking up from her plate.

Conversation lapsed for the remainder of the meal.

CHAPTER FIFTEEN

Sapphire wandered into the library as the sun set, searching each aisle for Evera. When she found her friend, she felt the tension between her shoulders relax for the first time all day.

'Glad to see you made it out alive from lunch.'

'How did you know?'

'The staff gossips more than you'd expect.' Evera pulled her into a hug. 'I had a feeling you'd end up here.'

Sapphire blew out a breath as she sank to the floor. Improper and unladylike, but she didn't really care. Evera joined her without hesitation.

'What's weighing on you?'

Sapphire leaned her head back against the shelves.

'I let my pride get the better of me today and jumped at the opportunity to duel Kaian.' Evera went to speak but Sapphire raised her hand in protest. 'I know. Trust me. But what was I supposed to do? Back down?'

'That *was* an option.'

'Well, it didn't feel like it.' She turned to look at her friend with a pleading expression. 'I'm not sure how I'm supposed to defeat him with beginner's technique.

Araxia insists we take it slow, that I understand the magic. I'm a fool.'

'You are not a fool. You are just . . .' Sapphire couldn't fight back a smile as Evera struggled to find the right word. 'Eager. You are eager. And luckily for you, you have friends in high places.'

Sapphire arched a questioning brow.

'Me. I am talking about me – your friend who has access to any and all books in this library. Including the books that detail duelling techniques that the queen most likely won't teach you, and might not want you to learn.'

'Evera, don't tease me. Are you saying –'

'Sit here while I go and retrieve them.'

'No. I'm coming with you. I'll carry them while you search.'

An hour later, Sapphire exited the library with a stack of books in her hands and her hopes higher than they had been when she entered.

These books spoke of magic she had never thought possible. They gave her new ways to use her powers, ways that were twisted and deadly.

They gave her answers, a fighting chance to prove herself worthy of her surname.

She sat at the desk in her room and read about how to remove all the water from someone's body or control the blood that ran through an opponent's veins. About drowning somebody from the inside out – filling their lungs with water until they were sputtering as they tried to breathe.

Thoughts of what was possible clouded her mind. A darkness took root in her, a hunger for power, a longing for destruction.

Drowning.

Suffocating.

Controlling.

The words on the pages blurred together until she could no longer decipher them. It was then that the familiar, chilling voice broke through the haze.

You're only beginning to wake, my child.

The words ghosted against her skin, and she slammed the book closed quickly, tucking it away in its rightful place in her washroom closet, and tried to shake the feeling of a presence that did not belong.

That night, she dreamed of the child for the fourth time in a row, watching as the girl ran from monsters Sapphire could not see. The sight of the girl in a tattered gown made her stomach turn – it reminded Sapphire of when she would hunt and then run to escape the Beasts.

Sapphire watched as the girl looked around wildly before stumbling over a log, causing her to fall hard against the ground. It was then that Sapphire saw the figure emerging. Shadows masked them as they made their way closer, and Sapphire watched as the child cried out in fear.

'Please save me,' the child begged. 'Please don't let them take me.'

Sapphire felt a pressure on her chest, and as the girl

stretched out her small hand, everything in her being said no. *Walk away*.

But she couldn't leave the girl, so instead, she offered her hand to the child as the shadows engulfed them both.

As their hands met, a shrill scream filled the room, and Sapphire shot from her bed, gasping for air. She kept her eyes closed in an effort to calm her erratic heart.

You are safe. You are in the kingdom. And you are safe.

But when she opened her eyes, taking in the world around her, the white walls and windows of her bedroom were gone. Instead, there were large trees that rolled as far as she could see – the ground was mossy and damp under her body. She stood up quickly, trying to find her bearings as panic settled in.

No.

As she began to walk, she found herself entirely turning around, but the trees never changed or thinned.

Lost. She was lost.

She sucked in a sharp breath, trying to get a grip on her building anxiety but failing spectacularly. Still, she paused in an effort to call upon the girl she had once been – the girl who felt at home in the woods. The memory helped ground her for a moment.

To her left, something moved in the shadows, and a small scream escaped her lips. She went to step away from the disturbance, but her foot caught on a fallen tree, and she fell hard to her knees. She cursed loudly as a sharp pain shot through her.

Laughter echoed around her, chilling her blood.

A wicked sound.

'Now, princess, what are you doing in the middle of the forest in the dead of night on your knees? Waiting for me?' Sapphire looked up, finding Ashes hovering above her.

Sapphire pushed herself up from the ground. She had to tilt her head upward slightly to meet the girl's menacing gaze.

Sapphire blinked a few times before taking a step back. 'I'm not sure how I got here. One minute I was asleep, dreaming of the forest – a small child running, trying to escape something . . . the next, I was here.'

'Fascinating,' Ashes said, squinting slightly in amusement. 'Well, do get home safe, princess. I'd hate for you to stumble across something dangerous.'

Sapphire watched as she almost slipped out of view before shouting, 'Wait. Please! Just . . . Just help me find the lake? Point me in the right direction, even.'

Ashes paused, turning on her heel shortly after.

'It must run in your family to beg Shadow Witches for assistance.'

'What is that supposed to mean?' Sapphire asked.

Ashes' gaze locked on to her then, pinning her in place, as the witch's eyes raked over her face.

'I asked you a question.' Sapphire stepped closer to the witch, fighting the urge to grab Ashes by her dress.

'Not one I'm interested in answering.'

Sapphire closed her eyes for a few moments, trying to remain calm, but frustration built in her like a weapon ready to be used.

'Will you help me or are you just wasting my time?'

'I never do anything for free, princess. What do I get in return?'

'I have nothing to offer you,' Sapphire bit out.

She felt the witch's thin fingers wrap around her wrist, tugging her closer.

'What a foolish thing to say, princess. Assuming you have nothing I could want.'

Sapphire was tall, but Ashes towered over her in a way that made her feel small. 'Wha-what could I offer you?'

'Plenty.' The witch smiled, looking down her sharp nose at Sapphire. 'Do we have a deal?'

'I don't even know what I'm agreeing to.'

'I suppose you'll just have to trust me.'

Never trust a Shadow Witch – a devil among men. That was what she had been taught. But she felt a tug of curiosity about the girl who hovered over her.

'You have a deal.'

The witch's smile shifted to something devious, and Sapphire's neck prickled.

'You truly are your mother's daughter, then.'

'What's that supposed to mean?'

Ashes took her roughly by the arm and began to walk, pulling Sapphire along behind her. 'Seek out your own history, princess. I have no . . .' she said, throwing a veiled look over her shoulder, a weighted pause lingering between her words, 'interest in being your governess.'

With a simple hand gesture, Ashes pulled the shadows from the trees, the moonlight providing enough light for her to see the lake in the distance. Sapphire sagged in relief, turning to say thank you, but Ashes was devoured by her own shadows.

Still, Sapphire whispered into the midnight mass before her, 'Thank you.'

She was almost at the lake when she felt the ghost of a touch on her back, pulling at her nightgown. And when she wheeled around, she almost screamed. A shadow person hovered before her. She stood frozen as it reached out for her, placing a phantom hand to her cheek.

'When I call for you, you come. Keep your word, princess.'

And then the shadows retreated to the forest, painting the treeline black.

CHAPTER SIXTEEN

Three weeks had passed since the lunch at the Princeps' estate, and they hadn't received word about the date of the duel. Sapphire didn't mind. She was glad to take advantage of the extra time. But she knew she wouldn't have much longer – and her dread was building every day.

She spent any free time she had in the library, poring over books and chatting with Evera until she had to return to Aleburn. Tonight, the candles had nearly burned out as they chatted.

'Are you feeling any better about the duel?'

'Yes and no,' Sapphire said, leaning back in her chair. 'Araxia thinks I can hold my own, and that's got to mean something, right?'

'Right.'

But Evera's tone was distant, and she wouldn't meet Sapphire's eyes. Sapphire needed more. She needed to prove herself. She grabbed Evera's hand and began dragging her towards the door.

'What are we doing?'

'I'm going to show you what I've learned from those books. I know you'll be honest with me.'

Evera's uncertainty lingered as they headed for the lake and it remained as Sapphire stepped into the water.

She had not taken time to change. Her dress became heavier the deeper she went, but she could feel the energy building around her – every nerve buzzing as the water met her skin. She stretched her hands out, prepared to run through what she had been practising.

The first move was simple – pulling all the water into her and then pushing it away to create large waves that could overwhelm anyone who joined her in the lake.

Simple. Easy. The water obeying its master.

'I'm glad to know the recommendations in that book were correct. But we should probably stop now.'

But it wasn't enough. She needed Evera to believe that she could beat Kaian. Even if Kaian was kind. Even if he was nothing like his parents. From the tips of her fingers to the very marrow of her bones, her entire being longed to establish dominance.

She thrust her hand under the waves, calling upon the magic in her veins and the magic that coursed through the ground under her feet. She called upon the Elders and the Gods that came before them, pleading with them to fuel her. To give her the kind of power that would bring the world to its knees. The type of power a queen would need.

Something heeded her.

As her outstretched hands began to move in slow circles, the water followed her. *Move with me. Follow me. Trust me.* Her fingers began to work quicker and the water followed at the same pace, spinning faster until she had created a whirlpool. The water roared with rage as it moved at her command. And she smiled to herself.

It wasn't proper. Araxia wouldn't approve. But, Gods, she was lost in it.

Lost in the sound of the rapids rushing past her, the feeling of the world bending to her will. In the sight of the water – hungry and consuming. In the idea of winning the duel with the smallest move of her fingers. At the vision of smiling in victory at Sadara. For a moment, she wondered if she could consume the world whole.

Right then, she understood Vasalis, the forsaken Elder who took on too much. The type of control and power coursing through her fingertips was impossible to replicate.

She understood the daughter of the water, who'd sacrificed herself to the Voltra Sea.

'Sapphire, please!'

Evera's strangled plea broke through the haze, and she dropped her hands stiffly to her sides. The water ceased swirling and became still without her guidance, and she stared out at the miles that stretched before her, blinking a few times to recentre herself.

Finally, she turned to Evera, who asked, 'Are you OK?'

Sapphire blinked a few more times before meeting her gaze.

'Yes, sorry. I'm fine.' She exited the lake, meeting Evera on the shore. 'What did you think?'

'I think you are a Canmore through and through. Kaian won't stand a chance.'

The girl smiled at her but it didn't reach her eyes, and

Sapphire felt apprehension build inside her, a lingering feeling that she had done too much. Once they had returned to the library and settled back in the large chairs by the windows, she studied her friend.

Evera looked anywhere but at Sapphire.

Chapter Seventeen

Her body ached, begging for a break from the constant assault she faced from the queen's training. But she was getting stronger, better. Her control was improving. Her technique becoming more focused.

But she couldn't outrun the exhaustion that clung to her.

This morning was no different. Her eyelids were heavy as she walked alongside Claye.

'Everything OK, princess? You've been pretty quiet this morning.'

'I'm fine. Just thinking,' She felt Claye's eyes on her, and she shrugged. 'Are you trying to analyse me?'

'Never,' Claye responded with a bit more bounce in his step. They paused in front of the door. 'Good luck with getting what you want.'

'How did you –'

'You're a bit easier to read than you'd expect. I don't know what you're going to ask for, but I do hope it goes well for you.'

Sapphire rolled her eyes and tried not to smile.

'You're going to make me late.' Claye just shook his head as he pulled at the door.

Araxia and Kip smiled as she entered. Good. They were happy to see her, so maybe today she would get a yes. She couldn't put her finger on why she was so nervous about asking to go out of the castle to see Evera, but she was. Maybe it was because she desperately needed to see her friend. She hadn't seen Evera since the training grounds session – the girl managing to slip out of the castle each time before Sapphire visited the library.

She couldn't fight the brimming thought that Evera was avoiding her, and the possibility was eating her alive.

It was a new feeling – relying so heavily on someone. Witrotean was not a world that offered the luxury of depending on others.

But she needed Evera's steady presence more than she'd like to admit. And after a lifetime of running from people, she had come to find security in her friend. Security she desperately yearned for, especially right now.

Araxia had announced it at dinner yesterday: Sadara's letter had arrived, and the date of her duel with Kaian was set.

Sapphire had been unexpectedly nervous.

She imagined herself locked in battle – struggling. She imagined eyes upon her, the same thought in every mind: a mortal girl who should've remained in mortal lands. But then she felt it, the unforgettable surge of power under her skin – the sensation of the world being at her call. Feral magic, untamed and unashamed.

The royal daughter. The heir to the throne.

So, despite her nerves, she told herself she was ready.

A plate was placed in front of her, bringing her

thoughts back to the table, and she began to eat with a shaking hand. Unsteady and unsure, she did her best to participate in the conversation, biding her time for the right moment. She waited until a lull hit the table. Araxia sipped her tea, and Kip studied the documents that had been delivered to him.

Sapphire cleared her throat.

'I need to talk to you both,' she said. She shied away from their gazes. Her voice was much louder than she had intended it to be. There was obvious worry in their eyes, and Sapphire offered a smile to reassure them.

'I think I've been doing well lately, wouldn't you agree?' Sapphire asked.

They both nodded, their postures relaxing at her question.

'Your progress has been impressive, yes. But why do you ask?' Kip placed his documents on the table as he spoke.

'Well,' she said, taking a deep, steadying breath. 'I would like Evera to stay the night.'

'Are you asking to have a sleepover?'

'I – yes. I am. I would like to have a sleepover.'

As so often, Araxia and Kip exchanged a look of understanding before moving forward. The queen reached out for her hand.

'Of course you can have a sleepover. I do hope you understand that you are not a prisoner in this castle. It is your home and we want you to be comfortable.' Araxia smiled at her and Sapphire tried to mirror the warmth the woman exuded but failed.

Her cold indifference to those around her had been forged by the life she had lived, those she had watched leave, the time she had lost, and the constant uncertainty.

Sapphire could never truly afford to offer warmth to all those around her. Self-preservation always prevailed. It was always needed.

And even now, she could not force herself.

Sapphire faked an illness to get out of training early in the hope of arriving at the library before Evera could leave. She burst through the door and a few scholars jumped as she shattered the tranquil silence, but she didn't care.

'Evera.'

The girl turned to meet her gaze and she didn't miss the look of dread her friend wore.

'Sapphire? How can I help you?'

Sapphire was suddenly nervous. Surely her desperation was pathetic? 'A sleepover.' Evera looked confused. 'I am inviting you to stay the night at the castle. Tomorrow. Please.'

Evera placed the book in her hand back on the shelf.

'I'd need to double check that my mother doesn't need help with my sisters.'

'Of course. Just send a note to my room tomorrow to let me know.' Sapphire bounced on her toes, feeling hopeful but Evera simply nodded and returned her attention to the shelf. A few suffocating, silent moments passed before Evera cleared her throat.

'I am quite behind. If you don't have a request, I do apologize but I must focus. Is that OK?'

Sapphire frowned, knowing a dismissal when she heard one.

'Of course.' Sapphire stepped back. 'Just send me a note tomorrow. I really hope we get to spend some time together.'

Evera offered her a tense smile but said nothing until Sapphire finally took her cue to leave.

Claye had delivered the letter a few hours ago, letting Sapphire know that Evera had agreed to stay the night and since then Sapphire had been awaiting her arrival. The sun had almost slipped away when the knock came. When Sapphire opened the door, both girls stared at their hands, unsure of what to say.

'I've been avoiding you,' Evera said with no preamble. Honest and straightforward.

'I caught on to that.'

'You deserve to know why.'

'You don't have to tell me.'

'Sapphire, stop talking. Please, let me do this.'

Sapphire clamped her mouth shut.

'I used to have four siblings. I now have three.' The tremor in Evera's voice was noticeable and Sapphire stilled. 'He died chasing power. And that night – when you were summoning your powers, the look in your eyes reminded me so much of the way he used to look. He could have burned the world to the ground and it wouldn't have been enough for him.' She paused and rubbed her neck like she was trying to convince herself to carry on.

'You – I can't . . .' She hiccupped, a soft sob bubbling on

her lips. 'Maybe we hardly know each other, but I care about you. And I can't imagine watching you burn out like he did. I can't lose someone else – especially not to the hunger for power that comes with this world. I don't want you to –'

Sapphire was up and moving before she had the time to think the decision through, wrapping her arms around Evera. She pulled her friend in close as Evera shook with sobs. And she remained there, supporting her as the girl struggled with a loss she would never shake.

'I – I never had the opportunity to have a family before I came here. But I did have . . . people who mattered. So, while I've never had a loss like yours . . . I am sorry. Sorry you had to face that and sorry that I ever made you think you would face it again.'

'You never talk about the Home.'

'I fear the guilt will consume me if I do. I . . . I left them. I left them and there was no one prepared to take my place.'

Evera reached out for her hand. 'You never chose to leave them, Sapphire.'

'But I left all the same.' Sapphire wiped a tear away with her free hand. 'Maybe one day I will be able to face it all. Maybe I can tell you about the Home and the world I once knew, but for now, it's simply a demon I am not brave enough to face.'

'You're braver than you ever give yourself credit for.' Evera squeezed her hand.

'I won't do it again,' Sapphire said, returning to the topic of conversation she could stomach. 'I promise.' And she meant it.

A few moments passed before Evera pulled away. Her eyes were swollen but she smiled.

'You're my friend. The closest friend I have,' Sapphire said too quickly.

Evera's smile grew, and she pulled Sapphire back into a hug. 'What a way with words you have.'

They fought back a fit of laughter that threatened to take them over, eventually succumbing to the feeling. They collapsed together on the bed, giggling, thankful that the hard conversations were over.

Still, a feeling lingered in the back of Sapphire's mind.

The feeling that she did not belong.

And she clung to Evera's kindness like a soul lost in a storm.

They spent the rest of the night confessing secrets and memories. Stories of their childhoods, which were so starkly different – Evera's filled with warmth and love, Sapphire's a fight – but still, they found more common ground than expected. Both had been caretakers for those younger than them, forced to grow up to provide . . . It was there that Sapphire felt a deeper connection than she had ever known.

They fought to keep their tired eyes open as the moon climbed high in the sky, not wanting the night to pass – but finally, Sapphire felt herself slipping into a deep sleep that only came with the security that Evera could offer her.

At the training grounds, Araxia was already in the water, which was entirely out of character. The queen had entered the water only once – on Sapphire's first day – remaining on the shore to instruct and encourage the rest of the time. The sight stopped her short, and Araxia waved to her.

'Come on, Sapphire. We only have a little light left. Let's get started.'

'Get started?'

'You're going to duel me.'

'Wh-What? I'm not ready for that.'

Sapphire took a step away from the queen, unsteady on her feet. And despite the water's chill, she began to sweat under her training suit. The idea of duelling Araxia, the queen of Eriobis and the woman who had taught her everything she knew, left her unnerved. She wasn't prepared, either mentally or physically.

'You are ready. And if you're not, you will be. We will duel every day. Multiple times a day if needed. I refuse to let my daughter walk into the arena unprepared – especially when duelling a Princeps.'

For a split second, Sapphire could see herself in Araxia. The fire in her eyes, the hunger in her voice. A charge surged through her.

'But we're both water . . . how will we duel?'

'Battling those of our own element can be one of the most difficult challenges. They know what to anticipate.'

Sapphire stared at Araxia for a moment longer, hoping she would reveal she was kidding.

She stared back with a flat expression, almost challenging.

So Sapphire stepped deeper into the water.

'Are you ready?' Araxia asked.

'Am I ready to duel the woman who has been teaching me everything I know? I'm not entirely sure –'

That was when she felt something tighten around her ankle, pulling her over. Araxia had water-wiped her. It was a trick she had learned recently – she could mould water into a rope and wrap it around her duelling partner.

When Sapphire broke the surface, Araxia was smiling coyly.

'I said, are you ready?'

'I am.'

CHAPTER EIGHTEEN

Her knees hit stone and a splitting pain surged through her – familiar and constant. She could feel the erratic hammering of her heart in her chest. And every time she went to make a move, the queen was prepared.

Outpacing her, outperforming, outworking. Outdoing her. Sapphire's bleeding knees were proof.

With bruised elbows and aching muscles, she lost again and again. The queen showed no mercy.

Pushing herself up from the lakebed once more, she wiped the trickling blood from her legs. Her eyes met Araxia's challenging gaze.

'Tired?'

The woman's smile was taunting, and Sapphire pressed her lips together in an effort to swallow the sour swell that was building up inside her. *Obviously*, Sapphire thought to herself while shakily retaking a defensive stance.

If this was any preview of her upcoming duel, she had half a mind to beg for it to be cancelled.

'Come on, Sapphire. Dig deeper. It's inside you – whatever catalyst you need. Find it. Use it.'

She wondered what would happen if she tapped into the

magic she had learned from the books she kept hidden, but she feared the repercussions. If she showed what she had learned, would they watch her more closely? She couldn't afford to find that out. Instead, angry tears spilled over against her will, and she looked away, trying to study the flat stones on the lake's floor.

Araxia's entire demeanour shifted in that second. Gone was the fiery look of a smug warrior, replaced by the concerned gaze of a mother.

What would happen if Sapphire just admitted that she was terrified of giving in to it all? That anger was the most consuming thing she had ever felt. Would the queen turn away from her, terrified?

'What do you feel when you're duelling? What are you fuelling yourself with?' Sapphire asked.

'Hmm.' It sounded like a melody from the queen's lips. 'I'm not sure I can answer that. Or if I should. A plethora of little moments shape us, mould us into who we are. That's why that power, that force, is unique to each person. Discovering that truth – understanding that deepest part of you that forces your limbs to move, your lungs to fill, forces you to live, it's – it's a rite of passage all of us must face. Never easy, of course,' she said with a soft chuckle. 'There is no power, no true power at least, without introspection. But mastering it is what separates the mavens from the acolytes. For me, I guess, if I had to pinpoint it, I'd say it arises from my competitive nature. I give in to my hunger to control what's around me.'

'What if what I feel when I'm working with the water isn't exactly of a – a good nature?'

'What do you mean?' The queen raised her eyebrows.

'Sometimes – well, a lot of the time – I feel anger. A deep burning rage. It almost scares me – to feel something so deeply. And I always fear that if I give in, it will consume me.'

Araxia tilted her head, a thoughtful look on her face. 'If you're focusing more on holding back in fear of what might happen, you'll never win. The water, the power, the anger can only consume you if you allow it. Believe it or not, anger isn't a foreign emotion that people dig into when working with the elements. I don't think it's something you should fear. Own it. Use it to your advantage.'

Sapphire clung to every word.

Over the past few months, a need had been born – to be the best, to wield power, to be worth the crown.

She had no reason to fear it.

As she turned to prepare for the next round, her body felt lighter, less battered. Her muscles buzzed with fortitude and drive as she extended her hands out before her, wiggling her fingers. The water rippled with her movements, and she felt a wicked hunger.

Sapphire took a deep breath, preparing herself to try once more.

Hours later, exhaustion weighed on Sapphire as she finally

made her way back to her room. She gathered the journals from their hiding places, and her muscles screamed in agony as she climbed on to the bed and stared at the jagged shadows the candlelight cast.

She peeled back the worn cover of the journal – the one with thin penmanship and a ripped spine. The journal that had preoccupied her since she had first felt it in her hands just days ago.

Her chest swelled with a mix of dread and excitement as she ran her fingers over the old, yellowed pages. Everything she had been searching for could be before her and she paused a few moments to gather her courage.

And finally, by candlelight, she began to read.

Sapphire's hands tightened on the worn leather as she immediately recognized a name.

Mikel.

Mikel, the man who had so boldly loved a Shadow Witch many moons ago. The man who had written passage after passage before disappearing entirely – like an ember lost to the wind.

Kya was Mikel's twin sister, and her journal was overwrought, with frantic questioning and searching for her lost brother.

My brother is an earnest, noble man. There is no
malice in his heart. He deserved to live out his days
here, with me, with our family. Where is he now?
It's been fourteen days since we last saw him.
Fourteen days. Where is my brother?

Sapphire flipped through the pages. Kya grew more desperate with each one. But when three months had passed, Kya's focus switched to something more sinister.

A Shadow Witch he loved. Tell me, did they seal him away with the rest when they built the Shattered Lands? Did they penalize him for following his heart? Did they punish him for what he could not control? Oh, Mikel, I will find justice for you. I will leave no stone unturned.

The woman had been braver than anyone Sapphire had ever known – facing long nights seeking out answers where she shouldn't have been. She searched the country for her brother, for closure, and it never came. Sapphire felt like she had ingested poison at the realization that Kya had died no closer to answers.

I hope a day comes when the barrier is brought to the ground. I hope those that took him from me lose something precious so they may share my pain. I hope a day comes where the answers I need are revealed. I will be watching from the other side.
And Mikel, I hope you are waiting for me.

That was Kya's last entry. Sapphire could barely keep herself steady as tears rolled down her cheeks, and she took a few moments to remember the brave twins to whom life had been so unfair. It was late, but her mind was buzzing. It had been some time since she had been able to beat the exhaustion, so she reached for another journal.

Marca, a man who was Fireborn and a distant cousin of Evera, had written his own journal forty-two years after the barrier had been built. He had an analytical mind – writing both fact and opinion. He kept a running log of those banished to the other side:

> *Shadow Witches, practitioners of Dark Magic, those who aided them, and those that turned against the armies of the Elders.*

And maybe Mikel? was added to the list in smaller letters.

The lands beyond the barrier were known to be dark and sprawling. A forest of never-ending terror now inhabited by some of the darkest creatures. Creatures that Marca could not bring himself to write about.

Monsters.

Witches.

Magic.

Marca questioned it all. How the barrier was constructed. If practitioners of Dark Magic truly deserved exile. If the war was more politics than a crusade for a better world. If they had stolen his ancestor, dragging him to the other side.

His musings filled the journal, questions bleeding off the page, questions that were now lodged into Sapphire's very core. He recounted how people had tried to break down the barrier, desperate to discover what was truly on the other side. But this led to injuries, to imprisonment, to death . . . All attempts had faded away.

She could feel his pleading through the pages. Pleading for answers and understanding. It left her feeling empty to think he probably never got it.

Still, all her reading – and the lack of answers – led her to one conclusion.

Sapphire needed to see the barrier in person.

She knew she was a fool. So, she supposed she shouldn't have been surprised when she made her way to the lake and dived underwater, headed for the shore of Ciliria. Not her best-laid plan, but she couldn't stay in the castle any longer. Not when she couldn't stop thinking about the barrier, about the journals, and if she was being honest, about Ashes.

She had spent too much time wondering why her mind constantly went back to the forest. To the shadows. To her. But it did – and maybe it was because Ashes seemed to be the only person in the entire kingdom who didn't care about her at all. The only person who didn't tiptoe around her or try to pressure her into greatness.

No, Ashes simply treated her like she would anyone else she couldn't stand. Sapphire almost craved it.

When she reached the familiar shore, she didn't break stride as she moved towards the forest. She was surrounded by trees now and despite her fear of what lurked in the beyond, she felt the weight of the day slide off her with each step. She was about twenty paces into the woods when she heard the distinct sound of someone or something nearby. She rushed to tuck herself away behind the nearest tree, squinting in an effort to make out whatever lurked in the shadows.

'You can't hide from the darkness that exists in these woods, princess.'

Sapphire bit her tongue to suffocate the scream that threatened to burst out of her. Whirling around, she found the witch looming over her. 'Running from something?'

Sapphire furrowed her brows, trying to consider what the witch could be implying, but came up with nothing. Ashes chuckled before reaching out a hand. Sapphire forced herself not to flinch as Ashes gently tucked a lock of loose hair behind her ear.

'This is not a safe place for princesses to play.'

'You speak to me as if I –' Sapphire sputtered. 'I am *not* a child.'

'No.' Ashes' eyes dragged down Sapphire's frame before meeting her gaze once more. 'You most certainly are not.'

Sapphire felt her cheeks warm and she angled her face away in an effort to collect herself.

Ashes asked, taking a step closer, 'Trouble on the golden throne?'

'I just needed fresh air.'

'We both know that's not true,' Ashes replied with a grin and the already black night became darker at the command of her shadows. Sapphire's eyes widened, fear gripping her. 'Power can be a terrifying thing, can't it?'

Sapphire opened her mouth to speak but closed it promptly – how did she know?

'I have no idea what you mean by that.'

'Of course, you do, princess. Otherwise, you wouldn't be in these woods interrupting my night.'

'What . . .'

'Power is nothing to fear.' The world around them darkened to an endless black and Ashes stepped closer, leaving hardly any room between them. 'Don't you crave it? The rush of it? The destruction?'

'How do you know . . .?'

Ashes reached out her hand, tucking one finger under Sapphire's chin. With a tap, she forced Sapphire to meet her gaze.

'What do I know?'

Sapphire felt pinned by the witch's stare and she opened and closed her mouth several times, entranced by the eyes staring back at her. 'Would you like to confess your secrets? I will listen.'

Something sparked inside Sapphire. Something dark and curious and she felt herself lean forward slightly, just close enough that she could feel Ashes' warm breath on her skin.

'What is it that you seek, princess?'

Sapphire's lips parted slightly but words did not come as she struggled to smother the answer she so desperately wanted to say.

I seek power. I seek answers. I seek you.

But she could not admit that so she shoved it down, forcing herself to take a step back. She desperately needed distance between them. Distance from whatever had awoken inside her. Ashes laughed like she could read her thoughts.

'Be careful in your duel, princess. I would hate to see that darling Princeps boy get hurt.'

And then, the darkness collapsed, and she was alone. The sensation sent her running for the shore, never breaking her stride as she met the water. But as she swam, she could have sworn she felt a monster watching her.

A monster in the form of the most beautiful girl she had ever seen.

CHAPTER NINETEEN

It was the morning of the duel and Sapphire struggled to focus as Claye escorted her.

'You're nervous.' It wasn't a question, more a statement laced with surprise.

'Wouldn't you be?'

'I guess. I'm just surprised.'

Sapphire didn't meet Claye's gaze.

'Is that so?'

'No matter how untraditional your past may be, you are a Canmore, princess. Women born from the magic of the Elders. The Princeps boy doesn't stand a chance.'

Sapphire wanted to thank him but let the moment pass. And she wasn't sure how to admit that while she was nervous for the duel itself, it was Ashes' warning that really set her on edge. The witch spoke in riddles constantly – but it was as if she knew something was coming. Something bad.

Outside, Kip offered her a small smile, and Araxia reached out for her hand, guiding her up the steps into the carriage. Sapphire tried to focus on the passing landscape. The shimmering lakes soon gave way to tall buildings that reached towards the sky. Merchants lined the streets, and temples with colourful stained glass were seemingly on every corner.

She begged time to stand still. But the Elders ignored her when she called upon them. And before long, the duelling arena, set in the city centre, came into sight.

She wasn't entirely sure why she was so surprised to see hordes crowding the entrance. They lined the street, and as the carriage rolled over the stone, guards worked to hold them back as they attempted to get a closer look.

And while she heard the cheers, she couldn't miss the whispers.

She understood it, truly. But it still left her feeling overexposed, her nerves buzzing under the thick fabric of her training suit.

They had shown up to watch it all unfold. To watch her be defeated, proving she had no right to the Canmore name. Like a child, she looked to Araxia, feeling overwhelmed. The queen took Sapphire's face in her palms.

'You are a Canmore. My daughter. My joy. They do not get the luxury of seeing you falter.'

The words were a command, and Sapphire fortified herself. Claye took her hand. As her feet met the ground, she turned her face to the sun and smiled.

Araxia and Kip flanked her as they walked towards the opening of the arena, and Sapphire was careful to greet everyone she could. Bowing her head in gratitude to those who called out her name.

The arena was simple and domed, with large arched

windows lining every wall. A small pool was in one corner, and a youngling tree in the other. Their weapons. She watched a man summon air, pushing the top of the dome up so that the arena was open to the sky.

It was real. It was here. And there was no escaping it.

Kaian and Sapphire were summoned to the centre of the arena.

'Both of you have accepted these rules with an Elder's oath?'

'We will obey,' they answered in unison.

'When the bell tolls, pull out.'

They nodded, accepting whatever came next. And as they shook hands firmly, they stared at each other, Kaian with concern and Sapphire with fear. Neither wanted this.

'Sapphire, if you don't breathe, you'll never stand a chance,' Kaian whispered under his breath, his hand tightening around hers.

As their hands dropped, Sapphire watched his eyes wander over to his parents – as always, there was an unpleasant look on their faces. When he returned his gaze to her, he had hardened, and she softened for him. A boy controlled by monsters.

'Good luck, Canmore. You'll need it.'

'I don't believe in luck.'

He blinked a few times, making an effort to hide a smile.

Her hands shook and her mind turned foggy as she drew her gaze back to Araxia, who awaited her in the corner. Doubt flooded her very being.

Fraud.

Illegitimate.

Undeserving.

She bit her tongue, tasting blood, until she had pushed the poison from her mind.

You are ready. Trained.

Royal blood. Magic blood. Waterborn.

You belong.

You will not fail. You will not fall.

She repeated the mantra in her head over and over until she saw the flag lifted into the air. The duel had begun.

Sapphire got in the first move. It started as a simple game of back and forth – each using more defensive than offensive tactics. Kaian wrapped ivy around her leg, pulling her feet out from under her. Sapphire replied with a water cannon that knocked him into the nearby wall.

She looked around the arena, finding the gazes of those who doubted her. She looked at Evera, begging for answers her friend did not have. She couldn't find Kip, but she never struggled to find Sadara and Tyden. They were always watching her closely, smirks on their faces.

Another vine wrapped around her waist, pulling her to the ground, hard, and she yelped as her elbow met stone.

She was losing in front of everyone.

The flag was raised once more, signalling that it was time for the break before the third round, but Sapphire remained on the ground, unable to find the energy to push herself up. She heard footsteps and looked up to meet Araxia's eyes. The queen extended her hand, and Sapphire took it with gratitude.

She bowed her head, not in prayer, but in total exhaustion.

They were headed into the final round, and she was three points behind. The judges tended to lean towards his swift and easy movements versus her jarring and stilted returns, and she wondered if just stepping out would look better. She could fake an illness or an injury.

She could.

But the world would know. And if they didn't, they'd assume.

She scanned the crowd once more, but her vision was blurred.

To hold back only disgraces the power in your veins.

She sat up straighter, trying not to appear startled. The voice was like the ghost of a whisper, like a light touch trailing up her spine.

Why do you run from your destiny?

She closed her eyes tightly, trying to force the presence out, but it did not go easily. A hand wrapping around her arm broke her trance, and she jerked away, nearly stumbling into the water.

'Sapphire, are you OK?' Araxia looked concerned.

'I'm going to lose.'

'It's your first duel. No one expected you to win.'

But Sapphire had hoped she would. And the fact that everyone here, including Araxia, had always doubted her stoked a flame inside her.

You cower to beings that should beg to bow before you. It's sinful, the dark voice whispered in the back of her mind.

The warning flag rose, and she walked to the centre of the arena to meet Kaian.

'Are you OK?' Kaian asked. He angled his face away from his parents, hiding his concern.

Sapphire didn't answer, her eyes finding the Princeps once more. Sadara raised her chin, smiling without a trace of kindness. She arched an eyebrow as if to say, *we knew you'd prove us right*, and Sapphire bit her tongue to stifle an angry scream.

Let it go, child. Let go.

As she walked back to her position, she met the eyes of people peering through the windows. They averted their gazes.

They thought she did not belong. To them, her royal blood meant nothing. To them, she had everything to prove. Everything to lose. To them, she was an imposter. A fraud.

She had been called many things since arriving in Eriobis. A daughter. A friend. A princess. All labels she had not asked for.

But she was more. She was a force. She was powerful. And she was worth the respect and the fear of those who gazed upon her.

Today, she would prove it.

You will not fail. You will not fall.

As the final flag was raised, she paused.

Show them. Show me, the voice sang.

And then she felt it – the loss of control. A bystander in her own life. And as Kaian sent another sluggish vine her way, she blocked it easily with a shield. As she began to close the distance between them, Kaian looked at her with a confused expression.

But she did not break stride.

Do you trust me, child?

'I trust you,' she answered to no one in particular. Kaian furrowed his brow, cocking his head from side to side, trying to understand.

She raised her hands to the sky and with a slight flex of her fingers, the world beneath her feet rumbled.

She felt it all – like raw power splitting her bones. A manic laugh slipped from her lips as her magic came to life around her.

Her magic. Hers.

A torrential downpour ripped into the arena. It soaked the dirt floor, turning the terrain into mud. Sapphire remained planted in place, stretching out her hands until her palms pressed against the wall of rain. It reacted in step as she pushed it forward towards Kaian.

She could see Kaian's fear, raw and feral, as she moved in closer to him. For only a moment, she considered that maybe she understood Ashes more than she thought.

My shadows could devour you whole.

Her magic longed to be set free.

So, she gave it what it begged for.

The storm shook the foundations below them, making her wonder, if only for a moment, whether she could cleave the arena in two.

She found Sadara's gaze once more, now panicked and strained as her son disappeared inside the storm.

Sapphire smirked.

She returned her focus to the monster before her – the monster of her own making – as it moved towards Kaian, pressing him firmly against the back wall of the arena.

It was only a few seconds before his knees buckled, and at the sight of his body on the ground, something snapped inside her. She gritted her teeth in an effort to control the storm, to make it stop, but it did not relent. Unforgiving and unyielding.

A heartbeat passed before the voice answered.

Oh, my child, this is simply the beginning.

She watched as the water began to spin, creating a cyclone – a roaring, raging sight, with Kaian as the target. It danced around him, mocking his fear.

'I said stop.' Laughter followed her demand.

You do not command me.

Water filled his lungs, and Sapphire fought to take control. She fought to close her hands, to end the storm she had created. She begged for it all to end – but it wouldn't. Her magic was entirely out of reach as she battled for control, its presence pushing against her. It pressed heavily on her chest. She watched in horror as the walls of the arena began to crack.

'Please,' she whispered.

Another sinister laugh followed.

'Sapphire Canmore. Pull out.'

Araxia's voice was sharp, and it finally shattered the hold the presence had on her. She dropped her hands and the cyclone collapsed, washing over Kaian before it disappeared. She stepped back, staring at her hands.

The arena was silent, and as she looked around, she realized many people had stepped back from the viewing windows. She saw terror in the faces of those who remained.

She felt the same when she noticed Kaian still collapsed on the ground a few feet away from her. His chest was not rising and falling. His smirk was gone.

A cry ripped from her, and she sprinted towards him.

'Do not touch him, Canmore.' Sadara bared her teeth, blocking her path. 'Crazy, just like that mother of yours. I should have seen it.'

She felt a strong hand on her shoulder as Araxia guided her away, her face tight with an emotion Sapphire couldn't read.

'It's going to be OK,' the queen chanted softly. To herself, to her daughter, to the healers rushing into the arena. Sapphire couldn't tell which.

The weight of the attention caused her to step closer to Araxia, like a child cowering.

'Let them stare. You are their future queen. They know that now.'

Crazy, just like that mother of yours.

Araxia guided her to the carriage and left, saying she would return shortly. Sapphire was about to mount the stairs when someone tapped her on the shoulder. She winced before she turned to find Evera, and relief washed over her.

'You promised me, Sapphire. You promised you wouldn't give in.'

The relief she had felt turned to icy dread as she reached out for her friend. Evera flinched.

'I – it wasn't – I didn't want to.'

Evera stared at Sapphire's hand on her arm, and the princess pulled it away quickly.

'Why didn't you stop?'

'I couldn't.' Sapphire's voice was only a raw, broken whisper. 'I couldn't make it stop.'

Evera frowned but softened slightly.

'What do you mean? Is there something you aren't telling me?'

The princess's shoulders sagged. *Yes*, she wanted to say. *Yes, please help me. I can't escape this.* But she feared if she'd admit it, she'd lose her friend entirely.

'I-I am still new to this. I am still trying to understand this . . . this power, who I am, and what it means to me. I will learn. I will. But please . . .'

Evera tapped her worn boot against the ground, contemplating Sapphire's plea.

'I think sometimes I forget everything you've been through.' The girl reached out her hand, and the princess accepted it. 'My expectations aren't reasonable. Just – I – I need you to remain here. I need you.'

Sapphire squeezed her hand, not needing to tell the girl that she would remain as long as Evera would allow her in her life.

'If it helps, I heard the crowd talking about you. Only the

queen's daughter could call on rain and control it like you did. If you didn't have their respect before, you do now.'

A soft smile spread unexpectedly across Sapphire's face. Being referred to as the queen's daughter sat with her much better than it had before. But as she looked past her friend, she saw the wary expressions of onlookers as they pressed closer, trying to get a better view. She quickly hugged Evera, promising to visit soon, and took Claye's hand as he assisted her into the carriage.

She collapsed against the cushioned seat, exhausted by everything that had happened. And when the door swung open again moments later, she was disappointed that it was Claye who joined her.

'Where's Araxia?'

'She's the queen, princess. She has to address the people properly.'

'Oh.'

'That was really something, princess,' Claye said as he settled in across from her. 'I know I told you I didn't have any doubts – but I wasn't expecting you to nearly bring the arena down.'

Sapphire wanted to laugh but she felt too exhausted to do so.

'Right now would be a great time for you to take one of those naps.'

Claye struggled to not grin.

'I'll offer you silence, for now at least.' He turned his focus to a stack of documents he had tucked away in his bag.

In the comfortable silence of the carriage, Sapphire tried to relax. Her body was tired, but her mind was alive and racing. The voice from earlier rang in her ears, and like a moth to a flame, she could not ignore it. When it came, she listened. When it controlled her, she could not escape.

It scared her that, deep down, she wasn't sure she entirely wanted to rid herself of it.

Back at the castle, the queen led her through a small door Sapphire had never noticed, and into an expansive winding garden. She wasn't sure where to look first: the blooming flowers, the robust roseberry vines, the manicured hedges that curved to create an elaborate maze. She had never seen this part of the grounds.

They walked slowly; their pace intentional as the sun warmed their backs.

'This is one of my favourite places to come to think.'

'I can see why. It's beautiful.'

'I try to tend to it myself most weeks if I have time. I enjoy the upkeep. My mother used to joke that I would have been better off being an earth wielder with my green fingers.'

Sapphire gave her a strained smile, unsure of what to say, and Araxia sighed as she led them over to a nearby stone bench.

Sapphire reluctantly followed.

'It is my job as your mother and your teacher to guide you through the hard moments. But if I'm being honest, while I know you are still learning to be my daughter, as much as I hate to admit it, I am still learning to be a mother. I don't always know what the best course of action is.'

Sapphire stayed quiet, unsure of how to respond to this type of vulnerability.

'This has been hard for you. I can't imagine how you feel – and it's not getting any easier. But your father and I love you. The power you wielded is something beyond me – beyond anything – or anyone – that I've ever seen.'

'Does that scare you?' Sapphire couldn't stop the question from rolling off her lips.

The queen, to her credit, didn't flinch. Instead she placed a gentle hand over Sapphire's, her words kind, but strained.

'We will figure this out, together.'

'I almost killed Kaian. I hurt him because I lost control.' Sapphire put her head in her hands, a sob winning out over her will not to fall apart. 'All those people today – they think I'm a monster.'

'No, Sapphire. No. Your power will be respected. And it'll just make you a stronger queen.'

Araxia's eyes finally met Sapphire's, and she noticed the queen looked tired. Sapphire's lip quivered.

'Since the day you were born, you were destined to be queen. All the unexpected circumstances in the world couldn't change that.'

Sapphire gave her a small smile, and Araxia stood up, smoothing the wrinkles out of her dress once more. A nervous habit that Sapphire knew well.

The woman began to head out of the garden, but Sapphire felt overwhelmed.

'Can you stay?'

Tears flooded the woman's eyes, and Sapphire admired how she did not fight to hold them back. They fell gracefully. Like they were nothing to be ashamed of.

'Of course I can.'

Araxia sat beside her once more, and Sapphire felt the weight of the day, of the last few months strike her all at once.

She laid her head on Araxia's shoulder. The woman stiffened but relaxed as she placed her own head atop Sapphire's. Since her arrival, she had been so focused on her own experiences she had never really stopped to think about how her return would impact Kip and Araxia. How they would struggle to make the right choices and fear that they were failing her. The thought made her chest ache.

They were quiet for some time. Sapphire felt growing fondness for the strong woman beside her.

'We'll figure it out, sweetling. I promise,' the queen whispered, gently nuzzling her head. 'We'll figure it all out together.'

'I've never had a mother before. I don't know what she should be or how it should feel. But – but whenever I close my eyes and seek out comfort or strength, you're all I see. I stare for hours into the looking glass hoping to find small pieces, scraps even, of who you are inside me. If there is another way, a better way, some skill I need to master, I don't see it. So, please, just – just don't give up on me.'

The confession slipped off her tongue, but her words, she had meant them.

'Sapphire.' Araxia's voice came clouded with emotion.

The queen turned and enveloped Sapphire in a hug. And Sapphire allowed it – enjoyed it – wanted it. A rock in the storm going on inside her soul.

Unknown power. A hazard.

But still, her mother hugged her tighter.

And that was enough for Sapphire – today.

Chapter Twenty

Sapphire and Evera were sitting in the garden enjoying the late-afternoon sunshine.

'I've never seen power like yours before.'

Sapphire sighed loudly, collapsing against the soft grass. Her leg bounced under her skirt, unable to stay still. Since her duel, the pace of training had slowed, and her body was restless without her usual routine.

She missed the water and the exhaustion it brought her. But when she approached the lake, she found herself too afraid to enter.

'You're going to have to get back in the water eventually, you know that, right?'

'I know. But . . . I just need a little more time.'

Evera returned her gaze to the sky, watching a bird fly overhead, and Sapphire appreciated that she knew when not to push the subject. Another beat of silence passed before Sapphire rolled over, looking at Evera. 'I read Kya's journal.'

The girl turned to her, their faces nearly touching. The castle had ears and eyes, little birds perched on every sill – and a private conversation took effort.

'What did you think?' Evera whispered.

'I want to see the barrier.'

'Pursuing trouble never ends well.'

Sapphire blew out a breath and rolled away from Evera to lie flat on her back again.

'Have you truly never wondered about it?'

'I mean, of course. But after learning about it in school, about the creatures that lie beyond the guard, I lost my interest. Some things are better left alone.'

'I want to see it.'

'Your parents will never allow it.'

'They won't know.'

Evera rolled her eyes. 'They know everything.'

The response was honest and deafening, and she knew Evera was right.

'She was a very distant aunt, you know. The woman who wrote that journal,' Evera said quietly.

'She reminds me of you a bit. I wish I could have met her.'

Evera smiled and returned her soft gaze to the sky.

She needed to know the country well to properly serve as queen.

That was the reasoning she'd repeated in her head as she pulled on the heavy blue cloak and sneaked out of her room that night. The hallways were dark and quiet, and she couldn't push down the feeling that someone was lurking in the shadows. The typically warm and airy castle was very different without natural light spilling through the windows.

She kept her head down, her pace fast, and she refused to stop until she was outside.

There, she paused only to pull the cloak tighter around her shoulders. The night air carried a chill, the moon was high overhead, and she did what she could to blend with the shadows as she moved towards the lake. She had studied the map closely.

The Voltra Sea cut off Astral, Aleburn's terrain had canyons and dangerous cliffs, and the Isle of Irobel would take days to reach.

No, the simplest way to get to the barrier was through Ciliria.

All she had to do was navigate the forest.

As she emerged on to Ciliria's shore, she spotted a familiar boulder and leaned against it for a moment to catch her breath.

But every minute wasted was a threat. She needed to be back inside the castle grounds before the sun broke over the horizon. So, she began.

It was darker than she recalled, so that she could barely make out the trees in front of her. It was hard, but not impossible.

She had to see the barrier. An urge that threatened to swallow her whole.

But every time the moon broke through the canopy, she found herself looking at the same wall of trees she had passed moments earlier.

She took a deep breath. She was prepared for this – she

had studied the map till her eyes had burned. She knew where she needed to go – she only needed to trust herself.

West.

She was supposed to head west.

Her pace increased, her confidence building with each step.

She was going to find the barrier.

She noticed the flicker of a flame a few paces ahead of her and quickly pressed herself against the nearest tree, try not to let her panic win.

But then she heard the sound of voices echoing through the forest.

She was not alone. No, worse – she was terribly outnumbered. Sapphire pressed her body harder against the rough bark.

She could turn around, try to find the water and swim home; but she wasn't sure she'd be able to find her way without proper light. Or she could swing wide and try to avoid disturbing the group before her.

Neither approach seemed very likely to succeed.

Short on choices, she decided to retrace her steps towards where she hoped the lake would be. When she whirled around, she felt her magic come to life, ready to protect her as she nearly screamed.

Ashes was only a few feet away. The same orb of dim light was floating in her palm and she had a curious look on her face.

'Now, if I didn't know better, I'd say you were trying to

run into me.' The witch's familiar smirk appeared, taunting her.

'You're the one who always finds me.'

'We have barrier bonds, princess. You tend to trip them. Every single time. It's my job to check them.'

'Barrier bonds?'

'More magic I can wield that you can't,' the witch replied with a smile.

Sapphire averted her gaze, hating that Ashes always seemed to have the upper hand.

'Now, what are you doing out here this time?'

'I don't believe it's any of your business.'

Ashes laughed as a shadow grew from her. It whisked around Sapphire, causing her to shiver.

'My shadows long for royal blood. And yet, you continue to tease them with these secretive outings you insist on having in the dead of night.'

Sapphire chewed the inside of her cheek. The first time the witch had threatened her, she had felt consumed with fear. But now, knowing that her own hands could cause as much destruction as the shadows, she would not yield.

'You'd be wise to leave me be.'

'Ahhh.' Ashes glided across the forest floor, towering over Sapphire before she even had time to blink. 'Have you found your backbone, princess? That will make this much more fun.'

The girls stood toe to toe, Sapphire's blood drumming in her ears.

'Well, what's your move?' Ashes smiled, exposing too

many teeth. In the shadows, Sapphire noticed they looked more like fangs.

'I refuse to waste my magic on you.'

The witch smiled in a sickeningly slow way. Sapphire fought the urge to cringe, but lost.

'Seems you've found your footing just fine,' said Ashes.

'I am of royal blood. A Canmore. A queen,' Sapphire challenged, channelling Araxia in every syllable.

'Future queen, highness. Time has yet to place that depthless duty upon those delicate shoulders. Thank Gods above for that small mercy.'

'Don't speak to me like that,' Sapphire hissed.

'What are you going to do about it, hmm? Will you take me back to the castle and punish me? Have your guards give me a good lashing?'

'I'd rather kill you myself.'

The words slipped past her lips, shocking her.

'Now, that's something I would love to see. What's your style, princess? Would you drown me? Lock me under the freezing lake? Or would you show mercy and hit me with a gale so strong I'd crumble on impact?' The witch bent down, nearly pressing her nose against Sapphire's. 'Your water-wielding does not scare me. I could rip the world out from under your feet. Ruin your mind. Steal your happiness so you would never feel joy again. Sit on your throne. Wear that glistening crown. Before you – or your *people* – could do a single thing to stop me.'

Sapphire laughed, shaking her head.

'You're not the only one here with a tempest inside them, witch.'

All her pent-up fear, anger, and rage came together in this moment.

'What a pretty little fool you are. You aren't strong enough to command me, princess. No high blood is.'

'An ordinary high blood, maybe. But I'm more powerful than most and I think you know that.'

Ashes froze and Sapphire smiled triumphantly. She realized this was her one chance to have the last word – to walk away. And she took it, turning on her heel and heading in a direction she wasn't sure of.

'Princess, wait.'

The way Ashes said the word *princess* brought her to a halt. There was less poison behind the title than usual.

'What were you seeking tonight?'

Never trust a Shadow Witch, she had been warned. But the Shadow Witch couldn't trust her either.

'I am looking for the barrier.'

Ashes cocked her head suspiciously.

'Why?'

'Are you done wasting my time?'

The left side of the witch's lips quirked upward, amused.

'Let's make a deal.'

The words sounded wicked rolling off her tongue. 'I'll lead you to the barrier if you show me that power you speak so highly of.'

'And how am I supposed to do that?'

'I have a feeling you'll figure something out.' A shadow brushed against her cheek.

The two stared at each other, unblinking, and Sapphire felt dread pool in her stomach. She knew better. She knew better than to say yes, to make another deal with this wicked soul.

But she needed to see the barrier.

'Fine. You have a deal.'

The witch reached for her hand, grasping it in her own – and they were both hidden by her shadows. Sapphire couldn't tear her eyes away from their intertwined fingers. Something about it felt so familiar.

'Then let us begin,' the witch hissed, pulling her through the forest. Sapphire struggled to keep pace with her. They moved too quickly, and where Ashes' turns were fluid, Sapphire's were jarring. Finally, they stopped in a clearing. The night sky was alive above them, like the stars and Gods were watching.

'Well, princess. Show me how you'd be my undoing.'

Sapphire suddenly felt . . . nervous. The witch watched her closely, a glimmer of mischief in her eyes. She leaned against a large tree, crossing her arms like she was awaiting a show. Sapphire looked to her hands, entirely unsure of how to proceed.

She took a timid step forward. 'And how am I expected to prove myself?'

'And here I'd thought, as this all-powerful being, you'd have the answer yourself.'

Sapphire sneered before focusing on the open ground before her. When she had summoned her powers previously, she had been angry, a bit lost, and the voice was present. She had no idea how to call upon it in this scenario.

She heard Ashes yawn dramatically.

'Tick-tock, little lamb. My patience and kindness are waning.'

'Would it kill you to hold your tongue for just a few minutes?'

Ashes sniggered, throwing her hands up in mock defence.

Sapphire took a deep breath and tried to clear her mind, calling up the magic she needed. Raising her hands to the sky, she closed her eyes tightly, summoning whatever power coursed through her veins. And then, she waited. Waited and pleaded for the thrum of power at her fingertips.

It did not come.

Sapphire was not sure how much time passed before the sound of clapping filled the silence.

'My, my, how impressive you are. How does one contain such power in such a delicate frame?'

Sapphire grimaced as she dropped her hands, not wanting to open her eyes. When she did, she jumped, as the witch was much closer than she had expected. Ashes grabbed her roughly by the arm, pulling her back. Sapphire's body slammed into her own. The witch put a single finger under the princess's chin, forcing their gazes to meet.

'Would you like to know what happens to liars in my coven?'

Sapphire refused to back down, but when she spoke, the tremor in her voice betrayed her.

'No.'

Ashes' grin widened at the sound of her fear.

'We carve their tongues out of their mouths so they may never tell a lie again.' Sapphire pushed away from the witch, but Ashes didn't budge.

'I need to see the barrier tonight,' Sapphire huffed.

'Your needs are of no concern to me. We made a deal. If you can't uphold your end, well, that is quite unfortunate for you.'

'I can. I will. I just need one more chance. Let me try again.'

'No.' The response was curt. 'I am exhausted by your childish attempts. We are done for the night.' The witch looked to the moon and then back to Sapphire. 'I'm not a dealer of second chances, princess. But for you, just this once, I offer you one. Tomorrow night.'

'So soon? What if I can't get away? I need time to pl–'

Ashes laughed, cutting her off as she stepped closer once more.

'Your problems are not mine, princess. I am not beckoning you into this forest.'

Sapphire wanted to bite back. She wanted to beat her fist against the witch's chest. She wanted to scream, but she needed to see the barrier. She couldn't mask the frustration in her voice as she spoke.

'Fine. Tomorrow night, then.'

Ashes nodded, her shadows dancing too close for comfort.

'I've warned you once – about making a deal with a Shadow Witch. Don't disappoint me.'

Sapphire clenched her jaw. 'And I'll warn *you* now – double-cross me and I'll kill you myself.'

'Tempting,' Ashes said with a curious smile. 'But, princess, if you killed me, who would you dream of at night?'

Chapter Twenty-one

Her maidens woke her up much earlier than she had hoped with worse news than she could have imagined. The Princeps were on their way.

Her stomach lurched. The events of last night were written across her face, manifesting in dark bags under her eyes. Her skin was dull, her hair knotted. She collapsed into a nearby chair.

Sapphire barely noticed when they laced her into a dress and laboured to cover the lingering bruises under her eyes. She didn't speak. She didn't meet their eyes. She did not argue. She followed the routine she knew well.

When the Princeps arrived, she greeted them with a simple nod as they bowed. Sadara's unpleasant stare lingered on her.

'Majesty, would you mind if the children went and occupied themselves? We have a few things we need to discuss – in private.'

Sapphire didn't argue as Araxia gave her a knowing look. Instead, she stood, excusing herself with Kaian in tow. They went through the double doors that led to the wetland gardens and walked in silence. As she took him in, she noticed he was limping. But that wasn't all – there were bruises on his skin. Noticeable bruises that had not come by accident.

'You're hurt.'

He gave her a gentle smile.

'After the duel . . . It's nothing I'm not used to.'

Sapphire felt ill as she realized what the boy was implying. An unfamiliar sadness rushed through her as she wondered if Kaian could ever truly reach the standards his parents expected.

'Come. Let's walk through the gardens.'

He nodded, keeping pace next to her. His face twisted as he struggled to match her stride, so she slowed.

'I'm sorry about the duel. I'm not exactly sure what came over me.'

'I already told you it was fine. It was a competition, and you had a lot more at stake. I understand.'

She gave him a grateful nod. 'Do you know what they're talking about?'

'Shadow Witches, if I had to guess. They've been occupying the forest in Ciliria for some time. Father is displeased.'

'Shadow Witches?'

She feigned ignorance – hoping Kaian would reveal something she didn't know.

'I'm surprised your parents haven't warned you of them.'

'I'm still going through my history courses.' Another lie. But one she could afford.

'Those courses teach you nothing anyway. Shadow

Witches were the root cause of the First War. And despite the advice of the whole royal council, three hundred years ago, the ruling queen decided to draw up a treaty with their remaining lineage. Their magic was somehow passed down and unrest grew as those of the coven bloodline yearned to practise the magic they knew.'

'But why would the rulers allow that?'

'Goodwill? Proof that the war was truly over? A token of good faith in the hope that the Shadow Witches took it and kept the peace? There have been plenty of explanations, but no one can really be sure.'

Sapphire chewed on her bottom lip, lost in thought. 'What makes them so awful?'

'Their shadows are beasts of their own creation that could tear the flesh from your bones, flaying you alive before you even realize you're dead. Their magic is dark, Sapphire. There's a reason why the Elders risked so much to seal them behind the barrier. They are just a venomous infestation that should have been taken care of ages ago.' He pointed to the large windows of the dining room where his father paced, his hands thrown in the air.

Sapphire shivered, the memory of Ashes' shadows brushing against her skin still clear in her mind.

'Have you ever met one? A Shadow Witch?'

His face shifted slightly. 'Once. And I'll never forget it. *Ict serventi cortus,*' he whispered, the language of the Elders rolling from his tongue with ease. 'Wickedness made flesh.'

To her dismay, Ashes' smile flashed in her mind.

213

Could wickedness look like that? Could wickedness be so . . . beautiful?

She blinked a few times, trying to shove the unwelcome thought away. But she knew it wasn't the first time she had considered Ashes' beauty, and was even more certain that it wouldn't be the last.

'There must be other issues, to force your parents to come all this way,' she finally said, hoping to move on from the talk of Shadow Witches.

'There's been some . . . . worry about the barrier. That the magic is weakening in Ciliria. I'm guessing they want to discuss how to move forward.'

'Is the barrier weakening?'

Kaian gave her a lazy smile.

'The Elders have protected our home for a thousand years, highness. I trust we are in no real danger and there is no reason for you to be concerned.'

A few minutes passed, and she felt the weight of someone's eyes on her. When she snapped her head up, she found Sadara watching her from the dining room, a sneer on her gaunt face.

Sapphire clenched her fists tightly until they ached.

Because she did belong here. A depraved woman like Sadara would not change that.

That night at dinner, she ate with unsteady hands, her thoughts racing. She laughed at conversations she wasn't heeding and tried to answer questions she hadn't heard. Anything to avoid suspicion.

When the sun slipped away, she lit a candle, braided back her hair, reached for the potion she had stolen earlier – and almost didn't take it. The witch had seen her eyes the very first day – but there was always a chance of meeting someone unintended in Ciliria. So, she swallowed the potion, still not used to the way it slid down her throat.

Taking her cloak from the hook on the wall, she buttoned it tightly around her chin in an effort to conceal herself. She hoped to move among the shadows undetected by any man, woman or creature she might pass.

But as she stared at her reflection in the looking glass, her hands continued to shake.

For a moment, she wondered if she should crawl into bed right now. Would she fall into a dreamless sleep?

Or was it all inevitable? Would she wake to find Ashes perched on her sill like a raven, her voice like a death knell as she came to collect on their bargain?

So, when she stumbled out on to the shore of Ciliria, the moon moving quickly to its zenith, Sapphire knew she would seek out Ashes.

She struggled to follow the path she had taken the previous night, and she found the deeper she moved, the more confused she became. She kicked up leaves as she walked, in an effort to disrupt whatever barrier bond Ashes created.

Sapphire cursed when her cloak snagged on a branch. She finally freed it, tearing it slightly, frowning as she did before she heard a twig snap to her right.

Sapphire whirled around. The darkness was so dense she could barely see a few feet in front of her.

She felt the magic beneath her skin pulsing, something she still hadn't got used to. She pressed the tips of her fingers together, trying to quell the anxious energy running through her.

Another crack of a twig under a heavy step was the undoing of her calm facade.

'Ashes?' Sapphire called.

To her left, leaves rustled as whatever it was circled her. Sapphire opened and closed her fists tightly, flexing and cracking the joints. The next noise came from in front of her, and she stepped backwards, tripping over the same large branch her cloak had snagged on. Pain shot through her, rushing up her arm, and a warm stream of blood flowed from her elbow.

Footsteps.

She heard them clearly as they moved towards her, and all the courage she had gathered was lost.

'You certainly know how to make an entrance, don't you, princess? You'll wake up every monster in these woods if you keep covering the forest floor in your blood.'

Ashes' voice was sharp, and Sapphire's breath hitched as she turned to meet the witch's narrowed eyes.

Ashes looked at Sapphire's wounded arm and licked her lips.

'There are beasts in the forest much worse than me, princess. It would do you many favours to remember that.'

Ashes tilted her head, studying Sapphire in the familiar pale light that glowed in her palm.

Irritated by the witch's warning chuckle, Sapphire didn't answer.

The two walked in silence, and Ashes looked up to the sky.

'It appears a storm could be coming.'

'I'm not scared of getting wet,' Sapphire muttered.

The witch smiled.

'Noted.'

Sapphire rolled her eyes, pushing forward. Ashes easily matched her stride.

'Where are you taking me?' Sapphire asked.

'Somewhere more private, and away from my coven.'

'Why?'

Ashes looked surprised by the question. 'I have my reasons.'

'But –'

'If you'd like, I can take you to them. Allow them to do as they will with a child of a high house. Would that be preferable?'

Sapphire's cheeks warmed, and she pressed her palms together in an effort to focus. 'No. I – No.'

'As you wish, princess.'

They walked in silence, Sapphire's mind restless as they moved deeper into the forest. She had no idea what to say as questions buzzed on the tip of her tongue.

'Why do you say high house?'

Ashes paused for a moment, studying Sapphire.

'I've just never heard anyone else call it that.'

'Before the First War, royalty and governors did not exist. The high houses – those who had the blood of the original elementals – were given the highest status. It was only after the war that the monarchy and governing families took hold.'

'Are you of high-house blood? Are any of the Shadow Witches?'

Ashes gave her an incredulous look.

'My blood isn't important.' She returned her gaze to the path, taking in a clearing. 'This will do.'

Sapphire stared at the small open area, suddenly nervous.

'And no one will find us?'

'No. No one will find us. There's a ritual happening tonight. All focus will remain there.'

'A ritual?'

'Yes. A ritual,' Ashes said impatiently. 'Much like you pray to your Elders, we speak to our ancestors. We ask them for prosperity and thank them for our magic.'

'Why aren't you there?'

'You ask a lot of questions.'

Sapphire shrugged. 'Aren't you the one who told me I should?'

Ashes sounded irritated as she spoke. 'I'm beginning to think you're avoiding your side of the bargain.'

'I'm avoiding nothing.'

Ashes wasn't looking at her. She was looking at the moon.

'We must begin or we'll never make it to the barrier.'

Sapphire gritted her teeth so hard it made her jaw ache.

Ashes was arrogant and sharp-tongued, and she felt that familiar sense of irritation and desperation bore into her chest. She wanted to wipe that damned smirk off the witch's face with her bare hands.

Sapphire walked to the middle of the clearing and took a deep breath, centring herself, and called upon the Elders to push her power past the limits others had set for her. She stretched out her fingers and demanded the world bend to her will.

A few moments passed, and her eyes darted to Ashes, who was looking unabashedly bored. Sapphire shut her eyes tightly, demanding focus.

The rain will come to me because I am the storm.

Her fingers remained outstretched towards the sky and she refused to look down.

'Please,' she whispered to no one in particular.

Then she felt it. The undeniable vibration of her magic. A small smile spread across her face. When the first droplet hit her skin, running down her cheek, she laughed.

'Come.' Her voice was defiant and commanding, and the rain followed quickly after, pouring from the sky and drenching them both. She allowed herself a stolen glance at the witch, and her haunting gaze remained trained on Sapphire – a flicker of doubt still there.

Sapphire could fix that.

She began to flex her fingers, slowly circling them. The rain followed – the storm giving way to a circular pattern. The quicker she moved her fingers, the quicker the water moved, and in a matter of seconds, the downpour had grown into something much more dangerous. A roaring cyclone, angry and looking to consume.

Here her mind was quiet. She relished it.

Ashes' eyes widened as the cyclone bounced around the clearing – as it sucked in loose branches and uprooted trees. Sapphire did not flinch.

As she pulled her hands back, the cyclone collapsed, flooding the clearing.

To her disappointment, when she turned to face the witch, she was met with a wall of neutrality. Her sharp features were fixed into an unreadable mask – displaying no reaction to what Sapphire had just done.

'I suppose I have my end of the deal to uphold.'

Ashes began to walk in the opposite direction, and Sapphire hurried after her. Ashes didn't seem to care, and that stung more than she wanted to admit.

'Nothing – do you finally have nothing to say? I find that so hard to believe.'

Ashes arched her brow, smiling slightly. 'I'm sorry. Was I expected to fawn over you? Would you like me to kneel before you, princess? Kneel and praise you, o glorious being?'

'No – I – well, I just thought you'd have something to say,' Sapphire said defensively. 'You always seem to.'

Ashes halted, turning to face her while tucking a fist under her own chin.

'I have nothing to offer that hasn't already been said to you, I'm sure. Come, we have to hurry if we want to keep our timing.'

Silence returned. She wanted to know more – more about the Shadow Witches, about the barrier, about Ashes.

'Just ask your questions, princess.'

'Can you read my mind as well, witch?'

'No. You're just quite obvious. So, ask your questions.'

A rush of excitement washed over Sapphire, and she did her best to mask it. 'What kind of magic can you do that I can't?'

Ashes narrowed her eyes. 'Have you not learned about the First War?'

'Of course I have.'

'Their version, I'm sure.'

'And what's that supposed to mean?'

Ashes let out a frustrated sigh. 'The Dark Magic you have been warned about began as simple magic. My people could do destructive things, yes. But so can you. They could strip powers, invade minds, and paint the world in shadows, but these were not things we pursued.'

Ashes' tone had an edge as she continued. 'Still, those of the high houses were losing grip on their control as my people grew more powerful. Elementals were welcome in our coven. Numbers were growing. They needed a plan. And the one they came up with was far more heinous than what one would expect. Burn the witches. They want your children. They will slip a knife between your ribs as you sleep. How easy it was to spread their rhetoric of fear. A common enemy is a universal pleasure. So, it led where all unfettered hate and unreasonable fear does – war.'

They took a sharp left, and Sapphire nearly stumbled.

Ashes grabbed her quickly, helping her upright. Sapphire stared down at the girl's hand wrapped around her arm, her heart rate picking up at the sight. She could feel the warmth of Ashes' skin against her own and she relished it. The slightest touch set her entire body on edge. She looked up at the witch and licked her lips, Ashes' eyes tracking her mouth as she did so.

And for the first time since she had arrived in Eriobis, Sapphire knew *exactly* what she wanted.

But then something scurried through the forest around them, breaking the trance, and they jumped away from each other before Ashes continued the conversation.

'The horror stories they created . . . Those monsters that came to life. Creatures born of dark intent, magic that would grind bones to dust – magic my people never wanted to use became their only armament. Every whispered lie had become a written truth. After months of fighting – after losing so much – my people were banished. To a land full of looming shadows. A purgatory and punishment for trying to survive. A land built by your people.'

'If that's true . . . how are you here?' Sapphire asked quietly.

'Our magic is older, deeper. It cannot be so easily forgotten. Slowly, the coven was reformed. A watered-down, apologetic, and fearful coven, but still – a coven. The original sisters practised in secrecy, descendants of those sealed behind the barrier.'

'And that was allowed?'

'Three hundred years ago, a treaty was made as a sign of

goodwill. It allowed us to exist, but our magic was to be governed by strict rules. We are tracked and watched to ensure we are – abiding.'

Sapphire chewed her lip, considering the witch's words. Questions raced through her mind, dancing on the tip of her tongue, but she knew that the time for her curiosity had passed. Instead, she focused on the path in front of her.

The world was so quiet it was unsettling. The witch always looked straight ahead. In the glow of the pale orb in her hand, Sapphire was struck by how unworldly she looked. Sharp features, long lashes, and lips that sat in a focused pout.

Striking. Fascinating. Wicked. And beautiful.

'I would assume that, in your many etiquette classes, they would teach you that staring is not polite,' Ashes snapped.

Heat crept up Sapphire's cheeks as she looked away. 'How much longer?' she asked.

'We'll be there soon.'

Sapphire clenched her jaw and stared at her feet.

'What is your plan? Are you simply going to see the barrier and return home?'

Sapphire ran her fingers gently over the embroidery of her corset, wondering how to come up with an answer. She didn't have one. Her impulsiveness did not allow her to get that far in her planning. Ashes took her silence as enough of an answer and resumed their quick pace.

That was, until the air shifted.

A surge of . . . something raced through Sapphire's body,

straight to her heart. She stopped, clutching her chest as she tried to breathe through the sharp pain. It surged again, and she collapsed to her knees. She tore at her corset, desperate to relieve herself of the building pressure.

Ashes stared at her, intrigued, but made no move to help.

The pulsating pressure was building, threatening to rip her ribcage open. She felt undone, fried, and terrified as she tucked her knees under her chest, writhing in pain.

Ashes continued to watch with an amused expression. Sapphire reached out a desperate hand, and the witch stepped backwards.

'Ashes, please,' Sapphire sputtered.

'Fascinating,' the girl whispered.

'Please. Help.'

One breath.

Then two.

She felt arms tuck under her, lifting her gently off the ground. Sapphire pressed against Ashes' chest. After twenty or so steps, Sapphire felt like she could breathe again.

She sucked in a few sharp inhales before speaking. 'Are we nearing the barrier?'

'Yes.'

'I-I think I could feel it.'

'That is impossible.'

'The magic was – it was building inside me. The pressure was – it was the barrier. I know it.'

'That's impossible,' Ashes repeated, her lip curling in a snarl, as she steadied Sapphire on to her own two feet.

'Why is that impossible?'

'It just is.' Ashes shook her head, looking over her shoulder at the barrier.

'I can feel it. Like vibrations filling every part of my body. I thought my chest was going to cave in. Like lightning crawling under my skin.'

Ashes' stare was heavy, unblinking, as she took a step closer. Sapphire wanted to sink away from her, but she remained upright as the witch searched her face.

'What? What are you staring at?'

'You.'

'Why?'

'If what you say is true, you're drawing in power from the barrier. And that, princess, is not something any high blood should be able to do.'

CHAPTER TWENTY-TWO

'Take me to it.'

Ashes shook her head. 'No.'

'I said, take me to it.'

'No,' Ashes repeated.

'We had a deal,' Sapphire spat. 'I upheld my side. You will uphold yours!'

'I will not have you lying broken at my feet! The barrier is over a hundred feet away, and you could barely stand being this close. I will not have your death on my hands tonight, princess. I will not.'

'Then I'll do it myself.' Sapphire stormed past the witch, but Ashes caught her hand, tugging her back roughly.

'I will take you,' Ashes said, leaning in closer, 'but I will not save you.'

'I never asked you to save me,' Sapphire seethed.

'Your memory is as limited as your sense – you begged me to save you only moments ago.'

Sapphire grabbed at the witch's neck.

But Ashes was always one step ahead. Grabbing Sapphire's wrist, she pinned it above her head.

'Now, now, princess – do try to play nice. This isn't the

right . . . situation for your hand to be around my neck.'

Sapphire yanked her arm back.

The air was tense around them as Ashes began walking in the direction of the barrier again. Sapphire stumbled as the feeling hit her once more, but this time she was prepared. She forced her shoulders back, taking stride after stride.

As they grew closer, the pain in her chest expanded into her stomach, and she bent forward, biting her tongue till it bled. She would not fall. She would not fail. Not now. Not in front of *her*.

Sapphire heard it before she saw it, the hum of magic filling the air. It reminded her of a time before the fall of Witrotean when the warm summer breeze would fill the Home and they would dance to the chatter of the insects.

But unlike those nights, this sound made her freeze in fear and double over in pain.

An unprecedented amount of magic slammed into her at once. She could feel it in the marrow of her bones, a thick lead lining her chest and threatening to smother her.

A warning. A warning that sounded with every step she took.

That's when the treeline thinned out and it came into view.

A brilliant blue wall touched the sky. It glowed, unwavering in its looming presence. She stepped closer and the pulse grew. Her vision was spotted as she stared up at it, and her entire body felt raw and exposed.

It was terrible. It was incredible. It was everything she

feared and everything she longed for. The magic inside her came to life, buzzing and brilliant. It was unbridled, inescapable. Her body screamed in protest, warning her to run. But her magic . . . her magic urged her forward.

Like calls to like, child.

Ashes remained only a few steps away, eyeing her closely. Sweat had broken out on Sapphire's brow, and her movements were laboured as she fought to stay upright.

She took another step towards the barrier and lost her vision entirely, the darkness terrifying. But she had never been able to see her magic more clearly – streaking out before her like tethers leading her towards where she needed to go.

Her blood drummed in her ears as she took another step, her legs shaking. Her body sent warning signs, begging her to step away, but she couldn't – like a moth to a flame, she needed whatever the barrier could offer her.

Her magic swelled inside her, her fingertips aching for release. Her chest rose and fell with the thrum of power that filled her core. It pleaded to be freed. It demanded to be allowed to take control.

Another stumble forward and her body sent what felt like a final warning shot before freefall. The pain made her stiffen – like claws digging into her mind. But her magic led her forward . . . and she knew she was no more than an arm's length away from the barrier.

Reaching out a timid, shaking hand, she braced for impact.

A hand clamped down on her shoulder, wrenching her

out of the sensation. She was dragged away, the heels of her boots scraping against the ground as she fought the force. She blinked a few times, her vision clearing, and watched as the barrier receded further and further. Her eyes found Ashes', whose hand was too tight around Sapphire's shoulder.

'Unhand me!' she shouted too loudly, pulling out of the witch's grip. 'You have no right –'

'I have every right when it is my life on the line. Touching the barrier is forbidden. Even I, a pariah of this forsaken country, know that. If you were caught, it would be my head the executioner held.'

'I am the future queen of this land. I will do as –'

'The future queen of this land should be able to find the barrier without the assistance of a witch. You are hardly prepared for your role, and you're a fool to think differently.'

'You cannot speak to me like that. You –'

'I can speak to you however I like.' Ashes stepped forward, so close that Sapphire could see a vein throbbing in her neck. 'You are no queen of mine. I will never kneel at your feet like the sycophants who swarm around you.'

Sapphire fought the urge to stomp her feet like a child. Ashes smirked like she could read her mind, and Sapphire looked past her to the barrier, longing for the feeling of absolute power it had bestowed upon her.

'When I am queen, you will regret every word you have said,' she whispered, eyes still trained on the blue wall of magic.

'If you become queen, my words will be the least of your worries.'

Sapphire snapped her focus back to the witch.

'What is that supposed to mean?'

Ashes gave a wicked laugh.

'Oh, highness, you will surely see.'

Claye found her sitting by the lake that morning. A comfortable silence settled between them as he observed her from a few feet away but relaxation did not come. The feeling of the magic from the barrier coursed through her, impossible to forget.

The sensation of her skin tearing, her bones grinding, her chest collapsing. Untameable magic. She yearned for it.

'Claye?' she called out.

The man took a few strides forward to join her.

'What can I do for you, princess?'

'What do you know about my disappearance?'

He paled, quickly averting his gaze. 'Why do you ask?'

'Would you not be curious?'

It took a few minutes for him to finally look back at her.

'I grew up in this castle, did you know that? My father worked here, as did his father. As a child, I used to run through these hallways and while it was beautiful, I found it was also hauntingly . . . empty. The lack of your presence was everywhere.'

She nodded, looking out over the water once more.

'Your parents mourned you daily. We all did.'

'I just can't understand any of it,' Sapphire admitted. 'I

can't understand how I disappeared, why witches were involved, or why those same witches would be trusted around me again.'

'I am not a scholar of Shadow Witch magic but I do know that it is . . . generational to an extent. The witch that caused your disappearance was of the same bloodline as the two who came to prove your legitimacy.'

'The witch that caused my disappearance . . .'

'Was executed,' Claye said, matter-of-factly. 'But her bloodline lived on.'

Sapphire stared up at him, unblinking, trying to process what Claye had admitted. Ashes' family was the reason why she disappeared. Ashes' family was why she had been forced to suffer and fight and grow up in a harsh and cruel world. Ashes' family took away the one thing she had always craved.

'Thank you, Claye. For being honest.'

'Of course, princess. Would you like to return to your room?'

Sapphire stood, smoothing down her hair with her hand.

'Yes. To my room.'

'Your wish is my command.' Claye offered a slight bow before escorting her inside.

Chapter Twenty-three

Once seated at the table, she could not untangle her thoughts despite her efforts. She bowed her head and pushed the food around on her plate as they tried to engage her in conversation. Short answers made it easy.

Yes, she was fine. Just a sleepless night. Yes, she understood that if that happened again, she needed to inform someone. No, she preferred not to rely on a sleep tonic.

She popped a fresh roseberry into her mouth as they struck up a conversation about the upcoming ball. It wasn't surprising, as she had spent more time in fittings and dance rehearsals than she had in training recently.

'May I add someone to the guest list?'

Araxia gave her a knowing smile.

'Evera and her family have been invited. We've provided a tailor to assist them with attire as well.'

Sapphire's heart swelled for only a moment before the shadows burrowed their way back into her mind.

After pacing for two hours, her body not allowing her to remain idle, she had decided she needed to escape the confines of her room.

When she threw open the library doors, she was relieved when it was Evera she found first.

'I had a feeling I'd see you soon.' Evera closed the book she was reading. 'We received your invitation to the ball. You didn't have to do that, you know.'

'I want you there. And Araxia and Kip actually made the decision before I even asked.'

Evera's smile grew, but Sapphire's shoulders sagged – the burden of all she had learned becoming too much. Evera noticed the uneasiness and escorted her quickly up the stairs to her small room.

As they settled into their usual spot, a couch hidden from view of prying eyes, Sapphire lay back and stared at the ceiling, unsure of where to begin.

'I spent some time in Ciliria. Well, the entire night. I'm exhausted.'

'To what end?' Evera asked, slightly taken aback by her statement.

'I was – I was with a Shadow Witch. Her name is Ashes. She's the witch who proved my legitimacy. I needed her assistance to get to the barrier.'

'Shadow Witches do nothing out of the kindness of their heart. What did it cost you?'

'She wanted to see the extent of my magic.'

'Shadow Witches cannot be trusted.'

Sapphire jutted out her chin, frustrated at hearing the same warning for what seemed like the hundredth time. 'But what else was I to do? I needed to get to the barrier.' She sat up, leaning against the wall. 'And I did eventually get there.'

'Was it worth it?'

'It was like –' Her throat constricted as she recalled the crippling feeling the barrier had brought. 'Like every inch of my body was set aflame. My nerves fully exposed. My chest was unable to bear the impact. But I couldn't walk away.'

Sapphire felt a bit better. Sharing the secrets consuming her allowed her more room to breathe, and she fought the urge to reach out for Evera's hand.

Still, she wasn't done.

'Afterwards, I had a conversation with Claye and he told me something.'

Evera waited for her to continue.

'Was Shadow Witch magic ever part of your studies?'

'To an extent,' Evera mused. 'I studied it a little as I prepared to graduate as a scholar but it was never my focus. Why do you ask?'

'I just . . . want to understand what they are capable of, I suppose.'

Evera nodded, and disappeared momentarily. When she returned, she had a thick book in her hand. She flipped through the pages until she found what she was looking for.

'Shadow Witch magic manifests in many different ways. Obviously they can bring shadows to life, create creatures born of nightmares – but they also have their natural witchcraft. The magic they held before they sold their souls to the darkness. Healing magic, potions, protective barriers. There are accounts of witches being able to inhabit the bodies of those whose lives they stole – taking on their bodies with little effort.' She pointed towards the page and Sapphire leaned forward to read it with her friend. 'The ability to shift bodies wreaked havoc during times of war. Witches would kill citizens, take their form, and live among the townspeople. This ability is one of the reasons they were eventually able to rebuild a coven. The Elders failed to uncover *every* witch that remained.'

Sapphire stared at the page until Evera closed the book.

'It makes you wonder why with such power they would sell their souls to the dark. Doesn't it?'

'People do many inexplicable things for power.' Sapphire's response felt distant – like someone was pulling the strings, forcing her to speak. 'Have you ever heard that their magic is generational?'

'Yes. Though that's not an exclusive Shadow Witch trait – it's actually simply a witch trait.'

'Well, the witches that performed the spell with my blood were descendants of the one that was involved in my disappearance.'

'That would make sense seeing that the spell performed was not Dark Magic but witchcraft. They would need that tieback.'

Sapphire chewed her lip as she considered the conversation. While the need for it made sense, bringing witches near her once more . . . after everything . . . she wasn't sure why the king and queen would allow it.

'What if they had followed in the footsteps of their ancestor? What if –'

Evera reached out for her hand, and the dam broke inside her, the tears spilling over with an unstoppable force.

They remained silent until Sapphire dried her final tear and turned her puffy eyes to her friend.

'I think the king and queen . . . well, it's a terrifying thing to realize your parents don't know exactly what they're doing – but I think they have always done what they thought was best.' Evera patted her back gently. 'No matter what has happened, no matter what others believe or say, I do think they have loved you fiercely.'

Sapphire paused, dragging her eyes upward to meet Evera's.

'What do others say?'

Evera looked caught off guard, sitting up a bit straighter. Sapphire could tell her tongue had slipped.

'It's gossip, Sapphire. Not worth you worrying over.'

'I still need to know, Evera.'

The girl closed her eyes and took a deep breath. Her nervousness made Sapphire's anxiety grow. The panic in her chest swelled uncomfortably.

'They say . . . Well, they say you are not truly of royal blood. That you were born of another womb, another element.'

'But I control water, just like my parents.'

'Which is why, after the duel, much of the chatter died down, but . . .'

'But what?'

'As you know, the women of Canmore bring forth one daughter each generation to take over the throne, but Araxia struggled, for years. There was a lot of talk of her being unable to bear children. But then, there you were.'

Evera took another deep breath, looking to her hands. 'No one ever saw her pregnant. It was as if you appeared out of thin air. The queen could have simply been reclusive during the pregnancy. Still, gossip will do as gossip will do.'

The feeling of belonging had been unfamiliar, but over the months she had warmed to it. Accepted it. But it slipped away from her now. Because if she did not belong to the queen, who did she belong to?

Hot tears took her over as she mourned. She had thought the feeling was hers to keep, but now she was robbed of something she had grown to love. She felt her heart breaking.

The first time they had called her Sapphire Canmore, it had left a bitter taste in her mouth. But she wanted to be Araxia's daughter. She wanted it more than she could ever remember wanting anything. Evera's grip on her hand tightened as the two lay down face to face.

'What if I'm not their daughter?' Sapphire whispered.

'You are their daughter,' Evera said forcefully. 'Even if there is truth to the rumours, blood doesn't make a family, Sapphire.'

What would they do if they found out she knew? Sapphire feared she knew the answer, and she didn't like it.

Even when sleep finally came, hours later, it was restless. She dreamed of dark creatures whose sullen touch left her broken. A flash of red hair and a taunting smile. Sapphire woke often, drenched in sweat and breathing heavily until the sun finally peeked over the horizon. Her feet found the floor as the room came to life and her footsteps led her to the soft, sandy shores of the training ground, close enough that the chilly water washed over her bare feet.

Absent-mindedly, she moved the water, creating shapes and ripples with the smallest gestures, and felt at home.

The water rippled as her emotions built, and she bit her lip to stifle her tears. The sound of footsteps caused her to jump, and she was shocked to find Kip standing nearby.

'Sorry, I thought you heard me when I said your name,' Kip apologized.

'Lost in thought,' she said, forcing a smile.

'I like to come here when I can't sleep too. Especially when I have to make big decisions.'

She studied him, no longer sure how to hold a conversation when the words she so badly wanted to say were on the tip of her tongue.

'I hope, when you become queen, you'll still find solace here. We need a place to clear our heads, in this role.'

'I hope so,' she half whispered, the words tasting stale in her mouth. The idea of being illegitimate, of not belonging to the royal bloodline, made her feel foolish to think of being queen.

'Are you OK, Sapphire? Truly?'

The question picked away at the wound she had been trying so desperately to close.

'It is . . . a lot. But Evera has been helpful. Every day I feel more adjusted.'

He sighed beside her. 'I wish more than anything that I could give you back the time we've lost. But time is not one to easily bend – even for us.' A small half-smile appeared on his lips.

'Do you know how I ended up in Witrotean?'

The question was a test to see if Kip's answers would align with the story Araxia had sewn into her heart from the beginning.

Kip didn't look irritated or even caught off guard, but instead, he offered her a small smile. 'I wondered when you would ask me this.'

Her heart flew into her throat as Kip shifted beside her.

'Your mother faced many health problems when it came to her pregnancy. And when you were born, worse ones followed.' He paused to look at her like he was trying to memorize her, as though she might slip away once again.

'I need you to understand, there was no other option.'

Despite the warm breeze, a cold sweat broke out across her brow as she waited for a misstep that would destroy everything she had come to know.

'We called upon a Shadow Witch, and we begged her to save you. Dark Magic, yes, but it was the only answer.'

The king looked small and embarrassed by the admission.

'When the ritual happened, something went wrong. One minute you were there – a beautiful baby – and the next you weren't, not even a puff of smoke. We begged the Shadow Witch to return you but she claimed she had no idea what happened. We pressed her for weeks, but she never offered us any explanation, and held firm all the way to her execution. We spent weeks in your nursery mourning what we had lost.' His voice hitched like he was fighting back tears. 'We held you in our arms for three minutes before you disappeared.'

'Did you ever look for me? Or did that room just become a place of mourning for what could have been?' she whispered, watching as the sun rose in the sky.

'Every minute of every day for the last eighteen years, we looked for you, sweet girl,' he said, his breath ragged. 'We never stopped.'

She felt her shoulders relax. Only Kip and Araxia would know what happened within those castle walls. So, with a small exhale, she let go of the inferior gossip and found the peace she needed.

CHAPTER TWENTY-FOUR

Despite the peace she had found on the shore with Kip, anger still simmered within her. She tossed and turned as she tried to tamp down the feeling but it boiled over, consuming her. She could not lie idle with what she knew, so, with a heavy sigh, she pulled on her training uniform, slipped past the guards, and headed towards Ciliria.

As she found her way on to Ciliria's shore once again, the moon was lost to a thick blanket of clouds, so that the forest was the darkest she had ever seen.

A roll of thunder split the air around her. Time was running out to find the witch.

'Ashes!' Her voice echoed through the forest. 'I need to talk to you. I know you're out there!'

Only silence answered her.

'I know you're nearby. And I know you know it's me.'

A gust of wind rustled the trees around her and she cowered, waiting for a creature to slither from the woods. As she stepped into a clearing, she looked overhead to see the clouds moving quickly.

'I'll stand here yelling all night. I don't care. Come and speak to me!'

The forest had gone still, and a grave sensation dug its way into the pit of her stomach. Something grabbed her arm tightly and she was yanked backwards.

'Do you have no sense of self-preservation at all?' Ashes roughly dragged her away from the clearing. 'You enchanting, insufferable thing.'

Ashes stopped walking and pulled Sapphire to hide behind a large tree. The witch leaned against her, placing a hand on her shoulder, shadows covering them. To Sapphire's surprise, they were not icy cold or suffocating. The darkness was almost a comfort, and she followed Ashes' gaze, horrified at what she saw.

A dog stepped into the clearing where she had stood, sniffing the air. It turned in their direction, and Sapphire gasped as she took in its black eyes and large fangs. Ashes slapped her hand over the girl's mouth.

It was then a serpent appeared – entirely too large and unnatural, its scales a shade of deep purple that reminded Sapphire of the flowers that bloomed in the gardens. She couldn't stop the shiver that ran through her body.

The two beasts' eyes met and they lunged at one another. Sapphire thought she might be sick as they ripped each other apart. She clapped her hands over her ears to avoid the guttural sounds they made as they tore flesh from flesh. It was then that Ashes led her away – their strides making no noise as they crossed the forest floor. When they finally stopped, Sapphire could no longer hear the gnashing of fangs and pained cries, a small mercy she was thankful for.

'Don't ever put yourself in danger like that again. Do you understand me?'

'Why do you even care?' Sapphire pushed away from the witch, her proximity too much.

Ashes tilted her head, and Sapphire wondered if, only for a moment, she had fractured the wall between them.

The witch placed a cold palm to Sapphire's cheek, and it took everything inside the princess to not hum with satisfaction as Ashes drummed her long, thin fingers against her skin.

'Because.' The witch leaned in closer, and Sapphire was transfixed. 'If anyone gets to take your life, it will be me.'

The words hit Sapphire sharply and she stumbled backwards as she reached for the magic that lived inside of her.

'Why were you risking death to find me, princess?'

Sapphire's words stuck in her throat and she swallowed hard. Rashness had cost her so many things. Her dignity, her secrets, the upper hand.

'I need to talk to your coven.'

Ashes laughed so loudly that Sapphire cringed. To calm her nerves, Sapphire rubbed her thumb roughly against her palm. The witch watched her with intrigue.

'Little lamb, what reason could possibly exist for you to seek out such a thing?'

'Answers.'

An expression Sapphire couldn't identify flashed over the witch's face.

'Answers – what answers, princess?'

'About my birth,' Sapphire started. 'And my disappearance.'

Ashes stepped back, staring.

'It's the beginning of the cycle of storms.' She motioned overhead, her eyebrow twitching in frustration or amusement, Sapphire couldn't tell which.

'So?' Sapphire pushed back stubbornly.

'So, that means I can't take you there tonight.'

'Because of a storm?' Anger fuelled her words now.

Ashes shook her head.

'These are not just *any* storms; our ancestors created them. A cycle of three to flood the lands and cleanse the ground of bloodshed. For all that we have lost. Tonight is the first.'

A bolt of lightning struck nearby like a warning shot.

'Your ancestors?' Sapphire questioned.

'Yes. Led by Ryvinika, the honoured one.'

'When will you take me?'

'Tomorrow.' A boom of thunder filled the air around them. 'The storm is almost here. It's time to go now, princess.'

'But how –'

The witch reached forward, absorbing the shadows into her body, and Sapphire gaped when she realized she was only a stone's throw away from the lake.

'Thank you,' she whispered into the empty air as she headed towards the shore.

The girl's shadows did not linger as Sapphire dived into the water.

As she swam, she kept one eye on the storm as it closed in on the world around her.

She pushed until her muscles ached, and she broke for air to pouring rain pounding the surface of the lake. A crack of lightning split the sky in two and she flinched.

She was close when she heard it.

A sound so deafening that no one could hear the scream that escaped her lips. She watched as another bolt of lightning sprang from the sky, striking downward and connecting with the water. She gasped for air as a searing heat wrapped around her, squeezing tightly.

She was going to die.

She was going to die in the middle of the lake – her body sinking to the bottom, her bones returning to the very element that she had been born from.

She waited.

But when she opened her eyes, she was still in the water.

There was no explanation for her beating heart, for the pulse she felt hammering in her throat. But as the wind picked up, she dived under and swam until her feet met the shore.

The rain pelted her skin as she stared up at the sky, enraptured by the storm unfolding before her. Another brilliant stroke of lightning filled the air and she stiffened.

The buzz.

Familiar and bone-chilling. The same buzz she had felt near the barrier, setting her nerves ablaze.

She sucked in a few deep breaths, trying to slow her heartbeat.

What are you capable of, child?

She closed her eyes tightly as the voice snaked its way into her brain, the familiar brush of an unwelcome touch.

'What do you want from me?' Her voice was small, lost to the storm.

Do you trust me?

No. She didn't.

A slight laugh reverberated in her mind.

Raise your hands to the sky.

As Sapphire lifted her hands to the storm, the voice offered her no guidance.

So she stood there waiting as the storm strengthened. The rain pelted violently against her skin.

The buzz intensified.

What if . . .

The thought lingered, begging to be explored.

What if she could do more than she thought she could?

If she failed, then she would return to her room and listen to the rain hit her window.

But if she succeeded . . . well, she wasn't sure. But she wanted – no, needed to find out.

Stretching her fingers upward, she let go. She saw the eye of the storm, and recalled the incantations buried in the forbidden books tucked away in her room.

It submits to you.

She flexed her fingers once more before speaking.

'Hear me.'

A gust of wind wrapped around her.

'Bend to my will.'

Thunder rolled in response.

Say 'ignite', child. And let the truth be known.

She closed her eyes tightly before the word rolled off her tongue.

'Ignite.'

Her pupils enlarged as searing white light ripped through the sky, crackling and striking the centre of the lake – the force surging over the surface as it rippled at the impact.

She stumbled backwards, looking at her hands and then back to the water.

The storm had listened.

I can help you, the voice purred, and she almost believed it.

CHAPTER TWENTY-FIVE

Claye announced Kaian's arrival only a few moments after he escorted Evera to Sapphire's room. Her two friends exchanged a worried look.

'What's going on?' Kaian looked at Evera but she threw up her hands.

'I haven't been offered any explanation.'

The two turned to face Sapphire and she felt her cheeks warm.

'Tonight, I am going to Ciliria to meet with the Shadow Witch coven.' Both of her friends opened their mouths to protest but she raised an assured hand. 'I am not asking permission. I am informing you in case something happens – you will know where to search for me.'

The two stared at her with bewildered expressions.

'I know it's hard to understand, but I need to do this and I just –'

'Sapphire, there is darkness in that forest – in those witches – that we can't even begin to understand.'

'I need answers, Evera. I have to go.'

'No. You do not. You have a family, Sapphire. You are the crown princess and want for nothing. I have no idea why you're so bent on unravelling this gift you've been given.'

Her tone was not harsh but steady, and Sapphire blinked, trying to find a reason the girl was wrong – but there was none. She looked at Kaian but he shrugged.

'Evera is right. The risks outweigh the rewards.'

Sapphire leaned her head back against the chair, staring up at the ceiling. Evera was correct. They both were. She knew that. But she also knew that tonight was an offer that would not be extended twice. She knew if she didn't get answers, she'd never stop thinking about it. Never find peace, not really.

They did not know the things she did . . . the feeling of the barrier, the lightning that bent at her control, the hairpin curve of Ashes' lips . . . Sapphire did and she wouldn't let them go.

'I need to go. I'm not asking you to understand. But I – I want to know where I belong. Why I can do things others can't. Why I disappeared to Witrotean and how I found my way back.'

Kaian and Evera exchanged a look – their resolve breaking.

'I am going.'

'Pig-headed, foolhardy, and certainly self-destructive,' Kaian said with a sigh. 'But I can't, in good conscience, let you go alone.' The two girls watched as he pushed away from the chair and headed towards the door.

'Meet me on the shore when night has fallen,' he called over his shoulder, slipping out of the room, the heavy door clicking closed on his heels.

The two girls sat in silence for a few moments until Evera took a deep breath.

'Some questions are better left unanswered. Are you truly that unhappy?'

The question gave Sapphire pause, and she turned it over in her mind. Was she unhappy? No.

Sapphire knew what unhappy felt like. Cold nights, an empty stomach, a home too small for so many girls. This was not unhappy. But still, she couldn't shake the crippling curiosity that brought her to this moment.

A childhood gone.

Powers she could not understand.

Chasing darkness was a risk, but it was worth it.

'I fear, without answers, I'll never truly feel like I belong. Here or anywhere.'

Evera rubbed her hands roughly down her face. As she sat up, she pushed her long braids over her shoulder.

'Walk away before you put us in danger. Promise me. Give me that much – and I'll go.'

'You have my word.'

Sapphire shoved the old rowing boat forward until it beached on the rocky shore.

Kaian walked towards them, dressed in dark green and blending in with the world around him. Evera gave him a timid smile.

The trio stared at each other, unsure of what to do next.

'Are we all set? You know where to find them?' Sapphire asked.

Kaian nodded. 'My father . . . he's convinced they're planning something so he's been tracking them. If his information is right, it shouldn't take us long.'

Sapphire rolled her eyes as they began to wordlessly move into the forest, the brush around them thick. In front of her, Evera tripped over something they could not see and she cursed, igniting a flame in her palm in an effort to watch her step.

'Extinguish it,' Sapphire whispered, Ashes' warnings of creatures lurking in the dark ringing in her mind. 'We don't want to draw any unwanted attention.'

Evera immediately snuffed out the flame, and Sapphire yearned for the light. Something about the darkness of these woods set her on edge, no matter how many times she had been here.

They had been walking for some time when Kaian stopped, Evera nearly running into him.

'We're nearly there. Just . . . be aware,' he cautioned.

They were close. She could feel it. She wasn't sure how, but it was as if Dark Magic permeated the air.

'Remember, you gave me your word. Nothing dangerous.' Evera's tone was tight.

'I remember. Which is why you'll be staying up here with Kaian.'

'What?'

Her friends said it in unison, and despite the darkness, she could see their faces slack with disbelief.

'You can't expect me to let you go down there alone,' Kaian said through clenched teeth.

'Of course I do.'

They stared each other down.

'Sapphire.' Evera's quiet voice broke the tension between them. 'You can't . . . They –'

'I have to do this.' Sapphire's voice was rawer than she intended.

Sapphire stepped forward, allowing herself to take in the world below. A large fire burned in the centre of the camp. Witches dressed in white were celebrating. The coven was here.

She stepped towards the path, forcing her feet forward before she lost her nerve.

A cold hand wrapped around her wrist, and she whirled around to face Kaian once more.

'I thought I told you to be smart.' Kaian's nostrils flared as he spoke. 'You cannot go down there alone.'

A wicked laugh filled the air as a hand wrapped around the boy's neck. Ashes appeared from her shadows, towering over him.

'Now, has no one taught you how to speak to a lady? Or am I going to have to teach you myself?'

Ashes' eyes found Sapphire's and she smirked – her hand tightening around Kaian's neck.

'Hello, princess.'

'Let him go,' Sapphire demanded.

'I'd love to see you make me,' the witch said, tightening her grip again. Kaian's face was red with effort as he fought against her, his hands wrapped around Ashes' slender wrist.

'Please,' Sapphire breathed.

She watched the familiar unreadable emotions cross the girl's face before her hand finally began to loosen. Kaian crumpled at her feet and sputtered as he struggled to refill his lungs with air. Evera rushed to his side, her eyes burning as she looked to the witch, but she said nothing.

Ashes watched them both, lip curled in disgust.

'Have no fear, high blood. She won't be alone. She will be with me.' The witch's eyes pinned him where he sat. 'And nothing touches her in my presence.'

'Over my dead body, witch. Like hell we'll just entrust her to you.'

'Oh, Kaian,' Ashes teased, her voice lilting in a laugh, 'you don't know how easily that can be arranged.'

Kaian clenched his jaw, his gaze flicking between the witch and Sapphire.

'You must know,' the witch said, finally turning towards Sapphire, 'they are not welcome in the coven. Only you, princess.'

There was no room for argument or bargaining, and Sapphire took another step towards Ashes with a timid nod.

Kaian reached for her once more.

'Don't walk into this alone and unprepared. What if –?'

'Ah, how I wish we were the monsters you and your family think we are, high blood.' The witch's eyes were wild and more unreadable than ever as she placed herself between Sapphire and the boy. 'No matter what the whispers in the wind have told you. Stay here, watch over us like a faithful little hound. But follow, and you will be treated as an intruder.' Ashes gave him a taunting smile. 'I almost wish you would. I'd love to see how terror twists that perfectly handsome face of yours.'

Sapphire tugged at Ashes' hand, not wanting her to push him any further.

'Are you sure you want to do this?' Evera looked at Sapphire with a worried expression.

'It's the only way,' Sapphire countered, more doubt in her tone than she wanted.

'No,' Evera pleaded. 'No, it's not.'

'It is for me.'

Evera stared at Sapphire, her eyes screaming everything her voice failed to say.

'You'll be here then, when it's done?' Sapphire asked. 'You'll wait?'

For a few heartbeats, Evera stayed silent, then her arms fell to her sides, defeated. 'You are my heart, Sapphire Canmore. My friend. I couldn't leave you if I tried.'

Tears threatened to spill over as Ashes began to tug her down the path. 'It will be OK,' she called back as the people who mattered most in the world to her began to fade from view. 'It will all be OK.'

Gods above, she prayed, *don't let that be a lie.*

'How foolish to bring them here, princess. I assumed you had more sense than that, at least.'

Sapphire bowed her head like a scolded child but decided to be honest. 'I was afraid.'

Ashes laughed, rolling her eyes. 'You've stumbled blindly through this forest, practically begging for something dangerous to come slithering out of the darkness to devour you. What's got you so timid now?'

'I – well. What if they – your coven – don't . . . approve. What if they –?'

Ashes stopped short, grabbing Sapphire by the chin and forcing her to look up. In the dim light of the orb, Sapphire's stomach clenched as she took the girl in.

'I would never purposefully bring you into a situation that isn't safe for you. I need you to understand that.'

'But you hate me.'

Ashes tilted her head, her lips tugging upward. 'I might. But I always collect my debts. So, for now, my word stands.'

Ashes dropped her chin and began walking again, and Sapphire frowned, missing the girl's hand in her own.

'Do they know I'm coming? Do they know what I am?'

'It was not my place to announce it.'

'I thought no one was welcome,' Sapphire said.

'You happen to be an exception, princess.'

'But why?'

'You'll see.'

Sapphire ran a nervous hand through her hair. Too much was unknown, there were too many unanswered questions, and too many riddles to solve.

The thought rooted her to the ground, forcing her guide to stop and face her.

'What are you doing?' Ashes questioned.

'I don't know if I can do this,' Sapphire admitted.

Ashes' usual hard expression softened slightly as Sapphire tried to steady her breath.

She waited for the witch to threaten her. Waited for her to make a jab. But Ashes was silent, her eyes slowly taking her in.

Mercy, she hated her.

Gods above, did she want to kiss her.

Sapphire studied the shape of her lips, the hollowness of her cheeks, the way a few loose tendrils of her red curls framed her face.

Wicked and alluring. Bewitching and impenetrable. Something Sapphire couldn't quite understand, and something she couldn't just ignore. She wanted to trace the lines of Ashes' face with her fingers, memorizing each dip, each span of smooth skin. She wanted to breathe the witch in, keep her. Lock her away in a corner of her heart that no one else could find. Hidden and hers. Hers alone.

'Whatever reason brings you back to this forest,' the witch paused, blinking a few times, 'is proof enough that you need to do this.' Sapphire wondered how Ashes would feel if she knew. That more often than not, it was her face that drove Sapphire from her bed and into the darkness. The words died on her tongue as Ashes dropped her hand and started walking again. 'It will also mean you will stop interrupting my nights. Your pesky presence will not be missed.'

Sapphire followed close behind, doing what she could to push the panic away. The trees soon began to thin, and through them, she could see the flame of the fire dancing. As they moved closer, Sapphire pulled her cloak tighter.

Ashes paused for a moment, looking at Sapphire, and

she shook her head. 'This isn't a place to hide, princess.' Her eyes were heated as she looked at the girl. 'This is a place to truly be free.'

Sapphire recognized Savina as she stepped forward.

'My daughter, who do you bring?' The woman's tone was sharp.

'The guest of honour, Mother.' Ashes looked at Sapphire, who kept her face tucked into the hood of her cloak. 'Well, princess, would you like me to do the honours?'

Sapphire took a deep breath before pulling the hood away, revealing herself to the women who watched her. Savina studied her, and the rest of the coven mirrored her, breaking out in quiet gasps.

No one spoke to her. The only sound was the crackling of the fire, and Sapphire took a step closer.

An older, dark-skinned woman moved forward. Her eyes were a honey brown with red rims, wise with years and experience. 'We have been awaiting your arrival.'

'You have?' She thought Ashes had given them no indication that she was to come.

The woman gave her an unguarded smile.

'Come. Join us by the fire.'

With tentative steps, she followed the woman to the circle of stones surrounding the flames and took a seat. The surface was smooth beneath her palms, and she struggled to settle.

She had been warned, since the moment that she arrived in this world, that Shadow Witches came with forked tongues and evil intentions. Their darkness was too much for any elemental to handle, but here, in the tightly packed circle, Sapphire felt welcomed.

It left her unsettled.

Across the fire, Ashes sat with her mother. The girl lifted an eyebrow at Sapphire as if to say *I told you so*.

'What brings you to our coven, princess?' It was the same older woman who spoke. Sapphire studied her ageing face and long grey hair.

'Just call me Sapphire.'

The woman bowed her head, nodding. 'And you may call me Esadora. I am the Elder of this coven.'

'It is an honour to meet you, Esadora.'

Once again, she felt her eyes flicker to Ashes, who was watching her intently. Sapphire took a few seconds to memorize how the fire cast delicate shadows across her pale skin, the way the flames danced in the reflection of her eyes.

'Now,' Esadora began. 'How can the coven serve you? What do you seek?'

Sapphire had prepared for this. Had rehearsed the conversation hundreds of times. She knew the answer. She knew what she needed to say, but the words lodged in her throat. She felt like if they escaped, everything would change again.

And really, was she ready for that?

Having finally found a home, was she ready for everything to shift?

Esadora smiled patiently, continuing to stare unnervingly at Sapphire.

It was too late to turn back now.

'I have many questions – about my birth, about my time in Witrotean, about my parents.' Sapphire tripped over the last few words. 'I need to know the truth about my life and how you played a part in it.'

The words rolled off her tongue with unstoppable force and Sapphire tensed, waiting for outrage.

But there was nothing except the slightest tug of Esadora's lips as she leaned forward.

'These are delicate subjects. Delicate questions that demand delicate answers. A Shadow Moon is required to reveal what you seek. And there should be no uninvited guests lurking above.' Esadora's eyes moved to the overlook as she said it.

'A Shadow Moon?'

'When the next Shadow Moon appears, it will offer us what we need.'

'When is the next Shadow Moon?'

'Forty-five days,' the Elder witch said flatly.

'How am I expected to wait forty-five days?'

'One cannot simply unravel the history of who you are, princess. It cannot be done without the alignment.'

Sapphire collapsed like a spoiled child.

The witch rose to her feet, the coven following. Sapphire remained seated, staring at Esadora.

'I-I need answers now. Please.' Desperation did not befit a princess, but right now, Sapphire couldn't be bothered to care. 'Please. Tell me something, anything.'

'Patience, my child, is a virtue you should hold dear.'

My child.

The words rang in her ears. She couldn't walk away without answers. Not now. She turned to Esadora, blocking out the remainder of the coven.

'There's a voice. It speaks to me at all hours. It – I can't. Please, I need answers.'

'A guiding spirit is a gift, princess. Knowledge bestowed upon you from a soul beyond the veil is an offering that does not come often.'

Panic was building inside Sapphire and she had no idea why. Her breathing was short and choppy.

'But who is she? Why does she speak to me?'

Esadora paused before reaching up and pressing her thumb between Sapphire's brows. Sapphire closed her eyes tightly, trying to force herself not to recoil. Finally, the elder witch hummed, nodding her head.

'Good intentions she brings. She speaks to you from a place of pure heart and guidance. You surely are blessed, princess.'

'I don't – I don't understand. Please – I just –'

'The Shadow Moon. Then, I will answer every question you have.'

Esadora stepped away from the coven as they gathered dirt from the ground, throwing it on to the fire and muttering words Sapphire could not understand. The fire was strengthened, and Sapphire was entranced by the growing flames.

She blinked a few times and found Ashes hovering over

her. The witch pulled her up and pressed a firm hand against her lower back, forcing her to walk.

'Have a safe journey home.' Sapphire turned to meet Esadora's gaze, seeing a playful look in the woman's eyes. 'We'll see you again soon, Sapphire.'

Chapter Twenty-six

Resentment wormed its way into Sapphire's heart as the light of the flame faded, the darkness of the forest swallowing them.

Resentment of the witches, of wasted time, of unanswered questions. Of Ashes.

Sapphire marched ahead, pulling the hood of her cloak up once more, this time in an effort to conceal the hot tears that stubbornly fell.

'You're not very skilled at masking what you feel,' Ashes said bluntly, something like genuine surprise crossing her face.

Sapphire huffed as another tear fell. 'We can't all be like you. Some of us feel things – deeply.'

Ashes chuckled, shaking her head as she stepped closer. 'I feel many things, princess.' The girl's eyes tracked down her body slowly and Sapphire felt her stomach clench. 'I've just never had the luxury of doing so without inhibitions. Being able to conceal your emotions is as good as any weapon.'

Ashes' gaze lingered on her, and Sapphire felt it again, the tug to reach out for her. To trace the small scar that ran through her brow. To finger her curls.

She responded with venom despite herself.

'I think you knew I wouldn't get answers. I think you enjoy wasting my time.'

Ashes, to her credit, did not flinch. She did not furrow her brow in irritation. She just remained still – the detached mask she wore never faltering.

'I could think of much better ways to waste your time,' she said with a smirk. 'If you no longer seek my help, then feel free to find your way back to your friends. Magic requires intention. Rituals demand met conditions. If we do not handle the situation with care . . . things, people, you – could be impacted.'

Sapphire turned away from Ashes and continued walking. No footsteps came after her.

When she turned to look behind her, she realized that she was alone.

Immediately, the forest seemed larger, more sinister. 'Ashes?'

Silence answered her, and she clenched her fist as the fear inside of her grew.

'Ashes, please?'

A brush of wind shook the trees around her, and she whirled around, feeling once more like prey.

'Ashes.' Her voice shook. 'I need you. I need your help.'

One.

Two.

'Manners suit you.' Ashes emerged from her left, palming a tendril of her own hair. 'Now, say it again.'

That familiar scent of smoke and honey hit her senses as Ashes stepped in closer.

'I need your help.'

'No.' Her voice was deeper and Sapphire shivered. 'The other part.'

The princess frowned. With her free hand, Ashes smoothed the lines that creased Sapphire's brow.

'Say it.'

Sapphire felt it. That familiar shift in Ashes' presence.

'I need you.'

'Good girl,' she whispered before stepping back, adding distance. 'Let's go.'

Sapphire watched her hair tumble from the witch's fingers as she turned to head towards the overlook.

She silently prayed that the witch would lead her anywhere else. Back to the flames, to the forest, to some dark hovel filled with monsters, it didn't matter. She would have given anything in that moment to have the girl consume her in the shadows.

'Are you coming?' Sapphire remained planted on the spot, considering her next move. But the sound of footsteps sent Ashes scrambling towards her, concealing them both with her shadows.

'Sapphire?' It was Evera's voice. 'Sapphire, are you there?'

'Let her go, witch,' Kaian growled.

'Kaian Princeps is awfully protective of you.' Ashes sniggered.

'I don't need protection.'

'No, you don't.' Shadows ran up Sapphire's back. 'At least not from him.'

Sapphire stared up at the witch. Ashes' skin was pale against the shadows that danced around them. This close, she noticed that there was gold threaded through the blue irises of the girl's eyes. The witch smirked.

'Tell me, princess, are you afraid of the dark? Or do you long for it? The touch of something wicked?'

A shadow brushed against Sapphire's lips. She felt it, cold and entrancing.

She had never been afraid of the dark, and she had half a mind to make that clear, but she heard Evera call her name once more, and the trance was broken.

'Let them see me, Ashes.'

The witch ran a gentle hand down the exposed skin of her arm, and Sapphire hummed, leaning in slightly. The witch was terribly enigmatic but something about her enthralled Sapphire, refusing to let her go. A few beats passed, the two staring at one another, and Sapphire desperately wanted to confess every thought she had ever had. But the witch blinked a few times and the moment passed.

'As you wish, princess.'

The shadows peeled away from them, revealing her two worried companions, painted by Evera's flame with a warm glow that didn't suit them. When they saw her, Sapphire stepped away quickly from Ashes.

'You're safe.' Evera's voice was tight as she pulled her into an embrace. 'We worried –'

'When I kill her,' Ashes' voice made Evera stiffen, looking at the witch with narrowed eyes, 'I won't make it so obvious.'

Kaian charged forward. 'You unbearable witch!' To Sapphire's horror, he raised his hand, calling upon the ground faster than he had in the arena.

Fast, yes, but Ashes was faster. Her shadows wrapped around him, squeezing him so tightly his face turned an awful shade of red.

Sapphire shot a fierce glance at Ashes.

'You are lucky the princess is here, high blood.' The threat was thick in the air. 'So very, very lucky.'

He struggled against the magic; eyes wide with panic.

'Ashes, stop.' Sapphire's voice was steady.

The shadows cut away almost immediately, racing back to the witch, dancing against her skin. She bowed mockingly.

Kaian stumbled over to them, and Evera held him upright as he gasped for air.

'Don't start fights you can't win.' The witch's words were like daggers. Kaian narrowed his eyes but said nothing. Ashes turned her attention to Sapphire. 'Always a pleasure, high blood. I'll see you at the Shadow Moon.'

With a simple blink, the witch was gone, leaving the three of them alone.

'The Shadow Moon?' Evera looked worried.

'What I asked – they can't tell me the truth without it.'

'She threatened to kill you,' Kaian spat, finding his words again. 'She attacked me. You will not be alone with her – with any of them – again.' He stood taller, running a hand through his hair, catching his breath. 'We have to inform the council. That my father was right, the witch –'

'Ashes.'

'What?' Kaian questioned.

'Her name is Ashes. And you can't speak of tonight. Not to the council. Not to your parents. Not to anyone.'

She looked at him with pleading eyes, and he stared back, uncertain. Finally, he cracked, sighing loudly.

'Sapphire, if the witch takes another step out of line, I will be reporting it.'

She reached for Evera and Kaian's hands and they accepted. She continued holding on until they had reached the edge of the lake.

CHAPTER TWENTY-SEVEN

'Princess, thank you for agreeing to spend the day with me on such short notice.' Kaian bowed as he spoke. His note had arrived, asking for her company, just hours ago. Kip and Araxia had offered to step in, to make up an excuse that could not be refused, but Sapphire had graciously passed.

She curtsied, offering him the smallest nod as the guards assisted her into the carriage.

'Miss me already? Or is this to be an interrogation?'

He looked caught off guard.

'Interrogation? About what?'

'About – you know – last night.'

'I didn't tell them, Sapphire. I gave you my word.'

'Then why would they invite me so suddenly?'

'Because today is a celebrated day in Ciliria. I want – I need you to see it.'

Sapphire relaxed slightly, leaning back against the cushioned seat, the blue lakes of Astral rolling by.

'I could've swum.'

He snorted.

'A Princeps allowing a lady of royal blood to find her own way? Think of my poor reputation if that news got out.'

'Pretentious baby.'

'I wear that like a badge of honour too.' He winked and they both fell into laughter.

'So, what are we actually going to do? I've seen plenty of Ciliria at this point.'

'Technically, I am supposed to take you to the celebration of the trees located in the centre of the village. But I doubt you'd want all that attention.' She nodded in gratitude. 'So, I figured we'd duel. I think I've earned a rematch.'

Sapphire swallowed hard as she recalled their last confrontation.

With no healers, no judges, and no one watching them, how could she possibly be sure she wouldn't hurt him?

'I'm just not sure if that's the best idea.'

'If you're scared of me, you can admit it. This is a safe space, Canmore.'

Sapphire rolled her eyes, returning her attention to the landscape beyond the window.

'That's not it. I just – I'd like to see Ciliria.'

He groaned.

'That's pointless. You've travelled this land several times over.'

'But if I'm to be queen, I should know it intimately. Don't you think?'

He threw up his hands in exasperation but did not argue.

The tour lasted for hours – broken up by short stops where Sapphire allowed herself time in the warm daylight to breathe. The forest was so different at this hour – full of magic and comfort and life. Not a hint of the witches or secrets that occupied it at night.

They came to a stop in a small clearing. The sunlight bathed the area in gold.

'It's beautiful here,' she said, plucking a roseberry from the vine and tossing it into her mouth.

'Well, I thought offering you a view was the least I could do after destroying you in that duel, so here we are.'

She laughed loudly and relaxed against the blanket.

'Destroying me, huh? Maybe one day I'll give you the chance.'

'I hope so. I want to go toe-to-toe without beginner's luck on your side.'

They laughed, and it echoed through the forest, but Sapphire was not afraid of who might hear.

'What was your favourite food in . . . what's it called?' he asked, sucking a bit of juice off his thumb.

'Witrotean. I'm not exactly sure if I had a favourite food. We ate what we had and did what we could to enjoy it. Then we had to start rationing. So, I picked up hunting. We only had a small dagger so I struggled, but from time to time, I would find a forest animal or a bird flying too low.'

'You, hunting? The horror,' he said with a laugh. Sapphire smacked his shoulder lightly.

A comforting silence settled between them, but Sapphire's mind was restless. Her questions kept growing, begging to be answered.

The Princeps bloodline and power ran deep – they were direct descendants of one of the Elders, Rosin Eliat, who was said to have had ties to one of the four original elementals who built Eriobis. This ancestry put them in a position of power – and made them privy to information that many weren't.

'What are you thinking about?' Kaian asked.

'Have you ever seen the barrier?'

He gave her a confused look.

'I have, a handful of times. Why do you ask?'

'I'd like to see it.'

'Not part of the tour, sorry.'

His voice was firm, with no room for bargaining or argument.

'Oh, come on, Kaian – the tour was never planned in the first place.'

'I can't take you there, Sapphire. My parents, yours – they'd have my head.'

'Well, can you at least tell me what you know about it?'

He sighed loudly, his finger tracing a blade of grass, looking uncertain.

'What is there to know?' His voice was bored.

'What's beyond the barrier?'

'Sapphire, what's trapped beyond the barrier isn't something people want to know more about. As queen, you will be sending that same message. Focus on Eriobis – not the darkness that lurks beyond the veil.'

'Curiosity, though – I can't be the only one with it.'

'Curiosity is the downfall of many. Better to release it from your heart and focus on what's actually in front of you.'

His tone was unusually sharp. The boyishness she had

come to know had been replaced by a coldness she could not stand.

'No one is ever honest with me. Why can't anyone just be . . . honest?'

He blinked a few times, then softened.

'No one knows what really lies beyond the barrier. Shadow Witches, yes, the worst of them. But the rest of the darkness that was buried along with them, well, the chronicles were burned, and the truth with them.' Her shoulders drooped. 'But there is one thing. A small detail passed down in my family – a simple folktale, more like – but something.'

She leaned further in to him.

'This stays between you and me. Give me your word.'

'You have it,' she said eagerly.

'Not even Evera.'

Sapphire hesitated for a moment, then two, before nodding.

'Mercy, you're good at getting what you want. You know that?' He looked away from her, shaking his head. 'My mother claims a book escaped the great fires. And while it was eventually lost, one detail has been passed down through the generations.'

She kept her eyes on him, her heart hammering in her chest as she waited for him to continue. He took a deep breath, returning his focus to her.

'Violet eyes. There are accounts of the inhabitants having violet eyes.'

CHAPTER TWENTY-EIGHT

As she walked through the dark forest, Sapphire's body begged for a break. For sleep. For rest. For a brief reprieve from the panic that had gripped her since she spoke with Kaian in that clearing.

She had spent an hour at the looking glass, staring at her now-green eyes. When the colour started to fade, she choked down another potion. She couldn't handle it – that violet reflected back at her.

She recalled the way Kaian's face contorted when he talked about it: a sneer, a furrowed brow, a look of disgust settling on his elegant features.

Disgust for someone like her.

Her breathing hitched – what would he do if he knew . . .?

A tightness in her chest made her bend forward, resting her head against the looking glass.

A barrier.

Dark Magic.

Violet eyes.

Her hands shook. Exhaustion settled. Panic permeated.

The only choice she had was to seek answers.

As the treeline thinned, she saw her, standing further along the shore and looking to the sky.

'Hello, princess,' Ashes purred, water gently lapping at her bare heels.

Sapphire joined her on the shore, staring upwards. Dense black clouds obscured the moon and the stars entirely.

'A storm is brewing.'

Sapphire nodded.

'This storm will take two weeks to form. The final storm of the cycle. And the most powerful.' Her eyes finally turned towards the princess. 'To what do I owe the pleasure tonight?'

A quick gust of wind made Sapphire shiver and long for the warm sanctity of her bed.

'I heard a rumour the other day.'

'A rumour?' Amusement resonated in Ashes' voice. 'What kind of rumour, pray tell?'

'A rumour about the creatures of the Shattered Lands.'

Ashes turned towards the princess, folding her arms as she tilted her head, taking Sapphire in.

'Speak whatever truth you must and be done with it, highness.'

'I heard . . .' Her voice was shaking, her fear evident. 'I heard they had violet eyes.'

Ashes' lips tightened, her eyes betraying her for only a moment. Sapphire knew her answer.

Anger like a cold, swift knife dug into her side, working away at a gaping wound.

'Not a single word. This whole time. You never uttered a single damn word.'

'They are people, not creatures.' The witch's tone was drenched in warning.

'You knew –'

'Of course I knew, princess,' Ashes hissed. 'What I don't know is why it matters to you.'

'My eyes!' she thundered. 'I have the eyes of a monster, that's why!'

'By the Gods!' A shrill, bitter laugh left Ashes' lips as she raised her hands towards the sky in mock exasperation. 'I'll give the high bloods one thing, their ridiculous propaganda is unmatched. Twisting history until it suits them.'

'Shut your mo–' Sapphire started.

'They weren't monsters.' The wind blew again, causing the water to ripple. The branches overhead cast jagged shadows across the witch's face. 'And I cannot answer your questions. I am bound by the coven's bonds.'

'Liar.'

'Come again, princess?' Venom dripped from her words.

'I called you a liar, witch,' Sapphire hissed. 'Your magic, the bond, your coven – enough. I think the only thing that stops you from answering my questions is your own sick satisfaction at watching me fail, making things harder for me. Lying and hiding things from me just like everyone else.'

'You should,' Ashes purred, closing the distance between them until her breath brushed along Sapphire's skin, 'think about your next words very, very carefully, princess.'

'I'm not the scared girl lost in the woods any more, witch.'

'You'll always be that girl, princess. Who's the real liar here if you think otherwise?'

Sapphire clamped her mouth shut. Angry. Exhausted. The hurt she refused to express out loud showed clear in her eyes. Bitter were the words, but Sapphire knew some of them rang true.

'Call me a liar all you like, but my answer stands the same.' The witch's eyes pinned Sapphire where she stood. 'But if I could offer you anything, princess, it would be this. History is determined by those that hold the quill. The living don't fear the dead rising to correct them.'

Before Sapphire could question what the witch meant, the distinct sound of a whistle, human and close by, startled them both.

Ashes stepped away, scanning the treeline over her shoulder.

'I must go,' the witch muttered as she turned to leave.

Sapphire had come for answers, but she had come for something else too. So she lunged for Ashes' hand.

Skin collided with skin. Sapphire felt it – a small charge between them. Ashes whirled around, her eyes mirroring her shock.

'What do you think you're doing?' Ashes' voice was strangled.

'I –' The surge of courage dissipated as she met the girl's fiery gaze. 'I need more, please, Ashes.'

Something shifted, if only for a moment. The hardness

that Sapphire had become so accustomed to slipped from Ashes' eyes. The witch stared at her, unmoving. But just as quickly, it passed as Ashes leaned forward, voice dripping with venom as she spoke.

'This kingdom may bend to you, but I do not.'

She had said as much before, but something about it – about the moment they clutched each other's hands – gave the words a blunt force. Sapphire dropped her hand and stepped away.

'You'd better go,' she muttered.

'Right.'

Sapphire did not wait to watch her go. Instead, she dived into the water to begin her swim home. Her tears mixed with the currents of Astral.

Chapter Twenty-nine

The storm arrived from the east, with gusting winds and heavy rainfall. The darkness swelling in the sky was an unwelcome sight.

'Damn it,' Sapphire cursed to herself, watching from the castle window. 'Did the witch have to be right?'

She padded barefoot on cold marble as she sneaked down long corridors, slipping into the shadows when she could to avoid passers-by.

No one noticed her as she continued to move, before long reaching the doors that led out to the lakes and training grounds.

Just a few stolen moments, that's all she needed. Walking to the water's edge, she watched as the lake darkened with the sky overhead.

When she stepped into the water, she felt her shoulders release some of the tension that had gripped them for days. Another step forward, and her jaw unclenched. Another and the tension in her neck was alleviated.

She had never planned to dive, but the water beckoned her and she listened, moving deeper until she was fully immersed.

When she resurfaced, the sky had a menacing flow about it. The thunder felt as if it originated from her chest as it rang out in the sky, and the first flash of lightning split it in two.

Ryvinika had arrived.

The wind picked up, howling as it raced through the hills of Eriobis. Rain poured down – like tears from Ryvinika's broken spirit.

Embrace me.

The voice echoed in her mind, and she whirled around, looking for the source.

'Who are you?'

A gust hit her, feeling too much like creeping fingers racing up her back.

Do not ask questions when you already know the answers.

'I'm tired of games,' she spat into the eye of the storm. 'Tired of riddles. Tired of questions.'

A flash of lightning across the sky looked too much like a grin, and she clenched her fist, digging her nails into her palm. A familiar sensation overtook her.

Imagine how your anger could change the world, princess.

But Sapphire was done listening, and she raised a hand to the sky to silence it. And for a moment, the storm listened. The wind halted, the air stilled, and the rain ceased. An eerie silence replaced the clatter of shaking branches and the rumbling of thunder.

Her arm began to shake as she tried to focus, but that

focus faltered slightly when she felt pressure against her outstretched hand.

It is not your time. Not yet.

A gust of wind hit her hard, causing her to stumble, and she cursed the skies. As she looked up, she could have sworn the storm had teeth, threatening to close around her.

The storm passed, but not without leaving its mark. Cliffs caved, branches shattered, and the orchards she had come to love were uprooted. And two lives stolen – two citizens of Aleburn who could not escape the storm's wrath.

Sapphire's numbness at the news could not take away the anger that consumed her and so, with her dagger strapped to her thigh, she headed once again to Ciliria with revenge and justice coursing through her bloodstream.

She reached the Cilirian shore and took in the looming forest, but did not stop. She unstrapped the dagger from her thigh and ventured into the woods as the sun sank below the horizon.

You will not fail. You will not fall.

Finding the witches proved harder than she had expected and she walked in circles as night overtook the world around her.

She stumbled and struggled through the forest ravaged by the storm. Downed trees and branches blocked known paths and opened others that were foreign to her.

'Princess, why are we always meeting like this?'

Sapphire paused for a moment, before turning to meet

tried to keep her breathing steady. The witch eyed her closely, the ghost of a smirk on her lips.

'Are you scared?'

'No,' Sapphire forced out.

'Liar.'

The blade dug deeper into her skin, but she did not bleed. Still, the pressure caused her to suck in a sharp breath. Ashes looked down at her, and Sapphire tried to stay steady, her knees buckling slightly. She told herself it was fear of the knife at her neck, but as she found the courage to meet Ashes' gaze, she knew that wasn't true.

The world around them darkened, Ashes' shadows flaring, and Sapphire lost sight of everything except the girl in front of her. The witch licked her lips as her eyes tracked across Sapphire's face, pausing when her gaze found Sapphire's mouth.

The witch leaned in a bit more, her warm breath mixing with the feeling of cold steel against her neck, as Sapphire was overtaken by the familiar scent of honey and smoke. They were now flush against each other, exposed skin on skin, and Sapphire couldn't ignore it. She couldn't resist it. She wanted, needed, more.

'What are you thinking about, princess?' Ashes smirked, already knowing the answer. 'Tell me,' she urged. Her fingers danced lightly across Sapphire's forearm. Ashes' voice was throaty, and Sapphire heard herself whimper. 'I want to hear you say it.'

Sapphire's eyes flickered between the blade and the delicate fingers caressing her.

'Would you like to know what I'm thinking about?' Ashes purred, and Sapphire's body betrayed her as her hips rolled against Ashes' frame. The witch laughed. 'Or would you like me to show you, Sapphire?'

Sapphire audibly whined, a high-pitched mewl escaping her at the sound of her own name slipping off the girl's tongue.

Gods above, please.

To stop or to continue, Sapphire wasn't sure any more what her silent prayer begged for. Ashes continued to look upon her, eyes narrowed, lips pursed like she was contemplating.

She took Sapphire's chin between her thumb and index finger, forcing her face to angle up.

'Damn it all,' Ashes half whispered, her eyes darkening.

The witch's lips met her own, and Sapphire heard the dagger clatter against the ground. One hand remained tightly gripping her chin, the other the curve of her waist, and Sapphire lost herself in the feeling.

A type of high she knew she would chase for the rest of her life. She deepened the kiss, grabbing handfuls of the witch's dress as she pulled her closer. Ashes obeyed, her full weight leaning in, trapping Sapphire against the tree.

Sapphire threaded her hands through Ashes' loose curls, tugging at them, and she felt Ashes' smile against her mouth before she bit down on Sapphire's bottom lip. The sensation caused her to jump slightly, and the witch took the opportunity to pull away.

Ashes reached out, tracing her thumb along Sapphire's

swollen bottom lip, and the princess fought not to beg for more.

'They're fools to let you out so late at night,' Ashes finally said against her ear. Her warm breath made chills rise on Sapphire's skin. 'You never know who's waiting in these woods.'

The witch picked the dagger up from the ground, handing it back to her.

'Trusting this won't end up against my neck again, princess.'

'I make no promises, witch.' Her voice was far more breathless than she wanted.

'Till next time, princess,' Ashes replied, taking Sapphire's hand and pressing her lips against the scar that ran across her palm.

With that, Ashes put her hands together, and the light of her orb dimmed, leaving them in darkness. Sapphire barely heard the witch's footsteps leave the clearing.

Chapter Thirty

Rayna offered Sapphire the familiar vial of potion as she stepped off the dressing box. 'For lunch?'

The girl nodded as she escorted Sapphire to the door where Claye greeted her.

'Mind telling me what's going on?'

'You have guests.'

'Don't tell me –'

'They are nearly here. We'd best get moving.'

Anxiety wrapped like a noose around her neck, tightening with every step.

The Princeps.

Claye said nothing as she turned to go, and when the double doors swung open, Sapphire's stomach clenched as she took in the scene before her.

Kip. Araxia. Tyden. Sadara. Kaian. He met her gaze – his eyes tired and sad. She offered him a small smile that he did not return.

'Come and take a seat, Sapphire,' Kip called.

There was a still type of silence in the room – not wanted or liked. A silent storm brewing between them.

As she turned to Araxia, the woman did not look

angry. Instead, she smiled, the tension obvious and foreign on her lips.

'To the future of Eriobis,' she said.

Glasses clinked, and Sapphire's movements were rehearsed and forced.

'And to new alliances,' Sadara followed.

Sapphire glanced over at Kaian, but he looked away quickly.

'What new alliances are we celebrating?' she finally asked after a beat of silence that was too long.

All eyes fell on her, and she squirmed in her seat.

'Sapphire, you are the future of the Canmore dynasty.' Araxia's calming breath did nothing to quell her nerves. 'The work your position will demand is tiring and trying, but even more so when you are forced to face it alone.'

The mood shifted with each syllable the queen spoke, the bitterness becoming tangible.

Araxia reached for her hand, and Sapphire did her best not to recoil. Despite the woman's joyful tone, her eyes told a different story, full of anguish and remorse.

'By combining the powers of our families, we believe that this country will take large strides forward.'

She swallowed the bile rising in her throat.

'And what does this mean?'

Araxia looked at Kip, a pleading look on her face. He cleared his throat.

'You will be courted by Kaian for the next few months, and then you will be wed.'

Sapphire dropped Araxia's hand, a rush of raw anger coursing through her. She glared at Kaian.

'You agreed to this?'

He opened his mouth to speak, but the smallest move from Tyden stopped him.

'Our son knows his duty.'

'I wasn't speaking to you,' said Sapphire.

Everyone at the table stiffened, unsure what to say next.

'I asked you a question, Kaian.'

He looked at her with such desperation in his eyes that she pitied him; pitied them both for being chess pieces on the board of Eriobis' future.

He looked to his parents, but their eyes were trained on Sapphire, their jaws clenched.

'What is best for Eriobis is the only choice there is to make.'

'You're a coward,' Sapphire hissed. 'Absolutely spineless.'

Sadara gasped and Araxia wrapped her hand tightly around Sapphire's arm.

'That is enough, Sapphire.' She turned to the Princeps. 'I apologize. We all know this type of news is always hard to process.'

Sapphire's eyes stayed trained on Kaian, and when he finally looked at her, she saw it.

Our lives are not ours, Sapphire, his expression told her. *They never have been.*

Something dark and venomous rooted itself in her, and the scar on her palm began to burn and she rubbed her thumb against it in an attempt to pull herself together.

The anger coursing through her was too much to tamp down, refusing to be snuffed out.

'Allow me a few moments to gather myself.'

Araxia turned to answer, but Sapphire was already up, moving for the door. The rippling pain in her palm grew with every passing moment. Once out in the corridor, she ran to the nearest washroom and locked herself inside.

She leaned against the sink for support, resting her head against the cool glass.

Ashes.

The witch had warned Sapphire time and time again about the world she had been born into, and Sapphire had chosen to ignore her.

Oh, mercy.

Ashes: the one person who had never treated her with caution, never tiptoed around what she wanted to say. The girl who had pressed her up against a tree and kissed her senseless not ten hours ago.

The girl who told her this kingdom did not deserve her.

Her heart ached at the thought of the witch and she hated it. Hated her. Hated it all.

She pushed away from the counter and met her reflection, staring down green eyes that were not her own.

Another sharp pain caused her to suck in a breath, and she clenched her fist tightly to dull the ache. When she reopened it, a small flame bounced in her palm. It danced, casting shadows on the wall of the washroom, and she stared at it with wide eyes.

It did not burn her.

She remained there, watching the flame flickering against her skin, unwavering and under her control. The sensation made her blood run cold; there was something unnatural about it all. She panicked, waving her hand around trying to make the flame disappear but it clung to her.

The world will fall to its knees. This is only the beginning.

She snapped her fist closed at the intrusion, and the flame was gone. She looked around the room, searching for answers, but none came. She reopened her fist once more, but the flame was nowhere to be found – the pain that she had felt was now just a dull throb.

You are powerful beyond your wildest imagination, child.

The voice was so clear that when she dragged her gaze to the looking glass, she half expected to find foreign eyes looking back at her. But she was alone.

The Elders never answered her.

The Elders never granted her prosperity.

The Elders never spoke wisdom in her ear.

The Elders never embraced her.

But the voice did – whoever, or whatever, it belonged to. The Shadow Witch had told her it meant her no harm.

It was time for a new God.

CHAPTER THIRTY-ONE

That night, she sat by the water, staring into the darkness. Footsteps behind her caught her attention, but Sapphire did not turn to greet them. A few moments passed before the woman found the courage to speak.

'We shouldn't have ambushed you.'

'No, you shouldn't have.'

Araxia sighed and sat next to her, tucking a knee into her chest and resting her head atop it.

'It is quite common – arrangements like this. But we didn't want this for you.'

'Then why do it?'

'We were not honest with our people when you disappeared. Maybe we should've been but sometimes the right thing to do is also the hardest and we didn't have the strength to be bold.' Araxia took a heavy pause, then struggled to continue. 'I always feared our lack of honesty would catch up with us – but I imagined it would come at the cost of my reputation. Of the Canmore reign. I never thought it would come at the cost of you and your future, Sapphire. I always thought the witches would speak out – I never thought the Princeps would . . .

Mercy, the Princeps knew about her birth. Maybe even more than that. Sapphire racked her brain, trying to remember if she had ever admitted to Kaian that her path and the coven's had always been intertwined.

'They're blackmailing you.' Sapphire did not attempt to mask the disgust she felt.

'Power makes people do things you'd never imagine. They saw an opportunity and have been planting the seeds, waiting for the perfect moment to take advantage of what they know.'

'And if we say no?'

Sapphire hated how childish her voice sounded.

'Then they go public with the information. The people – they won't be . . . understanding. It could lead to anarchy, an insurrection. Either way, the Canmore name wouldn't rule for long.'

'Is that really so bad?' Her question was honest.

'I used to ask myself that, long before I took the crown. I still do from time to time. If a life without . . . all of this could be one I would enjoy living.' She looked up to the sky, a frown on her face. 'But without us, without you, people like the Princeps take our place.'

She paused like she was considering whether she wanted to continue.

'I love Eriobis, Sapphire. I love it too much to be selfish.'

'And if I refuse? Refuse to marry him?'

Araxia finally looked at her, the darkness doing nothing to mask the pain in her eyes.

'I don't know,' she admitted. 'But I'm scared to find out.'

The honesty was jarring, and only silence followed as Araxia rose to her feet.

'If I could rewrite your story, I would, sweetling. But I'll never regret my choice to save you – even if it costs us everything.'

Sapphire did not turn to watch her leave.

CHAPTER THIRTY-TWO

When she met Kaian in front of the castle, he bowed, and Sapphire gritted her teeth. The dress she wore was a mix of green and blue – colours to showcase the union of the Canmore and Princeps names.

'Unity suits you, highness.'

'Unity is an interesting term for this.' She gestured to the monstrosity of a dress that Sadara had sent over the previous night.

Evera squeezed her hand gently and Sapphire tried to relax. They were heading out to visit the territories impacted by the storm, and Kip and Araxia had not argued when Sapphire had demanded that Evera join them in hopes to quell the tension.

'What does our visit solve for these people?' Sapphire said as she looked out of the window. 'Us laden in jewels and tailored dresses and robes as they mourn their homes and all that was lost.'

'It is a reminder that we support them,' said Kaian 'That they are not alone in these times. Since the . . . announcement of our betrothal, we will be expected to do these types of things, together.'

Bile rose in Sapphire's throat and she struggled to hold her tongue as he continued.

'Smile, bless the people, keep a level head. Remind them of the Elders' plan – how the Harvest Storm always seeds news gifts for the future.'

'Do you think that's true?'

Kaian shot her a wary look as the carriage arrived.

'Do you truly think the Elders took two lives as the price for prosperity?' Sapphire's voice had an edge of venom.

'I believe that the Elders always have a plan, and I will continue to trust that they do. As should our people.'

'You're a bigger fool than I ever took you for,' Sapphire spat. 'And stop calling them that.'

'Calling them what?'

'Our people. You don't sit on the throne, Kaian. Not yet, at least.'

He opened his mouth to say something but instead, she gathered her dress in her hands as she stepped towards the door. She smiled slightly when she found Claye waiting for her, hand extended like he had expected nothing less than this poor behaviour. She threw a scathing look over her shoulder. 'Besides, if I had just lost someone, I wouldn't want to hear that it was all for some bigger plan.'

Kaian paled as silence filled the carriage save for a rustling sound as Evera bounced her leg, from either nerves or discomfort. Sapphire cut her eyes to her friend, and Evera gave a smile that looked a bit more like a grimace.

The first location they visited was Aleburn. Sapphire sat with Yila, the woman who had been kind at her presentation lunch, as she poured her heart out. Cliffs had crumbled, homes had been destroyed, crops were no longer viable. Sapphire held the woman's hand tightly, looking to Claye to ensure he was taking note of everything Yila said. Aleburn had a special place in Sapphire's heart, and she wasn't lying as she promised to use whatever power she held to send aid.

Next was the Isle of Irobel. Sapphire had only been there once but knew the journey was long. She shifted in her seat knowing she would never be able to hide her resentment for the entirety of the ride.

'Do you have nothing to say to me?'

Evera, who had been half asleep, sat up straight beside her. Kaian tried not to be as obvious as he crossed his arms in front of his chest.

'Have I not offered you proper guidance, princess?'

'You knew. You knew and you gave me no warning. You kept a secret – one that impacted me – and you allowed me to be blindsided. I thought we – I thought you were my friend.'

Kaian's shoulders sagged, any last bit of properness washed away by her shaky confession.

'I am your friend, Sapphire. I – You are incredibly important to me, you have to know that.'

She snapped, looking out of the window. 'A friend would've never allowed that to happen.'

'I couldn't have stopped the courtship. You know that.'

'I don't believe you.' Her voice was too loud and strangled. She took a deep breath in an effort to steady herself. He looked down at his freshly polished boots as he reached out for her hand. She fought the urge to recoil as she recalled Ashes' hand laced in her own. Evera watched them closely as if she was afraid Sapphire would do something she couldn't take back.

'I should've told you,' Kaian finally admitted. His hand clung to hers like he was scared that if he dropped it, he might never get to touch her again. 'But I was terrified, angry, upset. You know my heart. You know Ciliria is where I belong and . . . You know my only dream was to preside over it, improve it . . . and now that dream has been stolen from me. And then there was you . . . Sapphire, you are just so . . . what is the fair term to use here? You are impulsive. I feared if I shared it with you –'

Sapphire pulled her hand away harshly at the words.

'You speak as if I'm a spoiled child who has never dealt with disappointment. I can handle my emotions. I won't allow you to make excuses for your choices.'

Kaian lowered his head into his hands, releasing an exasperated sigh.

'I – I am not making excuses, Sapphire. You are brave. That's the problem. Your courage is . . . There's no changing this fate. I am a coward. There. I admit it. I am a coward, a horrid friend, and entirely selfish.'

Sapphire finally looked at him. She hadn't noticed the slight bruising under his eyes. 'You owed me honesty at least, Kaian.'

'I did and I have regretted not offering it from the moment you walked into the dining room. I am sorry, Sapphire. I will say it as many times as you need to believe it.'

'I'll believe it faster if you offer me honesty now,' Kaian sat up straight. 'Have you been feeding your parents information regarding my involvement with the witches?'

'Sapphire, I would never do that to you. Think what you will of me, but your secrets are and always will be safe with me.'

The carriage came to a halt before she found the nerve to speak. Out of the window, a collapsed and ruined temple lay in heaps of rubble.

The altars, the offerings, the stained glass – all of it was shattered. Sapphire's stomach turned at the sight.

An older woman took her hand when Sapphire climbed out of the carriage. She had the sign of the Elders hanging around her neck. A Prodigal – one of those who dedicated their lives to the Elders and their teachings.

'We appreciate your visit, princess. Our mighty temple did not fare well.'

Sapphire stepped over a downed pillar, studying the debris.

'How does a building like this collapse under a storm?'

'We cannot be sure. Perhaps the Elders wanted a new place of worship.'

As they continued to walk, Sapphire couldn't keep her eyes focused. Too many pieces of the puzzle were not making sense. Finally, they arrived at the centre of the rubble, a perfect circle free of any disturbance.

'This is where we will rebuild. A sign of growth and a sign of where to begin.' The Prodigal dropped to her knees and began to pray, and Kaian signalled that they should follow. But as Sapphire knelt, she studied the untouched circle.

Do you like what you see, princess?

The voice was as clear as if the speaker knelt beside her, and she jumped slightly at the intrusion. Kaian, Evera and the Prodigal did not notice, continuing their prayer.

Every temple they build will crumble.

The air was suddenly thick, causing Sapphire to cough. She stood up abruptly, walking away from the clearing and Kaian followed.

'What is the history here?'

'I don't know what you mean.'

'The war – was it fought here?'

The Prodigal joined them, and narrowed her eyes at Sapphire's question. 'The war was fought here, princess, yes. Won here, in fact. The Elders led in bravery and triumph against those who turned away from the proper life.'

'Elders bless this land,' Sapphire sputtered. 'We will rebuild.'

The Prodigal smiled, and Kaian stepped away from her. Inside, Sapphire's blood was boiling.

Blasphemy on your tongue, my child. Do not praise those beneath you.

She pulled at the jewelled collar that hung around her neck as the words ghosted over her skin. The Prodigal bowed, thanking them once again for visiting.

But as Sapphire stepped into the carriage, she looked over her shoulder once more to find the woman staring at her, an unpleasant look on her face.

And for a moment, Sapphire could have sworn she saw purple eyes staring at her from just beyond the woman's shoulder.

CHAPTER THIRTY-THREE

Sapphire hated plenty about being a royal. The etiquette, the forced dinners and faked smiles – but she'd take a lifetime of all of that to never have to deal with wedding planning again.

She stood atop a dressing box as maidens poked and prodded her into a never-ending series of ill-fitting wedding dresses. She fought the urge to wrinkle her nose as she turned to see her reflection in a gaudy ball gown that looked as if a child had glued gemstones on to the bodice.

'That's the dress,' Sadara noted. 'Kaian will absolutely adore it.'

'I think it's more important that my daughter likes it,' Araxia said curtly. She stood to join Sapphire in front of the looking glass. 'What do you think?'

'I think . . .' A glint of red hair caught her eye across the room and her heart sank when she realized it was a maiden with another gown for her to try on. 'I think I need a break. Please.'

'But there are more gowns to be tried on and the wedding is approaching quickly. You must –'

'Sadara, I really must not do anything.' Sapphire's eyes

widened as she cautiously looked at Araxia, but the queen simply fought a smile.

'I do think a break would do everyone good. We can return with fresh minds later.'

Sadara levelled a gaze at them both but knew better than to argue. She wasted no time in leaving the room.

'These dresses are terrible,' Sapphire said as the maidens unlaced her quickly.

'These are Sadara's picks. But mine and yours will be next. I think you'll find them much more suitable.'

Sapphire took a deep breath as her ribs found their rightful place with the corset undone. 'I wish I was as brave as you are,' Araxia whispered, pushing a lock of hair out of Sapphire's eyes. 'Maybe then I could change your fate.'

She wished she could just rest. Her body was desperate. It was her mind that refused to listen. She counted the hours as they ticked by, throwing her body from one position to the next as her mind refused to slow.

She paced. She read. She stared: at the water, at the moon. Nothing worked.

Sleep would not come no matter how much she longed for it.

Currently, she sat in the armchair, legs tucked under her, sketching a portrait of Ashes absentmindedly – unable to focus on much else.

'You have my nose entirely wrong.'

Sapphire was about to let out a scream when a hand slapped over her mouth, smothering her cry. She pushed away from the intruder and whirled around to find the last person she expected.

'Ashes.' Sapphire self-consciously tried to smooth down her hair. 'What are you . . . how did you . . . ?'

Ashes ignored her, picking up Sapphire's sketch book. She smirked as she flipped through the pages, studying each closely. Finally, she snapped the book closed and returned her focus to Sapphire.

'An artist's muse. Now, that is something I never thought I would be.'

Sapphire grabbed the sketchbook back, shoving it under the chair cushion.

'You shouldn't be here.'

'You've been avoiding me and I'm terribly impatient.'

Tonight, she wore black, harsh against her skin yet jarringly beautiful.

'Yes, well, some things have happened that have demanded my attention.'

'Like a new courtship, I hear.'

'How did you –?'

'The joyous betrothal of the most infamous houses in Eriobis?' Ashes laughed, looking around the room. 'News like that spreads to even the darkest of places, princess.'

'I didn't choose this,' Sapphire said, desperate for the witch to understand the words she left unsaid.

'There is always a choice,' Ashes said, her tone cold and distant.

'Not for me,' Sapphire choked out.

Ashes countered, 'Especially for you.'

The witch began to walk around, studying the room.

'How exhausting it must be to live in such luxury. How brave you are to shoulder such a burden.'

Sapphire sighed as she walked over to her bed and sat down. A few moments later, Ashes joined her and Sapphire fought the urge to lean her head against the girl's shoulder.

'Blackmail.'

'Come again, princess?'

'His family. They are blackmailing my parents, forcing their hand.'

The witch let out a disgusted laugh. 'You can't trust anyone of high blood, Sapphire. How have you not learned that yet?'

There was no kindness in her tone. No understanding. And Sapphire moved away from her, putting distance between them.

'I am of high blood. So are you saying the same of me?'

'You have never been one of them.'

From the look on Ashes' face, Sapphire knew she had not meant to say that. Her lips pressed together, creating harsh lines around her mouth.

'What is that supposed to mean?'

The witch did not answer. Instead, she stared at the moon.

'Answer my question.'

Ashes shrugged, turning to face her.

'It meant nothing. High blood is high blood,' she replied, motioning to the room around them.

Unexpected sadness worked its way into Sapphire's heart, and she closed her eyes.

'You've never believed that before.'

Ashes' voice was smaller than Sapphire had ever heard it, a whisper carried away by the wind, broken. 'You're marrying him. Time will make you one of them yet.'

'I would never –'

'But you will,' Ashes replied, cutting Sapphire's defence short. 'You will. And one day, long after you've stopped visiting the shore, you will command the armies that hunt people like me. Eriobis' new king and queen crowned in laurels of blood.'

The anger that had bloomed in Sapphire's stomach intensified, and she shifted, trying to quell it. But she felt more than just anger. There was an unexpected edge of heartbreak. Ashes' words hurt more than they should.

'You know nothing of the queen I will be,' Sapphire snapped.

'You'll be no different than the last. Just another cog in the machine of death and devastation.'

Heartbreak and rage were a toxic combination. Rapid. Suffocating. And begging to be released. They rippled through her and did away with any sense she had left.

She watched as the pond in her room began to steam. And then, an angry flame erupted from her hand.

Ashes' eyes locked on her open palm, while Sapphire's eyes locked on Ashes'. They were frozen like statues in Sapphire's room.

'That's new.' Ashes' voice was steady. 'How long have you been able to do that?'

Sapphire opened and closed her fist a few times, trying

to douse the flame, but it persisted. 'It's none of your business.'

When the flame went out, leaving only her clenched, warm fist, the two girls were left alone.

'You're right. It's not.'

Sapphire deflated, the secret heavy inside her. She wanted Ashes to press her for answers, but the witch remained silent by her side.

'That's all you have to say?' Sapphire asked.

'What else is there?'

Sapphire shrugged. 'I don't know. I just thought –'

'I am your enemy.' The witch arched an elegant eyebrow, and Sapphire looked away quickly.

Sapphire knew Ashes should be her enemy. But still, the lingering memory of a soft hand on her lower back, lips against her own.

'You're supposed to be.'

The way the witch looked at her made her core warm, and she clenched her jaw in an effort to slow the building force within her. Ashes was entirely transfixing, consuming, and mind-numbing. Every time Sapphire met the girl's gaze, she felt whole and untethered at the same time.

Ashes didn't feel like home. She didn't feel like a safe place to land. But she did feel like power. Like rain on Sapphire's skin and magic throbbing in the tips of her fingers.

Ashes felt like being alive.

'If you only knew,' Ashes whispered as she inched closer, her breath warm against Sapphire's neck, 'how devastating you are when you look at me like that.' The witch's eyes roamed her face before landing on her lips, setting Sapphire's nerves aflame.

'Tell me, princess. How strong is that oath you took when they placed a crown on your head?'

Ashes' hand found its way to her thigh and Sapphire shivered. The touch of her skin was icy and jarring. Sapphire's eyes lingered where the hand rested.

She clenched and unclenched her fist, unable to cling to her resolve.

Instead, she leaned forward, pressing her own lips against Ashes'. The witch hummed in satisfaction, pulling her closer.

Sapphire yielded, allowing herself to be laid back against the expensive fabric of her bedspread. Her blood warmed and she leaned into the witch's hands as they found their way to her thigh, tracing delicate circles on her skin. Her breath hitched at the contact, a small moan threatening to break free, so she buried the sound in the witch's lips. Ashes took deep, reverent breaths at her neck, inhaling the perfume on her skin. Heat rippled wherever their skin met, and Sapphire lost herself in the feeling.

'I want –' Sapphire murmured into the witch's lips.

'What do you want, princess?' Ashes' voice was unhinged in a way that lit Sapphire's core. 'Tell me.'

'More,' Sapphire groaned. 'I want more.'

Ashes cupped a hand behind her head, pulling her closer, a delicious smirk on her face. 'Greedy,' she breathed, full of headiness. Ashes captured her lips again, wilder than before. Her other hand wandered under the hem of Sapphire's gown, finding soft, sensitive skin and as Ashes bit down on her lip, Sapphire threw everything down at that kiss.

Her desire, her desperation. Because, in that moment, she knew she would damn the kingdom, sell it and all its riches, and leave it to crumble in the annals of history for more of this, of the witch pressed against her. And for the feeling that had started to burrow its way into her heart.

Ashes pulled back, staring at her, and Sapphire whimpered. The witch took her hand and studied her scarred palm. Sapphire tried to shrink away, suddenly conscious of the jagged skin.

'Don't hide from me,' Ashes commanded, and her fingers wrapped around Sapphire's wrist. Sapphire watched as she pressed her cold lips to the scar. They remained there for a few moments before lingering over Sapphire's open palm, her delicate fingers digging into Sapphire's skin.

'You're not the only one with scars, princess,' Ashes mused, shifting the sleeve of her dress from her shoulder. There, Sapphire found jagged scars running across the witch's skin.

She reached out a timid hand and Ashes nodded, allowing Sapphire to trace the lines gently.

'Did – did someone *hurt* you?'

Sapphire stared at the pattern of risen flesh, trying to memorize the vulnerability the witch was offering her. But Ashes simply shrugged, pressing her lips against Sapphire's once more.

She wasn't sure how much time had passed when Ashes' body stiffened and she pushed away from the bed.

'I have to go.'

Her eyes darted around them as if she was searching for someone looking in on the private moment they had shared.

'But – I want –'

'I know,' Ashes said, her voice strained as she pulled Sapphire in close for a quick kiss that brimmed with promise. 'I know. But when my coven calls, I must go.'

'Do they know,' Sapphire questioned, unsure if she truly wanted the answer, 'that you're here with me?'

'You are a secret I prefer to keep to myself, Sapphire.' Ashes smirked but something was different. The witch was always difficult to read, but Sapphire saw the slight change in her expression. The smirk faltered, for only a second, and she knew that look because she herself had worn it often.

Guilt.

Remorse.

Sapphire reached out for Ashes' hand and squeezed it gently. She had kept her fair share of secrets since she arrived in Eriobis. She understood. She'd rather be a secret to the witch than nothing at all.

Finally, Ashes pulled her hand away and Sapphire watched as she padded over to the chair, pulling out the sketchbook once more, ripping a page from it before Sapphire could protest. 'Till next time. Your guards are sloppy and I do prefer you in the moonlight.'

And then, in a storm of shadows, the girl slipped from her room.

Once alone, Sapphire retrieved her sketchbook, trying to figure out which drawing Ashes had removed. She was surprised to see that the witch had taken Sapphire's recent self-portrait – the only sketch she had ever drawn of herself with violet eyes.

Chapter Thirty-four

The Canmore Waltz was a traditional dance that would be performed at both the ball and wedding, and currently the bane of Sapphire's entire existence. Her teacher tapped her back, reminding her to keep her posture upright, as Sapphire began to slump from a mix of exhaustion and boredom.

The music drawled on and she felt her eyes glaze over. This was her third lesson of the week. Her days had been filled with nothing but wedding prep and ball training. And it saddened her to realize that this was it – this was the life she would live until death took her.

Her future wasn't something she had spent much time considering, growing up – but since she had arrived here, she had begun to allow herself to plan. To dream. But she was back to square one – out of control and lacking choices. She hated herself for ever thinking it would be different.

'Sapphire?'

Araxia was standing behind her. The instructor stepped away.

'I was wondering how you're doing.' Sapphire did not

miss the slight tremor in the woman's voice. 'with everything.'

'I'm fine.'

'You're allowed to be upset.' Araxia's voice was tight. 'You're allowed to be unhappy, angry, even.'

'It's what's best for the family. For the Canmore name. What other choice is there?'

For a moment, Sapphire thought the queen looked more undone by her lack of anger than the actual situation, but it passed, and Araxia closed the remaining distance between them, pulling her into an embrace.

'Maturity and steadiness will take you far as queen.'

Sapphire forced a smile, unable to find the right words. Pulling free, she summoned her dance instructor and Araxia took her cue.

In her mind, she saw an image of a crown on her head, fire in her hand, and panic on the faces of those around her. Images of lightning fracturing the castle in two. She shook her head, but the visions grew more violent and more threatening, and eventually, she had to step away from the instructor once more.

'May I be excused?'

The man nodded and she headed for her room – nearly running down the hallway. Sapphire fought back her tears as the maidens rushed to undo her dress. She bounced on her toes as she tried not to fall apart.

Even though she was surrounded by handmaidens and the many staff that roamed the castle, she had never felt more alone.

Slamming the washroom door, she sealed herself away from the world and sank into a warm bath, allowing the water to still her mind, the images of the kingdom falling to ruin shrinking away.

Clarity.

She wasn't surprised when images of red hair and parted lips painted in moonlight flooded her mind instead.

'Have you heard any more about the Harvest Storm?' Kaian asked as they walked together in the garden, the setting sun warming their skin.

She shook her head.

He nodded, looking straight ahead. His hands were clasped behind his back and his spine was incredibly upright, a picture of a proper king. Handsome and kind. Patient and understanding. A friend.

A husband that would never know her true love.

'Do you think we'll be happy if we never love each other?' she finally asked. 'Not in that way, at least.'

He seemed caught off guard but not surprised at her question.

'Many kings and queens who were . . . friends and confidants, and nothing else, have reigned successfully. Who knows, never falling in love may be best for the job ahead of us.'

'For how long is the love of a friend enough to keep you happy? How long before it becomes a bitter taste on our tongues? A cage that we can never escape?'

Guilt flooded her. Guilt at the fact that he would be

marrying a monster masquerading in royal flesh. A monster that could call lightning and ignite fire and bend water.

Guilt so heavy it felt like she might choke on every lie she had ever told him.

'Please, don't think like tha–' Kaian started as she sucked in a breath.

'I've been lying to you.'

Kaian stopped, turning on the heel of his leather boot to face her. He reached out for her arm, wrapping his hand around the soft fabric of her dress at her elbow.

'If we can't have love, Sapphire, let us have honesty.'

She looked from his hand to his blue eyes – doing what she could to take deep breaths. He had promised her friendship . . . loyalty. And she believed him.

He was a Princeps. He was a Princeps but saw the world much differently from his parents. He was a Princeps, but Sapphire saw the young boy manipulated by people with darker minds.

And he was her friend. Her partner. Her future king.

She inhaled and exhaled, trying to speak clearly, trying to not allow her thoughts to cloud her judgement.

'Fire, lightning, water. I can control them. All of them. I'm not sure what that means, but that power . . . it calls to me. Every waking moment, I hear it calling to me.'

His hand slipped from her arm as he rubbed his temple before crouching in front of her, burying his face in his hands.

For the first time in his presence, she was afraid.

She knelt in front of him – her hand reaching out. He looked at her when he felt her touch.

'I-I shouldn't have said anything. I'm sorry. Please, don't . . . be afraid of me.'

He scanned her face, her hair, down to the tips of her fingers where they rested on his arms. He looked at her as if seeing her – truly – for the first time.

'Confused. Awed,' Kaian began. 'Curious. Baffled. I have a litany of emotions when it comes to you, Sapphire, but fear is not one of them.'

He ran a ragged hand through his hair, ruffling it. 'When – when did you realize?'

'The night of the first storm. I was in the lake and called upon lightning, and it shot from the sky just as I asked it to. I felt it. I felt it in my fingertips, in my chest. All of me felt it.'

'And fire?' Kaian asked, studying her features harder than he had before.

'The fire was . . .' Sapphire sputtered, suddenly nervous. 'Well, it happened after the announcement of our new . . . courtship.'

'I see.' A hint of sadness in his tone.

'Each time, each time that power surfaced, I heard a voice, encouraging me, telling me it was possible.'

'A voice?' Kaian questioned.

'I sound mad.'

Kaian shook his head, processing it all. 'It could very well have been a coincidence, Sapphire. And the fire – well, you could have been feeling overwhelmed. Perhaps it was your mind playing tricks.'

'I . . .' The words died on her tongue. 'Maybe you're right.'

He patted her hand gently, but she did not miss how quickly he moved away from her. She did not miss the silence that lingered between them. She did not miss his quick, polite goodbye as he hurried home. Kaian Princeps ran from her, leaving her alone in the garden.

As she swam, the world melted away. The feeling of needles against her skin, of lies grating against her mind, the memory of Kaian's concerned expression and Araxia's gritted teeth started to fade. And she continued to push forward, needing it all gone.

Her muscles ached, tears threatening her as she moved forward – trying to outpace something she wasn't even sure was real. The lingering feeling of her burning skin emerged as words of worship were whispered.

It was too much, and she swam until she reached the familiar shore. She should go to Kaian. She should talk to him about her confession, about the ceremony. She should seek comfort in him, her betrothed. But she couldn't. No matter how much her mind shouted to head towards the estate, her feet carried her deeper into the heart of the forest, searching for the one person she knew she shouldn't find.

It was an odd sensation to walk these woods in the daylight. The treeline thickened, concealing her entirely, and she silently begged Ashes to appear.

She trusted her feet to lead her where she needed to go. She trusted whatever lived inside her to guide her forward.

Ten minutes. Twenty minutes. Thirty. An hour. It passed in a blur of aching feet and bruised knees, but finally, she saw a flash of white. A girl gathering brush, alone.

She quickened her pace, refusing to let her slip away.

'Looks like I found you this time.'

Ashes did not startle, and she simply continued the task she was focused on, never turning to face her. Long gone was the softness of her features she had found a few nights previously. Sapphire fought the urge to frown.

Ashes placed the bundle of sticks on the ground, wiping her hands on her dress, before finally turning to face Sapphire.

'What are you doing here?'

The question caught her off guard, and she struggled to understand why Ashes was acting so cold.

'I-I don't know.'

'Yes, you do, princess,' Ashes clapped back, sitting on a large fallen tree trunk.

Sapphire could not help frowning. She was desperate to hear Ashes speak her name again.

'We had the mourning ceremony today. For the lives lost in the Harvest Storm.'

Ashes looked at her with raised brows as Sapphire continued.

'And the entire time, my skin . . . it felt raw against my dress. My nerves were exposed. My blood felt as if it did not suit my body. The Prodigal's words were stolen by a ringing in my ears.' She turned to look at the witch with a desperate plea. 'What is wrong with me?'

'Nothing is wrong with you.' The answer was sharp. 'Maybe the fabrics of the gown disagreed with you.'

Ashes stood, returning her focus to the brush she was collecting, and Sapphire watched her.

'You might as well say what's on your mind, princess,' Ashes called over her shoulder without even a glance in her direction.

'I think I'm losing my mind.'

The statement caused the witch to stop, her worried stare lingering on Sapphire. A flicker of the girl underneath the mask.

'Why would you think that?' Her tone carried an edge that Sapphire rarely heard from Ashes.

'I just – I fear if I tell you, you'll either think I'm insane or use it against me.'

With an eyeroll, she rejoined Sapphire on the log. 'You've got too used to your surroundings. Some value trust over leverage.'

Sapphire stared at her hands and ran her thumb roughly over the scar on her palm, her skin turning red under the force.

Ashes sighed as she roughly grabbed Sapphire's hand, intertwining their fingers.

'I am not your friend. But if you need to unload a burden, someone to help bear the weight of this life, I'm here.'

Sapphire's focus shifted to their touching skin.

Unload the burden. A safe harbour.

'Sometimes, I hear a voice. Her whispers in my ears are riddles and things I do not understand. But she always returns, and her words snake their way around my very being.'

Ashes' grip on her hand tightened. 'What does this voice say to you?'

'She warns me to not bow before the Elders, calls my praise of them blasphemy, and even in the storm, she spoke to me. Challenging me. I don't know who –'

'Ryvinika.'

'What?'

'Ryvinika is speaking to you.'

'Ryvinika? The Shadow Witch behind the storm?'

'Ryvinika controls the storm because it is hers.' Ashes cut Sapphire with a glare. 'This is all part of what was foreseen.'

'What was foreseen?' But the girl didn't answer her. 'Ashes, please.'

'I cannot answer your questions yet, you know that,' Ashes spat.

Like a spoiled child, Sapphire let out a low-pitched whine, burying her face in her hands, embarrassed. 'I just want to – to understand.'

A few moments passed before she felt familiar fingers taking back her hand, extending it. She watched through a blurry haze as Ashes placed a gentle kiss on her open palm, another on her inner elbow, and a final one on her collarbone. Her lips found their way to her tear-slicked cheek, planting gentle kisses until they found Sapphire's lips, meeting them softly. Sapphire leaned into her, allowing herself to get lost in the scent of honey and ash.

She closed her eyes, wondering if this was how the citizens of Eriobis felt when they prayed to the Elders she no longer believed in.

Finally, Ashes pulled away, their fingers still intertwined.

Ashes' tone was matter-of-fact as she cupped Sapphire's face with her free hand. 'We're doomed by this, princess.'

She felt the slightest brush of a thumb against her lip as Ashes traced it.

'I didn't know you'd be so beautiful,' Ashes whispered. 'I had no idea someone could be.' The vulnerability in her words shocked Sapphire. 'You will be my undoing. My damnation – but I accept my fate as long as it's at your hand.'

Tears brimmed in Sapphire's eyes, threatening to spill over. They both knew what this was.

How it would end.

'I'm scared. Of you. Of this. Of everything else in between,' Sapphire admitted softly.

'You may not trust me with most things, but please, believe me when I say the Shadow Moon holds the answers you seek.'

'I do.' Sapphire's voice was low.

'You do what?'

'Trust you.'

'Poor decision-making doesn't suit a queen.'

'For now, can I just be Sapphire? And just exist with you?' Without waiting for a response, Sapphire slid off the log to lie on the mossy floor of the forest. Ashes joined her, the witch's face hovering a hair's breadth from her own.

They lay still and in silence, gazing at one another. They had seldom been this close before.

'Tell me,' Sapphire's voice felt too loud for the moment, 'whatever it is you're thinking right now.'

'From the moment I first saw you, I've wanted this. Your face . . . it haunted me until it almost drove me mad. Half the time, when you'd call out to me in the darkness, I believed my shadows had summoned you to save me from that madness.' Sapphire averted her gaze, almost embarrassed by such a confession. 'What are *you* thinking?'

'I – well . . . Witrotean was not a place where beauty mattered. I've been called many things . . . a provider, a child, a burden but . . . pretty . . .'

Ashes chuckle cut her short.

'When they speak of this world, the stained glass of the temples, the highest peaks of Wilhelma, the sun reflecting off the Volta Sea, do they use the word pretty? No, Sapphire. I do not find you pretty. I find you magnificent, opulent, radiant. You are living art. Such a simple word does not capture you. It does not even come close.'

Leaning forward, Ashes placed a kiss to her left cheek, then her right, then gently found her lips. And she kissed her like she meant every word she had just said. She kissed her like she believed Sapphire was a wonder of this world.

'Do you think . . . one day we could meet outside the shadows? Outside this forest?' Sapphire asked. She wasn't sure where she had found the courage to do so, but she needed . . . something to hold on to.

'When I look at you, I wish the world was different,' Ashes muttered, looking away. 'I wish I could say yes, but, Sapphire, you had to know when this began. You had to know . . .'

Ashes' voice trailed off. Of course she had known . . . she had just allowed herself to hope.

Ashes swiped her thumb against Sapphire's lips. 'My coven believes that each soul exists in an endless cycle. That we live life after life, eternally moving forward through time. We might not have each other in this life, princess. But I'll find you in the next one and the next, and every single one that follows, however long it takes.'

Sapphire held out a timid pinkie. The witch stared for a few heartbeats before offering a rare unguarded smile, interlocking her own pinkie with Sapphire's.

An oath. No words; not in that perfect moment, at least.

Instead, they lay there, bodies entangled in the moss, Ashes murmuring sweet promises into her hair. 'Just you and me, Sapphire, for as long as you please.'

Sapphire was on edge as Claye escorted her down the long corridor.

The crown on her head was heavy, the dress fabric thick. She fought the urge to loosen the corset to make it easier to breathe.

Still, Sapphire had to admit that the seamstress had outdone herself. Shades of deep blue with jewels to match were sewn into the sleeveless gown, with the slightest dip at the neckline. She wished Ashes could see her like this.

'There is nothing the wealthy love more than feeling like a good person for a night,' Claye explained as he led Sapphire to the room where Kaian would meet her. She had tried to laugh but she couldn't bring herself to do it. She took a deep breath.

'Mr Princeps will meet you here in –'

'Now,' Kaian interrupted. 'Hello, Sapphire. You look beautiful.'

Sapphire nodded in gratitude but noticed Kaian avoided her eyes. Claye, sensing the tension, stepped out of the room.

'Are you ready?'

Sapphire turned to regard herself in a nearby looking glass, running her thumb over her scar.

'I'll be by your side the entire night.'

Sapphire knew he said it in the hope of relaxing her but it just caused her dread to grow.

'Thank you, Kaian.'

A soft knock at the door signalled that it was their time to join the ball and she rolled her shoulders, trying to put on a brave face. Kaian offered his arm and she accepted it and they began the act they had rehearsed hundreds of times.

Atop the stairs, she felt the crowd's eyes on her. She summoned every bit of courage she had as she took her first step, then held her breath all the way down. Kaian stepped to the side, allowing her to have her moment and she smiled as she had been trained to do before finding their seats at the table closest to the king and queen.

As introductions were made, Sapphire laughed for the first time all night when she realized that Claye had been right about the wealthy feeling like good people. The line for donations for those impacted by the Harvest Storm was longer than the line for the food, and the temple was packed with people praying for good fortune.

Sapphire hardly had time to study the room, though, as their table was flooded by those with congratulations and well wishes for their impending betrothal. She smiled and expressed her gratitude to each person present until she heard the first note of the Canmore Waltz. She watched with admiration as her parents took to the dance floor, performing the steps that Sapphire knew well. And she counted down until she felt Kaian's hand in her own as he escorted her on to the ballroom floor to join in.

One of his hands rested on her hip, and with the other he held one of hers. As they began to dance, Sapphire tried to refuse the thoughts that threatened to consume her. The thoughts about Ashes – about how she wished she could dance with the girl for the world to see. About how Kaian's hand did not fit the curve of her hip like the witch's did. How she'd give anything for Ashes to be here, to hold her, to kiss her in front of this room of people who didn't know her at all.

'Are you OK?' Kaian asked as he spun her back in.

'I'm fine.'

He pulled her closer to him as they neared the more difficult part of the dance.

'It's hard to miss the look of displeasure on your face,

Sapphire. I'm sure I'm not the only one who has noticed.'

Sapphire bit her lip, cursing herself for not focusing during such an important moment.

'I'm sorry,' she whispered. 'I'm just trying not to make a fool of myself.'

Kaian softened slightly.

'Allow me to just . . . take the lead here. You may be the most powerful person in this room, but I can out-dance you in any situation.'

She looked at him and tried not to laugh.

'You've got me?'

'Always,' he replied, spinning her outwards, and she nodded, relinquishing the final bit of control she had been trying to retain. The dance became less stilted in an instant. She smiled as her body relaxed.

'Pretentious?' she teased.

'And damn proud.'

Following the dance, Sapphire returned to her table and Kaian went to speak to his parents, leaving her alone. But that solitude was swiftly broken as someone approached.

'Who knew you could dance like that?'

Sapphire smiled as Evera stood before her.

'I can't. Kaian basically scolded me halfway through it.'

'Well, I, for one, thought you looked beautiful. Do look beautiful.'

'As do you. Red is most certainly your colour.'

Evera smiled as she ran her hands over the expensive fabric of the gown.

'I just – well, my entire family wanted to say thank you.'

Sapphire followed Evera's gaze to where Mr and Mrs Viotto were laughing loudly as they danced.

'You deserve to be here.' Evera nodded, looking at her hands and it struck Sapphire that now was the time to ask the question she had been considering for some time. The question that Araxia had grinned at and Sadara had scoffed at, but Sapphire didn't care. 'Evera, will you be my bridesmaid?'

The question caught the girl off guard and she took another step closer.

'I'm sorry. I don't think I heard your question right.'

Sapphire laughed, standing up and taking the girl's hand.

'I asked if you would be my bridesmaid.'

'But I'm not of noble –'

'None of that. You are my best friend. That, in itself, is all I need.'

Evera's eyes watered as she squeezed Sapphire's hand.

'I would be honoured.'

Sapphire hugged her tightly.

'Don't be too excited. You have to spend time with Sadara and that is enough to ruin any good experience.'

Evera laughed and shook her head.

'Worth it to stand by your side.'

She spent the remainder of the night greeting guests and wishing them good fortune. She danced a few times, chatted with Araxia and Kip, and fielded questions from overly curious council members.

And when the ball came to a close, she lingered with her parents as she bid each attendee safe travels.

She now stood in her room, unable to look away from her reflection. She was transfixed on the girl looking back at her, who did not seem to fit. The entire night had gone smoothly, and no immediate regrets came to her mind. Still, she felt increasingly unhappy as the minutes passed.

She didn't want to admit it. She didn't want to accept that she knew where the growing dissatisfaction was coming from.

She didn't want to – but she knew.

And as hard as she tried to shut out the thoughts, they lingered, clinging to her – refusing to loosen their grip. It was the same thought she had been wrestling with all night.

She wished Ashes could see her like this.

Her need for the witch's approval had not receded all night. Not during the many dances or many conversations. Every waltz, every toast, every moment . . . Ashes lingered. Inescapable.

But as she stared at the crown atop her head, she knew there was no choice. Not tonight, at least, as the grounds were still crawling with staff and guards. She'd never successfully sneak out no matter how thickly the clouds covered the moon.

So, instead, she sat by the window, sketchbook in hand, drawing images of flaming red hair and smirking lips. And trying to ignore the sinking feeling that maybe her choices would never truly be her own.

CHAPTER THIRTY-FIVE

Climbing into a boat on the night of the Shadow Moon, Sapphire settled in for the ride. It was a much slower process than swimming, but she didn't mind. She needed time to think, to gather her courage, and wanted to preserve her strength . . . just in case.

'Prompt as ever.' The voice didn't startle her as she looked up to see Ashes stepping out from the shadows when she finally arrived on the Cilirian shore. 'I'm here to be your guide.'

'I could've made it on my own.'

'I don't doubt it. But indulge me and my selfish vices.'

The witch stepped forward, closing the distance between them. When Ashes pressed her lips to Sapphire's, her body warmed at the touch. She deepened the kiss, her hands finding their place in Ashes' hair, and the girl smiled against her mouth.

'I have half a mind to keep you to myself tonight,' she whispered against Sapphire's lips.

'You're going to make me late.' Sapphire pulled away, her tone steadier than her feelings.

'Who am I to deny an opportune moment when it presents itself?' Ashes kissed her once more, her tongue dancing playfully along Sapphire's lower lip before pulling away and taking her hand.

'Follow me and stay close.'

From every direction, a creature stirred, birds called out, and small animals ran across their path, but Ashes never wavered.

'Can you tell me what's waiting for me?' Sapphire felt a rush of relief as she finally asked the question she had been thinking about all day.

'A ritual.' Sapphire halted and Ashes tugged on her hand, urging her forward. 'You won't need to use that dagger you have strapped to your thigh.'

Finally, the darkness broke, revealing too many witches to count seated in a circle around a large fire. They were about twenty steps away when Ashes dropped her hand.

'Pull your cloak up and follow me closely.' She searched Sapphire's face in the dim light of her orb. 'Breathe, Sapphire. Your questions will be answered tonight.'

'I'm not sure I can –'

The witch pressed her hand to Sapphire's cheek, instantly calming her erratic heart.

'You can and you will. I will be there. I won't let anything hurt you.'

'I'm still scared,' Sapphire confessed.

'Of what?'

'The truth, I guess,' Sapphire whispered.

'Good,' Ashes murmured back. 'That means you're not a complete fool.'

'I feel like one.'

'You're brave,' Ashes sighed, running her thumb gently across her cheek, 'and beautiful.'

Sapphire found Ashes' eyes and leaned into the girl's palm for a bit longer before pulling back.

A fire burned brightly in the dark as the coven came into view. Each witch wore a dress of pure white, with an oversized ruby hanging from her neck. An altar had been constructed in front of the flames, covered in huge jewels and hung with a garland. Large tomes were stacked neatly at its foot.

As Sapphire looked to Ashes, the witch clipped her own jewel around her throat, the glimmering stone flush against her pale skin.

As they stepped into view, the coven – and even the flames – seemed to still.

Ashes cleared her throat, signalling for Sapphire to remove her hood and step into the circle.

'Princess,' Esadora called out, walking towards her. 'You came.' Sapphire bowed her head in respect as the woman continued. 'The ritual is about to begin.'

Sapphire followed the woman, expecting to take a seat near the outer circle, but instead, she was led to the altar.

'Tonight, you are the Anointed One, princess. Gifts and offerings will be bestowed, and stories will be told. Are you ready?'

Sapphire blinked, only half following what the woman was saying. Still, she hadn't waited this long to turn back now. So, she nodded, and Esadora helped her take a place on the altar.

The fire doubled in size as she settled in and Esadora smiled.

'My sisters, tonight is the night prophesied since the beginning. A thousand years in the making. This child is the answer to the prayers you have been sending to our beloved Ryvinika. Bestow the prophetic offerings to the Anointed One. It is time.'

Sapphire watched with wide eyes as they lined up in front of her. One by one, they bowed their heads and placed their offerings at her feet. She searched for Ashes, finally finding her. The witch stared straight ahead, though – Savina watching her closely. When they arrived, Savina and Ashes did as the other witches had done, falling to their knees. A necklace, art, a bottle of wine: Savina offered it all before bowing her head, muttering words of gratitude for Sapphire's bravery and arrival.

Soon, it was only Ashes who knelt before her.

'You are the only queen I will ever bow to,' Ashes whispered, placing a small, smooth stone that was as white as the moon atop the pile of gifts that surrounded her.

Sapphire wanted to reach out for her, her fingers desperate to feel the girl's skin against her own, but Ashes simply bowed her head once more and moved aside, allowing others to pay their respects. The gifts grew – wildflowers and sparkling potions in jars. And she remained still, her eyes tracking every move.

Finally, Esadora arrived. With shaking hands, she placed a small floral crown atop Sapphire's head. The red clashed with the blue dress she wore.

'Do you accept these offerings?'

Sapphire scanned the piles that surrounded her.

'Yes. I accept.'

Esadora smiled and patted her hand.

'Then,' the fire grew, crackling wildly behind her, 'let us begin.'

Esadora turned her face to the moon, lifting her hands, and the coven followed suit. Sapphire could have sworn the moon darkened as they did so.

'Ryvinika, we call on thee to show the way of the world. Do you accept our humble plea?'

Sapphire looked to the moon, half expecting it to fall from the sky, but it remained and the silence around her was suffocating. But then, she heard it.

The voice. Clearer than usual, like whoever it belonged to was sitting beside her.

Tell them I accept, child.

Sapphire stiffened. Ashes had been right, it was Ryvinika who spoke to her. Esadora smiled, nodding her head.

Why me?

She asked the question in her head, and a tickle of laughter ran up her spine.

Speak for me.

'She accepts.' Sapphire's voice was tight with anxiety. 'I-I can hear her.'

A humming spread through the circle as their eyes remained on her.

Sapphire shivered despite the fire, and the coven dropped their hands.

'The world was once different. A world where people like us were not cast out but celebrated, feared, and exalted.'

It was then that the fire surrounded Sapphire, dancing around her feet, lapping at her skin, but it did not burn her. She opened her mouth to scream, but her voice was stolen.

She blinked as the flames came to life, painting a picture so vivid she felt ill. The rolling hills of Eriobis appeared, and images of people crowded the frame. Some manipulated air, others fire, water, and earth, and then there was one whose magic came to life in a very different way.

A Shadow Witch.

'But our people grew powerful. More powerful than any manipulator.' The flames shifted, revealing a woman twisting her hands wildly. An explosion occurred and the flame shifted again, revealing her and a large creature.

'Creatures born of shadows, spells born of magic this world had not known before, and Ryvinika was the best of them all. The magic that ran through her veins was pure. But her power frightened the high bloods.'

As it should have, the voice cooed. *I would have swallowed the world whole if they allowed it.*

The flames danced aside to reveal a gruesome scene. A battle in the darkness, unexpected and bloody.

'It was in the night that the manipulators attacked the coven. As we slept peacefully, they appeared, drowning, burning, destroying the souls that existed inside the coven. But Ryvinika was stronger, and she called upon her power to awaken the coven and defend our home.'

The shadow creatures came to life, destroying all enemies who stood before them. Sapphire flinched as bodies fell lifeless.

'And so, the war waged on, the witches led by Ryvinika. But before long, after countless, bloody frays, she feared they could not carry the weight of losing another precious soul. So she surrendered.'

An image of the coven being escorted through the very forest Sapphire stumbled through nightly came into view.

'And the Shattered Lands were born. Still, as the high houses built the barrier, Ryvinika pronounced a prophecy. One they should fear. One that would be their undoing.'

Sapphire shifted. Her eyes darted around, but she could not see past the flames.

Pay attention, child. All will be revealed.

Sapphire sat up straight, focusing on Esadora's voice.

'A blessed child would be born into royal blood – only to be ripped from her mother's breast. Lost to this world until her eighteenth year. This child would be gifted with powers, unrivalled by all but Ryvinika herself. This child would be the answer, the prophet of justice. This child would be the undoing of the world. The beginning of the end.'

Tears formed in Sapphire's eyes at the realization. She was simply a girl. She was no prophet.

Another whisper of a laugh and she closed her eyes tightly.

Oh, child. There is an answer.

'There are many secrets of the world, my sisters. Secrets that are destined to never be answered. But there is one that we do know. The princess is a child of the Shattered Lands. Stolen from the other side by trickery and deceit,' Esadora continued.

The fire once again shifted, revealing the barrier. The king and queen stood before it, soon joined by a man carrying a baby. As he handed the child over, Sapphire watched in horror as the man's throat was slit. His body collapsed at their feet before being rolled back through the barrier. The king and queen raised their hands to close it once more.

The sight made her sick, unravelled her thread by thread. This couldn't be real. This wasn't possible.

She was Kip and Araxia's daughter. A child of royal Canmore blood. This vision couldn't be true. She looked like Aylara, like Araxia. She was a Canmore.

'And just as Ryvinika had foretold ages ago, the child slipped away, the prophecy in action. Ryvinika's prophecy – a child born into royal blood – not of it. And when you returned here, eighteen years to the day, we knew you were the one we have been waiting for.'

The fire showed the image of Sapphire in the throne room, Ashes with the dagger in her hand. She tried to stand but something slammed into her, holding her down.

Face the greatness to which you were born.

'I do not take orders from you.'

The fire flared, a silent warning from Ryvinika to obey.

Sapphire did as the witch commanded as Esadora continued.

'Ryvinika, please guide us.'

Sapphire felt a shift, an alleviation of pressure she hadn't realized was there and she watched as the fire took on a form, walking to the middle of the coven.

'Hello, my sisters.'

The coven dropped to their knees. Ryvinika turned to look at Sapphire – and Sapphire almost emptied her stomach into the dirt. She looked exactly like her.

'I once had a sister, Aylara, who was desperate to free herself from the life she was born into. Ashamed of her Shadow Witch heritage. And so she took to praying in the elemental temples, joining the elementals at their tables, and when the time came for battle, she betrayed her own. She whispered our secrets – about the coven, about me – giving them exactly what they needed to defeat me. They stole my life – or thought they did, at least.'

Aylara.

Oh, mercy. The original queen. The woman who had fascinated Sapphire since her arrival. Her namesake. All those ripped pages . . . Aylara was a descendant . . .

'The Elders came to adore her – offering her a rare favour. The gift of the elemental powers she longed for. And so, the Canmore bloodline was born, water wielders who would bear one daughter per generation – the future queens of Eriobis. And her bloodline continued for centuries – until Araxia Canmore. Barren: heartbreaking for the dynasty. The possible end of the infamous Canmore queens. And that's when a plan was devised. Because while the bloodline of the Canmores grew . . . my own did as well.'

Ryvinika moved closer to Sapphire, who forced herself to remain still, forced herself not to look away from the woman's sinister stare.

'A deal was struck. A child of my bloodline would be brought forward in exchange for the freedom of those who resided in the Shattered Lands. The barrier would be brought down, and we would live in peace.

'And so, you were born. Small and feisty from the moment your cry pierced the world – stealing your mother's final breath as you left the womb. The child was presented through a hole in the barrier, where it was weakened just enough for a small passage accessible to those of pure blood, all while the Shattered Lands celebrated – preparing for a new life. But the queen did not hold up her end of the agreement; the barrier was sealed, reinforced even, locking away our people once more.'

The figure was close now – too close – and Sapphire could no longer feign bravado as she shied away from its menacing grin.

'And so Aylara Canmore was created. Named after my lovely sister. They tried to hide my blood running through your veins, but they failed. They will always fail because magic – power – is not so easily silenced.' Ryvinika turned to face Sapphire. 'For a thousand years I have awaited you. Months I have bided my time as you adjusted. But you have done well, my child – won the hearts of those around you. And when you take the throne, you can finally bring justice to this coven. A queen worth bowing to.'

The flame engulfed Sapphire, the feeling of burning fingers pressing into her eyes and an inhuman scream escaping her lips.

When the figure stepped away, she had expected the world to be dark, blindness to have taken her over. But the coven remained, staring at her in astonishment.

'Our hope and salvation. She with the violet eyes.'

Sapphire was hyperventilating, tearing at her skin with her nails. She reached for a looking glass from the offering pile and realized the green of her eyes was gone, and she fought the urge to vomit.

'It's not me,' Sapphire finally managed to squeak out. 'I am not the prophet you seek.'

But Ryvinika just smiled, walking over to her and placing a heavy hand on her shoulders.

'Call it what you like, my child. But you are the Anointed One. The goddess of strife and slaughter and the bringer of justice for our people.'

'I'm not one of you.'

'Rise to your feet.' Ryvinika's voice was harsh, and the coven stood. Their eyes were wide with admiration as they took in Sapphire and the goddess before her. 'The prophecy is in motion. May you burn the world as they have burned those who came before you.'

And then the fire went out, leaving them in darkness. Esadora brought it back to life, and Sapphire stood alone. Ryvinika had gone with the flame.

'I know the prophecy is a heavy gift, but –'

'I am no Anointed One. No bringer of justice or long-awaited prophet. I am the future queen of Eriobis, a Canmore.'

A grey-haired older woman stepped forward, her eyes tired.

'We pledge our loyalties to the queen we know. To the prophet. To the chosen one.'

'No,' Sapphire whined. 'I am not –' Her words were lost in tears as her shoulders began to shake, and she crouched to the ground, overtaken by it all. Her eyes darted around, searching for Ashes, who was nowhere to be found.

The coven surrounded her, careful to not touch her but close enough to offer her support, and she allowed their presence till she had no tears left to cry. Finally, she forced herself up on shaky legs, and grabbed the stone that Ashes had left atop the pile of offerings.

'I must go.'

'My queen, it is hours till the sunrise.'

'I need to go.'

Esadora bowed her head, and the coven parted, offering Sapphire a clear path to the forest.

Anger coursed through her – anger at the coven, at prophecies, at false truths, and maybe at fate. Without another word, she slipped her hood back over her head and barrelled into the forest.

Lighting a flame in her palm, no longer trying to deny her own power, she trekked along the path, trying to follow the steps that Ashes had led them down just hours before. Fifteen minutes had passed when a hand caught her arm, and she whirled around, nearly burning its owner.

'Sapphire, it's me.' She met Ashes' eyes, the light of the

flame casting menacing shadows on the girl's face. 'It's just me.'

'Did you know?' the girl spat, venom dripping from her words.

'Sapphire,' the witch pleaded.

'Did you know!' she shouted back, her voice echoing against the dense trees.

'I knew you were a part of the prophecy but didn't know the extent of it, I swear.'

Sapphire turned away from her.

'Please, Sapphire.' Desperation rolled thick from the girl's lips. She reached out but Sapphire pulled away.

'I wouldn't do that to you,' Ashes whispered. 'I would never do that to you.'

She regarded Ashes and believed the panic she saw. 'Do you believe it? Believe that I'm –'

'I believe that you're the Anointed One – but only you can decide what to do with that fact.'

'What would you do?'

Ashes sighed. 'My opinion doesn't matter.'

Sapphire put her head into her hands, trying to make sense of something – anything – she had learned at the base of that altar.

'I have seen,' Ashes started, rocking nervously on her heels, 'many atrocities in my life. Our homelands burned, our crops destroyed, our altars left shattered and broken on the floor. All while Eriobis thrived. If we were sick, we relied on our old magic to save us. If we were hungry, we prayed to those who came before us to help us survive. I saw my people banished to a barren wasteland meant to destroy us. While the people of this place you're so desperate to cling to sat by and cheered on our misery. Celebrated it. Their favourite sport to pass the time.'

'I didn't know,' Sapphire said quietly.

'But it never broke us. We exist because we believe in our magic. In our world. In our coven. And despite the hatred, despite the killing – despite it all, we still find ourselves capable of loving Eriobis.'

Sapphire flinched at the honesty, at the unconcealed brokenness that rang out in her voice. Ashes noticed. 'You wanted my opinion, my queen. You will hear it.'

Gently grabbing Sapphire's chin, forcing her to look into her eyes, to face her, Ashes continued. 'I think, if I was the one that was prophesied, the anointed, a true child of Ryvinika, I'd set this world ablaze and dance across the kindling. I'd rip the nobles from their houses to make them watch and laugh when they begged for mercy. I'd make them feel every scratch, every bruise, every tear spilled by my people.'

Sapphire tried to jerk back, but Ashes' fingers held her firm. 'I'd lay waste to everything I found.'

'Stop – please,' Sapphire begged, her eyes brimming with tears. 'Just st–'

'But I'm not the chosen one, Sapphire.' Ashes' eyes were wild as they ran across her face, studying her. 'You are. It is your path, you have to decide which way it goes. No one else can.'

Sapphire chewed her bottom lip, considering what that could mean for her, for her future, for her witch.

'What would I need to do,' Sapphire said softly, 'to fulfil the prophecy?'

Ashes bowed her head, her hand falling from Sapphire's chin before pressing her palms together, praying for something Sapphire didn't understand.

'The barrier.' The slight tremor in her voice betrayed her. 'The final words of the prophecy say that you'll be the one to tear it down.'

Chapter Thirty-six

She wished her surroundings looked more familiar, but truthfully, she wasn't entirely sure she was in the right place. It was still dark, and much of Aleburn looked the same in the moonlight.

Still, as she stood there, she sensed that this was the place where she had awoken months ago. The place where this had all begun. Anger, regret, heartbreak coursed through her. They felt toxic and all-consuming as she stared out into the flat lands before her.

A prophecy. An Anointed One. A stolen child.

Araxia and Kip had been lying to her since the day she had arrived. An angry sob overtook her as she remembered the first time Araxia had looked at her on the training ground. A look so full of love and support born from a demented history. She recalled the first time she realized she looked like Araxia. She remembered the first time she had called her mother.

The memories made her feel ill.

Liars. Traitors. Murderers.

Unjust and unfair – and she had fallen for all of it. She had trusted them. She had allowed them in, allowed herself to be their daughter. She had forgone her questions and suspicions, and she had done so because she was weak. For so long she had dreamed of a family, and at the first chance of having one, she had buckled. A fool draped in jewels and priceless fabric.

A strangled scream passed her lips and her magic flared, the ground around her bursting into flame.

She was not a Canmore. A Canmore couldn't set fire to the world. The fire swelled at the realization, devouring the very ground she stood on. Everything in sight was taken by the flames. Her flames. Not the flames of a Canmore heir.

She raised her hand, and felt the rain come next. It extinguished the fire, soaking her dress, and she gave in to her buckling knees, sinking to the ground.

The people hadn't believed in her when she arrived. The people had been wary.

And they had been right.

She was a fraud. She was a danger. She was born of what they all feared.

As she lay there, the rain intensified like it was listening to the sound of her broken heart. But the sadness was slipping away quickly, replaced by pulsating anger. The rain shifted to a hungry storm. Lightning split the sky in two.

She sat there and watched the world tremble under her own creation and she laughed. A broken, manic sound that filled the tense air around her.

'Maybe they've earned it,' she whispered to herself. 'Maybe I should bring the barrier down. This kingdom is founded on lies.'

She clenched her jaw when she realized that was what Ashes had been warning her of all along.

Hours passed. The moon still ruled the sky when she began making the trek back to Astral, but her feet took her in another direction, and before she knew it, the Viottos' cottage was before her.

The windows were darkened – no one was awake inside – and she felt another roll of nausea as she remembered her trembling footsteps when she had first arrived here. She was no longer that scared girl, but she was just as broken.

Hoisting herself on to the stone roof, she moved to the window she knew belonged to her friend and tapped on it gently. The window was thrown open a few seconds later, a sleepy and worried Evera standing there.

'Sapphire? What are you doing here?'

'I need – I –'

Evera stepped to the side to allow her entry into her room. Sapphire had hardly taken two steps before she collapsed into Evera's tiny frame. Devastation rocked her to the core. Evera held her tightly, rubbing her back. The girl asked no questions as she escorted her to her bed.

'Did they hurt you?'

Sapphire shook her head.

'Sapphire, what did they do to you?' Evera's voice was tight with worry, and Sapphire finally met her gaze.

She couldn't lose the girl in front of her. She couldn't handle that. If Evera walked away . . . she feared she might come entirely undone. She needed – reassurance. A promise that Evera would remain by her side even if Sapphire wasn't who the girl thought she was.

'I need your word. I need you to promise you won't abandon me – that you'll still be my best friend.'

Evera frowned. 'Of course. Nothing you could tell me would change that.'

Sapphire nodded, but she feared Evera would change her mind when she knew the terrible truth.

'Have you heard of the prophecy?'

Evera looked confused.

'A prophecy?'

'One exists within the Shadow Witch community. A thousand-year-old prophecy spoken into the world by Ryvinika, the woman they consider the original Shadow Witch, and the most powerful ever to exist. She revealed the prophecy as the Elders sealed her behind the barrier.'

'OK,' Evera said warily.

'It is said that a child will be born to bring justice to the Shadow Witches.' Sapphire took a shaky breath. 'And the coven believes that I am that child. That I am – a direct descendant of Ryvinika.'

'But how would that be possible, seeing that you are –?'

Sapphire cut her question short. Words spilled from her as she told her friend everything, from the visions in the fire to Ryvinika coming to life, a spitting image of herself. She told her about the offerings, the promises, the admiration.

And then, with the pale stone in her hands, her gift from Ashes, she explained the final revelation of the prophecy – the barrier falling at her hand.

Evera sat silently, taking in every word. Once she finished, she was quiet and thoughtful.

'Do you believe it?' Evera asked.

'Do you?'

Evera fidgeted with the ring on her finger. 'I don't know. It – it might make sense.'

At the admission, it struck Sapphire that Evera had a point. The Shadow Witches' involvement in her birth and her return, her eyes, the voice in her head. There were so many holes in the story they had woven, and so much information was fighting for space in her head that she hadn't pieced it all together – or tried to – to see that the fragments didn't fit.

She had known. She had been correct to question the king and queen, to not trust a word that left their lips. She had been right.

They had lied to her: over dinner, over lunch, in the gardens, in the throne room. They had lied to her while looking her directly in the eye.

And Araxia, the woman who she had come to love and admire . . .

Mercy, had they ever been honest with her about anything? Or was she just another necessary step in the continuance of the Canmore reign?

Did they even . . . love her as one should love a daughter? Or were they just desperate to retain control of a broken country?

Her heart ached at her own ignorance but burned with conviction.

'It would be much easier if I didn't believe them, wouldn't it?'

Evera nodded. Sapphire longed for her friend's wisdom. Evera's guidance was always level-headed and assured, always leading her in the proper direction, but the girl offered none.

'May I ask you a question? And you'll tell me the truth?' Evera finally asked.

'Of course.'

Evera shifted uncomfortably, like she was nervous for what she was about to say.

'If it was true and you were part of the prophecy, would you fulfil the final revelation?'

The question brought Sapphire pause, and she returned her gaze to the clouds and found the sky had cleared entirely – the moon bright overhead.

Would she?

Frankly, if she thought long enough about it – about the images that danced in the fire and the desperate confessions made by Ashes about their mistreatment – she might.

But she wouldn't allow herself to think about it. Not for long enough to drive her insane.

'No. I wouldn't.'

And she believed the words as they left her mouth.

But then she felt the smallest brush of hands wrapping around her throat, and her eyes darted around the room. Evera didn't notice.

Don't worry, my child. I've waited a thousand years. I don't mind waiting for you to realize who you are.

The return of Ryvinika's voice was too much for her to handle, so she pushed away from the bed, bouncing on her toes as if she hadn't spent the past few hours trapped in her worst nightmare.

'May I visit you in the library tomorrow?'

Evera agreed but Sapphire didn't miss the concerned look in her eyes. And she wondered if her own concern was as obvious.

Preparation.

That seemed to be all she did these days. Preparation for becoming queen, preparation for the wedding. The process chipped away at her, carving her into the perfect heir. Kaian stood beside her tirelessly. He took her hand when he was expected to. He guided her when she couldn't bring herself to navigate the small talk and political agendas hidden behind polite conversation.

Araxia slammed the gavel, signalling the meeting was over and making Sapphire jump. She hurried to gather her things before she could be cornered into a conversation she didn't need, and rushed out of the room with Claye on her heels.

'You have –'

Sapphire turned to look at him with a pleading expression.

'I'm begging you. Please. Allow me an hour off.'

'How do you expect me –'

'Lie, Claye. I expect you to lie. Tell them I am unwell, tell them it is my time of the month and I need rest, tell them anything. But I am begging you to grant me this one kindness.'

Claye sighed, running a hand through his hair.

'One hour, princess. That is it and then I'm going to come and gather you from the library.'

Sapphire half smiled at his certainty that that was where she was headed.

'You have my word.'

'The clock is ticking. Go.'

She hurried towards the library, her dress flying behind her. Only when she was safely inside did she allow herself to breathe.

'Claye set you free?' Evera asked, ushering her towards their private corner.

'For one hour.'

Evera smiled as she settled on the couch, Sapphire resting her head against a cushion.

'The governors were that insufferable?'

'Evera, if I hear about the oversupply of grain one more time –'

The door to the library opened and shut and Sapphire slumped down, trying to hide. Surely Claye hadn't already come to retrieve her? They both stared towards the entrance, only relaxing when they saw Kaian's familiar blond hair.

'You ran off without me,' he said as he sat across from them.

'I couldn't take any chances.'

The group laughed but an awkward silence followed and Sapphire finally sighed.

'You can stop acting like this. You are both aware of the situation.'

Kaian relaxed slightly. 'Are you going to tell me what happened?'

She dived back into the story, telling the night for the second time – Evera filling in details that she missed on this telling. Kaian listened with wide eyes, his shock apparent as the story went on. Once she finished, they found an area of the garden hidden from view and sat on the grass, the early afternoon sun warm on their skin.

'You can't possibly believe that is true,' said Kaian.

Evera and Sapphire exchanged a look that only they could understand, and Sapphire frowned. She wondered how she was supposed to move forward in this marriage. She wondered how she was expected to rule a country when she knew what she knew.

'I'm not sure what I believe.'

'Sapphire, you look exactly like your mother. Like Queen Aylara. And I've done plenty of studying – there's no other bloodline of your mother's anywhere in history. They orchestrated this to scare you, and it obviously worked if you believe that this could even be possible.'

'Kaian, have you not realized that the history we are fed is not always the entire truth?' Evera's voice had an edge that Sapphire didn't hear often. 'There are thousands of books in the library that are not available to anyone but the highest-level scholars. Those books could tell an entirely different story of our history.'

'Of course,' Kaian said. 'But this much history and

cover-up of mistreatment seem highly unlikely. Either way, the final revelation would be impossible. No one could ever bring the barrier down. It's the most powerful magic in the world.'

Sapphire chewed the inside of her cheek. To be doubted so boldly made something inside her stir. A thirst to prove herself, to prove her power. To prove him wrong. He meant well, but it stoked the monster inside her.

Foolish boy. He could never understand what you're capable of. Unless you prove it to him. Why don't you show him just what you can do?

The words sounded bitter in her mind, and she pushed the voice away.

A few more minutes passed, and she relaxed a little, grateful she had been successful. But then the familiar brush against her brain came, and the voice followed.

I know you because I once was you. But you won't make the same mistakes. You won't give them the chance to defeat you.

Kaian and Evera were arguing in hushed tones.

Sapphire closed her eyes tightly, trying to force the touch from her mind. A gentle hand on her arm caused her to jump, and she was met with the concerned stares of her two friends.

'Sapphire, are you OK?' Kaian asked.

'I'm fine,' she said, toying with the ends of her dark hair. 'I'm fine. Just tired.'

'You know, it's OK if part of you believes it. You know that, right?' Evera said.

Sapphire looked up from the flowers she had been picking. 'Are you sure about that?'

Evera shrugged.

'I hope so. Because part of me almost believes it, and I'm not sure what that says about me. I want to – to tell you it's not possible to still your worries. But I think everyone deserves to know the truth about where they came from, even if it's not to their liking.'

'And if it is true, what does that mean?' Sapphire said quietly.

'I don't know,' she said honestly. 'But I'll be here for you, regardless.'

Nine days had passed since the Shadow Moon, and Sapphire struggled to keep herself grounded.

Currently, she sat at lunch, gripping her fork a bit too tightly.

'Sapphire, are you listening? This is critical.' Sapphire snapped her eyes up from her plate, meeting the queen's narrowed gaze. 'Where has your head been? I feel like you've hardly been present.'

'I attend every meal, every etiquette session, every briefing you feel I am suited for. I'm not sure what else I could offer you.'

The older woman arched a cautionary eyebrow, warning Sapphire to watch her mouth, but Sapphire didn't care.

'Tell me what else you want from me. Tell me what I could do better. Tell me how I am falling short of this perfect, ideal image you had for your daughter.'

'Sapphire,' Araxia choked. 'I would never –'

Sapphire couldn't listen to another lie roll off the woman's lips. She couldn't.

'I apologize for not being the daughter you feel you deserve. The daughter you wanted.'

Araxia's expression was a mess of panic and alarm. She stood, closing the distance between them. At her touch, Sapphire pulled away.

'Something is wrong. Please talk to me,' the queen begged. 'Just tell me what you need . . . whatever it is . . . and I will do it.'

Sapphire's breath was short and desperate. 'I need to be excused.'

Araxia bowed her head with an expression so heartbreaking that it made Sapphire's stomach turn.

'When you are ready . . . I will be here. No matter the time or day, know I am here.'

Sapphire pushed away from the table with shaking hands. As she headed for the door, she refused to look back, afraid that if she did, she might break in two.

Sapphire could not shake the memory of the lunch with Araxia. It chased her through restless sleep and down the dark corridors as she slipped into the lake, heading towards the one place she had been avoiding, with the white stone Ashes had given her in her pocket.

She wasn't sure if it would protect her, but she hoped that it would help her find the witch, at least. As she entered the forest the numbness that had clung to her since the revelation of the prophecy remained.

And she wondered for a moment what would happen if she just lay down on the forest floor and let the world take her body, let her magic run back into the dirt she had apparently been created from, and ceased to exist.

'It's been some time since you've graced this forest with your presence, highness.' Ashes stood behind her. She did not smile as Sapphire turned to face her.

'How did you know I was out here?'

'The stone – I can track my own magic when it's close enough. I sensed it the moment you stepped on the shore.'

Sapphire nodded, stepping away from the girl, wrapping her own arms around herself. She couldn't look the witch in the eye.

'Look at me, Sapphire.'

Like a chastised child, she lifted her own eyes to meet Ashes'.

'You're still taking the potion,' the witch deadpanned.

'Of course I am. I –'

'You no longer have to hide yourself. Why must you insist on being so afraid of who you are?'

'You are a fool if you believe it is that simple,' Sapphire spat.

'I am no fool.'

A long-forgotten bitterness lingered between them.

'You didn't warn me,' Sapphire finally said. Her voice sounded tired and worn down.

'I gave you all I could offer you. I did my best.'

'It wasn't enough.'

Ashes closed the distance between them, taking

Sapphire's wrist in her hand. Despite her anger, the girl's touch was a balm to her frayed nerves.

'You know everything now. You know the power that runs through your veins, you know what was done, and you waste time being angry with me.' The girl stared down at her. 'I have been waiting patiently for the knowledge to be offered to you so I could – so we could exist in peace.'

Sapphire paused at *we*. It was such a foreign word – they were never able to consider the future where *we* could exist. But the feeling was fleeting as the familiar anger returned.

'Peace?' Sapphire gave a harsh laugh. 'You believe I will find peace with what I know?'

Ashes tilted her head before kissing Sapphire. Sapphire was too tired to fight it. The only peace she could find came at the brush of the girl's lips. The world slipped away as Ashes pulled her in close, backing her into a tree, and Sapphire locked her hands around the back of the girl's neck.

With the swipe of Ashes' tongue, Sapphire allowed the kiss to be deepened, and they melted into one another. She felt the weight of all she knew fall away with it, and she savoured it as the girl hiked up the skirts of her dress, her hand finding the warm skin of Sapphire's thigh.

A throaty moan slipped past Sapphire's lips and Ashes devoured it, a feral sense taking the girl over as she moved her lips to Sapphire's neck.

She slipped the thick strap of Sapphire's dress from her shoulder, tracing kisses over her collarbone.

Sapphire's head lolled back, and she closed her eyes

tightly. But it was a mistake as she instantly saw the images of fire and shadows, a barrier crumbling, and bodies strewn across the land.

'Stop,' Sapphire sighed. 'Please, Ashes. I need –'

Ashes stepped away abruptly, bowing her head.

'What do you need?'

'I need . . . I need to talk about this.' Sapphire realized she was on the verge of a panic attack. Ashes seemed to notice at the same time, pulling Sapphire to her chest and holding her there until her breathing gave way to a normal pace. 'I'm afraid that the prophecy is real,' Sapphire finally admitted. 'I'm afraid that this is the beginning of the end.'

Ashes gave her a dreamy smile.

'An ending is necessary for a new and better beginning.'

'And you think that if I bring the barrier down that it will be a better beginning? Eriobis can exist in harmony with whatever is beyond it?'

'It's written in the prophecy – prosperity for the nation of Eriobis, unity to be found.'

'Why wasn't I told that?'

'Because these are decisions you should be making on your own. Not for the greater good – but because you believe in a better world for the coven.'

'Will you get in trouble for telling me?'

'No. The ritual broke all bonds that held me.'

Sapphire nodded, studying the world around her.

'Have you considered,' Ashes began, 'that with this prophecy . . . it could mean our story might end much differently than we ever expected?'

Sapphire arched an eyebrow in confusion.

'You are the Anointed One, Sapphire. You and only you can bring me and my people out of the darkness we have been forced into. Only you can break the Elders' hold. You can make the world different – what we both wished for.'

'But at what cost?' Sapphire whispered.

Ashes took that cue to swallow her words, kissing her once more, and Sapphire let go of her questions and worries, allowing herself to indulge in the one thing that made sense.

CHAPTER THIRTY-SEVEN

It was a warm night. The glow of the stars overhead was enchanting as she approached the water's edge. It was late. Kip and Araxia were asleep, and the workers had gone home for the night. She was alone. And as she stared up at the sky, she couldn't shake the question: *Why?*

Why me?

As she looked out at the water, the faintest glint of violet caught her attention. She looked closer, tracking it as it made its way towards her. She did not shrink in fear; instead she remained on the shore, a few feet away from the water, waiting for the monster to visit her.

Ryvinika appeared, a ghost of her former self.

'Evening, my child.'

'Ryvinika.'

The figure stopped at the water's edge.

'You do not run from me?'

'I do not run.'

'You have questions you hope I will answer.'

Sapphire nodded, staring out at the water.

'Ask.'

Sapphire took a deep breath before finally turning to

look at the apparition beside her. 'If I do not accept the prophecy, what will happen?'

'The prophecy is not yours to accept or refuse. The prophecy is a part of you. You are, in many ways, the prophecy itself. It is inevitable.'

Sapphire stiffened. 'The future can always be changed.'

Ryvinika chuckled. 'My visions are final.'

'I won't bring the barrier down.' Sapphire sat up a bit straighter at the words, realizing she meant them. 'Not for you. Not for anyone.'

Sapphire could have sworn she felt the heat rippling off the witch. She shuddered at the sensation as the ghost moved up the shore until their eyes were level.

'Now, now, we both know that's not true. Not with your fondness for the witch.'

Sapphire froze, chilled at the mention of Ashes. 'She has no place in the conversation.'

'Of course she does. You might not bring down the barrier for the likes of me, but what about your beloved? How far would you go to protect your witch?'

Sapphire knew a threat when she heard one. 'Don't lay a hand on her.'

Ryvinika laughed again, eating away at Sapphire's patience.

'The monster you know, child, is the danger you should fear.'

Sapphire considered the witch's words, a heavy feeling settling on her chest. She felt Ryvinika's cold touch on her shoulder.

'I am afraid.' Sapphire hadn't meant to admit that out loud.

'Fear is not an enemy; it is a guide.'

Sapphire stared out at the lake once more, refusing to meet the woman's unsettling eyes as she began to move back towards the water. 'Destiny can be put off but never avoided, my child. Remember that.'

Sapphire kept her eyes closed for a few moments, and when she opened them once more, she was alone.

The lake no longer felt like home, and Sapphire rushed back into the castle and locked the doors behind her.

That night, her dreams were nothing but nightmares of war and destruction, and Ashes was at the heart of it. Her bones broken, her shadows stolen, her heart ripped from her chest. They hoisted her upon a wooden platform, and Sapphire screamed as flames were brought to life in the palms of her subjects – aimed at the girl she –

As fire met Ashes' skin, an inhuman scream ripped from her chest. Sapphire shot from her bed, rushing to the washroom. Staring at her own reflection, she tried to calm herself. Her skin was slick with sweat, her chest rising and falling harshly with uneven breaths.

She remained there until the sun broke the horizon.

Despite her exhaustion from a day packed with rehearsals and planning, Sapphire tossed and turned, unable to escape the vivid nightmare that consumed her every time she closed her eyes. She saw Ashes bruised and bloodied. She smelled smoke, heard the scream. Oh, mercy, that scream.

She needed to see Ashes, to feel her touch, and hear her voice. She needed to know that she was OK.

So it was really no surprise when she stumbled up the shore of Ciliria. She searched the dark forest, longing to simply see Ashes in the flesh. She just needed a moment of relief from the images of her death that were so vivid in her mind. She fingered Ashes' white stone in her pocket.

'I'm flattered you're still carrying that stone, princess.'

Sapphire whirled around to find Ashes leaning against a tall oak tree. She rushed towards her, wrapping her arms around the witch. Ashes pulled her close, raising her slightly off the ground in an embrace.

'I'm so happy to see you.' Sapphire breathed in the girl's familiar scent, her mind instantly slowing.

'Were you not expecting to?'

She considered telling Ashes about the visions of death . . . her death . . . that had been haunting her mind for days now, but she didn't want to ruin this precious stolen night.

'Of course I was. I just – can I not just be happy to see you?'

'I suppose it's better than a knife to my neck.' Ashes' lips quirked upward, her eyes playful as she pulled Sapphire closer. 'Maybe.'

Ashes kissed her and the world fell away like it always did. The witch's magic might be powerful, but her ability to make Sapphire feel like the only person in the world was beyond any power this world could offer.

'Now, to what do I owe the pleasure?'

Sapphire frowned at the question.

'Do I always need a reason to seek you out? Can I not just visit?'

'You can do whatever you please, Sapphire. Your presence is always welcome to me.'

Sapphire took a seat and tried to brush off her lingering irritation. She leaned against the witch, and Ashes wrapped her arms around Sapphire. It was peaceful, exactly what she needed, but her mind could never halt entirely.

She and Ashes had hardly confessed any secrets about themselves and their pasts, always too focused on unravelling the next mystery around them. But right now, Sapphire wanted to know more – even more than that, she wanted Ashes to know more . . . to want to know more. She sighed loudly, and Ashes tightened her hold.

'Go on. Tell me your thoughts.'

Sapphire shifted to look the girl in the eyes.

'I hardly know anything about you.'

Ashes tilted her head slightly.

'That is because my past is entirely unimportant.' Sapphire stared at her and Ashes sighed. 'I was born and raised into a coven of fierce women. My father . . . well, he's not pertinent.'

'Why is he not important?'

'Because he is dead.' The witch's voice was so calm that it made Sapphire shiver.

'How did he die?'

Ashes gave her a grim smile.

'For powers like mine, sacrifices must be made. Offerings to the ancestors. The man who was my father paid a price that I am grateful for.' Sapphire swallowed the lump that had formed in her throat, refusing to consider the implications of Ashes' confession. 'I was trained from a young age, made a warrior of the shadows. The rest is rather unimportant.'

Sapphire nodded, watching as she clenched her jaw. She wanted to know every small detail of Ashes' upbringing, but she didn't want to lose the opportunity for the conversation to continue. She waited for the witch to ask about her own childhood, but the question never came.

'The polite thing would be to ask me about my childhood, Ashes.'

'I've never cared much for being polite.' Ashes smiled as she said it.

'Your avoidance is more irritating than usual today.'

Ashes snaked an arm around Sapphire's waist, pulling her closer. 'Tell me about the place you came from.'

The words burst from Sapphire's mouth with unstoppable force – like she was desperate to bare her soul entirely. The darkness, the never-ending shadowed land. The beasts that hunted in the nights. She explained the famine, her days spent in the haunted forest, searching for scraps of food. She told of the Home, of Martia, of the girls who felt like sisters. Shared clothes, small rooms, too many beds crammed into one room. The silence returned, more poignant.

'Why have you never asked about my home? About how I got here? Everyone else seems curious.'

Ashes shrugged, a thoughtful look on her face.

'I am much more interested in the present day than the ghosts of your past, highness. But tell me a secret about that land. One you've never told anyone.'

Sapphire's heart fluttered. This was a new type of intimacy . . . not one of feverish, bruising kisses and desperate hands, but a sort of closeness they had never explored before. And there was only one secret to share . . . she knew that. She took a deep breath.

'I always had . . . these visions. Visions of death and destruction. I watched as lives were taken . . . by water, by fire, by lightning. They were inescapable, haunting. I became so accustomed to death, to the smell, the sight of it.'

Ashes had gone rigid.

'They came unexpectedly, pulling me under in a way that felt endless. I tried for so many years to save the people in the visions, to spare one life from hell, but I failed. I failed every single time until –'

Sapphire stopped short as she studied Ashes. Her red hair danced in the wind, her black dress was splayed across the ground. Sapphire cut her eyes to her thin, pale hands, and something so familiar struck her.

But, mercy, that hand. That hair.

Her final vision before her arrival. She remembered the smallest detail of the withered hem of the girl's black dress, the thin hand and well-kept nails, and the glint of red hair like a beacon of safety amidst the storm.

She reached out, palming a lock of Ashes' hair. It was so familiar; how had she not seen it before?

'Ashes . . .'

The colour drained from Ashes' face, her eyes dragging upwards to meet Sapphire's.

'I-I need to make one more confession.'

Ashes nodded.

'The visions . . . I-I believe I was dreaming of . . . you.' Ashes failed to mask her shock as she stared at Sapphire. 'I think whatever magic or prophecy or damn trick of fate brought me back knew. I don't think I came here to find my family, my kingdom – I think it brought me here to find you.'

The iciness melted entirely from Ashes' features, a smile breaking across her beautiful face.

'I thought you weren't a believer in fool's magic,' she whispered as she leaned closer. 'But if that's true, then I must offer fate my gratitude for the rest of my life.'

Ashes brought her into a lingering kiss that was full of longing and a desperation. She tugged Sapphire closer, lifting her on to her lap, and the touch of skin on skin made Sapphire's brain unravel. Every question she had melted away at the touch of Ashes' fingers on her thigh.

She had been dreaming of this girl before she had known her. She had been running towards her before she knew of her existence. She had been working to save her before she had ever set foot in this barren land.

Damn a kingdom. Damn a crown. Damn the Gods, the barrier, and everything in between.

Ashes, this Shadow Witch, was the salvation she had been seeking.

*

Days later, Sapphire wasn't simply avoiding sleep. She feared it. The nightmare felt so real, and she couldn't shake the sensation of dread that had settled into her bones. Still, exhaustion was a strong opponent, and despite her fear, she fell into a restless slumber.

Ashes. Screaming. Reaching out. Crying.

Sapphire could not get to her as a crowd ripped her in two. But then she noticed Ashes was not alone, and suddenly, Sapphire saw herself being held down as she lashed out, trying to free herself.

And then she heard the chants.

Burn the witch.

Burn the witch.

Sapphire watched as her dream self turned to look at Ashes. The desperation they shared was so raw and broken that Sapphire couldn't watch any longer. She sat up in bed before vomiting all over the marble floor.

Burn the witch.

She was out of bed in a matter of seconds, reaching for her training suit and pulling back her hair, strapping the dagger to her thigh. The chants from her dreamland rang out in her mind.

Burn the witch.

She slipped along the corridor, the shadows aiding her, though she passed no one.

Burn the witch.

As she met the water, she could not shake the feeling of being watched. She tried to ignore the warning feeling in her gut telling her to return to her room and wait till morning.

Burn the witch.

She began to swim, desperately pulling herself away from the shore. She willed the girl to be in the forest when she arrived.

Burn the witch.

They would not touch her.

Sapphire stumbled on to the shore, eyes searching the area frantically.

'Ashes?'

Her voice echoed through the forest.

'Ashes? Please.'

She tried not to panic, to not let the fear consume her, but Ryvinika's words rang in her mind.

The monster you know, child, is the danger you should fear.

'Sapphire?'

Ashes stood nearby. Her eyes were wide with worry as she stared at Sapphire.

'You're safe.' Sapphire jumped to her feet, throwing her arms around the girl, pulling her in tightly.

'You sound surprised.'

'They hurt you. They –' An unexpected sob escaped her lips, and she refused to loosen her grip on the girl. 'They burned you.'

Ashes stepped back, far enough to cup Sapphire's face in her hands. 'Take a deep breath, highness.'

She opened her eyes finally to meet Ashes' gaze, blinking back tears. 'Sapphire.'

'Hmm?' the witch cooed.

'My name,' Sapphire whispered between shuddering sobs. 'Can't you just call me by my name?'

'Tell me,' her tone was soft, 'Sapphire. Tell me what happened.'

Sapphire stepped away from her touch, blinking a few times. When she met the girl's gaze, she found panic there. Panic that did not suit her. So Sapphire obliged, her voice tight as she described the secret dreams. The heavy weight of the images that settled within her chest. Ashes' screams. The desperation. The emptiness that followed.

When she finished, Ashes did not immediately speak. She did not reach out a hand to comfort Sapphire. She did nothing but stare out at the black water, her eyes dark like the storm that was forming overhead.

The witch began to pace the shore, rigid with panic. She was murmuring spells or prayers that Sapphire couldn't understand. Sapphire's frustration swelled.

'No twisted riddles, Ashes. Tell me what is happening.'

The monsters you know, child, are about to show their teeth.

'Leave us,' Sapphire seethed, pushing Ryvinika away inside her head, and she moved towards Ashes. The presence left without a fight.

'Please, Ashes – just talk to me.'

'For years, the barrier has been weakening. Long before

either of us walked this land, the magic began to wither away. And despite the gifts and offerings presented by your people, the Elders have not responded. Surveyors studied the fractures, trying to make sense of the failing magic. There is no answer . . . or not one your people want to believe. Have you not noticed the king and queen's absence?'

'I –' Sapphire's voice caught, and she realized how foolish she had been lately. So wrapped up in her own world that she never even noticed the decline in family dinners, in lessons, in time spent together. She had never wondered what had taken their attention. 'I haven't noticed.'

Ashes let out a soft laugh.

'Whispers spread like wildfire. Whispers that my coven is weakening the barrier. Your people are blaming us. Me. It is much easier to have a common enemy than a common fear.'

Ashes was unravelling and Sapphire needed to make it stop. She felt an insatiable hunger to reassure, to comfort, to make promises she wasn't even sure she could keep.

'They are going to kill us.' Ashes' voice was certain, and it made Sapphire's stomach turn. 'This is their final attempt to eradicate us. The smudge on Eriobis' gleaming history.'

'The treaty is in place. My parents, they –'

'Sapphire, they may not deliver the blow that takes my life, but it will most certainly be delivered.'

The vivid images of Sapphire's nightmares came back. Graphic and detailed – lives taken, witches burned, cries of celebration and agony, a mixed chorus that made her ears ring.

'I – I will talk to them. I will tell my parents –'

'They are not your parents.' Ashes' voice was too loud, her words making Sapphire flinch. 'And what would you say? That you care for me? That you have grown fond of your very own Shadow Witch so they should spare my life?'

'I am smart enough to know that my heart cannot sway a country afraid of the unknown,' Sapphire bit back. 'I won't –'

'There is nothing you can do, Sapphire.' Ashes did not look afraid; instead, she suddenly smiled. Sapphire felt ill. 'But I will not go down without a fight. I will take as many souls as I can in my wake. In my final hours.'

'Wh-what are you saying?'

'I am the strongest of my coven. I was born to protect those who came before me, and I intend to fulfil the oath. If my coven collapses, I will bring the kingdom down with it. I will paint the world in inescapable darkness. And your people will curse my name for years to come.' She cut her eyes to Sapphire. 'I will welcome death, but I will not go alone.'

'They will kill you. You will –'

'They will.' Ashes smiled as she said it. 'But I'll bring their nightmares to life before they do.'

At the declaration, something inside Sapphire snapped. Weeks of pent-up emotion haemorrhaged forth.

Anger.

Fear.

Ashes looked triumphant in the face of death. She seemed at peace with leaving this all behind. But the witch was Sapphire's and Sapphire's alone. No one would take her away. She would rather be a queen of rubble than be robbed of the girl in front of her.

'No.'

Ashes looked down at Sapphire, narrowing her eyes.

'Come again?'

'I said no! You don't get to die. You don't get to be a martyr for your coven. I-I refuse it. I refuse to exist in a world where you don't.' Her voice grew stronger with each word, and she stood a bit straighter, staring down the witch who hovered over her. 'You might accept it, but I do not. I forbid it. I will not allow a future without you.'

'And what are you going to do, Sapphire?' The witch stepped closer, a wicked grin splitting her face once more. 'How exactly will you keep my life free of the executioners' grip?'

'I will –' She swallowed a lump in her throat as she considered her next words. If she allowed the words to escape her lips, all this would become too real. It would reveal how far she had fallen. How far she would go for the witch in front of her. The two girls stared at each other, time passing in measured heartbeats. 'I will cleave the world in two before they bring you harm. If you paint the world in darkness, I will ensure that the darkness never leaves. They will not touch you. And if they do . . .'

She trailed off, unspoken words heavy in her mouth.

Ashes hooked a finger under her chin, forcing her head back. Sapphire shivered at the proximity.

'Confess your sins.'

The night darkened as Ashes' shadows swallowed them both, into a world of their own making. A world that Sapphire would not relinquish.

'I will forsake them all. If they touch you, they will burn.'

A flame formed in her palm, and Ashes licked her lips, savouring the words and the undone version of Sapphire before her. The witch leaned forward, her mouth finding Sapphire's neck. She placed open-mouthed kisses along it.

'Let's bring this kingdom, this world, to its knees, my queen,' Ashes whispered before biting down on Sapphire's exposed skin. Sapphire's sigh of unbridled pleasure was the only response. It filled the forest as Ashes pressed her up against a tree.

Their hands were frantic as they pulled each other closer, desperate for more, for this moment.

Sapphire closed her eyes, relishing the feeling of Ashes' hot mouth on her own, the witch's hands gripping her tightly, touching her in ways only Ashes could.

Let's bring the kingdom, the world, to its knees.

Ashes' grip tightened once more, so that Sapphire's eyelids fluttered and her head lolled. And she allowed herself to fully realize a fact she had known since the Shadow Moon.

She would break every oath, every law . . . She'd bring the barrier down.

Mercy, she'd tear the Gods from their thrones in the sky to protect Ashes.

'For you,' Sapphire said, panting brokenly. 'For you, I will.'

Sapphire stormed into the castle and towards the throne room where her parents were holding council. Her boots were caked with mud, her hair undone.

As she charged down the corridor, the workers of the castle shot her worried glances but said nothing, and she kept her eyes straight ahead. Approaching the door, she was stopped by Claye. He grimaced as their eyes met.

'The king and queen are in a meeting, princess. No interruptions.'

'I must speak to them immediately.'

Claye shook his head, hiding a laugh at her rude tone.

'I apologize, princess. But we were told –'

She clenched her fist only once before the doors nearly blew off their hinges. Claye stared at her uncertainly, as if unable to work out what had happened. She stared at her hands, unsure of herself for a moment. Only when she heard someone clear their throat did she remember what she was doing there in the first place.

Before her, the king, the queen, and the senior councillors were watching her closely. She curtsied and moved quickly across the open room, refusing to shrink under their glares as she stood before the thrones.

'Sapphire, what do you think you're doing?' Araxia was the first to speak. 'We are in the middle of –'

'Call them off.'

Kip and Araxia shared a look and bowed their heads to the rest of the room. On cue, the councillors headed for the exit. No one spoke until the three were alone.

'What is the meaning of this interruption?' Kip was frustrated. She could hear it in his voice, but she kept her shoulders square and her tone steady.

'Warn the people of the consequences of killing the Shadow Witches. Do not allow innocent lives to be taken because of prejudice.'

'I have no idea what you speak of. Where –?' Kip started.

'I am not a fool. Stop treating me like one.'

'We simply are trying to understand where this is coming from,' Araxia stepped in. 'Please.'

'The barrier is weakening. Our people are planning attacks on the Shadow Witches because of gossip. They plan to . . .' Sapphire couldn't finish the sentence. 'You can't allow this to happen.'

Araxia took a deep breath, standing and descending the steps until she was eye to eye with Sapphire. She reached out, placing both hands on Sapphire's shoulders. Sapphire fought the urge to recoil.

'There is a treaty in place to protect the coven. Our people are aware that any attack against the Shadow Witches is treated like an attack on their neighbour. It has been a royal decree for decades.'

'They will only obey if you speak openly about it,' Sapphire pushed.

'We have always been vocal about our protection of the coven.'

The two women stood toe to toe.

'It's quite easy to turn a blind eye in the right situation.'

Araxia blinked slowly, like she was trying to dissuade herself, trying to convince herself that her daughter wouldn't imply that this was being allowed to happen.

'The Canmore line has never turned a blind eye. You should know that, Sapphire.'

'Even when it comes to the darkness in Eriobis' otherwise perfect past?'

Araxia's brows pulled together and lines of frustration gathered around her mouth.

'Where is this coming from?'

Sapphire levelled her gaze at the queen before looking away.

'I value all of our citizens, even those that may not agree with me. I believe it's important to send reminders to the kingdom in case it slips their mind. In case it slips your mind.'

Kip cleared his throat, breaking the tension between the pair. Araxia's face cleared before she returned to her throne. The king and queen looked at Sapphire.

'We offer you our word, Sapphire. The witches are protected under the covenant of the law,' Kip finally said.

'And if the law isn't enough? What will you do then?'

Araxia took a deep breath.

'Then we offer action. Responsibility on both our heads, and on the heads of those who breach the contract.'

'And what for the coven? What will you do if they lose one of their own?'

Araxia stared at her for a few seconds like she was trying to uncover the meaning behind Sapphire's passionate display.

'Sapphire, is there something else you'd like to say? Something you're not telling us?'

She sat there, staring at the pair before her, daring herself to implode. To burn the castle to the ground. To threaten them. To let them know that she knew everything they had done.

But she didn't. Instead, she shook her head.

'Swear the Elders' oath that a plan is in place.' She almost laughed, asking them to swear by the Gods she did not believe in. But she wanted to push them.

'We are your parents.' Kip looked baffled. 'Is our word not enough?'

Sapphire looked them dead in the eye and smiled sweetly.

'Not when it comes to something so important.'

'Alert the council they may rejoin us as you leave. You have the oath. Now, see yourself out.'

She did not bow as she left.

She returned to her room to consider her next move, but could not focus. So, instead, she marvelled at the feeling of wind leaving her fingertips.

Chapter Thirty-eight

Sapphire spent her nights learning what true fear felt like. Ashes was before her, and Sapphire was forced to watch as she was tortured at the hands of people she did not recognize. Their knives cut her arms, their elemental magic filled her lungs with water and burned her skin. And she cried out for Sapphire, begging her to keep her word.

Begging for her help. Those who kept her captive laughed as her cries rang out; Sapphire remained rooted on the spot, two pairs of hands holding her back. She turned around to find Araxia and Kip behind her, smiling as they watched the scene unfold.

Do you love her?

Ryvinika's voice cut through the madness, so clear and poignant. Sapphire closed her eyes tightly, trying to end the nightmare.

I said, do you love her?

Did she love Ashes? She knew –

My child, if you love her, you must wake up. You must go to her. Danger is born of the night.

Sapphire looked around wildly. Ashes' eyes were still

locked on her own, but she could not find the source of the voice.

Wake up and save your witch, Sapphire.

Sapphire was in her room, covered in sweat and gripping the covers so tightly her knuckles had begun to ache.

Go to her.

She was up and moving, grabbing her cloak and her dagger. Her gut twisted and it struck her that something was terribly wrong. But she did not take time to consider what she was doing. She immediately dived into the water and began to swim towards Ciliria, towards Ashes.

When she stumbled on to the shore, she did not call out for her witch. Instead, she moved into the forest, trusting Ryvinika would guide her.

'Take me to her.'

Then the world shifted. Sapphire was reduced to an onlooker in her own life as she was led by a mind that was not her own. She moved through the woods with confidence, taking sharp turns, with a precision that could only come from someone who knew the way.

The forest moved past in a blur of darkness, the moon obscured by an incoming storm. She tried to memorize the path Ryvinika led her, but she could not.

When they finally slowed, Ashes was only a few paces ahead, walking away from her.

'Ashes!'

The witch whirled around, and by the light of the flame in Sapphire's hand, she saw a look of relief wash over the girl.

'Sapphire, you never visit this late. I –'

'I know.' Sapphire cut her short, pulling her into a kiss. They lingered for a few seconds. 'I apologize. I – fell asleep.'

'Another nightmare?' Ashes tucked a stray strand of hair behind her ear.

Sapphire opened her mouth to speak, but the sound of movement nearby caught their attention, and the words died on her lips.

'Sapphire, I need you to hide among the trees. Now.'

At the urgency in Ashes' voice and face, Sapphire moved quickly, tucking herself behind a tree. She watched as the witch brought an orb of light to life in her palm.

'Sister, it is only me. No need for alarm,' Ashes muttered.

No response came and the uneasy feeling in Sapphire's stomach grew.

To her horror, two figures stepped into view. Not witches of Ashes' coven, but two men, their colours displayed – earthborn. Ashes didn't move, towering over both of them.

'Quite late for a midnight stroll through the forest. You never know what's lurking among the shadows,' Ashes mused.

The shorter man gave her a crooked grin.

'Oh, witch, we were hunting monsters. You were exactly what we hoped to find.'

With a flick of the wrist, one of the men shot a vine at Ashes, but her shadows quickly devoured it.

'Now, now, gentlemen. There's no need for this. I'm sure you have families that will mourn you.'

'We should carve your tongue out before we kill you.'

'Is my tongue truly worth your life?' The men laughed at the question, and Sapphire felt the familiar slow, smouldering burn of rage. Her fingers danced at her side, her magic begging to be set free.

'We do not fear you.'

'I am not the one you should fear,' Ashes replied.

The men's laughter echoed off the trees, ricocheting off Sapphire's skin. It stoked the fire that threatened to consume her.

'Then tell us, girl, who should we fear?'

Sapphire stepped from the shadows with a smile on her face and death dancing on her fingertips.

'Me.'

The men followed Ashes' gaze and saw Sapphire.

'Princess?' the shorter man wheezed before Sapphire's dagger buried itself in the side of his neck. Blood spilled from the wound as he grabbed for the hilt. She turned her focus to the other man, smiling.

'Apologize,' Sapphire demanded.

'Wh–what?' The man's voice betrayed his terror.

'Apologize for treating her poorly, for accusing her. For interrupting our night.'

'Princess, I –' His words were cut short as he tracked her movements, saw the flame flickering in her palm. She circled behind him and kicked the back of his knees, watching as he collapsed before Ashes.

'Grovel. Beg. If she grants you kindness, I will allow you a three-minute head start before I rip you in two.'

Ashes watched Sapphire, eyes dancing with approval. The witch smiled down at the man.

'I'm-I'm sorry,' he stuttered. 'We just want our families to be safe.'

Ashes arched a perfect brow, taking a step towards him. The kneeling man was forced to crane his neck to meet her gaze.

'You understand that, don't you?' the man begged.

Ashes squatted down, almost to his eye level. She studied him, head tilted, with a soft expression. She reached her hands out to cup his cheeks. The two stared at each other, moments passing in measured heartbeats until the witch smiled at him.

He breathed a sigh of relief.

Her smile grew.

'No.' Ashes' voice was deafening. The man froze, his body rigid. 'No, I don't think I do.'

The sound of bones snapping filled the forest. A sickening chorus of splintering fragments, of a death served quickly, rang in Sapphire's ears. Ashes held the man's limp head in her hands, looking up to Sapphire from her kneeling position, and grinned like a proud predator.

The witch stepped over the body to where Sapphire stood and pulled her into an approving kiss. When she pulled away, Sapphire set fire to the two bodies. They stood there, watching the flames grow. 'You kept your word.'

'I was told it's dangerous to make false promises to Shadow Witches.'

'Wise advice.' Ashes bent down, gathering the bones in

the same way as she'd held the brush the day the two had lain together in the forest.

At that exact moment, the familiar trace of an unwelcome touch ghosted up Sapphire's back and laughter followed.

Very good, my child.

They were going to kill her.

Tell me, how many lives will you take before you can no longer stand the guilt?

'You look ill.' Ashes stared at her with a concerned look.

'I'm fine,' Sapphire replied.

Bring down the barrier and prove there is nothing to fear. It is the only answer, for everyone.

Ashes turned to face her, and she was struck by a potent emotion that she couldn't ignore. *Longing* – longing for moments with Ashes that weren't . . . this. That weren't illuminated only by the moonlight and hidden amidst the trees.

That emotion quickly faded as Sapphire took in the bones gathered in Ashes' arms. Bones that had belonged to two living, breathing men only moments ago. Before she had killed one and allowed the other to be killed before her eyes.

She had killed him. She looked at her hands, which were stained with blood that was not her own.

Mercy, she had taken a life.

She sucked in a breath, but the panic grew too quickly, causing her to stumble. Ashes noticed, dropping the bones to steady her, but the sound of the pile hitting the forest floor sickened her. It was a rattling, unnerving ensemble of death. Ashes gripped her tightly as her body shook.

'Sapphire, I need you to look at me.'

Ashes' tone was commanding, cutting through the panicked haze that clouded her mind. Her eyes found the familiar haunting gaze of the witch.

'You did what was necessary.'

'I killed him.' Her voice was strangled.

'He would've done the same to me. To you. If he had the chance.'

'There is blood on my hands.' Sapphire's breathing was laboured. 'Please, get the blood off my hands. Please.'

Ashes guided her to sit on a fallen log before she disappeared into the forest. Sapphire's panic intensified. What if –?

But then Ashes reappeared, the skirt of her dress ripped to make a cloth that she had wet. She crouched in front of Sapphire, taking her hands. She placed a gentle kiss on her bloodied palms before beginning to wash them clean of the blood. They remained silent until she was done.

'There,' she whispered, pressing a cold hand to Sapphire's cheek. 'It is gone.'

'We killed them,' Sapphire repeated. 'How are you so –? Why are you not –?'

Ashes drummed her fingers against Sapphire's cheek with a haunting expression.

'There are certain depths of darkness from which I shield you.'

The two stared at each other, Sapphire's heart thundering in her chest.

'This is our secret to keep. Do you understand?'

Secrets. These days Sapphire was carrying so many she feared she would collapse from the weight.

'I understand.'

Ashes nodded, pressing her lips to Sapphire's temple before bidding her good night.

When Sapphire reached the lake, she found a place to sit atop a large boulder and she stared up at the moon. She could not return to the castle – not yet.

Child, did you notice anything about the men in the forest tonight?

Sapphire kept her head buried in her hands, refusing to acknowledge the question.

The monsters you know. The monsters you admire. The monsters who roam the very halls you do. The royal crest is only worn by those who directly serve the kingdom, no?

She waited for the final blow she knew Ryvinika would deliver.

They'll kill her. With smiles on their faces. What is your world without her?

Sapphire's stomach turned.

A world without Ashes. Without her gentle touches, stolen moments, without the intimacy they found in the dead of night among the shadows beneath the moon.

A world that would hold no interest for her. She racked her mind, trying to recall the night in detail. But all she could see were Ashes' eyes as she watched Sapphire taunting that man. All she could hear was the sound of bones snapping. She took a deep breath, trying to slow her mind.

It wasn't treason. It was an order.

Sapphire shut her eyes, trying to push the voice out of her head. She could not differentiate between Ryvinika's voice and her own, and the realization crashed upon her.

The monsters you know.

The monsters you know.

The monsters she knew.

Kip and Araxia on their golden thrones. Smiles on their faces. Lies on their tongues. Blood on their hands.

But not Ashes'. It would never be Ashes' blood.

She would make sure of it.

CHAPTER THIRTY-NINE

Ryvinika was silent in the days that followed.

Sapphire dreamed of death.

She tossed and turned, ripping the linens from the mattress as she fought to free herself from the torture.

In the morning, the bags under her eyes told of her struggles. Claye looked at her with a concerned expression but never spoke. It was as if darkness radiated off Sapphire, forcing her into silence.

But Kip and Araxia smiled as she took her seat at the breakfast table this morning. It had been weeks since they had all joined together for a meal. Tension was still tight between Araxia and Sapphire, but the queen patted her arm gently. So far they had kept their oath and the witches had not been attacked again. She knew she would have heard from Ashes if any more guards had been sent to the forest.

'Sapphire, we are so happy to finally be sitting down with you. We apologize for being so busy.' Araxia took a bite of the fresh fruit Sapphire knew was picked daily from the grove down the hill.

'No apologies are needed. I know your positions need focus and attention.'

'Still, we worry about you. We'd actually like to talk to you about something if that's OK.' It was Kip who spoke.

The couple shared a silent exchange that Sapphire could not read, and she waited for one of them to speak and let her in on the secret they apparently shared.

'We know you and Kaian have been spending time together.'

'Of course we have. We are partners now, are we not?'

Araxia nodded, looking to Kip to continue the conversation.

'Yes, you are,' Kip said. 'And we admire your maturity in taking on the role with ease. With that said, we are going to ask that Kaian only visit you here. No trips to Ciliria for the time being.'

Sapphire's fork clattered against the plate, making everyone jump. 'May I ask why?'

'There have been some unexplained events, including violence.' Kip looked to Araxia, who nodded like she was allowing him to continue. 'Two of our men disappeared there a few days ago.'

'There's no trace of them?'

'None at all. It's like they disappeared into thin air.'

'What were they doing in the forest?'

'They were sent to observe the Shadow Witches' current position. We send them out monthly just to track the coven's location.' Sapphire narrowed her eyes, and Kip threw his hands up. 'Sapphire, you have to understand, as the leaders of this nation, we have to know where all of our citizens stand. Even those who may not agree with us.'

So, she had not imagined the crests, and Ryvinika had not been lying. And Sapphire and Ashes had taken the lives of two men sent out to do her parents' underhanded work.

'I'm sure they just got off course. The forest is dense and it is easy to lose your way. I'm sure they will return soon enough.'

'We must pray to the Elders for their return. Let's bow and take a pause to speak to them now.'

Moving in front of the golden statue of the Elders, Kip and Araxia knelt before it. They asked for the Elders' graciousness and kindness to return the two men home. But Sapphire did not bow. She stared at the gold-plated statue. And as she smiled at the Gods, the prayer she recited in her mind was not for them but for the girl who kissed her in the shadows.

'I do not fear you. I do not bend to your will. I will tear the sky in two. I will destroy the world you built before you touch my witch.' Some disembodied pressure struck her back, and her knees buckled, but she remained upright. *'I kneel before no one but her.'*

For a moment, she could have sworn that the eyes of the golden statue moved to her. She almost hoped they did. They would find anger, darkness, power, and the eyes of a Shadow Witch who she refused to let go.

'Sapphire?'

She snapped her attention back to her parents. Their eyes shifted between her and the statue she had been staring at.

'We just wanted to make sure you understood. No

visiting the forest until we can figure out what is happening. We've already written to the Princeps.'

'I understand.'

The monster you know.

Her parents would do well to heed that advice.

The wedding was approaching and it felt like a noose tightening around Sapphire's neck. It was only a matter of weeks before she and Kaian were supposed to walk down the aisle and pledge their loyalty to one another and the country they served. Dress fittings were over, as were ballroom dancing classes – instead, she spent her time locked away in rooms being prepped for what came after that special day.

More responsibility to the crown she had grown to hate.

The Princeps spent most of their time at the castle as well – their presence was a constant reminder of the choices being made for her – but she knew she'd make her own choice soon, and that would be the only one that mattered.

She shook her head, trying to clear her thoughts, trying to focus. Currently, she was sitting in her room with Kaian and Evera – the three of them sprawled out on the floor as Kaian spoke in a reassuring tone.

'I would've heard if the barrier was weakening, Sapphire. I'm sure this is just another gossip scare.'

It wasn't like she could admit that Ashes had been the one to bring her the news. She couldn't risk anyone finding out about her nights spent on the shore.

'Nothing has been said in Aleburn or the library either.'

Evera crawled to Sapphire, taking her hand. 'You know I'd tell you if I heard even a whisper of this.'

'I know.' Sapphire gave Evera a small smile and squeezed her hand.

The worry slipped away for a few blissful moments as she rejoiced that both Evera and Kaian could exist with her in her room. But then the cold rushed back in. The reminder of Ashes, bloodied and bruised. The girl's panicked eyes as realization set in. Her fear. Her desperation.

'If the barrier fell, what do you suppose the world would be like?'

Evera and Kaian snapped their attention back to her and then exchanged a worried look that she did not miss. Neither hurried to speak.

A tense pause followed, but finally, Kaian cleared his throat. 'If the legends are true – if the monsters still linger beyond the barrier – then war. I believe it would be a world full of war.' The three stared at each other and Kaian stood, shaking his head. 'My parents are growing worried. It seems there's a darkness in Eriobis that no one can shake.' Evera looked to the ceiling.

'My parents won't even allow me to go on my usual rounds in the forest. Two men disappear and it's like suddenly everyone is a target.'

Sapphire moved away from Evera, trying to appear busy tidying her room. The skirt of her dress was making it difficult to move and she cursed silently. She felt their eyes on her, like they were waiting for her to speak but she couldn't find the words so she continued to pace.

'Why are you acting so . . . standoffish?' Evera asked. 'Please take a seat – you're putting me even more on edge.'

Sapphire obliged and sat in the empty armchair across from Kaian.

'I can trust you both, can't I?'

Evera smiled at her. 'You shouldn't even have to ask that.'

But she needed to.

'I want to tell you something. But I need you both to swear to me that your loyalty is unconditional.'

Something in the atmosphere shifted, and the two nodded in unison, sharing a worried glance. She wanted to believe them. She knew this honesty might cost her more than she'd like to admit – but she needed to talk to someone because she was teetering on the cliff of insanity.

'I have befriended Ashes.'

They both frowned. 'The Shadow Witch?' Evera's voice was small.

'Yes.'

Kaian rubbed his face in frustration. 'Sapphire, you know those witches –'

'I need you to let me finish.'

He clamped his mouth shut and leaned back in the chair.

'I was spending time with her a few nights ago, and two men stumbled upon us in the forest. They attacked her. Threatened to kill her. And –'

'Do not say what you're about to say.' Kaian's voice was low with warning, and he grabbed her roughly by the arm. 'Don't, Sapphire. Don't admit it.'

'But –'

'There are eyes and ears everywhere. Places you can't imagine. Do not.'

Sapphire swallowed the confession and looked out of the window, suddenly unable to meet either of their gazes.

'Sapphire, you can't trust her.' It was Evera who spoke. 'No matter what she tells you, or what they show you, or how kind they seem.'

'Ashes is . . .' Sapphire opened and closed her fist three times, trying to decide if she wanted to continue. 'Maybe if you just took some time to understand her –'

'No.'

Kaian stared at her with narrowed eyes.

'Excuse me?'

Kaian rose to his feet, hovering above her. 'For centuries, Shadow Witches lived up to their reputation. And you will not change that. I won't allow it.'

A fire deep inside her stoked the anger in her chest. She dug her nails into her scarred palm in an effort to not give in. Still, she couldn't slow its burn. It devoured her, pulsing through every nerve ending.

Silently, she rose, standing nose to nose with her husband-to-be. And when she smiled, she watched as Kaian's expression shifted to something else entirely. Fear, realization, desperation.

She swallowed, trying to dispel the poison she felt building inside her.

He will control you. A queen is but a puppet for the man who sits beside her.

No.

Kaian was her friend. Her advocate and her confidant. They had made a promise.

High bloods never keep their word.

Ashes' words rang in her ears. Ashes had warned her that he would try to control her. That she would lose her voice and her power – her decisions made by her husband and a council.

'You do not command me,' Sapphire said in a low voice. 'I do not answer to your orders.'

'I am your partner. We make decisions together, and I have the right to tell you when you are acting . . . unwisely.'

'You're not even listening.'

'Then talk, Sapphire. Tell me why I should trust this Shadow Witch you're so fond of.'

Sapphire stared at him with wide eyes, unsure how to explain that she dreamed of Ashes' lips, her skin in the moonlight. She could not gather words, and Kaian gave her a sideways glance.

'Exactly. I advise you to focus on your people. The ones you will do right by and serve faithfully.'

With that, he pushed away from his seat and walked towards the door. Once Kaian was gone, Evera spoke.

'I'll listen.'

The words caught Sapphire off guard, and she stared at her friend in disbelief.

Evera patted the free spot beside her, and Sapphire crawled on to the bed, her body suddenly exhausted. As she turned to look at Evera, her friend stared at her with worried eyes.

'You really care about her, don't you?'

'I do.' Sapphire didn't hesitate. It was like a rush of fresh air to speak of her feelings for Ashes. To be fully herself. To admit that she adored the Shadow Witch that walked barefoot through the forest and praised the moon.

'I am not here to judge you, but you have to understand that I am . . . confused.'

Sapphire wanted to tell her of the nights in the forest, in the clearings. Of a blade to her neck and promises on her lips. She wanted to tell Evera everything.

So she did, and when she finished, Evera picked at the non-existent dirt on Sapphire's quilt.

'I hope you understand that I can't –' Evera took a deep breath, closing her eyes. 'I am struggling to find the balance between being your friend but also a voice of reason. Kaian is much better at the latter.'

Sapphire gave her a half-smile and Evera spoke again.

'You have your whole future ahead of you. You know that, right?'

She nodded absentmindedly, looking out of the window. The whole world ahead of her – a world she would improve. A brighter future. She just hoped Evera would understand.

CHAPTER FORTY

It had been a long time coming, she mused while walking along the shore, staring up at the circling clouds. Her mind had been made up weeks ago. Her next step was the only way to push the world forward. It was the only way for her to learn who she truly was. It was – the only way . . .

A new world where there was no barrier, no hunting, no anger, where different people could coexist.

A world where respect flowed naturally and people understood. A world where she could love Ashes.

The prophecy had called for a better world.

One she would deliver.

Still, a piece of her selfishly wanted to watch the barrier crumble under her hand. She longed for that feeling – like the weight of the world was in her palm again. Saviour or ravager. Lamb or lion. Her path was hers to command.

The prophecy will come to fruition. Your magic cannot be kept from the world.

The witch was right. Every day the dull ache, the pressure, and the nerves all increased, pushing her towards the edge. She wanted Araxia – she wanted to ask her to make sense of what was happening.

But after the night in the forest, the two men with their spiteful grins and the royal crests, trust had been just out of their reach. And deep down, she feared if she admitted it all, she'd break the promise they had made that day by the lake.

Footsteps interrupted her thoughts, and she turned to find Kaian standing behind her.

'I owe you an apology.'

She returned her eyes to the lake, not wanting a conversation.

'I swore to myself I wouldn't be my father. That I would treat you as an equal; and when we last talked, I didn't. You didn't deserve that. But I will always tell you what I think is best. I hope you do the same for me.'

'Sit,' she said with a sigh. 'I think this whole arrangement might have been easier if we hadn't been friends. Maybe that's why your parents sought a duel between us, hoping we would become enemies.'

He laughed, shifting closer to her. 'I think that's exactly what they hoped for. I mean, you did almost drown me, so . . .'

She bit back her own laugh, shaking her head at the memory. Even with the marriage contract in place, nothing had changed in her heart for Kaian.

'I accept your apology.'

He smiled, pulling her into a hug, and she leaned into him with a small grin.

'The coven,' he started, his voice tight. 'If this is something you are serious about, then I want to try to understand it.'

She stared at him for a moment, admiring who he was – a king who would be kind and faithful. A king that Eriobis did not deserve.

But the small memory of Ashes' hand pressed against her lower back returned. The girl's lips slightly parted. The way her hair looked like a live flame in the moonlight.

Once she had settled, once she had pushed away the fear, and the sensation of fire being pressed into her eyelids, she suddenly wondered if that was the connection she had been craving since before she arrived at Eriobis.

Family that understood her, knew her, accepted her.

'Can we just,' Sapphire sighed, exhaustion thick in her voice, 'enjoy our time? For today, at least.'

'How about a swim?'

Sapphire laughed, slipping into the water before Kaian could move, and he followed her – their expensive garments most likely ruined but she didn't care. And for a moment, she felt an unexpected sadness settle on her heart. The sky opened and the long-awaited rain began to fall. It was not angry or ruthless. It was a steady fall that made the mundane world around them more beautiful.

Her friend.

Her intended.

And one of the many hearts she would soon break.

The day passed, quick and easy and filled with a warmth that Sapphire hadn't realized she missed. But, when it was done, and Kaian was gone, her heart pulled her back to a place – to a person – she couldn't ignore. The image of Ashes sitting on the shore burned into her mind.

This night was no different as she poked her head above the water, catching the view.

She smiled to herself as she got closer. Stepping out of the water, she wrapped her arms around the witch, savouring the scent of honey and ash and the way Ashes' calloused hands felt wrapped in hers.

'The coven received a visit today.' Ashes' voice was low, angry. 'Your parents' lackeys. They had questions about the disappearance of two of their men.'

Sapphire stiffened as the sound of bones snapping in a quiet forest rang in her ears.

'They left without answers. No need to get that –'

'I'm going to bring down the barrier.'

It was the first time she had confessed it aloud, and the words were heavy.

Ashes looked to Sapphire, eyes bright.

'You,' Ashes kissed her neck, 'magnificent,' a kiss to her cheek, 'powerful,' her other cheek, 'creature.' The witch breathed the final word into Sapphire's lips. Her hands found their place at Sapphire's lower back and in her hair.

The kiss was maddening, consuming, intoxicating. She may have been born to fulfil a prophecy, but, in that moment, with the witch's warm lips against her own, she liked to believe she was born for her as well. To find her. To love her. To run through the shadows of this world together.

'I feared –' Ashes said as she pulled away. 'I feared you wouldn't –'

'For you. For us. For a better Eriobis.'

'For us, my queen.' Ashes pressed a gentle kiss to the back of Sapphire's hand.

And then they heard footsteps emerging from the forest.

Ashes opened her hand quickly, dousing them in shadow. Sapphire felt safe in the darkness and, moving closer, the witch slid her hand around Sapphire's waist, pulling her close. They didn't dare speak or move, instead watching as three figures emerged from the trees. She recognized two of them – Sadara and Tyden. The third was a woman sporting a royal crest on her shoulder.

There was something unsettling about the three of them standing at the shoreline, their shoreline.

'They are south of the estate. South of the villages as well. Not close enough to cause problems or be heard if trouble arises.' The woman's voice was lower than Sapphire expected – authoritative and confident.

Sadara spoke next, her face tight. 'I'm not sure how much clearer we must be. Eradicated, destroyed, and removed. I want the coven gone. It's the only option. If we're not careful, we'll lose our grip on everything.'

Ashes' hold on Sapphire's waist tightened.

'We'd need three days to properly prepare.' The guard sounded afraid.

'And if we don't have three days?' Tyden snapped.

'Things like this must be handled with a certain . . . discretion. Soldiers with the necessary skills and the ability to stay silent.' Sadara's eyes swept over the lake and the shore, landing where Ashes and Sapphire were huddled. After lingering for a second, she looked back to the woman beside her. 'My son's wedding is approaching. I won't have this overshadowing it.'

Silence followed before the woman cleared her throat.

'The minutes are already slipping by. Three days. And I expect *all* the witches to be dead.'

The woman nodded, turning on her heel and striding purposefully into the forest. Sadara and Tyden remained.

'With the Shadow Witches gone, it will slow down, right?'

Sadara sounded afraid as she looked at her husband, searching for reassurance.

'It's the only way to end this. We must stop those monsters before they ruin this world.'

Tyden took Sadara's hand and guided her away from the shore. Sapphire and Ashes remained there, masked by shadow, for some time after.

When the shadows dropped away, she looked to Ashes.

'We must go now. I can – I will bring it down tonight.' Her voice shook as she spoke, betraying her.

Ashes shook her head, caressing her cheek.

'I must warn my coven. We need time to prepare to protect you. Time to prepare for the shift. Two days. I need you to wait two days. Can you do that for me?'

Sapphire nodded, taking a deep breath. 'Go. Warn them.'

Ashes pressed her lips against Sapphire's, kissing her as if it was the last time. Sapphire mirrored her desperation.

She couldn't lose this. Not now.

'For a better world, Sapphire.'

'I – Ashes, I –'

'I know,' the witch whispered, squeezing Sapphire's hand. Sapphire pulled her into a tight embrace, trying to memorize every curve, every scent, every last detail of her. As the witch turned to go, Sapphire desperately reached out for her. Reached out like she had been doing for years before she realized who Ashes was.

The witch turned to face her.

'I promised you once that I would always find you, did I not? I have a habit of keeping my word, princess.' She untangled her fingers from Sapphire's and closed her eyes for a few heartbeats before returning her gaze. Something about the witch's unguarded expression didn't suit her. 'Fate is a cruel and ruthless mistress, but the oaths I take are unbreakable. I will always find you, Sapphire.'

Sapphire felt a lump form in her throat as she struggled to find words. When she felt she could respond, Ashes' mask of indifference had returned.

'I must go, princess. Return to the castle and remain there. This forest will be unsafe in the days to come.'

She went to argue but Ashes was already blending into the shadows. Sapphire remained on the shore, allowing her tears to fall without shame. The Princeps . . . with the insults, their sneers, their blackmail.

She smiled.

Ryvinika had always said: 'It's the monsters you know.'

She almost pitied Sadara and Tyden for not realizing that.

CHAPTER FORTY-ONE

Two days later, Sapphire awoke and slipped on one of her favourite dresses. It was a deep blue that reminded her of the waters at night – a representation of herself to the rest of the world.

Her hair was pulled back from her face. Jewels were secured at the crown of her head, and curls spilled down her back. She looked entirely the part of the Princess of Eriobis.

A fitting day for the prophecy.

The bringer of justice, the prophecy had called her.

But she decided to be the bringer of peace, of a new world, and equality.

That shift helped her breathe as she moved down the corridor. And it prevented her from coming completely undone when Evera walked into the parlour.

'What are you doing here?' Sapphire's voice was harsher than she intended, her teeth clenched.

Evera sent Sapphire a warning look. 'You asked me to take the day off. But if you don't want me here, I'll just –'

'No. Stay. I apologize. I'm . . . in my own head.'

'What a place to be.' The two girls whirled around to see Kaian walking through the archway. 'Ladies.'

Sapphire rolled her eyes, glancing between the two, who shared a knowing look.

'You planned this?'

Evera and Kaian bit back laughs as they exchanged another knowing glance.

'We're getting you out of the castle for the day. We have a full programme planned.'

'And what will we be doing?'

'Enjoying all that Eriobis has to offer.'

She met their gazes, and knew she couldn't risk being too obvious. She softened her expression.

'Tell me we'll be visiting Ciliria. I miss it.'

Kaian nodded with a smile on his face. 'That's where we're having lunch. I have a picnic basket packed with all your favourites – including pastries and that roseberry jam you love so much.'

Sapphire bowed her head in gratitude as she began to consider her next moves.

'Now, let's get moving. The carriage is waiting.'

'How did you –'

'Claye agreed that you need a day out. He . . . pulled a few strings.' Evera took Sapphire's hand as they began to make their way to the front of the castle, chattering about something Sapphire was too distracted to take in.

As she stepped into the carriage, Ryvinika came to life.

Tell me, child, do you trust me?

Sapphire nodded as the world outside the carriage began to move past her.

A hint of satisfied laughter followed – the feeling of something brushing up against her mind.

Today, we change the world.

To Sapphire's dismay, they stopped at the temple in the city centre.

'Offerings first,' Kaian explained, extending his hand for her to take.

Hand in hand, they slipped out of the carriage to find onlookers excited by their presence. Many reached out to them, asking for prayers and healing, while others expressed gratitude. Sapphire played her part well, nodding and smiling as she followed Kaian to the open gates.

Once inside, a pressure settled upon her. It was as if two hands were pushing her down. The presence was unwelcome and she shifted, trying to be free of it.

'Are you OK?' Evera asked. Kaian had dropped her hand now that they were out of view of onlookers, and Evera had taken his place.

'I'm fine. Why?'

'Are you sure?'

Sapphire nodded, shutting her eyes tightly and hoping to find some relief.

They want me to leave.

Sapphire stiffened. She looked around the temple, her eyes landing on a statue of the Elders looking down on her. She stared at them, challenging them to speak to her.

They remained unmoving, unwilling, and unaccepting of who she was.

So she bowed her head in an effort to pray, but Ryvinika stole her mind once more, her voice louder than any half-hearted prayer that Sapphire could muster:

She does not fear you. She does not bow to you. She will serve justice and bring peace to Eriobis. And its citizens will no longer live in fear.

Today, she will bring down the barrier that you built. Your temples will be levelled, altars burned. Today, the world will learn. And it will be at my child's hand.

Ryvinika purred but Sapphire felt a sickness settle into her bones. She could have sworn she heard a new voice ring out.

You will not.

Her focus snapped and she vomited. She opened her eyes to find a puddle of blood in front of her and Evera and Kaian gazing at her. She stared at the blood, frozen.

Get out.

Sapphire stood quickly and began to make her way to the door, fighting back the urge to throw up once again on the polished marble floor of the sanctuary. She tucked herself away from the prying eyes beyond the gate and vomited once more, coating the stones beneath her feet with blood.

Evera and Kaian hurried up behind her and reached out frantically to hold her steady.

'Sapphire, what is happening?' Evera's voice didn't sound like her own.

'Get me to the forest, now.'

Neither of her friends argued, escorting her to the

carriage. Once they were among the trees, Sapphire could breathe, and she inhaled sharply a few times, desperate to rid herself of the feeling that had come over her in the temple. Desperate to rid herself of the Elders' tainted touch. Kaian and Evera's eyes held unspoken questions; questions Sapphire could not answer.

And when the carriage stopped, she was the first out of the door, not breaking her stride as the other two hurried to follow her.

'Sapphire! What are you doing?'

She didn't slow, but she heard their footsteps behind her. *Move fast, child. It's coming.*

She lowered her head and trusted the presence to guide her feet in the right direction.

'Sapphire, please! At least tell us where you're going.' It was Evera crying out behind her, and Sapphire turned to meet her eyes.

Evera registered the magnitude of their current situation. 'No. Sapphire, no!' she burst out. 'Think about this!'

But Sapphire did not answer.

'What's happening?' Kaian half shouted as they stormed through the forest at her heels.

Sapphire knew Evera was looking to her for an answer – for guidance. Her allegiance had been sworn to Sapphire before anything else – but Sapphire didn't have time to waste.

Not when she could have sworn she felt the footsteps of oncoming soldiers.

Not when the Elders knew what she was about to do.

Evera waited – waited for an answer, for confirmation, for anything from her best friend. But when it did not come, Sapphire knew the girl would get there herself. She knew she would answer the question Kaian was asking because Evera was afraid.

Sapphire could not blame her.

'She's going to try to bring down the barrier.'

There was no *try*. She would bring down the barrier. She would stop the oncoming attack. And she would force Eriobis into a new era.

'Sapphire, have you lost your mind?'

Maybe.

But the power inside her was lit, and it demanded to be released.

Kaian and Evera followed her deep into the forest, never pausing. Ryvinika kept her feet moving.

Overhead, the world darkened. Threatening clouds obscured the sun. A storm fit to birth a new world.

That's when it slammed into her.

The pain was bone-splitting. Agonizing. Like it was stripping back layers of flesh, exposing her entirely. Her knees shook at the impact but she steadied herself. The pause gave Kaian and Evera the time they needed to catch up with her. Kaian took her by the arm.

'What are you thinking?'

'I am thinking,' Sapphire pulled her arm from his grip, 'that this is what I was born to do.'

Kaian. He reached for her but she pulled away.

'I will bring it down.'

Thunder rolled overhead and she knew it was coming.

Move, child. Time is running out.

Ryvinika's voice pushed her forward, and she began to move once more. She could feel the barrier, the magic digging beneath her skin, taking up too much space in her chest. Her breathing was laboured as she pushed forward, the storm growing stronger above her with every step.

Kaian grabbed her again.

'The Shadow Witch did this. Didn't she?' he demanded of Sapphire, though he must know the answer. 'Why? What does she have –?'

Kaian's words came to a stop as he realized.

'She has your heart.' Sapphire stared him down, daring him to speak against her witch. 'Tell me I'm wrong. Tell me right now.'

'You're hurting me.' His grip tightened on her arm. 'You are not wrong.'

He looked at his hand and released his grip but did not step away.

'Don't do this.' His voice was strained.

'They are going to kill her. Your parents plan to kill the coven.'

'You don't kn–'

'There is a promise of a better world. A prophecy of a land without barriers. A land of peace.'

'Shadow Witches know nothing of peace.'

'I need you to let me go,' she whispered, her heart breaking.

'You're a fool for many reasons, Sapphire Canmore,' his

voice was strangled, 'but even you are not foolish enough to believe I could ever do that.'

Tears welled in her eyes as he stepped back from her, Ryvinika tugging at her to move forward. And she cast a lingering glance at Kaian before she began to move again, never once checking over her shoulder to see if her friends were following.

She knew they were.

Finally, the forest gave way, and she stepped into an open field. The barrier hummed and glowed, and for a moment, she couldn't help but admire it. It was the greatest work of magic the world had ever known, but it did not belong here. And she was going to fix the mistakes of the Elders and set the world right.

She began to move forward once more, doubling over as the invisible pressure of the barrier crashed into her. This time Ashes wasn't here to support her. Her teeth chattered, and the closer she got, the more she struggled as her magic begged to be set free.

Ashes promised a better world for everyone – for them. The thought kept her moving.

'Sapphire, please. Please don't do this.' Evera was crying as she caught up, the fear so clear on her face.

'I will be OK. It's all going to be OK.'

'Look at the storm. The Elders are angry. Please, do not push them any further,' Kaian begged.

Would you like to show him, my child? What your anger can do?

It was a moment of weakness, she supposed. But she did

want him to see her – all of her. She wanted to kill the doubt that lingered in his eyes, to make him worry more about her capabilities than her failures. She wanted Kaian to see.

She felt the familiar touch of Ryvinika pressing on her eyes. She did not scream or stumble. And when the witch was done, she slowly turned to meet Kaian's blue-eyed gaze.

'No.'

He stumbled backwards, gasping for air and attempting to find his bearings. 'That's not possible. Your eyes –'

'I am not a monster, Kaian. I am your friend. Your partner.'

'Sapphire . . .' Everything about his tone had shifted.

'I am asking you to trust me.'

He shook his head, and tears shimmered in his eyes.

'I cannot. I cannot let you make this mistake.'

'It's not a mistake.'

She felt the push of Ryvinika once more, and a roll of thunder sounded across the land.

It was time. She knew it was time. She turned away from her friends and focused on the barrier. But a hand on her arm pulled her back.

It was Kaian again. His eyes were desperate and afraid. 'You can't do this.'

'I can and I will.'

'Please, Sapphire.' His voice was raw and broken as the rain began to fall. Her heart ached as she saw the fear sink into his eyes. Kaian was afraid – afraid of her.

'I have to do this. Can't you see?'

Kaian reached out once more, but she avoided his touch, afraid that if she allowed it, she might break in two.

'I am asking you to choose me. Choose Evera. Choose your parents. Choose Eriobis and walk away from this.'

Sapphire looked to the barrier once more – his words ringing in her ears as her stomach churned.

'I'm sorry,' she muttered as she extended her hands towards the sky. 'But I choose . . . myself.'

Lightning tore through the sky, meeting her open palm, and the prophecy began to unfold.

Chapter Forty-two

The lightning directly struck her open palm, a palm already scarred, but she did not flinch. Instead, she summoned another strike. The storm responded quickly, a bolt meeting her other palm, and with a fluid movement, she shoved her hands forward and watched as the lightning slammed into the barrier.

She called upon the world to support her. And the world answered. She watched as the ground beneath her split in two, the force racing towards the barrier and slamming into it with a loud boom.

More lightning.

More fire.

More rain.

More destruction.

She did not control the magic, but she trusted it to guide her as she continued to be a vessel for the power that gave birth to a better world.

She heard only snatches of Evera and Kaian's desperate screams as they begged her to stop. Their words were quickly carried away as she focused on the barrier.

She felt the surge of power as she lifted her hands

towards the sky, and three different lightning bolts came at her call. With all her might, she released them towards the barrier. A blinding light followed. An ear-splitting groan filled the air, and she watched as the barrier rippled and split in two, collapsing – revealing a world unknown.

Sapphire collapsed to the ground. Blood dripped from her nose, and her hands shook.

Evera and Kaian ran to her, pulling her off the ground. They were trying to decide what to do when a loud, bone-chilling howl came from the Shattered Lands. They froze, staring at the forest ahead.

Sapphire stumbled backwards, suddenly unable to breathe.

She knew this place. The muted colours, the dying trees, and the large stone house that sat in the middle of it all.

She knew it because she had spent eighteen years there. She knew it because it had once been her home.

Witrotean was sprawled out before her, and she recognized every inch of its desolate landscape for as far as she could see. Ryvinika appeared from the shadows, a sickening smile spreading across her familiar features.

'Hello, my child.'

No.

Sapphire's knees buckled.

No. Not that voice. Not the voice that had taught her right from wrong, had taught her the Saints' prayer. The voice that had bidden her goodnight for years, that had bestowed wisdom on her until Sapphire had disappeared.

The person who stood before her was Ryvinika. But that voice – that voice was Martia's.

'How –'

'You certainly did not fail, Sapphire. Isn't that what we always discussed? You will not fail, you will not fall. I suppose my visions couldn't be swayed like you hoped.'

'Martia . . .'

'Oh,' Ryvinika laughed, her own voice returning. 'Don't tell me you were fond of that old hag? I would have assumed in the two years *I* raised you, I taught you better than to be a fool.'

Sapphire stared up at the woman, trying not to allow the wave of her latest realization to cause her chest to cave in.

There are accounts of witches being able to inhabit the bodies of those whose lives they stole.

Martia . . .

Sapphire racked her brain for memories of the day that had once haunted her. The day she had forgotten over time. The day the Beasts had arrived at their door and the Mothers had locked them away under the stairs. Sapphire remembered the women's cries of agony, their prayers as they begged the Saints to save them – she had heard the Beasts roar, heard their teeth meet flesh. Death permeated the air around them.

No one had understood how Martia had survived that day. But instead of questioning it, they had considered it a gift from the Saints. But Sapphire now knew it was no such thing.

Martia hadn't survived that day.

Ryvinika had made sure of it.

Martia had died – all of the Mothers had died so

Ryvinika could get to Sapphire. Was the war . . . the Beasts . . . the death . . . was all that blood on her hands? She stumbled backwards, closing her eyes tightly.

She had left them – all the girls at the Home, Lyna . . . Susanna. She had left them and rested with jewels clasped around her throat and food always on the table, and had slept in a safe place with no fear of monsters.

She had left them to fend for themselves in a nightmare that was created because of her.

She wished Ryvinika would kill her – call upon the creatures or summon her magic and stop Sapphire's heart at that very moment. She could not shoulder the guilt she now knew.

When she opened her eyes, Ryvinika was smiling as if she was savouring Sapphire's world falling apart. But finally, the witch's focus drifted past Sapphire and her smile grew. Sapphire forced her gaze from the familiar world before her to find the coven exiting the treeline, making their way towards them – setting fire to the forest as they came.

At the head of the procession was a familiar figure, with fiery red hair and narrowed eyes, her black cloak flowing behind her as she crossed the open plain between them, looking every bit the monster that Sapphire had been warned of.

Ashes stared straight ahead, never glancing at Sapphire. Her eyes were fixed on Ryvinika, her expression a mask of indifference – so stark compared to the gleeful women who surrounded her, clapping and chattering excitedly. Sapphire kept her gaze locked on her witch as the world darkened around them.

Ashes was a few steps away when she finally looked to where Sapphire stood. She did not falter when she met Sapphire's stare.

'The prophecy is fulfilled,' Ryvinika called out and the coven cheered. 'Now we begin. Now we take back what should have always been ours.'

Ashes did not smile, did not praise her. She remained stoic, staring blankly.

'What have you done?' Sapphire pressed when Ashes was near. Her voice was steady, though she did not feel that way.

'I did nothing at all.'

Ashes' voice was hollow, empty.

A cry split the air.

It was a warning. A warning to run, to hide, to be anywhere but here. And then the ground beneath their feet shook as the creature came into view.

A shadow creature the size of the tallest tree stood at the border, waiting for a command.

'Look at me!' Sapphire demanded. 'Why would you do this to me?'

'I did nothing, princess,' said Ashes. 'Your choices are your own.'

Her eyes did not dance as she spoke, and there was no bite to her tone. She sounded drained.

'You told me to trust them. To trust her.' Sapphire pointed to Ryvinika, the woman who looked so much like herself. 'You gave me your word – that peace would come if I just followed the prophecy. This is not peace. This is –'

Her eyes flickered to the flames that consumed the forest. The forest where she had spent many nights. It was ablaze, her naivety burning with it. 'There were never plans for peace, were there? This . . . you always intended this. To trick me, make me your fool. You *lied* to me.'

'You chose to believe me.' Sapphire's eyes widened at the impact of the words and she found Ashes' gaze. If it had been all those months ago, when their paths first crossed, Sapphire would've thought nothing of the slight shift of Ashes' expression – but Sapphire *knew* her now.

Only for a moment, she saw a glimpse of the girl from the forest and she almost reached out a desperate hand, but as quickly as it had come, the glimpse was gone.

'Was any of it real? Anything you told me? The oaths you took? Your –' Sapphire choked back a sob. 'Did you ever care for me at all? Or was this just part of your plan? Whatever must be done. No matter who gets hurt.'

'Saph–' The name died on Ashes' tongue as her focus cut away, looking at the witches that now circled them. The coven watched them closely and Ashes' gaze was almost panicked, her eyes roaming frantically until they found Ryvinika. Sapphire watched as Ryvinika gave the smallest tilt of her head and Ashes' hardness immediately returned. Rigid and cruel, the witch tried to smile as she delivered her next blow. 'I always told you I was your enemy, did I not?'

'You were never my enemy. I thought –' It gutted Sapphire that Ashes' face showed no remorse. She offered no look that only they could understand, no explanation. 'I never wanted you to be my enemy.'

'Nothing could've changed that fate.' The witch's voice was hardly a whisper.

Ashes had once told her that fate was a cruel and ruthless mistress. Maybe she had been right.

'What have I done?' Sapphire's voice was barely a whisper.

She stared at the witch. Her chin quivered but she held it high because she was not the scared little girl Ashes had once known.

Still, something inside Sapphire shattered. Maybe it was the hope she had been clinging to, or maybe the belief in a better world, or perhaps the anger she had been choking on for much too long. Or maybe it was none of those things.

Maybe it was something bigger. Something more permanent. Something she had not expected.

Her heart.

She had assumed heartbreak would be quick and ruthless. A rush of emotions that would drown her instantly. The type of pain that made you drop to your knees and beg the Gods for relief, for answers.

But heartbreak was no such thing.

It was a slow, agonizing process of small, jagged cracks splintering her core. A new, raw version of herself was clawing its way out.

It was mourning. Mourning for a lost love, lies told, and the person she had once been.

There was no cry of anguish, no coming undone. She did not choke back tears or collapse into an inconsolable heap. No, this feeling, this heartbreak, was simple.

She remained upright, her hands by her side. The world around her continued to exist. Her heart continued to beat, and she stared into the unwavering eyes of the one person who she thought would never betray her.

But she had. Sapphire blinked a few times, trying to process it all.

Betrayal, she decided, smelled like fresh soil and a storm on the horizon. Heartbreak smelled like honey and ash. And both were beautiful, deadly, deceptive things with haunting eyes and a wicked smile. All those nights, all those memories, all those promises . . .

Oh.

Her witch had never been hers at all.

That realization was the final blow, and she desperately reached for the anger that simmered in the pit of her stomach. She clung to it, afraid that if she felt anything else in that moment, she might remain there forever. Rooted to the very spot where Ashes had left her, returning to the ground that had birthed her magic.

'I will end your life, witch. Mark my words. I will watch the life drain from your eyes before this is done.'

'Then do it, Sapphire. Kill me.'

Sapphire's hands shook as she looked from them to the witch. She could do it. She could. But all she felt were strong hands on her hips, shadows brushing her skin.

'I will become the monster you made me.' Sapphire stood a bit taller as she said it, pushing her hair out of her face. 'I will haunt every waking thought and every dark path you take.'

'I pray I will be so lucky, princess.'

Sapphire couldn't quite understand what that meant.

Savina tugged roughly at Ashes' arm, and Sapphire watched as they left. The witch took one last dead-eyed look over her shoulder, and Sapphire stared back. Unfaltering, unblinking, and unafraid, she pointed a finger at Ashes.

'It's the monsters you know.' Her voice was strained and tired as she returned her attention to Ryvinika. The shadow creature next to her unfurled its huge, unnatural wings and took flight west, headed straight towards the castle.

She was a pawn.

A fool.

And she had played right into their hands.

A type of rage she had never known coursed through her, and an unnatural scream ripped from her throat.

Not her kingdom. Not her people. Not more blood on her hands.

From her days in Witrotean, she recalled the words of her vision. The words that had left her curious and confused. A message she could not decipher.

The storm is you.

She did not call upon the sky to aid her. Instead, she called upon the storm within her to reveal itself, and she watched in awe as lightning shot from her hand. She gripped the bolt, aiming directly for the shadow creature that travelled overhead, and it wrapped around the creature's torso. A cry from another world filled the silence as she watched it fall, shaking the ground on impact. It fought, writhing in the dirt, and she tightened her grip until it stopped moving entirely – the shadows dissipating as if the creature had never been there.

She returned her gaze to Ryvinika.

'If it's a war you want, I will give it to you,' the witch said.

Sapphire clenched her fist. Another bolt of lightning struck right in front of Ryvinika, causing the witch to stumble backwards.

'You have not known war against someone like me,' Sapphire choked out.

For a moment, Ryvinika dropped her usual smirk, and curiosity and hesitation were clear on her familiar features.

'I can't wait to see you try, child.'

As the witch turned to retreat into the Shattered Lands, darkness raced towards them, but Sapphire did not flinch as she held up her hands. A blast of wind knocked the shadows away, revealing the border of the Shattered Lands – of Witrotean – once more.

Ashes stood near the Home. Her red hair whipped in the wind as she pulled her hood over her head. Sapphire watched as the witch turned away, retreating in the direction her coven had headed. But Sapphire didn't move.

She stared at her childhood home. The place that had raised her, broken her, mended her, and broken her once more. The place she had left behind. The people she had left behind.

Oh, mercy, what had happened to the girls of the Home?

Lyna and Susanna? What if –

She didn't finish the thought before rushing towards the Shattered Lands. She had only taken a few steps when she felt someone grab her hand. She turned to find Evera standing there.

'You're thinking about them. About the girls in the Home.'

Sapphire nodded, tears welling up, threatening to spill.

'If they are there, you cannot help them. Not right now, anyway. We need to figure out our next steps.'

Kaian joined them, helping Evera usher Sapphire towards the forest.

'We hurry home. We say we were having lunch in the clearing and heard the barrier fall. And we protect this country. We protect our home.'

At Kaian's words, the implications of her actions hit her full force.

'We have to get home, Sapphire. We have to get home and alert them. We have to alert them all.' It was Evera speaking to her now.

Home.

She no longer knew what the word meant. Not with the world she had once known behind her and the world she had destroyed before her.

Evera tugged at her arm, and Sapphire began to move, her friends leading the way as they ran, Evera controlling the flames that threatened to consume the forest. Sapphire felt depleted, like there was no magic left in her veins, and her friends slowed their pace to allow her to keep up.

'She promised,' Sapphire whispered.

'And she lied.' Kaian's voice contained no sympathy, but Evera squeezed her hand gently.

In the silence, she realized how lonely her mind was without Ryvinika there.

The thought faded quickly as another unwelcome presence ghosted over her skin.

She jumped, looking around to find the source, but there was nothing.

Please, do not be alarmed.

The voice was similar to Ryvinika's but softer, and Sapphire paused as Kaian and Evera watched her with concern.

I am Aylara.

Sapphire stiffened at the name.

The original Canmore queen.

Ryvinika's sister.

The fall of the barrier was inevitable. You cannot carry that burden if you plan to win a war. Please, let me help you.

'Why would you? I'm not a Canmore. You've seen what I've done.'

Kaian and Evera stared at her, attempting to figure out who she might be talking to.

The voice replied with a gentle laugh. *You are more Canmore than most who have come before you.*

'What do I need to do?'

Return home. Speak to your mother. Offer her one word: Vincatti. She will know what this means. You must go now.

424

Sapphire felt the presence slip away, and she charged forward, ignoring the anxious questions of her friends.

These were the last few moments she would know before war. The last few seconds of peace in the country that she had just betrayed.

The doors of the castle swung open, and she found her parents, relief washing over them as they took in the trio.

But the relief soon gave way to worry as they met Sapphire's eyes, so Araxia rushed to pull her into a tight embrace. And Sapphire allowed it as she sobbed. She allowed herself a moment to be a child . . . broken.

Sapphire stepped away from them, taking Araxia's hands into her own. Someone had once said that the Canmore women were a force to be reckoned with and their power was not of this world.

Sapphire was ready to prove them right.

'Vincatti,' she whispered, and Araxia's grip tightened.

But the queen nodded. She looked to Kip and made the simplest of gestures. He went stiff, then bellowed for servants to ring the tower bells.

War had arrived. And Sapphire would not rest – not until those warning bells stopped ringing for a war of her own making.

ACKNOWLEDGEMENTS

So many people had a hand in bringing this book to life. So, while I'll try to sum it up quickly, just be aware I will inevitably fail and spend the rest of my life trying to express said gratitude.

First and foremost, I want to thank every single person who decided to follow me on TikTok. Might be a weird place to start, but the truth is, without all of you, this book would not have landed in the hands that it did. I started posting in February 2022 without a plan but with a big dream, and so many of you invested in me while I stumbled through the process. You all offered me patience, and you did not have to. You came back and encouraged me every single day, even when I offered nothing in return. And you stuck around when I couldn't give you answers that you deserved.

And because of you, I truly am living my wildest dream. Your belief, your encouragement and your love for the characters pushed this book across the finish line and I don't think I'll ever be able to say thank you enough.

Next, I have to say thank you to Erin who, regrettably, had to deal with every up and down of this book. From the panic of planning and writing, to the late nights where I walked her through every plot point, to the months of anxiously waiting to see if I would get a book deal – she dealt with it all. She'd get me dinner when I felt I couldn't leave my keyboard, made sure I drank water when I was in the deep depths of my creativity, and would always remind me to stop and enjoy the moment when I got overwhelmed. I'm afraid to think about what this book would be without her, but I'm guessing it would be trashed somewhere and never see the light of day. Thanks for always being the first line of my support system.

Next I have my friends. Katie, Patrick, Brooklyn, Courtney, Emily, Morgan, Bridget, Brennan, Jess and names I am no doubt forgetting. You all have stuck by my side and cheered me on every step of the way. Thank you for loving me in all stages of life and for always celebrating me, win or lose.

And Galia; we met in the most unexpected way, but I am forever thankful for our niche little mutual hobby. You have humbled me a hundred times over, made me question my ability to write, and made me *want* to cry (but I never did) – but all of this made me a better writer. Your feedback was critical to this story and its success, and I am forever grateful for our five-hour FaceTimes and your willingness to always tell me what I need to hear even if I don't want to hear it.

Now, Steph, what can be said? You invested in me when you didn't have too. You gave me hours of your time, hours of your effort, and insight that this book would not have moved forward without. Your feedback and edits helped make this book what it is, and I am so grateful that you were willing to work with me even from across the country. But even more than that, your belief in me truly helped change the way I see myself. You are always the first to celebrate my wins, to remind me of my value and to shut down any of my negative thinking. In so many ways this book would not exist without you. I am so grateful for your friendship, your guidance and your kind heart.

To my team at Penguin, it's been a *wild* ride but I could not have asked for better people to be on it with. Your hard work and dedication to this book is something I will never forget. So, thank you to my editorial team: Carmen McCullough, Katie Sinfield, Ruth Knowles and Sarah Connelly. My production team, Rianna Johnson. My marketing and PR geniuses, Jannine Saunders and Harriet Venn. My rights team, Beth Fennell. And I cannot forget my extremely talented cover design team, Sophia Watts and illustrator Kii.

Finally, Charlotte. I could write an entire book explaining why I am so thankful, but I will try to keep it brief. When you popped into my inbox in August 2022, I was buzzing with excitement. As I've said a hundred times, it was the first step to my dream coming true. But what I never expected was for *you* to be so wonderful. Your guidance, dedication and love for this book has made this experience so incredible. From answering every single question I ever had (which was a lot) to fighting for me and my vision, you truly are a gift to this industry. And I'm beyond lucky to have you on my team.

And lastly, my final thank you goes to you, reader. You're the one who makes it real.